A
Time
of
Death

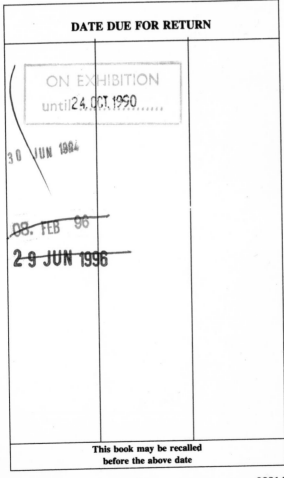

DATE DUE FOR RETURN

ON EXHIBITION
until 24. OCT. 1990

30 JUN 1994

08. FEB 96

2 9 JUN 1996

This book may be recalled
before the above date

90014

THIS LAND, THIS TIME

I   Into the Battle

II   A Time of Death

III   Reach to Eternity

IV   South to Destiny

Dobrica Ćosić

A Time of Death

translated by
Muriel Heppell

A Harvest/HBJ Book
Harcourt Brace Jovanovich, Publishers
San Diego   New York   London

English translation
copyright © 1978 by Harcourt Brace Jovanovich, Inc.

Library of Congress Cataloging in Publication Data

Ćosić, Dobrica, 1921–
A time of death.

Translation of Vreme smrti.
1. European War, 1914–1918–Fiction.
I. Title.
PZ4.C835Ti3   [PG1418.C63]   891.8'2'35   77-73047
ISBN 0-15-190448-0
ISBN 0-15-690445-4 (pbk.)

The Prologue that appeared in the hardcover
edition of *A Time of Death* (Harcourt Brace Jovanovich, 1978)
is a condensation of *Vreme smrti,* Volume I, which now
appears in full in the paperback volume *Into the Battle*
(Harvest/HBJ, 1983)

Printed in the United States of America
First Harvest/HBJ edition 1983

A B C D E F G H I J

Translator's Acknowledgment

I should like to express my thanks to Mr. Sava Peić, of the staff of the Library of the School of Slavonic and East European Studies, University of London, for his valuable help in the final revision of this translation.

M. H.

A
Time
of
Death

1

TO THE AMBASSADORS OF THE KINGDOM OF SERBIA IN ST. PETERSBURG, PARIS, AND LONDON:
IF WE DO NOT OBTAIN MUNITIONS FOR FIELD CANNON AND HOWITZERS IN THE SHORTEST POSSIBLE TIME SERBIAN ARMIES FACE INEVITABLE CATASTROPHE STOP SERBIA EXPECTS COLLAPSE WORSE THAN EIGHTEEN HUNDRED THIRTEEN IN FIRST RISING STOP HELP MOST URGENTLY NEEDED STOP OUR ARMY CANNOT HOLD OUT TEN DAYS BEFORE THE ENEMY REACHES KRAGUJEVAC STOP THEN DISASTER STOP PLEASE IMPLORE MUNITIONS BE SENT IMMEDIATELY STOP DO NOT FORGET TO SAY SERBIA UNDER ATTACK FROM SEVEN AUSTRIAN DIVISIONS STOP IF WE HAVE MUNITIONS AND BOOTS WE CAN DEFEAT TEN DIVISIONS STOP PAŠIĆ

From Rudnik, General Mišić looked on an extraordinary scene: Podrinje, Mačva, and Pocerina had turned round and were streaming toward Šumadija and Pomoravlje, as though the Austro-Hungarian army had overturned that part of Serbia, with its villages and towns, and shaken it out—sky, river, and mud—to the accompaniment of the rumble of artillery. And now—from hills and valleys, amid mingled cloud and falling leaves—every living creature, everyone capable of flight, and everything that could be carried or dragged, were moving along the one road that led between fences and plum orchards, and fields of unharvested corn, to the center of Serbia. In this upheaval the road itself was fractured, disappearing into woods, villages, and empty fields. Down this glutinous, well-trodden defile—between blackened hedges and bare boundary stones, amid the mounting terror of both humans and animals—men and cattle, carts and dogs, poultry and domestic animals were all hurtling downward. All in the same direction. Opposite him.

For today he alone was traveling in the opposite direction; he alone was going toward the place from which everyone else was fleeing. Since leaving Kragujevac, he had not met or overtaken a living soul. It seemed that not even the crows were flying westward toward the battle front. Cold gusts of wind whipped up the rain; the mountaintops were already powdered with snow. Everywhere he encountered uneasiness in children and animals, and reproach and hatred in the glances of women and old men. He did not hide his face with his military cap, nor with the curtains of Prince Alexander's car. He met and endured every single look.

A number of telegrams had reached the High Command the previous evening: the road to Loznica, along which Field Marshal Oscar Potiorek, commander of the Balkan Army and the Serbian Punitive Expedition, had traveled by car, was now adorned with priests and old men strung on gibbets; the ditches alongside the hedges were stuffed with the corpses of children and mutilated women. As Vojvoda Putnik handed him the telegrams he had again uttered the warning which he had given with every unfavorable report from the front since the fall of Šabac:

"Now don't forget, Mišić, this Field Marshal Potiorek has written in one of his vindictive communiqués that the Serbs are a dirty, stinking, rascally race. You must remind the Serbian officers of this. You must remind them constantly, if you don't want to end up as the groom of an Austrian sergeant major."

At this point Stepa had related how the Austrians had tied an old miller to the wheel of his mill, raised the sluice, and released the water to turn the wheel, then sat around and stabbed him with their bayonets—in revenge for the killing of Franz Ferdinand and Sophia.

The chauffeur sounded his horn; he had done nothing else since they left Kragujevac. His adjutant poked his head out the window and shouted to the people to get out of the way and let the general pass. The mention of his rank and the fact that in the presence of their suffering he was traveling by car, were more distasteful to him than the curses and evident hatred of many people he passed. He was one of those who must bear some of the guilt for the great misfortune which had overtaken them.

The road became increasingly crowded with refugees from the west, and the sound of artillery grew even more distinct. It was already past noon, and he would not be able to reach Mionica before the light failed. Yet he had to get there, in order to be invested with his command by General Bojović and get down to work that very evening.

How would he present himself and impose his attitude on the First Army, so that from the very beginning they would all be aware of his presence and know his intentions—everyone from the division commanders down to the medics and the men in the supply trains? How would he convey to them that he would do only what could be done, and what was best for them? What was his primary idea, now that he was in command—some simple idea that would be grasped by every soldier, that would save the Serbian army? Attack. Yes, that was his dominating idea. But attack could succeed only under specific conditions. Attack could also lead to defeat. The external circumstances, the weather, the relative strength of the opposing forces—all these determined the significance of an attack. The stupidest cadet at the military academy learned this, and every lieutenant had to know it for his examination in campaigning and strategy. If he was in Field Marshal Oscar Potiorek's shoes, what orders would he give for the next day? He would order an attack: yes, he would pursue the Serbians, giving them no time to organize themselves; he would pursue them till there were none of them left. But he and Field Marshal Oscar Potiorek did not act on the same principles as commanders; he had already noticed this in the battle at Cer. What orders would Oscar Potiorek give to the Serbian army that evening, if he were in Mišić's place? He must have a clear notion of this. However self-confident he might be as a man, if Potiorek was a good officer—if he had learned any lessons from military history—before he wrote out his orders for the next day, he must reflect: what does the commander of the First Serbian Army intend to do?

He sat staring at the refugees, smoking continuously, and quietly urged the driver to hurry as much as he possibly could. But when the car spattered women and children with mud, and drove cows off the road into the ditch, he told his chauffeur that he was not driving Field Marshal Oscar Potiorek but a Serbian officer born in Struganik, under Bačinac, above Mionica. When they came upon an overturned cart, he stopped the car and told the driver and his adjutant to help the unfortunate occupants, and himself opened the door and gave advice. This kindness was more often than not greeted with reproaches, occasionally with silence, and only rarely with gratitude. If Spasić shouted at the old men and women because of their rude and insulting remarks, he said,

"Leave them alone, Lieutenant. Unhappy people can't help behaving badly. But as long as they do this, they can endure and continue to struggle. As long as they curse me, the people have not lost hope."

In the confusion caused by the attempts of covered carts full of children, geese, and turkeys to pass each other on the road, the car slithered into the ditch, and stayed there. The refugees turned a deaf ear to the driver's desperate appeals for assistance to get the car out of the ditch; weighed down by their bundles and sacks, walking under umbrellas, the men and women trudged on despondently, continuing their muddy way into the trackless distance. He got out of the car and politely asked some women and boys to help push the car out of the ditch. They walked past him with angry sidelong looks. Mišić then appealed to some more passers-by. They paid no attention. He raised his riding whip at a group of old men and townspeople, but spoke without anger:

"Come on, folks, help me! I'm in a hurry to get to the front."

"Are you the King?" asked an old man who was leading a cow and holding his grandson by the hand.

"No, I'm not the King, but I'm a Serbian general."

"It's you generals and Pašić that have got us into this mess," added a townsman under a mauve sun umbrella.

"No, it's the Austrians that have got you into this mess. We're trying to get you back home, if you only had the sense to see it!"

"And where are your cannon? You've taken the skin off our backs with taxes! You rob us worse than the Fritzies. What do you think you're doing with Serbia?"

They stood around him, blocking the passage of the covered carts. Mišić was not offended by their words. Yes, it was all right: they were angry, they hated him, so they could stick it out a bit longer. He let them vent their spleen on him and so ease their suffering. He was about to say: you can tell what human beings in general are like when they suffer, and what the country folks are like at a wedding, and the state when it's at war! But someone from the edge of the crowd burst out:

"That's Živojin Mišić, you idiots! Aren't you ashamed of yourselves? It's Mišić from Struganik!"

The angry bystanders fell silent. They stared at him and at his general's uniform, then began to jostle one another trying to get out of his sight as soon as possible. But those who felt most strongly shouted with unabated anger:

"Why on earth didn't you say you were Živojin Mišić? You're not Saint Nicholas, whom we all know when we see him. You're no great credit to us. We should know you by your mustache. Come on, folks, let's help this fine man on his way."

"General Mišić, is there any hope for us? Can you stop them, for God's sake? What's going to happen to us?"

"Yes, there *is* hope, my friends. And we'll stop them, just you wait—if everybody does what decent people ought to do, and if we all do our duty! Well, I'm in a hurry, so I wish you a good journey!" He could see from their faces that there was a lot more they wanted to say to him, but he had nothing more to say to them. He could hear the Austrian howitzers exploding, with the salvos that presaged an attack, so he added: "Share your misfortunes, and don't let them get you down! And help the army by your patience and faith. You'll soon be home again, I'll vouch for this with my life!" He gave them a military salute, then made his way through the silent circle back to the car, which managed with difficulty to move out of the puddles and hurried on uphill, honking as it went.

On the upward slope they encountered a column of empty munitions carts and groups of walking wounded; the car was halted again, as the soldiers did not get out of its way. For the first time he saw the soldiers of his army. They would not let him pass, even though they knew that only the Commander in Chief or Vojvoda Putnik could be in the car. The wounded were arguing with the civilians, and paid no attention to the honking of the car or the shouting of Lieutenant Spasić. He pulled his cap further down over his forehead; now he didn't wish to be recognized. The adjutant got out of the car to deal with a supply train which was jammed up against an overturned cart carrying refugees. The firing of the Austrian howitzers continued.

But this was Glavica! It was here that he had taken his captain's examination, on the fighting tactics of a rear-guard battalion. He had passed with the highest marks. And what was he going to do now with his army? He was not just fulfilling the oath given to the King: that was a trifling obligation in the face of such great suffering. This time he had to take his examination in front of these people fleeing in the rain, not knowing where they were going, in front of those weeping children who were hitting their cows, these barefoot wounded, and soldiers without boots or overcoats—in front of all these people who had met him with curses ever since he left Kragujevac. He felt a strong desire to see Glavica again, and from under its wild pear trees to look at the area in which his army would operate. Quickly he got out of the car, jumped over some bushes, and leaned against an old pear tree— the only one in the clearing, beneath which his examiners had sat. The

General Staff had named the elevations, and the positions of the brigades and squads, without looking at their military maps, since that was their own country.

Here among these hills he had herded goats; he had wandered through the meadows during his vacations; as commander of a division in Valjevo, he had conducted military exercises. He stood under the pear tree, leaning against its trunk, and removed his cap. Before him were mountains and hills, intermingled with cloud; the Kolubara curled its way down the valley; Valjevo was a white blur in the distance. Occupied territory now. More than once he had stood under this pear tree, looking at the countryside with the eyes of an army officer, and thought: no countryside is more suitable for fruit trees and for acts of destruction—for nurture, defense, and burial. The mountains were suitably spread out to accommodate army divisions, the rising slopes appropriate for battalions, the descending folds just right for platoons. The Kolubara was somewhat muddy for the rear guard, while a vanguard could cross it without pontoons. This was the terrain of his army—and also of the Sixth Army of Field Marshal Oscar Potiorek. Here Potiorek must first be halted, then pushed back toward the Drina and the Sava. But how, and when? How could this be achieved with an army reduced to half its strength, and lacking artillery? If he could not surpass his opponent in strength of will and intelligence, how else could he manage it? His good luck with money and women was well known, but there was no sign of it yet in the fate of the nation.

But what should he do today, indeed that very night? What could the Serbian commander do that Field Marshal Oscar Potiorek would not foresee? A great battle must begin with a great idea: quietly, with blows proceeding from the intelligence of the commanding officers—that's what he had told cadets in his lectures on strategy. He had passed over in silence the fact that every good commander has two opponents: the enemy and his senior officer. He would have to pit himself against two opponents: Vojvoda Putnik and Field Marshal Oscar Potiorek. He would not subordinate himself to Putnik, and he would try to read Potiorek's mind and anticipate his actions. But what about the division commanders and the chiefs of staff? They were also opponents whom he must master. And what was he to do against the thousands of despairing and wretched men who comprised his army, whose one thought was how to get home as quickly as possible?

In front of him the road leading downhill overflowed with a seething mass of soldiers and civilians, animals and field guns, empty munitions carts, and refugees mixed up with the retreating army—an army exhausted by battles followed by withdrawal, and which had broken loose from its wounded and bewildered commander, General Bojović, and was now scattered over the roads and villages, looting as it retreated, melting away with its back turned to the enemy.

His first task would be to end this chaos and turn the rout into a withdrawal. He would bring some order into the prevailing misery, and give to defeat some shape and direction, so that disaster and defeat would at least be more bearable. He would try to find some meaning in this vertiginous and confused situation, and meet it squarely, face to face. What was Field Marshal Oscar Potiorek preparing for tomorrow, when he reached the Kolubara? In which direction would he move his main force? Toward Belgrade or toward Kragujevac?

His adjutant reported that the road was now cleared. Looking straight in front of him, he returned quickly to the car and lit a cigarette. They moved forward, but at an ever slower pace. Along the road soldiers were mixed up with women, animals, and peasant carts. He turned his eyes toward the forest: yes, he must begin the struggle for survival by creating order out of disorder—there was no doubt about that. The soldiers must be separated from the refugees and women and children; their suffering must be kept apart. The soldiers must be made to march in a column, and without delay.

The rain gave no sign of stopping, nor did the pounding of the Austrian artillery. It was beginning to grow dark on the heights of Mednik. Everything was being driven in on itself, into a concentrated sense of foreboding.

Baćinac. Was that wild cherry tree still there—the one from which he had picked cherries that day the goats got lost, and his uncle beat him so hard that his mother had to carry his bruised body to the sheepfold? Further down, underneath Baćinac lay Struganik, his father's house, his brothers, and the cemetery. It was over three years since he had heard anything of their worries and troubles. In three days at the most, the Austrians would remove everything from the sheepfolds and cellars of Struganik. They would set fire to the largest house there, the white house where he had been born, with its open hearth smelling of wood smoke and old ash. And they would burn those big black dough trays in which flour was stored. Even when he became a lieutenant, he had still retained his childhood fear that in those trays, concealed in the flour, there lurked the old demon of Struganik.

The car came to a halt before a mass of soldiers, civilians, and animals who had stopped in their tracks, blocking the road; they were all looking at an officer who was chasing one of the soldiers. The soldier jumped over the ditch and stood near the first plum tree in the sloping orchard beyond the road. The officer fell into the muddy water in the ditch. The soldier stopped, went back, and bent down to help the officer up. The latter quickly got up, pulled out his revolver, and shouted hoarsely:

"Lay down your arms!"

The soldier cast a long, tearful look over the refugees and soldiers, then turned around and faced the bare plum tree in the rain. As his eyes met the repeated command of the officer and the raised revolver, he removed his rifle from his shoulder, then hesitated as to whether he should remove the bag containing ammunition and some stolen bread. Slowly he went over to another plum tree and rested his rifle and bag against it, then returned even more slowly to the first tree. There he stood, with his mud-stained hands hanging down, in his broken sandals and torn breeches, his threadbare jacket and cap, wet through and leaning against the plum tree, gazing without fear or defiance at the hills, from which came the roar of the Austrian artillery.

The officer took off his belt and began to beat the soldier on the head and unshaven, haggard face as hard as he could. The soldier's cap flew off; he clung to the tree with his arms, leaning his neck against the trunk and resting his head among the branches. He braced himself against the blows, but never flinched; between the strokes from the officer's belt, he could see the people and the animals.

The soldier's platoon was standing on the road; they could hear the swish of the belt. Then more groups of soldiers came along and stood there, silently watching the scene in the mud; a number of women, also some sheep and cows, and people carrying suitcases, gathered around them. The old men made use of the pause to rearrange the baggage in their carts and adjust the weight of their bags. All the children in the covered carts were watching the officer beating the soldier.

Then Tola Dačić arrived on the scene in a cart and stopped, got out of the cart and pushed his way through the crowd: could that man leaning against the plum tree be one of his four sons? When he had assured himself that the man whose face was covered with blood had nothing to do with him, he stood at the edge of the underbrush and spoke in indignant tones to the mute, shivering, mud-stained crowd:

"Just look at your shame! And remember this is what happens to an Austrian spy. That's why we're refugees now in our own country, without a leader, while the Austrians plunder and burn our houses, and kill everything left alive. Just take a good look, learn your lesson, and pass it on to your children!"

"What do you mean, a spy? You've got spies on the brain. This is a wretch, a barefoot peasant. What can he sell when everything's lost anyway? He's not tied up, but he's not resisting. And where's your rifle, you blind bat? Our poor country! What a mess we're in, with our miserable army! What's become of Serbia? And you soldiers, why are you just standing and looking? You should be ashamed of yourselves! Why don't you kill that scoundrel with epaulets? Go on, soldier, run for it; if you're a man, run away. Go on, hit, you Hun, we've deserved worse than that!"

Blows from the Austrians. Blows from the officers. And the rain beating down, too. Blows everywhere. As for the Serbian army, God help it.

General Mišić, whose car no one had noticed, told his driver to advance. The car moved down the road and stopped suddenly in front of the crowd, which retreated into the ditch and the bushes.

The adjutant got out of the car and opened the door for the general. Mišić threw away his unfinished cigarette and stepped quickly over the ditch into the orchard.

The belt swished for the last time and struck the soldier on the hand; as the officer let it go, it fell between him and the soldier, who released his hold on the tree and stood, submissive and motionless, with his face bleeding and his arms hanging down beside his torn breeches. He stared at the red tails of the general's overcoat and at his epaulets, which the officer had already seen in a swift sidelong glance. The officer bent down to pick up his belt, then quickly straightened up, turned around, and stood at attention in front of General Mišić, who was observing him closely: no, he hadn't been this man's instructor in strategy, nor had the man served in his division; probably he had obtained the rank of lieutenant without passing an examination—anyway he didn't recognize him. Yet he *did* recognize him: a frightened parvenu "gentleman," but quick with his fists. It was to carry a saber, and not to fight for freedom, that he had become an officer. He could hear whispers behind his back:

"That's Živojin Mišić. Yes, it's him all right. Yes, and his yellow mustache. He's the man to get us out of this mess. It's too late, I tell you. It's never too late if you really want to do something. I tell you, he'll drive a stake right through the Fritzies!"

Mišić walked over to the lieutenant, seized one of his epaulets, and tore it off. The lieutenant was thunderstruck. Mišić seized the other epaulet and threw it into the thornbushes. The lieutenant stuttered:

"He was trying to make the soldiers run away. And he refused to go to the rear guard, sir."

"I didn't ask you about that. What's your regiment?"

"Sir, I'm a platoon commander in the Third Battalion, First Regiment of the Danube Division."

"Report to your commanding officer for reduction to the ranks. When you've learned what it means to be a soldier, report to your regimental commander to see whether he thinks you can be trusted with a platoon. And remember this: God can be cruel and unjust, but not a commanding officer; his duty is to be both kind and just. Now get out of my sight!"

Then he turned to the soldier and looked at his beaten, bloodstained face. He was a man from the mountains, tough, no stranger to pain and suffering, who could take even more: he could still turn toward the Drina and haul himself forward. Mišić raised his hand to the brim of his general's cap and saluted the soldier. He spoke to him quietly, so that only he could hear:

"This is a fateful day for you, soldier. Wash your face and get into the car. And hurry!" he said to the incredulous soldier, whose mudstained hands were dangling. He went back to the road and stood on the slope in front of the soldiers and refugees:

"God help you, heroes!"

They looked at him speechless in the falling rain accompanied by the sound of the Austrian cannon. They did not immediately return his greeting, and some did not do so at all. He looked at them sternly, and with some anxiety. Yes, they too could turn toward the Drina and go forward, he thought. It was not so much that they were afraid. What have we to hope for? their eyes asked him. He answered:

"Form a column, and move on. It'll be night soon. You should find somewhere to sleep and have supper."

"We'll eat mud and drink water from the puddles. We'll sleep in the thornbushes."

They all turned to look at the soldier who had broken in with these menacing words. Mišić had no wish to see him: he knew it was a man who was ready for anything, who would never quit his post.

"Tomorrow you'll have something hot for supper, and a swig of *rakija*—brandy's good for you. Where you sleep will depend on the Austrians. If they don't attack and kill you, you'll have a dry place to sleep."

The officers gave orders to the soldiers in whispers. One of the refugees burst out in a threatening tone:

"And what's going to happen to Serbia, Živojin Mišić?"

"Folks, don't you see what a general is? A general all right, but he's the same as us. He's Živojin Mišić, but he looks just like any Serbian soldier!" exclaimed Tola Dačić. "If you take off his overcoat and cap, you could see him behind any plow or hoe. He's no better than any of us. So if you can, don't pay any attention to what he says. He's just a downtrodden peasant like we are. I dare you not to believe what he says!" continued Tola at the top of his voice.

The soldiers, who were forming a column, stopped and stared at the general.

"We've got to work and to think, boys. There's a lot for all of us to do. First we've got to halt, and turn our faces instead of our backs to the Austrians. We've got to look them in the face like men. Then they'll get scared and turn their backs to us, and you'll be able to get home again."

"That's right, General Mišić, that's the only thing to do," said Tola, separating himself from the women and cows and moving toward the general. He wanted to shake him by the hand, then tell people in Prerovo how he had talked personally with General Mišić; it might be a good thing for his sons, too.

General Mišić saluted and hurried toward the car.

"What are you waiting for? Get in, man!" said Mišić to the beaten-up soldier from whose face blood was spurting. "What's your name?"

"Dragutin, sir. But where can I go like this? I'll make everything dirty, sir."

"Then wash yourself first. But hurry, Dragutin. You can stay with me and help me. When we get to headquarters I'll tell you what your duties are," said Mišić as he got into the car, followed by Dragutin.

The engine snorted and the car moved forward. Then Dačić shouted:

"I want to shake you by the hand, General Mišić! I've given the country four soldiers, so I think I deserve to shake hands with you."

Mišić ordered the driver to stop, opened the door and held out his hand to Tola: "You deserve that and more, my friend. Long life to your sons. Good-by!"

"And will you remember my hand with its calluses—a working man's hand, General Živojin? My name's Tola Dačić and I come from Prerovo."

"Yes, I'll remember all right. Have a good journey."

"Just a minute, general, there's something else I want to ask you. How old are you, Živojin Mišić?"

"I'm fifty-nine, Dačić." Mišić shut the door and the car started off.

"That's fine. You know the beginning, and you can see the end. May time clear gently with you, Živojin Mišić!"

Tola placed his hand on the roof of the car, which spattered him with mud.

"Drive as fast as you can!" ordered Mišić. He lit a cigarette. "Dragutin, who do you have at home?"

"I had a son nine years old, and my father. The Austrians killed them in the summer, when they crossed the Drina. Then they burned my house and the other buildings. I've one more brother, a bachelor, who was killed where you can cross the Sava. And maybe my wife is still alive, and one little girl, three years old—maybe, maybe not."

"Let's hope they're alive, Dragutin."

"God willing, everything is possible."

"What are the soldiers saying these days? Who are they angry with?"

"They're angry with fate, sir. Some curse and some don't say anything. They're afraid things might even get worse."

"We'll pull through, Dragutin."

"You know best."

"But you must know it, too, Dragutin. Do you smoke?"

"Since they told me what happened at home, I don't even feel like smoking a cigarette."

"As soon as we get to headquarters, go see the doctor and get some ointment for the cuts on your face. They might freeze in the cold."

"Oh, it will pass, sir. The man might have killed me; still, he's all right."

"Did you do something wrong?"

"When doesn't an officer think a soldier's done something wrong? If I was an officer, who knows but I might've been even worse?"

"You speak like an honest man, Dragutin. I hope you'll act like one, too. You will be my orderly."

The car stopped again: some soldiers were taking geese from a peasant woman, who was crying for help, and cursing the government and Pašić. The driver honked, and Spasić poked his head out and shouted at the soldiers, who were now hitting the woman while the woman pelted them with mud; the geese were quacking. Spasić got out of the car and seized by his collar a tall, powerful soldier who was wearing an Austrian officer's overcoat. In the sudden silence before the car engine started snorting again, the soldier pushed Spasić into the ditch as he shouted:

"I don't care if Mišić's there! I don't care if it's God Almighty! We've had no rations for three days, and this woman has some geese. When the Fritzies find her, she'll give them roast goose and something else of hers as well. Give me a hand grenade, and I'll let her keep her geese!"

That's another man who'll hurl himself against the Austrians, Mišić thought, satisfied by the man's words and strength.

"Dragutin, here's two dinars; give them to the woman for her goose. And call Spasić."

Dragutin came back with the soldier, who was carrying the goose under his arm. He stood at attention and saluted the car, looking to see who was inside.

"God was on your side, my man!"

"Sir, I couldn't believe that you were really General Mišić. I made a bet about the goose. And I'm hungry, too. I could eat the highway!"

"What's your regiment?"

The soldier gave him a hard stare: what does he want to know my name for? He won't give me a medal or promotion—a box on the ears, more likely. Sibin got it, so let him look for him if he must look for somebody.

"My name is Sibin Miletić, and I'm from the village of Šljivovo, near Palanka." He looked hard at the general: no, he wasn't angry.

"And what troop are you serving in?" Mišić was delighted: what a man!

"I was a time-setter in the artillery section of the Morava. Since leaving Šabac I've been a gunner. Until the Austrians captured our battery, that is."

"And how in God's name did that happen?"

"Well, first they trained their howitzer on us and killed everybody but me." He fell silent, and looked at the general's mustache: no, he doesn't believe me. "You know better than anyone, anything can happen in a war. Just then I had to relieve myself."

"Lucky for you!" said Mišić with a smile.

"Then I was transferred to the infantry, which I don't think was fair." It was all right—the old boy was smiling. What should I ask him for? Or should I drive a nail into the coffin of that silly ass Major Rakić?

"We'll soon have new cannon and plenty of ammunition, so you'll be back in your proper place. Meanwhile, Miletić, do what you can with your rifle. That's also one of a soldier's tools. Good-by! Hurry back to your platoon. And kill that goose, or it'll die on you."

The car jerked forward to the accompaniment of the horn. The soldier stood still in its tracks, with a certain feeling of victory. He looked at the multicolored tracks in the mud, then at the black, lurching mass which was pushing through the crowd of refugees, soldiers, and animals. He could see the general's head framed by the car window. He walked forward in the track of the car, feeling vindictive. Still bewildered, the soldiers looked at him. He spoke in a low voice, but angrily:

"Who can know how to act right, and what's best to do in this mess? Why did I tell that lie for nothing? May Sibin Miletić forgive me, God rest his soul! And all because of a damned goose that I could catch whenever I feel like it! I didn't even say anything about the cannon, which would do me some good. And for General Mišić to catch me just now!"

Angrily, with his bayonet he cut the goose's head off and threw it into the underbrush. The soldiers and civilians watched him in bewilderment for a few moments, and Aleksa Dačić, holding the goose by its neck to reduce the dripping of blood, said to himself and to them:

"Who'll believe that I talked with General Mišić man to man? And he said plain as can be, 'You've shown the Huns your backsides long enough!' Didn't you hear? You should keep quiet while the old boy is talking. Well, good luck to him, and to Sibin Miletić. The general will remember him as a dead man, though. What an idiot I am! He'll need to know who I am, when he recommends me for the Karageorge Star!"

He moved along the road in front of a flock of sheep and a fiacre full of women, paying no attention to the driver when he shouted to him to get out of the way. A man is born the son of a peasant, and once in a lifetime sees a real live general—but sees him when it would be better if he hadn't! Why hadn't the general appeared at Mačkov Kamen, blast him? He should have seen me when I laid low a battalion of Huns with buckshot. But taking a goose, of all things!

"Now Pajo, and you, Miloje, you saw me talking with General Mišić. What I said is my business. When Major Rakić asks you, you just say that he called to me from the car and that we talked while he smoked a cigarette wrapped in a piece of newspaper. And that's all you know. Nothing to argue about, and we'll share the goose like buddies."

The driver of the fiacre sounded his horn, and he and the ladies shouted to Aleksa Dačić to get out of the way. But all the time he managed to keep walking in the tracks of the car. That was what he felt like doing, to follow the tracks of the general's car until dark. The war might soon be over, everything had gone to pot, and he hadn't even become a corporal. His battery commander had twice proposed his promotion to corporal, and recommended him for a medal for his performance at Mačkov Kamen. But nothing came of it, Major Rakić had spoiled it all, damn his guts. What if he landed him one in the dark, somewhere like this, on the road? A rifle could go off—who would know which? Three months of war, he was going deaf from the noise of cannon, and still not a single star. And some people were already sewing them on for sergeant. And they've never heard the howitzer shells whining over their heads! It wouldn't help if God Almighty was his uncle, now that that blasted Rakić had got his boot on his neck. He'd even got him transferred to the infantry. By the time his commanding officer got to know him, and the battalion commander heard about him, Serbia and the war would be finished. When they had begun he had sworn to himself, while looking at Prerovo, that he would go back there either as an officer or as a rich man with a cellar full of ducats. But he wasn't going home without either the stars or the money.

"Stop that racket! I'm not going to get out of the way. If you touch me with that fiacre, I'll put a bullet in your belly. It's women you've got inside there, not shells. You can go around me if you're in such a hurry!"

Perhaps it wasn't such a bad thing that he'd been transferred to the infantry. Now that everything had gone to pot, and there were no leaders, he could go wherever he liked. Why not take something from two or three of these fiacres? They're not carrying just rugs and rice and sugar in those bags. Women like that are probably hiding a bag of ducats between their tits. In all those bags, they can't be carrying just dresses and shoes. Fine ladies from Šabac! They're fat, so their money chest must be fat too. He'd get his hands on those boxes as soon as it got dark! The big box could be forced with a bayonet. When they passed through a town that night, and went to the shops to get coffee and spices and other groceries, then he'd fill just two sacks. Who needed all those things now? And the money chest—a whopper! A few blows with a pick ax, and it would burst open like a pumpkin. Then he would make himself scarce and head for Prerovo; he would go there at night and leave before daybreak. No one would see him, and he wouldn't tell a soul what he'd brought and where he'd left it. If he got killed, it would all go to the devil anyway!

"Where do you think General Mišić is off to, Pajo? He hasn't come into this ruckus just for the ride. It's never too late for us to die. Just remember what I'm telling you. He'll have us at the Drina again. How'll he manage it? Why, haven't you heard all the officers saying the same thing, ever since we joined the army? You must be ready to die for your fatherland, they say. But who's going to pay taxes, if all us peasants get killed? Now listen, when it gets dark, keep close to me. It's those bags in the fiacre I'm thinking of. What do we need eiderdowns for? Only things that we can stuff into a bag and our pockets. Don't worry, they won't get away. It's getting dark now."

At the entrance to Mionica the car thrust its way through a mass of soldiers and baggage wagons. Soldiers and civilians alike were cursing, and struggling to buy the bread and *rakija* which the local people were selling. The refugees clamored to get through, breaking down fences as they did so. Pedestrians and animals rushed through yards and gardens, amid the bawling and cursing of housewives. The chauffeur honked in vain. The adjutant shouted to the officers on the road to make some kind of order, so the general's car could pass. The officers looked at one another, then darted into the close-packed platoons and battalions, but the soldiers paid no attention to their orders and threats.

General Mišić looked closely at the suffering faces of the soldiers. Besides despair, he could see there only one kind of fear characteristic of soldiers: fear of the enemy. Nowhere could he discern that other kind of fear: fear of the commanding officer, and of failing to do one's duty. It was by this fear that a soldier defended himself against thoughts of death, and fought the enemy in all circumstances. Each soldier felt he was experiencing defeat and suffering alone, and that he faced death alone. He had lost faith in his officers, hence in the state and the fatherland; the loss of this faith also meant the collapse of that militant national self-consciousness which had enabled these same soldiers to defeat the Turkish and Bulgarian armies. Hopelessness was now eating into their souls like a cancer. From midday on he had been traveling alongside soldiers, and nowhere had he seen any sign of the firm hand of an officer. The officers had withdrawn into the rabble, and were distinguishable only by their uniforms, or by the fact that they were on horseback. The people had streamed into the soldiers and infected them with their own fear and disorder, with the weeping of women, the wailing of children and animals. They had added their sufferings to those of the soldiers, imposing on them a burden of affliction too heavy to be borne, and depriving them of the conviction that they could defend their fellow countrymen and families. For the soldier, self-sacrifice had lost its meaning. It was urgently necessary to separate the refugees from the troops; that must be his first task. But there was only one road, and that was narrow and almost washed away. Always there was only one road for everybody and everything. And if Field Marshal Oscar Potiorek should cut that road during the night, then the First Army would be completely scattered.

Spasić was pushing his way with his fists through some soldiers who were preventing a munitions cart from getting out of the roadway. That's not the way to behave, Lieutenant! But he would not say this just now. He must not begin anything which he could not bring to a successful conclusion. Every order he gave must be such that it could be carried out. Otherwise the First Army would remain simply something marked on the military maps of the High Command. In the uproar and confusion he lost sight of Spasić. The chauffeur honked continually. Dragutin was not looking at what was going on in front of the car; he crouched down, hiding himself from the eyes of the soldiers. It was distasteful to him that he was in a car, and in the company of a general.

"Dragutin, call the lieutenant."

A crowd of furious, drunken soldiers in torn, mud-stained clothing rushed at the car to push it over, cursing the government and the gentry. This was a nice welcome for the new commander in front of the army staff. Mišić pressed his face against the window so that people could see him, but the infuriated soldiers didn't notice him. With a firm movement he opened the door, got out, and faced the angry soldiers. They suddenly grew silent and rigid, and let go of the car. Now he could greet them:

"God bless you, heroes!"

Some of them returned his greeting—not all, he noticed. But they all moved down into the ditch, through which ran a muddy stream. They were waiting for something. He would not speak a word to them now; he returned to the car. The officers cleared a way for him to pass, standing at attention in the mud.

"I apologize, sir. But this is complete chaos."

"It's simply a difficult situation, gentlemen. And if the officers behave as though it's chaos, it will become chaos," he said as he got into the car.

Once more they came upon a scene of confusion. To take over such an army from a demoted and ambitious commanding officer—whose vanity was certainly no less than his wisdom, and whose courage exceeded his knowledge—would be an agonizingly difficult experience at the end of a difficult day, and the beginning of an even more difficult night. And this was the region where he had been born: he knew every tree.

Crawling slowly, they managed with difficulty to reach an inn, in front of which the horses of the staff were tethered to some lime trees. Orderlies stood under the eaves, staring at the car which came to a stop beside them. Mišić got out and greeted the soldiers, and then saw that the bridge over the Ribnica was thronged with soldiers and supply trains. Soldiers and civilians were fighting one another to get across; a streaming mass of people, carts, and soldiers had already overflowed onto the riverbank. He could hear the oaths of the women.

This was the crux of all that unforeseeable chaos which was most densely concentrated here, and would thin out along the road in all directions—to Šumadija and to Pomoravlje, spreading with it the horror of defeat in the field and the hopelessness of a fleeing people. There on the Ribnica bridge—the only bridge by which his army could retreat, and the enemy could pierce the flanks of the Second and Third Armies—the struggle for survival must begin at once. The first battle is always against oneself. Whoever loses that one will also lose the last one.

He walked toward the inn, but slowly, with unsteady knees: did he really have the power which the High Command believed he had? Had he not arrived too late? Was it not already the end of the last battle? Why were the orderlies looking at him so slyly and grimly? It took him a long time to accomplish the fifteen or so steps to the threshold of the inn.

He could not get into the inn, which was full of peasants and townspeople. The chaos in the army had its origin in the chaos of the staff, and the fact that the army had got mixed up with the refugees. The anxieties of the army must be separated at once from those of the civilians; they must not be allowed to mingle and to goad each other. He stood in front of the door and listened to the abuse of the civilians.

"Why didn't you accept the ultimatum, if you've got nothing to fight with? You've driven the people to their destruction, and now you're running away in front of them. Where do you think you're going, anyway? You've surrendered Valjevo. Why don't you take up your positions and die honorably? Where do you intend to go next? And what about all the war taxes we've paid, and you haven't got shells for three months? Why are the soldiers without clothes and boots? What's that Pašić thinking of? It's a disgrace! And where are the Allies? To hell with England, France, and Russia!"

"We defeated the Turkish Empire and Bulgaria, and we'll defeat Franz Josef, too! But don't bother your heads with worries that are no concern of yours."

It was General Bojović speaking. He couldn't see him. Presumably he would not receive his command over the army in front of this assembly! This was not the sort of staff headquarters which he wished to enter.

"Spasić, tell that crowd in the inn that I've arrived," he said to his adjutant, and fastened all the buttons of his overcoat, then stood at the entrance of the inn.

Spasić pushed aside the civilians. "Get out of the way, General Mišić has arrived!"

The people inside parted and turned toward the exit to see him. In the half-darkness of the inn he could hardly recognize people's faces; he knew the names of some of them, and who they were. Still they did not come out, and when they did they moved slowly. He coughed in the doorway. A hush and whispering spread through the café: The civilians began to move, while the officers who were drinking *rakija* at the tables got up and stood at attention. He stood motionless, still not speaking, waiting for the room to empty. The civilians—people he knew from Mionica—greeted him by raising their hats and fur caps. He barely returned their greeting. He looked at them severely, pushing them close against the wall; one by one they began to move rapidly and silently past him, staring straight ahead, crushed, like criminals, and then disappeared into the seething crowd on the highway. He waited until the last civilian had shuffled out, still not moving a muscle.

Under a window in a corner of the inn, General Bojović lay on a sofa with his leg in bandages. At last their eyes met; a sharp igniting of glances loaded with memories of clashes and insults when they had both served on the General Staff during the war with the Turks. Bojović still did not greet him: well, let him endure his disgrace to the bitter end. He could feel a sense of superiority and victorious scorn rising within him: Bojović had obtained the order from the High

Command; he had been dismissed not only because he had been wounded. If he could not stand up, he could at least raise himself on the couch. He knew well enough who was the senior on this occasion. The service rules held good for General Bojović, too. In the sudden silence the windowpanes rattled from the artillery fire; a volley could be heard in the distance. The racket continued on the highway; the squeaking of carts, and the refugees shouting at the soldiers, the cattle, and each other.

"Come in, Mišić!" said General Bojović crossly.

Mišić said nothing, and looked at the officers in turn: he knew them all. Hadjić, the chief of staff, was a careerist blown up with conceit and snobbishness. He would occupy himself with administration and writing reports to the High Command. There were some able men there. Since Mišić had been retired in 1913, the man beside the beam, Major Savić, had stopped greeting him in the street. And that fat Djurić had turned his head the other way, pretending he had not seen him. Lieutenant Colonel Rašković had stopped coming to his house. Professor Zarija—now what was he doing here? He suffered from fatty degeneration of the heart and so had withdrawn into the staff. An artless chatterbox—good company during a sleepless night; he was smiling with pleasure. Captain Lukić, a gambler and a womanizer, had whistled to him derisively from the stairs of the officers' mess when Putnik had dismissed Mišić from the General Staff. Apart from him, the rest were competent officers.

"What are you waiting for, Mišić? I'm wounded, and I'm older than you," said Bojović, still more crossly, leaning on the sofa with his elbows.

Mišić continued to observe the officers and weigh their qualities. His expression revealed the scorn he felt: no order in the staff means no order in the army, gentlemen staff officers. He walked between tables with unfinished glasses and carafes of *rakija* and came up to Bojović, whom he first of all saluted. Bojović barely grasped his outstretched hand.

"How is your wound?"

"You should leave that question until last."

"I have done so, in fact. Before I asked, I had seen what I needed to see on the highway. And here in Mionica, when the soldiers under your command tried to overturn my car. And here in the inn, too."

"Still, I see you have arrived alive and well," interrupted Bojović.

"Yes, I'm alive, but covered with mud and extremely worried."

Bojović lifted himself up and sat sideways, with his wounded leg stretched out on the sofa. He began to shout:

"For a whole month I've complained to Putnik and to you that my army is exhausted, that half my officers are dead or wounded! I've begged them in vain to send us ammunition for the artillery and clothes for the soldiers. And how many times have you yourself said: 'You must make do with what you have!' With what, Mišić? With whom was I to defend Valjevo? My men were sick and tired, they collapsed in the ditches. There was no one to carry off the wounded, no one to bury the dead. Those same soldiers who were victorious at Kumanovo and Bregalnica—now, after Mačkov Kamen and Jagodnja, are marauders and deserters!"

Mišić was familiar with this tone and knew all these facts. The only thing that interested him was what the staff officers thought about these facts, so he sat down at the first table and looked at them without blinking. There were other facts he must begin to talk about here: facts which it was difficult to see; facts which did not express defeat, but awakened hope and a powerful impulse toward endurance and survival. Why was the chief of the operations section smiling at him so ironically? Some of them were glowering and offended. He lit a cigarette.

"Last night my entire regiment scattered. And Putnik gives orders that deserters must be shot. Can I shoot the whole regiment? Would you please be so kind as to carry out Putnik's order!"

"I don't think it will be necessary to carry out that order. As regards the other things, I'll do all I can. The car is waiting and I suggest you leave at once, so as to get through to Glavica while there is still some light left."

"I want to hand over the command in the proper manner," said Bojović, scarcely raising his voice as he lifted up his wounded leg with his hands.

Mišić wanted to finish the takeover as quickly as possible, so he said: "I am well aware of the state of the army, and the chief of staff will inform me of any changes that have taken place today. I wish you a good journey and a speedy recovery."

Bojović angrily pulled at his long, pointed mustache, and gave Mišić a withering look. Then he got up, supporting himself against the sofa. His adjutant ran up and took hold of him. Bojović pushed him away with his elbow:

"Take my things. I wish you success in your task, Mišić!"

Mišić extinguished his cigarette, got up, and held out his hand.

Bojović simply saluted, then turned to the officers, who were all standing at attention: "Gentlemen, I thank you for your co-operation. You have honorably performed your duty to King and country. I am sure you will do the same under the new commander of the army."

While the officers came up to Bojović to take leave of him, Mišić went out onto the steps leading to the café. The bridge above the swollen Ribnica seemed even more hopelessly thronged with refugees; the baggage carts and herds of cattle seemed unable to disentangle themselves on the bridge: it was a scene of whirling confusion. From the direction of Valjevo, even denser crowds of soldiers and refugees, intermingled with animals, streamed along amid shouting and wailing. And the enemy artillery was energetically and methodically performing its task alongside the infantry, keeping up its concentrated firing in the lower Podgorina. First he must make order here in the staff, and then outside on the bridge. He would begin with the bridge; that would be the starting point for bringing order out of chaos and transforming the rout into an orderly withdrawal to be controlled by him, and not by Field Marshal Oscar Potiorek. What directives should he issue first? Not a command, but just some words, some thought. The rain and his forebodings became fused in the gathering darkness. He heard the car move away, and turned toward the officers.

"Sit down, gentlemen," he said, and himself sat down at a table which commanded the entire inn.

Major Savić, the man who had not greeted him after his retirement, came up to his table to collect the half-liter carafe and glasses. Mišić let him perform this menial task, but did not look at him.

"Colonel Hadjić, give us the latest reports from the divisions. And your most recent orders."

Colonel Hadjić ordered lamps to be prepared and the tables rearranged so that military maps could be spread out.

"Arrange the lamps so we can see each other clearly. I know the positions of the army. I don't need a map. If you don't know the positions by heart, then read them out. But only if something has changed since this morning."

Speaking in a hoarse voice, and clearly suffering from a cold, the chief of staff somewhat confusedly indicated the positions of the First Army and the directions of attack from Potiorek's Sixth Army. Mišić drummed quietly on the table with his fingers, lost in thought; and as Hadjić indicated the positions of the divisions and regiments, he could see the country as though on the palm of his hand: a firm line should be formed in clearings of the forest and the ridge as far as the foothills of Suvobor; if they could not attack at once, then they would lure Field Marshal Oscar Potiorek deeper into impassable country, where his artillery would not be able to follow. Overlapping steep slopes, crisscrossing streams, interweaving slopes—not a step further! There only the countryside and bad weather will work for us. Suvobor and Maljen are the army's reserves: my strategic reserves.

"And what is happening in the army of Field Marshal Oscar Potiorek, Colonel? Would someone please bring me a cup of lime tea?"

"The enemy continues to act with great energy, sir."

"Have their reserves been brought into the front line? What about their supplies? How do they feel on the sodden Serbian soil?" he asked, staring at the officers. Why were they smiling at these questions?

"Well, I wouldn't say they find it easy. As for bringing up their reserves, we don't know."

"It doesn't seem that they are having all that much difficulty in moving forward, Hadjić. Have any of our Slavic compatriots come over to our side?"

"Recently, only those with no alternative. A few of the educated people among the Croats."

"And what can you gentlemen tell me as a group about the enemy? Are they rampaging around Valjevo?"

"We don't know anything about Valjevo. Today the Austrian howitzer was firing in positions it did not occupy yesterday. It's very difficult to find out anything more. We haven't any new prisoners, as we're retreating all the time," said the man sitting near him.

"You know so little about the enemy that you can't give sensible orders to the divisions! The army's sunk in fear, and the command is groping in the dark. The Austrians are pursuing, and you're running away, and looking at maps to see how far they've got. Hadjić, give this order to the divisions at once: tonight all regiments are to send out strong reconnoitering groups to bring in enemy prisoners. By noon tomorrow I wish to have exhaustive reports about the enemy."

"We're up against material difficulties, artillery, and greater numbers, but not brave soldiers or superior command. That's the general consensus, sir."

"A general consensus of that kind gets us nowhere at all, Colonel. Because the superiority you refer to will always be on the side of the enemy. That superiority is the basis of their policy of attack and their operational plan. Without it, Austria would never have attacked Serbia. If we wait until we're on a level with the enemy in numbers and equipment, or count on this, they'll push us into Macedonia by Christmas. We must be quite clear about one thing, gentlemen, that we can successfully resist our enemies only if our command is twice as intelligent and our will twice as strong—if the morale of our troops is higher. What I mean is that both our command and our troops have to perform better. There's no other way."

He stopped speaking and looked at them in turn; he could see smiles on some faces, though some were frowning. He counted those who showed that they believed what he said; they were the majority. He continued confidently in a quiet but firm voice:

"First of all, it is essential to transform this chaotic flight into a strategic withdrawal. That means giving up unfavorable positions in order to take up better ones and create conditions for a full-scale attack toward the Drina. Our country is too small for us to follow the example of Kutuzov and count on the weather and the vast extent of our territory. And while you're working with me, don't forget this: our army is a peasant army. Our soldiers are defending their homes and children. They're fighting for their lives, for survival. For this purpose, the Serbian army can endure everything and dare everything. But its command must know precisely what orders should *not* be given to such an army. I think that as long as the war lasts I have nothing more important than this to say to you. Now we must get to work. We must at once have some sort of order in front of the bridge over the Ribnica. I want to see an army passing through Mionica, not a rabble. Let the people go over first, and when the women and children and animals have gotten across, then the army can go. Savić, you go to the bridge and make order."

The stout, burly major got up slowly, sought support from the chief of staff with his eyes, then said:

"May I suggest, sir, that someone of higher rank should be with me on the bridge?"

"No, Major. It's not epaulets that can make order on the bridge now, but a strong man who is sure of himself."

"I'll do my best, sir."

Mišić looked at him as he laboriously went out; he was listening to the shouting on the bridge, and the evening attack on the Morava Division.

He sat down by the window, through which he could see the bridge over the Ribnica. His first operational order to the First Army must be carried out. This was his first battle: if he lost it, who could tell what else he would lose tomorrow? The darkness was deepening. Beside the bridge Major Savić, his saber unsheathed, was rushing ineffectively at the crowd of refugees swirling over the bridge. Above their heads deep-toned, long-drawn-out explosions of shells reverberated, while volleys of gunfire from the Kolubara mingled with the rumbling of carts into agitated movement along the muddy highway in the rain.

Major Savić brandished his saber and struck some soldiers streaming from the bridge, who paid no attention to his shouting and blows.

Hitting people was a mistake, the wrong way to go about it. In the barracks a soldier gets a box on the ears for disobedience, but he should not be struck while on active duty. No one had the right to humiliate that wretched man now.

The chaos became even more dangerous. On the other side of the Ribnica—the side from which the Austrians were advancing—crowds of new arrivals were spread out on the riverbank. He could no longer hear or see Major Savić. He turned toward the officers, who were standing against the wall or around the tables, silently watching as he stared at the bridge. He would send two or three sensible men out there. He selected several such officers, and told them not to behave like Savić.

"I wish to report, sir, that the commander of the Morava Division has announced that the positions on the Kolubara must be abandoned immediately. Tomorrow morning the Austrians will break through onto the road and cut off our retreat."

"That must not happen, Hadjić."

"We must make it possible for the soldiers and supply trains to cross the Ribnica. There are two batteries of the Morava Division there. The people can cross tomorrow."

"You mean we should leave them on the other side tonight?"

"There's no alternative, sir, if we don't want to risk the batteries and all the supplies of the Morava Division being captured. That would be disastrous."

"We mustn't let the people be taken prisoners and herded off tomorrow. And when you give your own opinions, choose your words more carefully, and more like a Serbian."

"But we must sacrifice something."

"We must act so that nothing need be sacrificed," replied Mišić, and turned back to the window; taking hold of the grille, he stared again at the bridge. What if those three men do not succeed either? He must not lose the battle of the bridge, the battle to restore order. He would send Hadjić there, too: that "elitist officer," as they considered him in the High Command. He continued to watch, waiting to see what the three men would achieve. He could hear them giving orders, but the words were lost in the bleating of sheep on the opposite bank of the Ribnica.

Professor Zarija came quietly up to him, smirking in his uniform as though it had been stolen. His face and lips swelled with the desire to talk. In peacetime—mornings, in the outdoor café of the Moskva Hotel—he could tell you what the fine folk of Belgrade had even dreamed about the previous night; maybe he would be equally knowledgeable now about the army, or at least about the staff.

"Sit down, Professor. Are you all right, apart from your cold?"

"I'm very glad you've come, sir. And you've arrived at the eleventh hour—even later," he said in a quiet, confiding voice.

"I would say that when it's a matter of the time, it depends on the watch and the manner of reckoning. Everyone has his own twelfth hour."

"I'm clerk to the staff here, so you can imagine how much I know about strategy and tactics. But I can see a few things. Perhaps we'll be saved now by those words of Njegoš: 'What cannot be, now will be.'"

"Well, I think that what poets have described as impossible is the one thing that people must do to survive. And for Serbians, Professor, the impossible is to show greater wisdom than the enemy, and to endure more than he can. To do what can be done. And that always means doing more than the stronger party. When it's a question of survival, I don't know any better strategy and tactics for us Serbs." He turned away from the professor and again stared at the bridge, sipping his lime tea.

For a moment the officers he had sent out managed to halt the movement on the bridge, then the infantry streamed forward in an even more uncontrollable rush.

"I think, sir, that all this is just a waste of valuable time," said Hadjić, the chief of staff, in a tone of unrestrained anger.

"I don't think so, Colonel. We must spend a certain amount of time on the bridge. That's on the watch of Field Marshal Oscar Potiorek."

"Not even a machine gun could stop that elemental chaos."

"But the commander of the army must do so."

"You must decide, sir, when and where the staff of the army will withdraw. It would be a good idea to make preparations while you are undisturbed."

"In the present circumstances, and contrary to the rules, the staff of the army will not leave Mionica tonight. We will stay here until daybreak. The army must see, and the people must know, that we are here."

There was a sound of revolver shots on the bridge, and a sudden burst of shrieking. On the other side of the river cows began to bellow. The battle on the Kolubara raised its menacing voice. As they walked past the inn, a group of soldiers and women, some of them with children in their arms, threatened those who had stopped them on the bridge with revolvers. Mišić took this as a threat to himself. The power of that threat was not only in the despair of these soldiers. Everything he saw before his eyes, every thought that passed through his head, everything he heard and remembered combined into one explosive threat of imminent catastrophe. He had once fallen into that same Ribnica, fallen in fright from a willow tree one stormy night when his teacher had punished him, sending him to fetch a jug of water from a cave because he could not bring himself to beat a schoolmate for stealing walnuts; now he might fall into the same river that night—for the last time! He would tempt fate—indeed he must do so, and he wanted to do so. Now it was too late for him to change his decision. The entire staff would take it as a sign of failure. He would be defeated over his very first decision. Should he send Hadjić out; in fact should he send all the staff onto the bridge? And what if they didn't succeed either? This was not the moment to risk all of them losing their authority. At least it was not yet dark. Then it would indeed be impossible to accomplish anything, and this unending stream of chaos and despair, born of defeat, would surge all night toward Rudnik. He would go out himself. Now, this moment, on the bridge, he must affirm his strength of will and test his power. His hand must seize by the throat the confusion and fearfulness of the army and the people. That panic must subside in the face of common sense and courage. More revolver shots were heard, accompanied by bleating, bellowing, and bursts of fire from howitzers; the entire northern area was ablaze from the infantry battle of the Morava Division.

He got up, moved away from the window, and ordered General Bojović's horse to be got ready for him. He refused Hadjić's offer to accompany him. A mud-spattered, ungroomed black horse was brought to the front of the inn.

"I hope I never see a horse like this again," he muttered. Then, with an effort he managed to conceal, he rode off into the middle of the highway, right into the crowd of soldiers who were floundering along in the mud with whatever speed they could muster. He stopped, so that they could see him and let him pass. Then he waited until those exhausted and hopeless soldiers, with their caps pulled down over their ears, could grasp that in front of them was the commander of the First Army. On the bridge, the fighting between soldiers and civilians continued. The officers came up; they recognized him, stood at attention, and greeted him. The soldiers also halted, stared, then saluted.

"You're in God's hands, and you're brave men. Halt at the crossroads, and draw up in formation in the orchard there," he said, without raising his voice.

They seemed surprised, and moved forward uncertainly. But in front of him a rent appeared in the crowd rushing toward the bridge, and the well-trodden highway became visible. He advanced slowly along this short, narrow cleft, with his adjutant at his side and Dragutin walking behind the horse. He could scarcely squeeze into that dense, funnel-like space under the lowering sky, with the riverbanks a living mass of people who might at any moment topple onto him and crush him; he settled himself more firmly in the saddle and shortened the fully stretched reins. There was a break in the wave of people from the bridge, affording him passage and a moment of authority; he speeded up his horse and without hesitation made straight for the bridge. There he stood rigid: never had he been in such danger; never had he stood so high above the Ribnica, which roared beneath him. On the other side of the river the bell tower of a church swayed with the random motion of his riding whip. He felt a desire to strike that humiliating fear which deformed him as he melted into the twilight, and which transformed into frightening specters the faces of all those people coming toward him, looking askance at him with hatred in their eyes, driven on by the exploding of shells, the bleating of sheep, and the beseeching cries of women on the riverbank and the highway.

"I command the soldiers to halt. Stop! I am the commander of the First Army!"

The mob suddenly came to a standstill, as though confronted with an unexpected abyss, and fixed their gaze upon him.

"Are you really going to leave the women and children at your backs? You've abandoned your villages to the Austrians, and now they'll slaughter your children and livestock on the road. What is this fear that is deforming your souls, soldiers? There's no place to run to; our country isn't big enough for flight. And what will happen to us if we do run away?"

The great mass of people could not hear him speaking in his

ordinary voice, nor could they see him as they rushed forward to cross the bridge, as if to find there their final salvation; they surged forward against those who were standing in front of him. But these latter—indignantly, silently—prevented them from moving further.

Tears of hope welled up in his eyes: the First Army was beginning to act! From those people—the first to recognize him: people who did not wish to go further but wanted to hear what he had to say—there flowed a wave of stillness and silence which poured over the bridge onto the other side of the Ribnica. He was seized by a sudden compassion for the soldiers, who were humiliated by both the enemy and himself.

"Soldiers, turn around and face me!"

"Do you really want us all to die?" interrupted one of them. At once he felt easier; he could have embraced that bewhiskered sergeant.

"I want as few of you to die as possible, Sergeant. I want us all to work together to pull through. It's those who run away without thinking that perish; those who fight back and who think, stay alive. The Austrians haven't reached the Kolubara yet, and you're rushing off as though they were coming into Mionica."

"Get out of the way! What do you want from us, Mišić? Go back to Kragujevac! Or go off to Niš or Salonika! Let us save ourselves as best we can! Those who've died so far have died for nothing!"

Those must be civilians; he sought them out with his eyes. Under pressure from the mob, the bridge had become jammed with soldiers: dark, unshaven faces, with singed caps pulled over their ears. If the first ones let the mob through, they would knock him off his horse and trample him. But he did not shout; he just spoke in a firm, severe tone:

"I want my army to cross the bridge after the last of the refugees. The First Army must remain an army even when things are going badly. It mustn't add to its troubles. Can you hear me, soldiers?"

His voice was drowned by shouting: "We're going home to defend our own houses! We can't do any more for the government. Let Pašić and the French defend it! Are you going to stuff corn into the cannon? I'm barefoot, and I took this jacket from a dead man; anyway it's too small for me. I've been living on *rakija* three days, but I have to fill my flask at bayonet point! All my folks at home have been killed—so what am I fighting for, General?"

The staff officers shouted to the soldiers to be quiet, and also yelled out his name, saying he was the commander of the army.

"Now soldiers, tell me your troubles."

"We've nothing left to die for, General, and nothing to fight with. But at least we can save our own lives."

"Good God, men, I haven't come here to send you out to die! I've come so that we can work together to save ourselves. We have to get ourselves organized into platoons and battalions and regiments. I give you my solemn word, you're finished with running away; your troubles will soon be over. Help is on the way, and shells, too."

"Is that really true, sir?" shouted a man whose face he could not see.

"Yes, of course it's true. I'm not asking you to work miracles, only to do the same things as your leaders are doing." Tears welled up in his eyes, and his throat contracted. "I don't love this country more than you do, and my head isn't worth more than yours. Do as I tell you, and you'll see how things will be with the Austrians a week from now."

"What do you want us to do?"

"Let me cross over to the other bank, and you follow me," he said, and got off his horse. He handed the reins to Dragutin, and walked slowly behind those who had begun to turn around and push the others to allow him to pass. One by one they were left behind him; then they pushed Dragutin to make him stop with the horse so that they, his soldiers, could be as near him as possible—a man who did not threaten or scold or curse them, who was not like any other commander they had known.

You can see what a man's like by everything he does: he came right into the middle of our blasted mess when our cart was tearing down the underbrush and stuck himself in front of the shaft, but perhaps he had his backside hindmost, but not under the shells which were spurting all over this chaos. We don't know where we're going to go in this cloudburst; our teeth will rot from this rain and tomorrow the frost and snow will rip the top off our ears and fingers and toes. We'll stay in this ditch forever, in the same grave maybe. It will be like he says maybe. It will be even better with him, just as he says; then there's nothing and nobody to rely on. We'll just see what this man with the yellow mustache will do, the one who turned up here in front of us in his new overcoat and boots up to his knees and his orderlies and his staff, just when everything was black as night and we'll never see daylight again. And what can we do when we had a dog's life before the war and now in the war.

They wouldn't even let the staff officers surrounding Mišić keep them away from him, but fought, pushed with their elbows, and crowded together, paying no attention to the commands from the staff to let them pass.

He walked slowly and softly, keeping himself well under control, as though stepping on eggshells, as he moved westward toward the Austrian divisions which were smashing his forces with their evening charges: perhaps at this moment and at this very point—the bridge over the Ribnica—the First Army would turn toward the Drina and Mačva, and begin the attack against the evil within itself, carrying on tirelessly as long as a single Austrian remained in Serbia. There were many who could do this: he could sense this in some cases by their voices, in others by the way they held themselves or from their mud-stained hands. If only they could sleep for three nights in a dry place, and eat hot food from a pot; if they could rest until ammunition and the students arrived! In their heads and hearts there was darkness and confusion. A victory was absolutely essential—and confidence in the command. Yes, that was what they needed. A hot supper and a good night's sleep. In front of him were a supply train, and a column mixed up with fiacres and cattle. He crossed over to the other bank and then was on the road. As they mentioned his name, the soldiers were hitting the women and civilians, who were hurling themselves forward to cross the bridge as soon as possible.

"Officers, draw up your platoons on the left, toward the gypsies' houses. Artillery and supply train, move over to the right side of the road. The rest of you wait a bit. Where are you going in such a mad rush? The army is with you; they're looking after you."

The officers ran down into the meadows and cabbage fields on the riverbank, calling out the names of their platoons. The soldiers looked at Mišić, still waiting for something, then slowly and reluctantly came down. He stood in the middle of the road, surrounded by officers. People were lighting the lamps in the houses in Mionica. There was no letup in the rain, nor in the artillery fire from Brеždje or the gunfire from the Kolubara. He must get everything under control, calm this senseless confusion, and convince them quickly that they shouldn't flee in this disorderly way, but retreat in good order.

On the riverbank beside some bare poplars, a line of soldiers was slowly forming: the first sign of order. The line grew, meandered in the grainfield, and swelled in the half-light. Already there was a platoon.

"See if you can find some food and *rakija* to distribute among the soldiers. Savić, do your best to find some. Go hunt up the quartermasters. Milosavljević, you help the artillery and supply train to get organized. Ask if there's food for the animals. Get some in Mionica from whoever has any. Now the refugees: the animals cross the bridge first, then everybody on foot. After them the carts. The fiacres from Valjevo last of all."

The passengers in the fiacres heard this and grumbled. He was not going to explain. He watched the first battalions of the Morava Division take shape on the riverbank, saw a regiment gather, a division gradually form. Yes, the First Army was growing.

"Officers, light fires. The men must get warm. And soon we'll have some bread here."

He lit a cigarette. In the gathering darkness along the bank of the Ribnica, people were breaking up hedges, smashing garden fences, and pulling out stakes; then fires appeared on the ground, kindled with the greatest difficulty, barely flickering. A whole row of fires was extinguished by the rain. Poplars and willow trees bent specter-like toward them, while behind the trees roared the dark, swollen river. The women and animals were crossing the bridge. That was how he wanted it.

"Would you mind, sir, if I played my flute?" whispered Dragutin.

"Have you got one?" He fell silent: would the music perhaps offend the unhappy people? But many people would see it as thumbing one's nose at their situation, and in such defiance lies the power of the Serbians. Yes, Dragutin understood very well what the soldiers needed now. "Get cracking, Dragutin! Do your damnedest!"

Dragutin pulled a flute out of his bag, and with faltering notes began to play a song from the plains. Some women hurled curses at him from the ditch.

"Take no notice, Dragutin, just go on playing. You're worth a battery of howitzers to me right now."

Dragutin played louder and with growing confidence. The soldiers making their formations could hear him, and those already drawn up huddled over the fires on the riverbank. Some of them were angry; others shouted, "Go on playing!"

"It's all right," Mišić whispered to himself, and went on smoking. Peasant carts and cattle began to appear on the bridge. That was what he wanted. He moved over onto the shore and stood beside the stone bridge. The rain poured down. The officers and sergeants called out commands to their platoons. Mišić gazed at them. There were not yet two full battalions; they were growing, but slowly. The soldiers were coming down from the road with difficulty, still mixed with refugees.

He would have promoted to first sergeant any soldier who laughed aloud at that moment. In jest, he would give him a medal.

Dragutin began to play a kolo. One of the officers swore aloud, and scolded him. "Don't do that now," Mišić whispered to Dragutin. If only he could give each of those soaked and frozen men a plateful of hot beans, or at least fill their flasks with *rakija*. He came down from the embankment, tramped across the grainfield through deep mud, and walked slowly past the columns of soldiers who were bent over, stiff with cold even in front of the flames which were struggling to keep alight in the rain. He couldn't see their faces, and this troubled him. Presumably they could see him, so he greeted them, then began to speak slowly and quietly:

"Our country is small. There's nowhere for us to flee. The Austrians haven't invaded Serbia to remove injustice or get rid of people that are no good, but to exterminate the Serbian people right down to the roots. Just think what's happening now in the towns and villages they've taken from us! It's far worse than in Jadar and Mačva last summer. That's because we gave them such a thrashing at Cer."

The soldiers remained silent; behind them roared the swollen Ribnica. He would have heard them breathing and their teeth chattering but for the noise of the river, the increasing clatter of munitions carts on the road, and the rumble of cannon. He raised his voice a little:

"If we want to stay alive, we've got to stop them and push them back over the Drina. And we can do it. I give you my solemn oath that we can do it!"

Sporadically the soldiers coughed. They were frozen, without overcoats and boots. And soaked through, after ten days and nights in mud and trenches. If only he could make them a pot of hot *rakija*, well sweetened. He summoned the battalion commanders:

"Listen, the soldiers must have something hot to eat. We haven't time to cook beans, but send the quartermasters into Mionica to get some pots and *rakija*. And tell them to get a sack of sugar from the grocer. Then, as quickly as possible, have them prepare hot *rakija* here where the men can see it, and give it to them."

He returned to the highway. He could see Dragutin still playing defiantly while old men and women swore at him, and the artillery squad, too. Well, let them be angry and offended, let them hate anybody and everything, provided they were not downcast and despairing. The gunfire from the Kolubara had stopped, but behind Breždje the artillery was still active. If that night, or before noon the next day, the Austrians cut off the First Army's line of retreat along the highway, who could tell when and where they would stop their advance? Walking in the ditch past the munitions carts, he returned to the inn accompanied by his silent officers.

Inside the inn he sat down beside the blazing fire of the stove to get warm and dry his clothes; through the flickering light of the lamp he could see the smiling face of Professor Zarija. He placed himself where he could be seen, and called to the professor. His was the one smiling face he had encountered that day between Kragujevac and Mionica— the only smile he had seen over the last few days, except for his little Andja with her kitten in her arms. He would send her some walnuts from Struganik. A cup of lime tea was brought to him. He called to Professor Zarija to come nearer, and offered him some tea.

The chief of staff informed him that the enemy, with two regiments and three batteries of howitzers, was firmly established on the left bank of the Kolubara.

"Do you think they intend to cross the river at dawn?" he asked, wanting further information.

"I'm sure they do."

He remained silent. If that happened, they would be in serious trouble. The supply train and heavy artillery would be lost, and many people taken prisoner. The army would become an even more tangled mass, and would be scattered beneath Suvobor. Then it would be even more difficult to accomplish anything.

"What about those damned Allies of ours, sir? If they're not bothered about Belgrade and Kragujevac, I suppose they're at least concerned about Salonika and the Dardanelles."

"It's a case of every man for himself," snapped Mišić; then they fell silent.

He heard a gun being fired close by. He pricked up his ears: the supply train and the refugees were milling along the road. There was another revolver shot from the direction of the bridge. The chief of staff sent his orderly to find out who was shooting.

Mišić decided to take up positions near the Kolubara immediately and to strengthen the rear guard. He must on no account allow the Austrians to cut the highway from Mionica to Gornja Toplica the next day. He asked for another cup of lime tea; then he would go.

The officer who had gone out to investigate the shooting returned with Dragutin. The officer spoke in a loud voice to the silent group around the stove:

"They were firing at him in the dark!" he said, indicating Dragutin, whose face with its marks from his beating embarrassed the staff officers.

"Were they really firing at you, Dragutin?" asked Mišić.

"Yes, they fired at me twice, under cover of dark. While I was playing."

Mišić looked fixedly at the embers peeping through the door of the stove. Those two bullets fired in the dusk were intended for him, Živojin Mišić. He remained silent for a few moments, then said:

"Well, come to think of it, no one's in the mood for music right now." He got up. "Let's go have a look at the rear guard of the Morava Division."

2

The dusk wove in and out of the hills, orchards, and groves. Behind General Mišić, who was riding with a group of men, the snorting of horses and the heavy beat of their hoofs resounded through the meadows, grassland, and wastes.

Although he couldn't see it, he knew well the ground over which they were riding, and the landmarks they were passing. It was his own country; everything was his that night. He could feel, see, and hear the earth. The horses of his staff were treading upon a land of centuries of laborious toil, where men sweated as they dug and grumbled over their plows; and always there was the same foreboding, the same continual fear in the frowning, angry men under their caps and fur hats, men with sunburnt faces and bent backs. Ah, there they were now in the underbrush; and over here were some soldiers sitting or lying beside fires in a dugout, with the rain pouring down on them.

"God bless you, soldiers! Get yourselves warm. Have you dried your socks? That's the way to keep healthy—keep your socks dry. Why don't you wake up those men sleeping in the mud? You could cut down branches, and bring kindling from the pastures. I know you're tired and haven't slept for several nights. But boys, you must have strength enough not to lie down in the mud and puddles. As soon as we've halted the Austrians, you'll be able to rest. Corporals, here's some packets of tobacco, pass it out around."

His horse bore him on, and would not let him make promises. The route he was following was impassable for carts and heavy animals when it rained. The sticky soil bit into his horse's feet; he was afraid it would tear out the hoofs.

"God bless you, soldiers! Why don't you make a better fire? The Austrians have stopped on the other side of the Kolubara, you needn't be afraid. And if they do cross to the right bank, they won't get far. Anyway, we've got to stop them, and then drive them out of Serbia. How will we do it? With everything that makes us Serbs what we are. Now tell me, can the Austrians go without sleep longer than we can? Can they move over our hills faster than we can? In mud and snow? Can they stand more hunger and cold than we can? And is the army which is killing an honest and innocent people, and plundering their homes in the name of Franz Josef, braver than one that's defending its families and womenfolk? I'm not asking you to answer me. When I've gone you can answer the question for yourselves: who is bound to lose this war?"

He spurred his horse forward, so that he could hardly keep his saddle as he moved toward the fires and enclosed fields. How barren and meager was this land! If it were not well fertilized by anxiety and endurance, not even a thornbush could have sprouted there. Now the blood and sufferings of the soldiers would fertilize this sandy soil. He was stopped by a startled sentry calling from an enclosed field:

"It's the command here, don't shout like that! God bless you, soldiers! Now how do you think the Austrians are feeling just now, in this rain and muck? Just imagine how you would feel on such a night if you were somewhere near Vienna, in a stream or in some bit of wood, not knowing the language or where you were going? We're stronger than they are, stronger by far. Only we've got to see that we don't forget it. We must never forget that they are more frightened than we are. But we must think better than they do, and act better, too. You must do your utmost to hold these positions until dusk tomorrow. Don't worry, in ten days' time we'll be singing a different song. Good-by, boys!"

Their silence and their rare words, expressing doubt and hopelessness, made him shudder. Yes, a victory was absolutely necessary. At Baćinac, perhaps, or Milovac? No, the highest ground in front of Suvobor and Rajac. He would take up firm positions there, wait a bit, then throw the enemy back across the Kolubara. Then, perhaps, from Baćinac and Milovac, they could begin the march back to the Drina.

"Yes, Professor, those barking dogs you hear are in my village. We'll be passing quite near it."

He was following a path of reddish-brown soil. It cracked and groaned, quite unyielding.

It was along this very path that his mother had carried him with a gaping wound, first to Mionica and then to Valjevo. He could recall the incident as though it had happened that very day: his mother had related countless times how an infuriated gray bull which attacked children and sheep had gored him. The bull had pierced his stomach with its horns and lifted him up, intending to either carry him off or throw him over its back. But his mother had flung the pail of milk over its head. The bull then took fright, dropped him in the pool of milk, and rushed away toward the sheepfold. His mother had stared at his entrails and the milk now mixed with blood, too terrified even to cry out. Then his aunt came up, took him in her arms, and ran toward the house, shouting, "Give me a needle and thread!" When his aunt began to sew his torn stomach, his grandfather appeared waving his stick. He said they must take him to the doctor in Valjevo, even though he was the last child—the thirteenth—and the puniest. It was only then, they said, after hearing his grandfather's words, that his mother began to weep and wail, and then carried him off to Valjevo. She related at great length how she had carried him home afterward wrapped up in a white cloth; she had walked slowly, step by step, so the stitches wouldn't cut into his wound. From time to time she had laid him down—a beetle wrapped up in white cloth—on the grass beside the underbrush, taken off her head scarf, and kneeling in front of him, prayed to the Mother of God. Maybe it was then that she had begun to call him "Beetle."

This path, which he was traversing with great difficulty, would be quite impossible for the artillery and supply train of Field Marshal Oscar Potiorek. That path was now doing its bit toward the survival of the First Army.

"God bless you, soldiers! Have you got some wood? Can't see any around here? Then pull down the garden fences. Over there, a bit higher up, there was always a haystack. Take out some of the hay, and don't lie on branches on this wet grass. Yes, Sergeant, I am Živojin Mišić—since yesterday evening, commander of the First Army."

From Valjevo and the Kolubara came the sound of two revolver shots. Then more.

This vast underbrush, which he had been so scared of as a child, now constituted the boundary of the country. And it too was fighting in its defense, catching hold of the Austrians, tearing their overcoats, scratching their hands and eyes.

Somewhere nearby, lower down beyond the large fire, there was a well which had long ago dried up; he wanted to see it again, and turned his horse in that direction.

It was only at noon in the summer, and in the company of a few of his boldest companions, that he had dared to look down into this well's dark depths. At the bottom there was a Turkish devil, among the skulls of Turks who had been cut down by rebels; it would wait until nighttime, then jump out and roam along the streams and the crisscrossing paths. "What's he doing now?" they would ask at the top of their voices, speaking to the boldest of their number as he leaned over the well. "He's crouching down and dozing," that hero would reply in a whisper, in order not to wake the devil. "And how big is he?" shouted the boys behind the hero's back, looking carefully around, ready to rush among the flocks of sheep, or hide beneath the bellies of goats and kids. "Well, he's no smaller than a horse." "But how is he different from a horse?" "He's got clipped ears, and his head is like a log. And wow, how his eyes are shining! You should see them!" Then they all fled. Only once had he ventured to look into the bottom of this well; he had cried out, "He's fallen asleep!" and pelted him with clods of earth. Then they had all thrown stones at the log-like head of the sleeping Turkish devil.

From the valley, in the direction of the Kolubara, came a burst of machine-gun fire. Then silence. At infrequent intervals a dog barked.

"Stop here a moment, Colonel. That black patch over there is my brother's apple orchard. There may still be apples there, not gathered. Let's go see."

He dismounted, and handed the reins to Dragutin; they could not see each other, but they could hear each other over the snorting of the horse. He slipped as he walked toward the fence, caught hold of a slimy stake, then continued alongside the fence, looking for the gate. There is only one place in the world which a man can call "my apple orchard," one place where he can fall down on "my earth." The first tree on which he lighted seemed to have the shape of a bird, the most wonderful little creature in the world. It was from this apple tree that he had first looked down from a height at his friends, his brothers, his aunts, and the cows, and gazed at them for a long time. This earth, on which he had walked barefoot, was muddy and cold in a different way; it felt different when one fell on it. His boots slipped constantly on the wet grass between the fence and the road, so he grasped the cold, damp, mossy stakes and for a long time held them close; it was as though he was clasping the hands of his brothers and friends, his own folks from Struganik. His soldiers. Old men. Dead men.

For Field Marshal Oscar Potiorek, that night there was no place which he could call "my path," and on which he had planted his bare feet; for him there was no place that was "my apple orchard," where even in the darkness he could see the pink piles of apples; for him, no barrier that was "my fence," covered with a silvery, grayish-green moss. He, Field Marshal Oscar Potiorek, could not smell in the rain "my" rotted stake, on which he had torn his linen shirts as a child, and won his first victories as a human being and a man, by climbing or jumping over it. He walked beside the fence, greeting every damp, lichen-coated stake. The stake and the fence: they were the peasant and the village, made from the earth and sun, driven into the ground to guard what is "mine" until they rotted there. And even when they had completely rotted away, they continued to indicate a boundary in a law court. A boundary and a defense; a sign of strength and identity before the village and the world. Each peasant had a different kind of fence; by his fence you could distinguish a man of substance from a poor man, a young householder from an old one, the house of a widow from one full of men. Every fence had its dog; he could remember them by their eyes and bark, he had watched them and listened to them across the fence. And then that firm embrace of the stake, that dark brown circle round the white houses. Having none of these things, Field Marshal Oscar Potiorek hated them.

He came upon the open gate; it was at war, too. He passed through the apple orchard, touching the old, bent branches. They were bare and wet. No, the apple trees were somewhere else, to the right of the gate. Small, rosy apples which did not fall before the first snow, and lasted until the cherries came. Their flesh was white and tart, and had a wild fragrance. He pulled himself under the crown of the tree, caught hold of the trunk, and shook it; it was thick, the same age as he was, and did not feel his pressure. He shook the branches: was that something falling? He did not want to strike a match. It was getting dark, but he could see everything. Only what is "mine" can be seen in this dim light. He walked along the fence to the place where the apples were usually piled, and encountered the scent of the apples. He breathed his fill. He wanted to lie down there as he used to do—not only when he was a child, but when he became a lieutenant, then a captain; right up to when he attained the rank of major, he always came home on leave at the time of the apple harvest. In the evening he would lie down on fallen leaves on the dry earth, between piles of apples, breathing in their scent and watching the Milky Way flooding the sky, while the village settled to its nightly rest. Once he became a colonel, he no longer came home for the apple gathering; now he was a general, and he couldn't even lay his head on that pile. He knelt down on the wet, life-giving earth, gathering up the apples. He ate them hungrily.

The officers wandered about the orchard, striking matches and looking for apples. A shot was fired in the distance, from the depths of the night.

Here in this apple orchard he and his elder brother had measured grips on their grandfather's club to see which of them would have to go to school, because an order had gone forth that the Mišić household must send one child to school in Ribnica. Trembling, they had seized the stick and pushed, hating each other, in front of the ever anxious eyes of their grandfather: the one who secured the last grip at the end of the club would have to go to school. Their grandfather had warned them severely to place their fists properly; otherwise he would decide that the one who cheated would have to go. When the grip of the two childish palms left only a small bare space on the club, and it was obvious that the elder brother would have to go to school, he complained loudly. Then the grandfather had muttered through his teeth: "Why are you shaking like that, Živojin? Go on, take hold of the club; you can grasp it with your fingers, and that's enough for you. You're small—not much use with the animals, and still less with a hoe and a scythe. The house won't have any good from you, so if we must send a child to school, then you're the one, Živojin." Hurt by this injustice, and disappointed in his grandfather for as long as he should live, Živojin had rushed through the apple orchard, wailing loudly. He hid among the weeds. Night fell, but he still didn't want to go home; he would hide until he grew up, and then become a rebel. Yes, he would become a rebel, but on no account go to school. With a lighted torch in her hand, his mother found him, and took him into her arms: "Poor little Beetle! It's better for you to go to school than for those heartless creatures to eat you. Everything attacks you—the children, the animals, the grownups. Just hide away in that school until you're a bit bigger." They had both wept, and then he fell asleep in her lap. His mother had sat on in the weeds until daybreak. In the morning his eldest brother had seized him by the hand; carrying a bag of flour and beans on his back, he had led him over the hill, then through the big wood to school.

The officers called to him; they had found a pile of apples.

"I've found some, too! Fill your bags. Dragutin, fill your saddlebags with apples."

He made a space in the pile of apples; he must sit down on them; his wet knees were numb with cold. The apples made a crunching sound under him. He listened: they were rolling down the hill. If his grandfather could have seen him sitting on these apples, not even his general's epaulets would have saved him. He felt an overwhelming desire to see the red skins of the apples, so he struck a match: in the pink gleam of the apples, light of summer and autumn burst momentarily into flame, then an even murkier, murmuring darkness enveloped both him and the apples. The rain tinkled over them. The Austrians would eat them, and what they left would rot. He took a bite from some of them and breathed in the scent of their flesh. It was two years since he had been in the village, but he wouldn't drop by his home that night. When his job was done, when the children of Struganik had nothing to fear but a Turkish devil at the bottom of a dried-up well, when only hunters and merrymakers fired shots over the hills, then he would come to Struganik and sleep one night in his old home. He would roast potatoes and pile up nuts in front of the hearth, and have hot milk with cornmeal mush for supper. He would get really warm, and listen to the talk of the women and the old men of Struganik. He would send apples to Louisa, and nuts to Andja; he would pick them and pack them with his own hands.

The horses shook themselves in the rain; they had got cold, after sweating. The officers and his staff were eating apples. He must get up and move on. He stuffed some apples into the pockets of his overcoat.

Again he was riding at the head of his staff; he held the reins firmly, and sat bolt upright in the saddle. The path was narrow and worn; his horse stumbled and sank to its knees in the mud. He wished he could traverse this path on foot.

It was along this path that his mother had carried him to the meadow, or led him by the hand, carrying a hoe and bags full of bread for the laborers. She was always sad and complaining: "You're such a tiny little thing! If I can just live until you grow up, so the goats and rams can't hurt you, and you can protect yourself from the bull and the big animals! I want to stay with you, Beetle, as long as the fine folk frighten you, and your aunts talk at you—tearing my heart out—saying that you're good for nothing. 'He's your thirteenth child and good for nothing!'—that's what my sisters-in-law shout at me. If I could only see you with your scythe among the reapers, then I could die at ease, Beetle."

Some shots sounded from the last position of the Morava Division's rear guard.

He stopped his horse at the crossroads where the paths met above the village. The tramping of hoofs suddenly ceased; the exhausted, sweating horses whinnied and shook themselves in the rain. Here his mother had stayed behind when he was taken across Suvobor to Kragujevac tied to a packsaddle, first to attend the grammar school and after that the military academy.

"No, there's nothing the matter, Colonel, nothing at all. Can you see that height, or at least its outline? If you can't see it, do you know which is the highest elevation in this district? No, not Straža. Baćinac. Yes, it's marked as Elevation 620, you remember, on the map. One division must make a serious attack on Baćinac—the Danube Division, second levy. And we'll place the Morava Division in a firm position on Milovac. From Baćinac and Milovac we'll begin moving back to the Drina and the Sava."

All the men around him remained silent. Had they no faith in the army, or did they not agree with his choice of positions for starting an offensive? The horses shook the rain from their manes, stamped their feet, and panted. Down below in the village, two dogs barked. No sign of light anywhere. The stream roared in the deep darkness.

It was under these walnut trees, when he returned from the war with the Turks (he was a lieutenant then), that he had gone out with his mother to this meadow, one Sunday in autumn, to gather walnuts. They had sat on pungent-smelling fallen leaves, and he had arranged the walnuts in heaps, while his mother had shelled them so he wouldn't get his hands dirty. She had looked straight at him and kept asking the same question: "You mean to say, Beetle, that you actually fought the Turks? You're a fine lad—you saw the Turks with your own eyes? And you gave orders to the soldiers, Beetle, and those men did what you told them to? My, I wish I could have seen that! I would like to have seen it with my own eyes, Beetle—you giving orders to the soldiers, and them obeying you. Did you say forty soldiers had to do what you said? You're sure you're not laying it on a bit for your old mother, Beetle?"

"I just want to smoke a cigarette, gentlemen. Then we'll go on."

Whenever he received a promotion, he had had the same conversation with his mother, and answered the same questions. "And are you now giving orders to two hundred men, Beetle? Do you mean to say it's now five thousand soldiers? You don't think this will bring you bad luck, Živojin? I like it that you've turned out so clever, and people do what you say. And that you don't have to dig this wretched soil, or drag beech trees down from Baćinac. And that you're a gentleman, and the government takes care of you. But I'm really afraid when a man has so much power over others, and one of my own kin at that. No good can come of it!" That autumn he was a major, and they had again gathered walnuts; she had shelled them, and he had piled them up.

The wind shook the branches and whistled over the hilltops. In the darkness he could faintly discern the huge crowns of the walnut trees. He breathed in the pungent scent of their leaves. In the distance two guns were shooting.

But when she learned that he was in command of a brigade, she never even asked any more about his work or rank. She would say nothing on this subject, and when his brothers or the neighbors started to talk about it, she would immediately leave the room. Thus as the years passed and he advanced in his military career, she would look at him with growing anxiety, gazing for a long time right into the center of his eyes, as though she wanted to see something there. And when she came to these crossroads to see him off, she was always more quiet and worried. The last time before she died, she couldn't get any farther than the gate. But she had spoken the same words as when they parted the first time, when his brother had hoisted him onto the white mare between a sack of food and saddlebags filled with dried meat, because all the men and older people in the house had agreed he wasn't suited to the work of a peasant, and so had better go to the town and seek a living that didn't need a hoe. On that occasion his mother had embraced him, and pressed him against her breast, and said, weeping: "May the Lord look after you, Beetle!" Those words came back to him in every moment of loneliness and anxiety. And on her deathbed, almost the last words she spoke were, "It's only Živojin I'm worried about!" "But why are you worried about him, when he's the best off of all your children?" "Well, maybe he is; but still, I'm afraid for Živojin. He's over other people."

In the distance the two guns were still firing. The wind howled, shaking the heavy, creaking branches of the walnut trees. The stream roaring down from above, from the village, swirled toward him. If his mother Anđelija were alive now, what would she say to him tonight, now that he was a general and in command of an army? A shudder ran through him.

The officers around him were talking about something, and asking him questions. He couldn't understand what they were saying. His cigarette went out.

"Let's go now. I'll lead; I know the way."

A spasm of shuddering ran through him, and his eyes smarted with tears. Never in all his life, right up to the present moment, had he listened to more significant words than those spoken by his mother when he left Struganik. Not even the words of love uttered by Louisa, nor the first words spoken directly to him by his children, nor the words of praise from three kings; not the news of the victories at Kumanovo and Bregalnica, nor Putnik's announcement: "From today on, Mišić, you are to be my assistant." Nothing, absolutely nothing, meant so much as his mother's words: "May the Lord look after you, Beetle."

"I suppose you know from your military survey maps that there isn't any better route for the direction in which we are going, Hadjić. The artillery must come this way as well. There's not one of our roads that the Serbian artillery can't manage. No, our paths are impassable only for the Austrian artillery. No, I'm not angry. But let me repeat: the supply train of Field Marshal Oscar Potiorek is bound to sink in this mud. All right, we'll say no more for the moment. We'll discuss this when we're settled in the staff headquarters."

His horse fell in the mud, and extricated itself with difficulty; he could hardly keep in his saddle. One of his staff fell in a puddle. The horses were getting frightened; the underbrush crackled, there was a sound of people crying. But he didn't stop; he pressed on slowly, and it suited him well that there was only Dragutin behind him, coughing slightly, babbling quietly and imploringly to the horse, and urging it to be careful—talking to it as to a member of his family.

That was a real man—a brother to the plants and animals. Everything that was part of the earth was his; everything which comes from heaven belongs to man. Somehow he had even had the strength to play his flute on the bridge. How had he felt then? How had he brought himself to do it? That was a good lesson for the army staff. He'd like to tell the military instructors at the academy that they should work with music and songs, not blows and curses.

Dragutin said something, but the horses' hoofs drowned his words. Mišić did not venture to ask him what he had said: hadn't it come to the point when it was all the same to the soldiers what ills they suffered, and who caused them? His staff had caught up with him.

The stream roared menacingly in the darkness. He could never forget that sound: the roar of a stream in the dark.

"Don't worry, Colonel. I know this path. I can see it in the dark."

He lit a cigarette and left it between his lips, then fanned the glowing spark so that it became a spot of light going along in front of him over Suvobor. And along the path. The path was as narrow as a trench, clothed with tall underbrush dug up to protect it.

Where was he going that night? Into what was this path twisting and turning through the darkness? And through it he must wind the whole of his scattered army. No pausing either.

At dawn the rain suddenly stopped. The clouds broke up on the edges of the battlefields and the mountains. A soft light spread over the wet, mud-stained soldiers and refugees, who mingled with one another along their route of retreat between the dark, silent heights and the valley along which the battle flowed and the Kolubara wandered.

The movement along the road became slower and quieter: the people, soldiers, and animals wound their way between the sun and the front; between the silence and Rudnik, Suvobor, and Maljen; between the infantry and artillery battles, as if they had become indifferent to the fact that at any moment they might be spattered with shells and shrapnel. Notwithstanding war and defeat, humans and animals wanted for as long as possible to see and feel the light and warmth of the sun; the decaying smell of weeds and damp earth; the fragrance of the sky, whose depths concealed the warm winds of spring, summer, and autumn, that brought flowering and ripening; and the light, thick scents of fields, meadows, and orchards. Women and soldiers, old men and children, seemed to want time to stop that noon: if they stood still, then the sun would stand still for them above the mountain crest between Suvobor and Maljen. Everything would stand still.

They stopped. They stood with their faces turned toward the sun and the silence. Behind their backs were battles and gunfire. But they breathed in the light, the autumn, the earth. Crowded amid the underbrush, huddled together in mud and puddles, everyone was alone. The women and children looked at the plum orchard beside the road, full of horses and soldiers; they looked at the soldiers sitting on their saddles beside the muddy, unsaddled horses, all sleeping with their backs against the old plum trees. All the troopers in the orchard had tied their horses to the trees, but only one was sleeping still in his saddle, his arms clasped around a plum tree with the reins thrown back over his head, so that the resting horse was tethered to his neck.

As though their glances had burned up his sleep, Adam Katić suddenly awoke. Dragan was there in front of him, caught by the sunlight: a muddy, sorry sight. Suddenly he felt sad: the finest horse in the Morava Division no longer looked like itself; even his mane was stuck together with yellowish soil. Of the flower mark on his forehead, only a dirty stain was visible. Along his belly and cruppers ran a finger of dried mud. Dragan was looking at him reproachfully, with motionless nostrils, clearly offended; his flanks were sagging: the poor creature was hungry. Adam got up from the saddle, stroked Dragan's forehead, then brought him a bag full of oats; Dragan gave a shudder of disgust, champed, but would not eat, then gave a sigh. How could he eat in this disfigured state—he, the finest horse in the Morava Division, spattered with mud like a wild boar?

Quickly Adam took his currybrush, comb, and a bundle of straw, and began to rub him down and clean him. Dragan's nostrils began to quiver with pleasure, and their eyes met. Some little suns were playing about in Dragan's blue eyes. Adam dropped his brush, and tenderly took the bony face in his hands and looked hard into his eyes: hills and clouds were sailing around the suns under the vault of the sky. Yes, Dragan would save his life again, as he had done last night, when he was the only one from the rear guard to jump over the chasm into which some of his companions had tumbled while under machine-gun fire. Only Dragan had leaped over the chasm like a sparrow hawk, landed in a puddle, moved off at a gallop, and stopped of his own accord in a sheltered place beside a water mill.

Now he found himself inside someone's apparently green and invisible eyes: he met that green, luminous glance, and plunged into it. From the road, from the edge of the ditch, among a crowd of cows and old women, and a little boy who was holding onto her skirt, a young girl was looking at him, a girl more beautiful than Natalia, if it was possible. He let go of Dragan's head and began to walk toward her, toward her thoughtful, staring eyes, then stopped: it was the first time he had seen such green eyes, and never had he seen such a beautiful girl. He began to tremble. He returned quickly to Dragan, turned his back to the girl, and went on deftly rubbing down his horse. Unable to believe his eyes, he turned again and looked at the girl. She was looking at him and the horse, sternly and thoughtfully, as she had done a few moments previously—but more at Dragan than at him. Yes, she was more beautiful than Natalia, smaller and more slender. The little boy leaning against her must be her brother. Her grandmother was leading a cow. And her father and mother? He looked for them in the crowd of old men and women, among the carts, sheep, and pigs. No one resembled her.

It embarrassed him that he was looking at her so long and intently; he returned to Dragan and continued rubbing down his flanks, his powerful chest, his hair, his long shoulders, his strong knees, his sinewy white fetlocks. While crouching, he turned around: she was still looking at Dragan, and she was much lovelier than Natalia. He looked down at himself: he was dirty, his clothes torn, his boots gaping. He ran his hand over his face: he hadn't shaved, poor fool—that's why she wasn't looking at him.

He took his knapsack and hurried away behind a shed to shave. If only she didn't run away! But he would catch up with her, and find out her name and where she came from. The war must end by Christmas.

After shaving, cleaning himself up a bit, and fastening his buttons, he returned quickly to the orchard. She was still standing there, only she had gone down into the ditch and was holding onto some milkweed twined around a broken plum tree. She was looking at his horse. He went up to her. She stopped him with a quick look, and smiled. Incredible! He could not return her smile, his jaw was rigid; he was trembling.

"What's your name?" he stammered.

"Kosanka. What's the name of your horse?"

"Dragan."

"He's lovely."

She looked at Dragan, while he waited for her to ask him his name. Someone called her, and she went away without a word. She hadn't even looked at him! He hurried after her, seizing the bare branch of a plum tree. She was rapidly disappearing into the crowd of people and animals which, as though struck by a whip, had suddenly started to move along the road. He caught up with her, out of breath; she was startled at first, then greeted him with a look from those green eyes and that smile of hers, but it was a much longer smile, and different from the one in the orchard. A warm trembling seized him under his torn, mud-stained jacket, as he continued to walk beside her. He hadn't slept for two nights, and he might easily have had a concussion yesterday; but even if he couldn't hear properly, he could see all right. She was silent, too, and was looking straight ahead.

"Where do you come from, and what family do you have?"

"What's that got to do with you, soldier, what family she has? You'd better get back where you belong!"

"I'm asking you as if I was your son: where are you going? Perhaps I can help you. In fact I'm sure I can." It bothered him that his voice was trembling, and he couldn't get out that sudden, life-saving thought that he would send them to Prerovo, and they could stay there in his house until the war was over and he came back. He took longer strides so as to see the old woman's eyes and what she was looking at;

her head was bent, and a blue scarf concealed her eyes. He dared not let the girl out of his sight in this confusion. Let the war end as it might—for him it had ended with her.

"I'm serious. My name is Adam Katić and I come from Prerovo, near Palanka. My father's a merchant there, and my grandfather is also called Adam Katić. Maybe you've heard of him. I'm an only child."

"So you're an only child, are you? No one to look after but yourself," said the old woman.

"You go straight to Prerovo, and to my house." He put his hands on her shoulders, bent down, and whispered into her scarf: "You can see for yourself that no one knows how all this business will end. Where will you go with Kosanka and the boy? They'll drop dead in the mud and snow. I'm telling you the truth, I've never lied to anyone."

"Get out of my sight, soldier! Go wait for the Huns, and don't hang around women's skirts, you pisspot!"

Bewildered and hurt, he stopped, then turned around so that he could see the girl's face—it would give him comfort and hope. She was looking straight in front of her, her head bowed under a large kerchief, keeping a firm hold on the boy, who was loping along, his eyes flashing.

"Listen," he said to the old woman, "your suffering has made you lose your wits. I mean nothing but good for you and your folks."

"But why should you wish any good to me?"

"Well, I just happen to feel that way. And I suppose your brain isn't so addled that you'd refuse a chance to save your lives. Now remember my name: Adam Katić, Prerovo, near Palanka. Say that Adam sent you. We met on the road, and I sent you to my home. Nothing more. Here's my photo as proof." He took out of his wallet a photo of himself in uniform on Dragan, and pushed it between the old woman's breasts. She threw the photograph in the mud.

He could hardly restrain himself from pushing her into the mud, too. The girl continued on her way behind the horses and sheep, her head bowed, pulling the boy with her. Overcome with shame, Adam bent down and picked up the photograph, then stood up and looked at the girl, slight and slender in build, and much, much lovelier than Natalia. Would he never see her again? Was she now leaving him forever? No, that could not be! He caught up with her, and for some time walked by her side. He was waiting for her to say something—anything—to him, for her to smile at him once more, or at least to look at him. He didn't care that the old woman was swearing at him as she walked behind. What could he do? It was broad daylight. He turned around: the sun was moving over toward Maljen and the Austrian artillery battery, which was keeping up a rapid fire. He must return to his squadron: there might be an order to move on.

"Wait for me by the church in the village where you spend the night. By the school, if there isn't a church. If there's no school, then wait for me beside the inn. And if there isn't an inn, go to the house by the crossroads in the middle of the village. And if there isn't a crossroads, then go to the house nearest the bridge. And if there isn't a bridge . . . There's no bridge . . . What if it's a mountain village with no bridge? Then go to the last house at the end of the village, on the road to the Ljig, Kosanka." He put his hand on her shoulder, making her jerk; but it was he who jerked her, before she managed to move away, he was sure of it. "If you don't spend the night in the first village, you will in the second; it will soon be dark. Then do everything I've said. Go where I've told you and wait for me; I've never yet lied to anybody."

She nodded.

He bent down, so that his face was closer to hers, and they walked side by side. Perhaps their bodies touched, perhaps she whispered something to him; he was lost among the flecks in the limpid, shining green of her incredible eyes.

He returned by way of the ditch to his squadron, which had remained lower down in the orchard, far beyond the bend near the end of the village. He stepped through the puddles with his arms hanging down rejectedly, without looking at the refugees who gazed in amazement at this soldier—the only person they had met coming along the ditch in the opposite direction.

The squadron was lining up in the orchard. The section commander caught sight of him and shouted at him, cursing him soundly. He ran up to the infuriated Second Lieutenant Tomić, who was waving his whip while chewing some candy. Adam did not greet him, but hissed straight in his face:

"Now listen, Lieutenant. If you use language like that to me again, I'll part your head from your body! Do you hear? I won't be spoken to like that!"

Second Lieutenant Tomić went on chewing his candy and brandished his whip over Adam's head, but did not hit him.

"So you're behaving like a rebel, is that it?"

Adam turned his back and moved off toward Dragan. It was Dragan who carried out the second lieutenant's orders: Adam did not hear them. They were running toward the Kolubara and the machine-gun fire. Wherever they ended up, he would go after the girl as soon as it was dark.

Now they were riding in front of thick clumps of trees on an extended slope, the last one in front of the valley and the Kolubara, from which direction the Austrians were pressing forward. Slowly and hesitantly they entered a copse, where it was already dark. The officer told them that they were the end of the rear guard, and would not withdraw from there until the division took up new positions.

"Get to your places, and no one's to move! Everyone answers for the man on his right," shouted the commander.

Adam didn't wait for the roll call to finish. He patted Dragan's neck, mounted, and went off at a walk through the waste, listening to the roll call behind him, and the machine-gun fire from the direction of the Kolubara. As soon as he got out of the waste, he gently spurred his horse, and hurried over the clearing toward the high ground and the road, from which floated the sound of people shouting at their animals, the creaking of carts, and some throbbing or beating. He could not follow the road, so he kept to the fields, staying close to the cursing and groaning, the laborious movement which his eyes could but faintly discern.

In front of him dogs were barking, and he could see a few dim lights: that must be the first village. She wouldn't be next to the church or the school, he was sure; but she would be there at the end—that is, if she wasn't next to the inn or the bridge, or in a house by the crossroads in the middle of the village. How would he see her in this murk? She could have told him where she would be; but she dared not, because of that old hag. Still, she could at least have nodded a bit more emphatically. She had been trudging along—perhaps she had nodded and he hadn't seen. But because of the people, the carts, and animals he would have to go through the ditch. People cursed him because he was riding, and because his horse scattered them. He pushed his way through the sheep and cattle. How would he find her on such a dark night?

"My God, folks, if this one-eyed hole hasn't got a church or a school, what is it called, anyway? No crossroads and no bridge? What's the matter with everyone tonight? Don't be cross, you old hag, I can't see you. Get out of the way, can't you hear the horse? Don't swear at me, I'm not a refugee—I'll trample you down. I'm just asking where the inn is here. And the bridge? And the crossroads? But how can you not have any of them, and how can every house be on this road? All right, then, where's the last house? Look here, girl, I'll give you ten dinars for a lantern. Nice people you are—and we're giving our lives for you! Is there a living soul in this yard? Answer me—you're Serbians, aren't you? At least tell me if this is the last house? Well then, how far away is it? Come on, Dragan, gallop!"

It was beginning to rain. I'll find you, Kosanka, if I have to look for you till daybreak, even if you're in the division commander's knapsack! He should have called out her name as he rode through the village. Perhaps he had gone past her. There were fewer carts and people on the road. He stopped his horse.

"Kosanka! Kosanka!"

He heard the murmur of voices, carts creaking, a splashing sound from the cattle. A man was complaining loudly; some women wailed. Come on, Dragan. Dim shapes of trees became visible: this must be the last house. A dog barked; he could hear shouting and curses. His back was wet. The hedges, fences, and clouds were all intertwined. The creaking of carts and despairing cries indicated that the road was near; he broke into a gallop once more. His ribs hurt, and he could hardly breathe. He slowed down to a walk.

"Kosanka! Kosanka, where are you? I'll find you before daybreak, my darling! On with you, Dragan!"

He could see a big fire, and spurred his horse to a gallop. It was a haystack on fire.

"Where is everybody?"

Flames leaped into the clouds; the dark depths of the forest rushed at the blazing haystack; the fire scattered them, contracted and compressed itself into the heap of straw. There was not a living soul to be seen. He guided his horse toward the light. He continued on his way, still at a walk. He had never before been deflected from his purpose, and he wouldn't be tonight.

Dogs were barking; this must be the first house. He called out, but there wasn't even a dog. He continued on his way: no sign of houses or lights, just total silence. Even the road was empty. He stood still; the horse was panting from exhaustion. The wind was tormenting a stray branch. He forced his horse to a gallop, but only for a short time; suddenly the horse was stuck fast. Frightened, he whinnied as he exerted all his strength to extricate himself; Adam could hardly stay in his saddle. Behind him was the dark night, and the sound of occasional shots. Perhaps he had turned off the main road. He went back to the solitary house.

He dismounted and led his horse through the ditch alongside the fence. The gate creaked: it was open. He took hold of it, but jerked

back his hand; he had grasped the wet back of an animal. He struck a
match: it was a dead dog on the open gate, hanged. Pale brown and
wet, it hung down, its head touching the ground. He went into the
yard, but he couldn't cross it, he couldn't go a single step farther. He
stood still and listened hard: somewhere near him a door was creaking
in the darkness, creaking and banging. He dropped the reins, removed
his rifle from his shoulders, and set off toward where the creaking was
loudest. He found himself standing in the stink of congealed dung—
the dung of cattle, sheep, and horses. He lit a match: at the entrance
to the stable was a broken wooden pitchfork. A shudder passed
through him. But he must press on to that sound of short, thick
creaking and banging. He lit another match: there was a dead cat on
the door of the house, hanged on the door handle. It was pushing
against the door, which swung back and creaked as though the cat was
miaowing. He shook the door with his foot, struck at the darkness,
crossed the threshold, and stood still, then stared at the one-time
dwelling of some poor family, at the filth beside the walls of their
house. He struck another match: there were torn, empty pallets
thrown on the ashes of the hearth, broken and overturned stools,
empty kneading troughs, a broken sieve. Murmuring darkness engulfed him, the cat whined against his leg. He could not turn back; he
was caught fast in emptiness and death, as in a vise. He managed to
strike yet another match: there was human filth in the middle of the
house, between the shattered sieve and the broken pieces of earthen-
ware. The darkness roared, rushing down at him through the hole in
the roof. A cry broke from him, then he groaned aloud, jerked himself
over the doorstep, leveled his gun, and fired at the house. He waited to
hear moans. He was trembling, and could hardly hold his gun. The
door creaked and banged; behind him his horse stamped. He ran up to
him, mounted as quick as lightning, and drew the reins taut, while
still holding his gun. The horse stopped dead.

"Hey, folks!" he cried out to hear his own voice. Then he forced the
horse onto the road and galloped off toward the Kolubara and his
squadron.

TO SPALAJKOVIĆ, MINISTER OF THE KINGDOM OF SERBIA TO ST. PETERSBURG:
GET ON YOUR KNEES BEFORE THE CZAR OUR SAVIOR STOP TELL HIM SERBIA
IS ON HER DEATHBED STOP PAŠIĆ

At dusk General Mišić and his staff arrived in front of an inn at
Gukoš where the army headquarters had been temporarily established

in the course of the retreat. Exhausted and hardly able to dismount, he threw the reins to Dragutin and stumbled forward, his legs tingling, his face gloomy. On entering the inn he stopped to receive the report of the chief of staff.

"A while back we received an urgent directive from the High Command with six items."

"Who signed it?"

"Vojvoda Putnik, sir."

This directive must contain something against me and my plans, he thought. He did not want to hear it now; at least he could allow himself that. He didn't want to hear of any directives from the High Command until he had thought out his own plan, and issued his orders to the divisions for the next day. He looked at the sky; it was heavy and overcast: would it rain or snow? Down below, near the Kolubara, he could hear shots and machine-gun fire.

"All right, Colonel. I'll hear you later. Where are my quarters?"

He was escorted through the village inn to a well-heated room, where the innkeeper was waiting for him, showing unseemly pleasure at having him in his house. He offered him some hot *rakija*. His face was wreathed in smiles as he announced that supper would soon be ready.

"Make me some lime tea, if you have any. Nothing else. And don't bother to light the lamp. Put some more logs in the stove, and leave me alone."

He took off his overcoat and left his knapsack by the window. Why hadn't Field Marshal Oscar Potiorek attacked more fiercely today, and pursued him really hard? He had let him bring his supply train and artillery across the Ribnica. He hadn't cut off his main line of retreat. Was he perhaps tired, exhausted? Or maybe after the Second Army's withdrawal to the right bank of the Kolubara—a withdrawal made without permission—he was preparing to strike a blow at the wings of the First Army, so as to squeeze it into a small space below Suvobor, and then deliver a crushing blow.

He sat on a chair in front of the stove, in which a fire was burning, smelling of bitter-oak. He liked that green, pungent smell of clean, cool earth, and of sap from the trunk of the oak. The new bedcovers smelled of wool and dyes. He knew well that smell of peasants' guest rooms, redolent of kindliness, feast days, and intimacy. He would have liked to lie down, stretch out, and doze a bit, before writing the orders to the division for the next day. But he couldn't lie down on a clean bed in his boots and with mud on his clothes. He settled himself on the chair, leaned his head against the wall, and closed his eyes. He listened to the fire, and breathed in the scent of bitter-oak and bedcovers. What should he do tomorrow? What had he done today?

Since dawn he had been at the positions, on horseback or on foot; he had visited all the staff headquarters, had made a point of being seen by as many soldiers as possible, and of having as many officers as possible hear his voice. He did not reproach anyone for any failure, or for not carrying out orders. Certainly not! Only commanders who waged war for glory and profit did not share defeat with every soldier. He listened to them as long as they wanted to speak, weighed their faith in himself and the troops, considered how long they could continue to hold out. To the platoon commanders he always put the same question, speaking confidentially and in a whisper, so that the officers on his staff could not hear: "Tell me, won't you, who are soldiers cursing? Tell me the truth!" He looked at them attentively, straight in the eye, and pondered every reply. "They curse the government, Pašić, the Allies. And they curse themselves, sir." Perhaps now and again some cunning fox lied to him, but many gave the same answer. "But how is it that no one curses the Austrians—the enemy who are doing such terrible things to us?" he asked. Their elaborate and detailed replies notwithstanding, he came to the disquieting conclusion that fear and suffering had killed their hatred; for it is well known that in human beings even hatred is consumed by great fear. But they still had some valid reasons for defending their dignity: they would not admit responsibility for defeat. They believed it was the fault of Pašić and the Allies, and were bitter against them because they, the soldiers, had suffered so much. Well, they were right, but it was obvious that their whole being as soldiers was in a state of disintegration. "Tell the soldiers that ammunition for the artillery is on the way. Our cannon will be more active than last summer. And there'll be clothes and boots, too."

He made this promise to every officer. It was little enough to inspire their confidence, little enough for the soldiers as well. It was not the best or wisest thing to make promises at a time of defeat. A commanding officer should make promises only to himself, and only once. Supposing the ammunition didn't arrive? In that case we just have to struggle on, to carry on the fight with what we have. With cudgels, with bare fists, with our nails. Because we do want to survive. That was what he must say to everybody. From that, faith and will power would be generated—from within oneself and out of oneself. That was the highest and deepest force working for survival. The commanders of the battalions and regiments all made the same complaint: more and more deserters. Whole platoons had fled from their posts. They had refused to carry out orders. They had raised their guns against the officers. They had all made much of this, as though they were boasting of the number of deserters and their bad behavior. This attitude forged by disaster boded no good; their eyes were dilated at the thought of evil. They were seeking pretexts for not carrying out the orders of the higher officers; they refused to take any responsibility. In great misfortune there is a certain state of mind that causes people to desire greater sufferings and burdens—a sign that the spirit of resistance has completely died in their hearts.

"And is it surprising that the morale of the army has collapsed, when the general situation is so unfavorable? When nothing that makes up a soldier's life is functioning properly? I ask you, gentlemen, what army in the world would not have disintegrated after all they've been through between the Drina and the Kolubara? But we haven't collapsed yet, and we won't collapse. We'll stick together until we have ensured the survival of our people."

"And what are we to do, sir?"

"You must do your utmost to change the living conditions of your men in every respect, and as soon as possible."

The bravest, or perhaps the most desperate, replied: "That doesn't really depend much on us here in the lines, sir. It's a matter for the government and the Allies."

Again, that misuse of the subordinate position. He reprimanded those who spoke in this way sharply:

"You leave Pašić and the Allies to mind their own business, and see that you behave properly as officers. See that as many soldiers as possible have a dry place to sleep, and that they sleep as long as possible. If you stay in the same place for an hour, cook some beans or prunes—whatever food you can find; but let the men eat hot food from a pot. A change usually begins with the pot and full rations. And they should mend their clothes and footwear regularly—and shave, and kill their lice. People should care for themselves first, then their fatherland. They've got to look like human beings, then life is worth while and freedom a necessity. As for the generally bad situation, I take responsibility for that. It will be changed, within a few days at most."

But that was a long time. He looked hard at them: many eyes had remained calmly fixed on himself, but some—by no means a few—had looked down at his overcoat or his feet, accompanied by a trembling born of disbelief. To those he would say in his ordinary, everyday voice: "Don't get so upset. I know what a tremendous job lies ahead." Then he passed on, thinking in detail of the officers he had met and talked with. He knew all the regulars, either from the military academy, where he had taught them, or from service with units he had commanded, or from examinations for promotion. He allotted to each his own task, thinking out their role in the future work of the army according to their character and abilities. Because one soldier cannot do everything. The reason for the existence of an army is that it can achieve the most if every individual in it does his utmost, and what he knows how to do best.

Throughout the day, riding from post to post, he had stared at the sky, which was swirling in gloomy uncertainty: if only the rain would hold off for at least two days, to give them a chance to pull their small amount of artillery and the supply train up to the heights, where they would be more sheltered than on the vulnerable road. If only the soldiers could have three days without getting wet, so that they could dry their footwear, and have bright fires at their posts. On the highest ground he got off his horse, walked some distance away from his staff, and for a long time stood gazing anxiously toward the Kolubara, Valjevo, and Povlen. Why had he stopped in his tracks last night? Why was Field Marshal Oscar Potiorek not advancing today? Was he changing the direction of his attack? Did he intend to make for Belgrade, or was he going to throw his forces across Maljen in the rear of his opponents, dig in on the crest of Suvobor, then drive them down to the streams and mud flats of the Kolubara? Only by means of an attack could he frustrate that intention of the enemy, whose plan would wipe them out if it succeeded. The attack must be launched from Baćinac and Milovac, the two commanding heights on the wings of his army. He would take up a firm position there, and launch the big attack on November 21. November 21? That meant in three days' time—the latest possible date. The attack could not be postponed. Perhaps these few days were the last in which the First Army was capable of attack. Later—in a few days' time—it would not be able to attack: it would be without men, without faith, without any wish to attack, capable only of retreat and disintegration, each man wanting only to get to his own home. He must tell every officer today that the Serbian army would not be defeated on the Kolubara, nor on Suvobor or Rudnik, but only when it no longer had the strength to attack, wherever that might be. But why was he still silent, why did he not inform the staff of his decision to start the attack from Milovac and Baćinac on the twenty-first?

The reason was that none of the division commanders and no one on the staff had any thought of attack. People were completely subdued by the immediate conditions, the general situation, and the facts of defeat. There was not a single objective circumstance, not a single event which justified the idea of attack. During the last ten days every battle had been lost, and every move by the enemy had forced them to retreat. To the staff his decision to attack would appear irresponsible, crazy. It would be interpreted as an expression of his personal character, his ambition and vanity—his desire to show himself wiser than Putnik, Stepa, and the Regent. Furthermore, he had refrained from announcing his decision because he was completely nonplussed about what Field Marshal Oscar Potiorek intended to do after taking Valjevo, Povlen, and the left bank of the Kolubara. If he were in Potiorek's place—how many times had he not pondered this with his head in his hands?—he would have continued pressure on the Kolubara with all his forces, marched over Maljen, hurried up to the Suvobor heights, cut off the First Army, and then hit hard at the Second and Third Armies in front of Rudnik. That would have caused immeasurable hardship. He could not think of a single military reason why Potiorek should act so slowly and hesitantly. Or could this man have some great overriding idea which it was impossible to discern?

Dragutin brought his cup of tea, and rattled the spoon to wake him. He opened his eyes: Dragutin looked clumsy and ugly, standing there with the cup in his hand while he stirred the tea. Even the poorest and most downtrodden peasant did not know how to behave like a servant. He was not suitable for that kind of work; he lacked the soft hands and deft, slender feet that it required.

"Will it rain, Dragutin?"

"It'll snow, sir. If it had held off for two days, the soil would have absorbed the moisture, and you could have got the plow going and sown some wheat."

"But in ten days' time, even if the weather was good, I suppose it would be too late for sowing?"

"If there was nothing to make the ground damp, and if the weather was mild like it was yesterday and until noon today, you could sow up to Saint Nicholas' Day. But the weather's changing."

Mišić sipped his tea, and listened to Dragutin counting on his fingers how many days it was to Saint Nicholas' Day. This peasant had not yet lost his belief that they could win: he was thinking of his sowing, putting it off in the hope that the land could be liberated for sowing before the snow came.

"And do you think, Dragutin, that we'll be able to win back Mačva, the place you come from, before it snows?" he asked, suddenly turning to him.

"You know that better than me, sir," he replied, bending down to put some wood in the stove.

The ruddy light of the embers suffused them both, the firelight moved the walls out, making the room seem higher and wider.

"Do you think the rain will hold off till daybreak, Dragutin?"

"I don't think so. A while back I was in the stable to put down the straw for the horses. Because of the manure. It looked as if it was just about to rain. There'll be snow on Suvobor and the high ground. If you wave your hand, the cloud makes your finger tips tingle."

Mišić smiled with pleasure. He had never heard such a forecast of rain! He wanted to go on listening to Dragutin, but the chief of staff entered:

"May I speak to you, sir?" he said, waiting for Dragutin to go out.

"Listen, Colonel," began Mišić, without waiting for Dragutin to leave, "I want to hear your opinion. I have decided that the army shall launch a decisive attack from Baćinac and Milovac at dawn on the twenty-first." Colonel Hadjić gave a semblance of a smile, but not one of pleasure and agreement; he opened his mouth to say something, but Mišić interrupted him: "During the next three days we must get the army organized, concentrate its forces, shorten the front, bend the center further in, onto the slopes of Suvobor." He stopped and placed his cup of lime tea on the window sill. The two men looked at each other as the flames from the stove played over their faces; Mišić could not tell what Hadjić was feeling while he talked: "We'll place the wings in strong positions on Baćinac and Milovac, and draw the enemy into the hilly, broken ground where the going is difficult. We'll lead them on into our foothills, then launch a large-scale, decisive attack. Have you given any thought to this?"

"But, sir, I have in my hand telegrams from the Danube Division, second levy. Vasić announces that the enemy are moving toward Struganik and Baćinac."

He did not wish to admit this blow; he continued in a firm and haughty tone:

"All right, we were expecting that yesterday, Colonel. Indeed, I'm surprised it didn't happen even two days ago. I can't understand why Potiorek is so hesitant." He got up; Hadjić's darkening face made him feel uneasy. "With what forces is he moving toward Baćinac?" he added.

"With strong forces, sir."

"Those words don't mean anything. To a weak and frightened officer, a platoon represents a strong force. Please check at once the numbers of those strong forces."

"It is reported from both Danube Divisions that the regiments are suddenly losing strength. There are many deserters; they're throwing away their weapons. Self-mutilation is increasing all the time. Vasić reports that the morale of his division is in a critical state."

He turned his back on Hadjić, not wishing to hear his description of the Danube Division's morale. He picked up his teacup, sipped his tea. It was a good thing he was familiar with the rhetoric of Miloš Vasić: the self-confident political rhetoric of a colonel who could never forget that he had been Minister of War, and had once been more favored than Mišić, his present superior. And he was the very man who must act on Baćinac, and defend this vitally important position on the army's left wing.

"Precisely because the morale of the troops is uncertain, we must win a victory as soon as possible, in order to instill confidence into the army. We need a real victory, and we can achieve this only if we attack. There is no other alternative, Colonel. You must begin to draw up the plan of attack this very evening. Take Baćinac and Milovac as your starting points."

He sipped his tea audibly. Yes, an offensive begins in the army's staff; that's where the first enemy positions are—they must be conquered at the start. The staff must be urged to think only of an attack, and to work for no other purpose. He heard Hadjić's affirmative reply, given after significant delay:

"Yes, I understand, sir. And I mentioned that I have an urgent directive from the High Command."

"Will you first please inquire from the divisions in what strength the enemy are approaching Baćinac? Then you can give me the orders from Putnik."

As soon as Hadjić had left the room, he took an apple from his knapsack, moved over to the window, and stared at the evening sky. He listened: some orderlies were coming from the lines; others were riding out into the night. What if Baćinac should fall tonight? If it did, then he could not launch the big attack on the twenty-first. He stopped eating his apple. He simply dared not allow that to happen: Baćinac must be defended at all costs. From somewhere in the direction of the Danube Division a howitzer was firing—not his, there was no ammunition. The little that was left, a few shells for each gun, he had ordered to be kept back for when the army attacked.

Hadjić entered the room: "I haven't been able to establish contact with Vasić, sir. I've been calling him continuously. And we have a new directive from the High Command."

He turned around to Hadjić full face: "Has the ammunition for the artillery arrived? Or the students?" He spoke provocatively, caustically, against himself.

"No, sir. It's an order issued to all staffs, from army staffs to regimental, directing that court-martials be set up to judge deserters from the front."

"Who signed it?"

"Vojvoda Putnik."

Mišić moved over to the stove, and knelt down to add more logs. But the stove was full; not knowing what to do, he began to poke the fire. Hadjić coughed and moved from one foot to the other behind his back. Mišić gazed at the embers, thinking to himself: So that's it—instead of clothes and munitions, court-martials! Summary procedure! No! While I'm the commanding officer, there'll be no court-martials in my army. Judgment in court is for thieves and traitors far behind the front, not for exhausted and despairing men who for two months have been beaten and chased by more powerful forces with full stomachs. No one in this country has the right to judge the people for failing to do what cannot be done. He straightened up.

"Half of our army has already been judged by various Austrian gentlemen—Potiorek, Frank, Šnjarić, and Sarkotić. I've taken note of the order. Court-martials are the last resort of a commanding officer, and I haven't got to that point yet. Please press on with getting the reports from the divisions. And tell all the regiments to capture some enemy soldiers tonight, and to submit exhaustive reports about the state and dispositions of the enemy by seven o'clock."

Left alone, he moved over to the window. You can't launch an attack, Vojvoda, with court-martials by the staff. Summary executions don't arouse a will to victory. Had Putnik not foreseen this? How dare he judge the people? They should not be sentenced in court-martials on behalf of any kind of freedom, or for any government! No one should either liberate or save the people against their will and beyond their strength. Everything resides only in the people, and all action must begin with them. He gave a start: Vukašin Katić thought this, too! No, he thought, I look at things differently. It's a question not of freedom, but survival. Did Putnik really have to issue this last order?

At dawn, when they reached Boljkovci, it seemed as though the houses would dissolve in the water. The hills, looking like little molehills, were sliding down into the valley and into roads mingled with hedges, and disappearing into the Kolubara and the Ljig. A great mass of water had eroded the forests and worn down the trees; it needed only the wind to blow and knock everything down. A shudder ran through him as, seated on his horse, he looked through his field glasses at the terrain of his army: the Kolubara valley had turned into a swamp, while Suvobor and Maljen were white with snow. And between the snow and the swamp—in rain, snowdrifts, and slush—lay his unraveled army: he could feel its presence, and see it as a whole— anxious and shivering, naked and barefoot, wet and hungry, caught in mud in the valleys and by the snow on the heights, powdered by the snowdrifts on Maljen. Every movement was slowed, and the army was dazed from fear.

While riding through the mud and slush, they could hear short, scattered bursts of gunfire; no one in his staff was talking. In such silence they reached the inn at Boljkovci. He felt a bit more relaxed when he had settled himself in his room with a window, right next to an old, black apple tree. He was alone and disconsolate. Although it was warm, he did not take off his overcoat because of the shivering fit which had seized his whole body on the journey. First of all he should telephone, to ask for news about enemy prisoners. But he didn't want to ask, he would wait until he was told about the situation on Baćinac. He sat there alone by the window, smoking, still wearing his coat. He was thinking hard about the attack on November 21. Would the High Command help him with one more division? He would put this request to Putnik once more, at daybreak.

Reports were beginning to come in from the lines. They were all worse then the previous day. Today Field Marshal Oscar Potiorek was active—threateningly, treacherously active: he was approaching the main positions, withdrawing under the heights, crossing the streams, moving up his artillery. As the day stretched out toward noon, reports were brought in of increasingly long and dense Austrian columns: he was feeling his way, sniffing, here and there applying a little pressure. He was testing the depth of Mišić's defenses, shaking the outer ring of sentries, breaking the thin lines. That was easy. He would take what he wanted to take, and stop when he wanted to stop. It seemed as though he did not yet want a large-scale battle; he was tormenting them with uncertainty. His greatest threat was directed toward Maljen, which his columns were approaching without a break—moving toward the army's weak spot, where the defense lacked force and firmness. Mišić didn't have troops to hold him in the foothills; all he could do was have the Maljen section dig in on the heights, then wait for a battle to the last man. To the last man? Long ago, when he had been commanding a platoon in the Serbo-Turkish war, he had asserted that he would never issue an order to "fight to the last man." Such orders were given by commanders who were waging war for its own sake and their own advancement, but not for life and liberty. But to hold Maljen, they would not have to "fight to the last man."

The latest reports forced him to the conclusion that today the enemy was taking serious action. It was as though Potiorek had divined his intentions, and was striving to occupy the most sensitive and critical positions. Slowly but surely. He became infuriated. Was it that Field Marshal Oscar Potiorek had rested, and was now drawing up his troops for the big attack? Perhaps he was intending to move tomorrow, and had outwitted him? That was what he, Mišić, suspected and indeed thought. But in his position, could he allow himself only to suspect and assume the enemy's intention? The stronger commander could allow himself to be confronted by something unforeseen, but the weaker one—in this case, the Serbian—never. What were the facts at his disposal? It was past noon and there were still no reports from the divisions about information obtained from prisoners. He asked the division commanders to bring him reports about the enemy's position within half an hour.

He refused lunch but ate two of his apples, the ones from his own orchard. He walked about the room, smoked, and looked out the window: the ground was slushy, the haystacks and the stakes in the fences were powdered with snow. The chief of staff reported that during the past night, and up to three o'clock that morning, the First Army had captured only a single enemy soldier—a Czech. His information was of no importance. Mišić restrained his anger; he wouldn't even ask how many of his men had surrendered to *them*. He requested the same order to be given to the divisions for the coming night. He called the High Command and asked to speak to Vojvoda Putnik. Colonel Pavlović informed him that Vojvoda Putnik was engaged.

This infuriated him: Putnik was always in a superior position! From the time when he had taken his captain's examination, and for three subsequent promotions when Putnik was one of his examiners, until today when he was in command of an army, Putnik was always above him.

"Can I give the Vojvoda a message?" Živko Pavlović, Putnik's assistant, asked this question twice.

"Tell him I want three divisions under my command this very night. And ammunition! Get on to the government again and say it's urgent. If no shells arrive within five days, the war will be over. One side will have to stop firing."

Angrily, he slammed down the receiver without saying good-by, sat down by the stove, and stared at the fire. He poked it and listened until he could see the flames; a ceaseless procession of carts carrying refugees was passing along the road beside the inn. There was no resisting this despair; only when the army moved to attack would the flow of refugees be halted. But how could he do it without artillery? An attack on the twenty-first was unthinkable without ammunition for the artillery. Unthinkable? Rubbish! An attack from Milovac and Baćinac was essential and could not be postponed. They would attack with stones if they had nothing else. He could hear the commotion of the operator in the next room:

"Hello! Hello! Morava Division, second levy! Hello! Danube Division, second levy! Hello! Danube Division, first levy!"

He lifted the receiver and listened:

"We've lost Orlovac. And Milovac is under fire."

"What, Milovac?" said Mišić. "Already?"

"The Austrians are moving toward Milovac."

"Then a regiment must attack the enemy from Milovac as they approach. Send one off immediately."

"How can we do that without artillery, sir?"

"That's your business, Colonel! But Milovac must be defended. It *must,* do you hear?"

Mišić sat beside the stove, staring at its doors. The embers were disintegrating into ash. The firelight was darker, his face was burning. From somewhere in the darkness of the village came drunken singing. Was it from the men in his supply train, or were they peasants? Despairing men, anyway. He stirred the embers, rekindled the fire with acacia logs, and breathed in their scent.

The chief of staff entered the room and informed him, in quiet and hesitating tones, that Colonel Vasić, the commander of the Danube

Division, second levy, wanted to speak with him. Feeling that something was wrong, he lifted the receiver with some agitation:

"Well, what's happened on Baćinac?"

"Two Austrian platoons have dispersed my regiment—two platoons of Croats. They've captured my cannon, taken over a thousand prisoners, including officers. It's a total collapse, sir."

"I asked you what's happened on Baćinac?"

"The enemy are there."

"You mean on Baćinac?"

"Baćinac fell at half past four."

"Have the enemy occupied the whole of Baćinac, including the summit?"

"The remnants of the regiment have rushed down to the streams and are fighting barehanded with their officers. No one is obeying orders. They've killed an officer who tried to stop the rout."

"Please tell me if we've lost the summit of Baćinac."

"Yes. All Elevation 620 is gone."

"Vasić, to us that isn't Elevation 620—it's Baćinac. And my orders are that it's to be recaptured tonight. By assault. Daybreak must see only the corpses of Austrians there."

"And how am I to recapture it, sir?"

"With your soldiers, Colonel. With the Serbian soldiers and officers under your command."

"It just can't be done. Don't you realize that my regiment is completely scattered?"

"Then collect your staff officers, Colonel, and lead them in an assault on the summit of Baćinac."

"The officers too have lost the will to fight. The rabble of refugees are shooting at everyone holding a command. Tomorrow my division won't exist any more. *My* division!"

At this point they were cut off.

He dialed the Danube Division, second levy. There was a buzzing sound, and he could hear the operators shouting to each other. Then more buzzing, crackling—then silence.

"Hello! Hello! Army staff?"

"Mišić speaking. I can hear you, Vasić."

"I said I doubt whether I'll have a division by tomorrow."

"You've already told me that."

"There's nothing I can do."

"That doesn't matter now. There's only one thing you must grasp: if your division collapses, then the First Army is finished. And if the

First Army collapses, then, Vasić, the consequences for the Serbian army and the people don't bear thinking of. We're fighting for our very existence!"

"There's nothing I can do to change the situation, sir."

"Right now it's not our business to know how powerless we are; it's our business to have faith in ourselves and our soldiers. We must have faith, and we must do something—we must act like people who are determined to survive."

"You have no need to doubt my patriotism."

"I have no time for that, Vasić. And that's not my duty toward the division commanders. What I require now is that you carry out my orders. We can talk about patriotism when the war's over. Baćinac must stay in our hands. On the twenty-first we shall move toward Valjevo, starting from Baćinac and Milovac. On the twenty-first, do you hear?"

"The Maljen sector is in a desperate state, too. They're stuck in a snowdrift, without food. Since noon, men have been deserting. There's a blizzard, too. Traffic can't get through. No village where they can spend the night."

"Tell them that there are some sheepfolds behind the Debelo Brdo—quite a few sheepfolds. They can settle the bulk of the troops in huts until daybreak."

"But I can't make contact with them, and they couldn't get to the Debelo Brdo anyway. It would take them all night. I told you the snow's drifting, and blocking the paths."

"Well, find some way of telling them to withdraw tonight to the Mečija slope. There are stone pits there where they can light fires."

"But who can find stone pits in the blizzard and darkness?"

"Then let them go down to the village of Planinica, and just leave sentries on Maljen."

"There are refugees crossing the Maljen sector, fleeing toward Planinica. They're infecting the troops, too—calling out to the soldiers to join them. That's what's so terrible."

"It's no less terrible, Colonel, that the two of us are talking so much. Please act on my orders—which are that Baćinac is to be in our hands!"

Left alone, he took an apple from his knapsack and stroked it. Its rosy skin gleamed in the firelight from the stove. But he could not bite it; he just stared at it.

So Baćinac has fallen! he kept repeating to himself. He returned to the table, sat down, and placed his hand over the receiver of the telephone, waiting for the news that Baćinac had been recovered. The operators were shouting at one another. When the operators were not shouting, he could hear the wind in the branches of the apple tree by his window.

Aleksa Dačić was sitting on a gnarled tree in a stream, in the darkness and slush; he was wet through, and vexed and humiliated by the recent flight from the summit of Baćinac. The soldiers crowded around him were shivering, their teeth chattering; they were hungry and frightened. Their officer, Luka Bog, spoke threatening words from the darkness:

"No one is to stir! I'll kill anyone who tries to run away, I'll kill him on the spot!"

The regiment had in fact been driven off Baćinac more by shouts and curses in their own Serbian mother tongue than by enemy fire and bayonets. From up above they could hear the singing and joyous cries of the Austrians, who were talking in Serbian, while in the stream down below, Serbian officers were brawling and shouting, and shooting at those who tried to run away. Groans tore at the thick darkness.

"Have you ever been in a worse mess, Aleksa?"

"Shut up, Slavko."

"Now I've lost my other shoe, and my socks are all torn."

"Well, put up with it."

"But how long?"

"Ask Putnik and Mišić. Ask the King. Or Pašić. But leave me in peace."

"You've no heart and no balls, you shits!" shouted Luka Bog. "Who do you think you're running away from, damn your eyes! They're not even Austrians—can't you hear?"

Luka Bog struck a match to light a cigarette. From Baćinac above them they could hear machine-gun fire, and a song with Serbian words which they couldn't make out. Around Aleksa was the sound of chattering teeth and whispering:

"What have they got to be so happy about? I'd like to see Franz kick their Bosnian asses! They've got Baćinac, but they haven't got Belgrade. From the racket they're making, you'd think the war was over. Well, perhaps it is. It damned well isn't, you idiot. Between here and Bitolj there are three hundred hills as good as Baćinac. This is the last one, for me. They don't talk like Bosnians. Then what are they? They're swearing just like Serbians, the Bosnians don't swear like that. It's only the Croats who swear at us like that. Anyway, it doesn't matter. Oh yes it does. It's all the same shit as soon as they talk our lingo. But it's the end of the road for us. We'll be finished tomorrow. Or in a week's time at the very most."

"But we're not finished yet, damn you!" Aleksa could no longer restrain himself, what with the happy shouting up above and the whispering around him.

"Get back, blast your eyes, even if you are in the water!" shouted Luka Bog. "Until I give the order, you can just freeze there!"

"Give me a bite, Aleksa. I'll give you a dinar for half a piece of hardtack."

"What makes you think I've got some hardtack, Slavko?"

"I know you have. I felt it in your bag."

"I don't have to feed you because you're defending my throne. My bag isn't a government supply store," said Aleksa, though he did in fact have some hardtack in his bag. They hadn't received any rations that day, and he had had cramps in his stomach since noon. Slavko would hear him if he ate it alone, but if he was going to share it, why had he risked his life to get the wet, slimy stuff? He had dragged himself across the stone quarry on his stomach and elbows through a rain of bullets, and returned to the hawthorn bush where the battalion commander's orderly had been killed, and taken the hardtack and some clean undershorts from his knapsack. How could he share it? Who knew when they would get their next rations in this confusion? Behind his back he could hear people talk about deserting.

"Who wants to sneak off?" he asked aloud.

"You managed to earn a stripe last night, didn't you, Aleksa? And perhaps something else as well."

"I got my promotion when we were on Tekereš, you damned fool, and at Pecka I earned the right to keep it. And for what I did outside Valjevo, I deserved to be made a sergeant. You know damn well that a poor man can't do things by halves in this life."

"And is that the only reason you haven't sewn on your stripe?"

"I'm not bothered about that. And you're not going to give me the slip tonight, let me tell you!"

"Where are you, Dačić?" shouted Luka Bog from the darkness, behind the glow of his cigarette.

Aleksa did not answer: who knew what that idiot was thinking up now? He had smashed up the entire third platoon between the Drina and the Kolubara, with the exception of just a few men. Then, when the commander of the second platoon was killed, he was put in command of that to finish it off, too. Maybe he would send some of them out that very night to catch some Austrians and take them to the battalion staff to be interrogated.

"I suppose Dačić hasn't run off, that fucking bastard?"

"No, sir, I haven't run off, and don't intend to. But don't go sneaking after me in the dark. I don't miss when I shoot, however dark it is."

"Well why don't you answer, then?"

"I'm shitting, sir, so I can't stand at attention."

"And you can damn well eat your shit. Choose three men from your section, and take them to be sentries at the quarry."

"The Fritzies are there."

"They're above the quarry, Dačić. They're on the upper side, and you're to dig yourselves in at the lower end, and don't stir till I replace you."

Aleksa muttered a curse. Every night that idiot thought up something to kill off someone in the platoon, and whenever he was really crazy he thought of him. Still, he would have to get up.

"You choose the three men, sir. I haven't the rank to choose men to be killed."

Aleksa crawled through the snow and mud down the slope, toward the glowing point of Luka Bog's cigarette. Bog called out the names of the soldiers, then finally shouted:

"Follow Dačić!"

As if to spite himself, Aleksa set out by way of the stream, floundering along in the water and slush. Furtively he began to eat his damp, slippery hardtack. Up above, the Austrians were still making a noise and firing an occasional bullet.

"Don't cough, and watch out where you put your feet," he warned his companions as they passed through the quarry, which was densely strewn with bushes. He went ahead, with his gun at the ready. He stumbled over something soft.

"Stop! Here's some bastard who's paid his debt to King and country."

"Is it a Fritzie, or one of ours?" asked Slavko.

Aleksa passed his fingers over the dead man. His bare chest was powdered with snow.

"They've even taken his shirt," he whispered. "Good luck to thieves who work so quickly! They've taken his britches, too."

He moistened his hands in the intestines and the frozen mess round them, then wiped them on the grass and rubbed them with snow.

"Shit is shit. It's all the same if it's Austrian or Serbian."

"Here's another," whispered Dragiša.

"They're lying around us like sheaves, aren't they?" whispered Slavko.

"You can strip them, but you've got to share everything you find," said Aleksa.

"I'd rather die myself than take something from a dead man," whispered Slavko.

"All right, then, get on with it. But do your sentry duty first, so the Fritzies don't take us by surprise from up there." Aleksa proceeded through the quarry, running his fingers over the corpses; their clothes and footwear had been removed. He found a bag with two grenades in it, which he took; also a flask with some *rakija,* which he drank. He pulled a tent flap from under a man whose jacket had not been taken, being full of shrapnel holes.

"This one's alive," muttered Buda.

"Ask him who he is."

"Yes, he's breathing, poor bastard. Are you a Serb?"

"What's the use of asking that now?"

"I don't care whether he's a Serb or not. He's a man, anyhow. Who are you? Yes, he's a Serb all right. That's one of our guns. What shall we do with him?"

"You're not suggesting we carry him back to the dressing station?"

"He's one of our people, Aleksa."

"All right, when we're relieved you can carry him seventeen kilometers to the dressing station."

"I'm going to!"

"That's enough of that. What have you found? Don't let me have to search you!" Aleksa wiped his hands on the grass.

"I've got a pair of wool socks."

"And I found a flask, but no *rakija* in it, only water."

"I found a jacket. When it's daylight I'll see if it's whole."

"No food?" asked Aleksa searchingly.

"Not a scrap."

"I don't want to have a search now."

They swore they had nothing. Some tracer bullets flew over their heads and disappeared somewhere below in the darkness, like snuffed-out candles. They made their way toward the quarry face; they could sense the proximity of the enemy, so they moved more and more slowly, forming a firing line. They walked around the bushes and the corpses. When they reached the quarry face, Aleksa checked them: they were only three.

"Where's Buda?"

No answer.

"Where's Buda?" he shouted.

"Don't shout! Go look for him."

The Austrians fired a few shots in their direction from the top of the quarry; they fell flat and took cover behind the projecting slopes.

"If anyone tries to run away, I'll bust his head open!" threatened Aleksa. Then he went up to Slavko and Dragiša in turn, and gave them a bit of his hardtack. He did not want to take cover, or even to lie down. He sat on a stone and wrapped himself in the tent flap; he was furious with Buda, who had surely escaped while they were still in the bushes. The Austrians pushed two stones over the edge of the quarry which rumbled down toward them in the dark. They all jumped up, not knowing where to go or seeing any place to take cover. But the rolling stones came to a halt just in front of them.

"I don't intend to be killed by a rolling stone, Aleksa."

"Well, Slavko, I'd certainly rather the Fritzies pelted us with cheese and loaves of bread. But you'd better not move from here. Stick to the stone like lizards, and keep a lookout to the left and the right. I'll watch straight ahead."

He sat down on a stone and covered himself with the tent flap; he wanted to sleep. Slavko and Dragiša were docile fellows, they wouldn't blink an eyelash. Well, let them gape at the dark.

From time to time, enemy sentries launched a stone which rumbled down rapidly toward them; he continued to doze. Slavko and Dragiša poked him when it seemed that a stone was rushing right at them. That's good, he can sleep peacefully; the two of them wouldn't dare close their eyes because of the stones. The wind began to blow in the quarry.

Someone gave him a poke. He gripped his gun, threw off the tent flap, and jumped up.

"It's me—Slavko."

"Why did you wake me up?"

"It'll soon be dawn, and there are only the two of us."

"Where's Dragiša?"

"He's run off, too."

"And why did you let the son of a bitch do it?"

"Why should I stop him? I roused you so that we can disappear into the mist before daylight. If the Austrians don't kill us with stones during the night, they'll fix us with bayonets in the morning."

"I'm not going to run away, Slavko. I won't admit to being beaten by the Fritzies."

"But what can you do when they're stronger? It's not your fault that they're the bosses and have everything."

"No, it's not my fault, but I'm not giving in to them. I may have had to work for Djordje and Adam Katić to earn my bread, but I'm not going to be the slave of the Fritzies."

"Now's the time to save your skin, you fool!"

"Now's the time to save something that's worth more, you ass!"

"Our regiment's done for. You heard last night how many officers surrendered, including the regimental C.O. And who are you in all this?"

"I don't care. I don't care if Živojin Mišić surrenders, and Vojvoda Putnik and King Peter. I'm not going to!"

"Can't you see that it's all over with our government and our freedom?"

"Maybe. But I'll go on fighting the Fritzies after the war, too."

"But who the hell are we giving our lives for, I ask you?"

"Look here, I'm a Serb. I'm a Dačić from Prerovo, and no one on this earth is going to lord it over me while there's breath in my body. I'll bend my neck to no man. I want my freedom, so that I can do whatever comes into my head. Now leave me alone to sleep a bit longer."

The Austrians again rolled down a stone from above. It was a huge stone which came tumbling straight at them. They jumped back and ran behind a wall; again the stone came to a stop in front of them. Its rumbling was followed by laughter from the quarry above them.

"Hear him? He doesn't even want to shoot. Wants to kill us with a stone like we were snakes," whispered Slavko.

"We'll stuff that bastard's throat with mud, and make him pay for tonight's entertainment! What's that murderer Luka Bog thinking about?" whispered Aleksa, hopping on one foot. His wet feet had frozen, and his clothing was like an icy skin. The wind howled. He still felt sleepy. "I'm going to doze a bit more," he said. "You keep a lookout to the right." Then he crouched down and covered his head with the tent flap. Again he imagined that it was summer, that he was in a warm haystack beside the Morava.

Slavko put his hand on Aleksa's head and whispered: "I'll give you a ducat if you'll wound my foot."

"You're not going to desert, you fool!"

"I'll give it to you right now. A real gold coin. Do you want to feel it?"

Aleksa did not remove the tent flap from his head; his breathing made his face feel a little warmer. He said aloud:

"I'll shit on your gold coin!"

A loose stone thundered down, shaking the quarry: he could not hear Slavko's whispers. Perhaps he really had a ducat. Yes, a ducat—a ducat!

"I'll give it to you like you were my brother. Do you know what a ducat's worth today?"

"But why do you want me to wound you—so that the Fritzies will take you with a hole in your foot? Why don't you run off as you are? You're no good for anything anyway."

"I can't break my oath."

"What oath?"

"That oath to serve King and country till death, which we gave in front of the priest."

"Ah, so that's a big thing for you! I'd like to piss on your oath, and on the priest's cassock, too. Keep a lookout on the left. And down below. It's time we were relieved."

"But what's to stop you from wounding me in the calf of my right leg? And you'll get a ducat for it, Aleksa. It might save your life one day."

"And why do you want me to wound your right leg?"

"I'd be more sorry if it was my left."

"So you want me to decide which leg you'd miss more. Let me sleep." He curled up and pulled the tent flap around him. Land would be cheap after the war—empty, with no men to work it; women and children couldn't till the fields. For a ducat he could buy a hectare of land along the Morava. Slavko was whispering something into his ear, into the tent flap:

"Please Aleksa! It'll soon be light."

"Why don't you want to lose your left leg?"

"I feel that way about everything on my left side. And it makes no difference to you."

Slavko's hands were trembling violently as he pulled the tent flap off Aleksa. Aleksa felt sorry for him, but if his own hands had not been shaking, he would have boxed his ears. They looked at each other, but without seeing each other's eyes, or their shuddering and trembling. They could hear each other's breathing; their breath collided. Aleksa noticed that Slavko was breathing in gasps; he also heard the thick and heavy wind howling through the quarry. Yes, land would be cheap when there were no men to work it. He could get ten hectares for ten ducats, and would never have to work for the Katići again.

"Let's move a bit further to the left. They can't do anything there when they hear your gun."

"Stop shaking, Slavko, or I'll hit you," he said as he walked after him. When they stopped he seized him by the shoulders: "Why don't you run off as you are, fit and whole? You're a coward anyway. Run off into the stream before I kill you!" He pushed him away with all his strength.

Slavko tottered, then said again in a whisper: "I told you, I can't break my oath. If a man breaks his oath, his children will pay for it."

"Stop shaking like that, or I'll smash your jaw!"

"If the Lord doesn't catch him, He'll catch his children. And I've got two boys. Do you want the ducat now or afterward?"

"Why don't you shoot yourself? What are you slobbering over me for?" Aleksa gripped him by his shoulders and began to shake him.

"It's a sin for a man to kill himself."

"But it's not a sin to pay someone else to do it for you! That's all right, isn't it? I won't do it unless you give me two ducats," he said, letting him go and moving away.

The Austrians rolled down another stone. A tracer bullet flashed through the sky, then went out.

"But I haven't got two ducats. I'll give you all I have. It's my wife's, one she had as a girl. When I went off to the war she took it from her neck and sewed it into my belt. What more do you want from me, you skinflint?"

They were both silent. Aleksa thought he could see pinpoints of light in the gloom. Either day was breaking, or he himself was bursting apart from his suffering and his anger.

"Anyway, let me tell you that I'm not going to carry you to the dressing station. You'll have to drag yourself there. I'm not going to leave my post."

"But we're all human, and it's only right that you should carry me to the dressing station."

They could hear the Austrian sentries' coughing, borne down to them by the wind.

"Slavko, I don't give a shit for your ducat. I won't carry you."

"All right, then, don't. But get on with it, for God's sake—it's getting light." He dragged himself under the wall.

"Give me the ducat!"

Slavko felt for his hand and dropped the ducat into it.

"You're sure it's a real one? If not, I'll smash both your feet."

"I told you, it was my wife's before we were married. What do you think, Aleksa, would my thigh be better? But don't hit the bone!"

"It might cut a vein, and then you'd bleed to death."

"All right. Then aim at the calf. But you can't see! It's dark!"

"Lift up your foot."

Slavko groaned. "Please, whatever you do, don't hit the bone! Can you see my calf? Have a good look, for God's sake!"

Aleksa felt his shin bone. "You're so thin, you wretch. How can I miss hitting the bone? There's nowhere for the bullet to go. I'll have to wait till it's light. And what if the Huns take you prisoner in the dressing station? What if you can't get to the hospital in Kragujevac?"

"Don't worry about that. Just get on with the job, for God's sake!"

"You're so thin and it's still dark. I'll smash your foot like a dry twig."

"Then let's wait."

Slavko moaned and groaned, and whispered a prayer to Saint George, his patron saint. The Austrian sentries pushed down another stone; its rumbling mingled with that of the wind. Aleksa tightened his grip on the ducat, until it touched his bone. If only he could somehow get thirty ducats, that meant ten hectares; or twenty ducats, five hectares, oxen, horses, and cows. For a hundred ducats he would have to make holes in a hundred Serbian feet. But what was he waiting for? One ducat for each Serbian. To hell with the army and the country! To hell with freedom! Slavko's no man, and I'm not either.

"Stop moaning!" he burst out, and spat at Slavko.

Slavko was silent.

"And what's that Luka Bog thinking about, for God's sake? Why doesn't he send someone to relieve us?"

"I tell you, Aleksa, they've all run away."

"Maybe they have. But I'm not going to. First I'll smash your foot. Then I'll drag myself inside the quarry, so that even a howitzer can't hit me. And I'll shoot at the mouths of those Fritzies for swearing at us in Serbian, and singing and throwing stones at us."

"Shh! Do you hear? They're talking about something."

"That's the wind."

"I think you can see my calf now."

Aleksa got up, moved one pace away, and unstrapped his gun.

"Move further away, so that there won't be any mark from the powder, or I'll be court-martialed and shot for wounding myself."

"Don't shake your foot so! I'll smash it to bits!"

"Just a minute. I want you to promise me something—on oath. But who can you swear by? You're not married?"

"I can swear by myself, you idiot! What do you want?"

"If I die from this wound, write to my father and my wife—you know the address. Say that Slavko was killed during an assault, by a shell."

Aleksa said nothing; he was frightened at the way his gun was shaking. He felt very cold from the sleet and the north wind.

"Swear to me that you'll write that letter."

"Lift your foot up a bit, my hands are shaking, blast you! I'll hit your guts."

"Then don't shoot, if your hands are shaking. Wait. Oh damn, I can't remember all of the Lord's prayer!"

"I piss on your Lord's prayer."

Aleksa could hear Slavko's teeth chattering. It would be easier to wound him when he wasn't expecting it. He moved away a bit, leveled the muzzle of his gun at Slavko's leg, and fired. Slavko fell down in a heap, shrieking:

"Oh, help! Help!"

The Austrians spattered some bullets in their direction from the top of the quarry.

"I asked you to hit my foot, you bastard! I didn't ask you to make mincemeat of me!"

"Stop that now, or I'll put a bullet in your head!"

"I can't move, I'm done for!"

Aleksa really felt like putting a bullet in his head, right into that mouth that was groaning in such a shameful and disgusting way. But he just spat again, and sat on a rock. The Austrians started shooting again. Aleksa jumped up and leaned over Slavko, who groaned.

"Go on, now *you* spit at *me*. Spit at me, because there's nothing to choose between us, Slavko."

Slavko continued to groan. The Austrians pushed down a stone, and shouted noisily.

"You can't even do that. Then drag yourself to the stream." He got up and lit a cigarette. The wind howled through the quarry. It began to snow, but only a few dry flakes which bit at his face.

"Aleksa, I can't move at all. Wrap up my foot, or I'll lose the little blood I have, and then I'm finished."

Aleksa extinguished his cigarette and put it back in the packet. He took one of his bandages and clumsily wrapped up the shin bone without looking at the wound. Then he took up his gun and bent down:

"Get on my back. Ride piggyback when I tell you."

Moaning and weeping, Slavko somehow managed to get onto his back, and he carried him down the quarry. The Austrians sensed what they were doing and began shooting at them. Aleksa did not hurry, nor did he attempt to hide. Let them put bullets in both of them! He lurched along the thin cover of frozen snow, then grabbed hold of a juniper bush. Suddenly he stopped:

"Now I've left my sentry post!"

He shook Slavko from his back, found a few dinars in his pocket wrapped up in a piece of paper, and handed them to Slavko.

"Here! Let's hope someone finds you, you idiot. Drag yourself to the stream, and cry out that you're wounded."

He removed his gun from his shoulders and hurried along toward the quarry, where day was breaking.

TO PAŠIĆ, PRIME MINISTER OF THE KINGDOM OF SERBIA, NIŠ: YESTERDAY I HANDED THE CZAR IN TSARSKOE SELO TELEGRAM NUMBER 6927 IN THE NAME OF THE REGENT AND NUMBER 7058 IN YOUR NAME STOP I REWORDED BOTH TELEGRAMS MORE STRONGLY STOP MY RECEPTION WAS EXTREMELY CORDIAL AND INTIMATE STOP I TOLD THE CZAR AUSTRIA WAS PLAYING HER LAST CARD AND MUST LOSE STOP THE CZAR SAID AUSTRIA WOULD LOSE THE GAME STOP THEN HE EXPRESSED ADMIRATION FOR OUR ARMY AND MARVELED THAT IT HAD HELD OUT TILL NOW STOP COMPLAINED THAT RUMANIA HAD NOT YET DECIDED WHAT TO DO STOP HAS NO FAITH IN BULGARIA STOP ALL RUSSIA SEES SERBIA'S LOYALTY WILL DO EVERYTHING FOR HER STOP RUSSIANS ARE DESCENDING FROM CARPATHIANS AND AUSTRIA WILL HAVE TO WITHDRAW FROM SERBIA TO DEFEND PEŠT STOP I TOLD THE CZAR OF ATROCITIES COMMITTED BY THE OCCUPYING POWER AND ASKED RUSSIA TO PUT PRESSURE ON HUNGARIANS STOP CZAR AGREED AND SAID HE HAD ALREADY DISCUSSED THIS WITH GRAND DUKE NICHOLAS STOP BEFORE LEAVING I KISSED THE CZAR'S HAND STOP I THANKED HIM WARMLY AND REPEATED THAT ALL SERBIA'S HOPES REST IN GOD AND HIMSELF STOP SPALAJKOVIĆ ST. PETERSBURG

At dawn General Mišić dozed off, with his head resting on his right forearm and his left hand still on the telephone. He was listening to Baćinac, united with it through the wires, which also brought him the scent of the grass on its bare heights, and the view of the Kolubara valley encircled by mountaintops and hills, undulating gently toward the Sava in waves of anxiety and hope.

As soon as it was light the ring of the telephone, long delayed because of dense fog, pierced his brain, hurried down his spine, and filled his veins, ears, and eyes with Baćinac.

"Hello! Is that the staff of the First Army? Vasić speaking, commander of the Danube Division, second levy."

Mišić said nothing; he held on to the table, keeping the receiver under his chin. Only when he had recognized all the objects in the room, and noticed the murky light of the dawn, and the black crown of the apple tree through the window, did he speak in a hoarse, quiet voice:

"Mišić speaking. What is it, Vasić? Why haven't you shifted them from those copses of wild cherry and service trees? But how can I send you reinforcements? No, I can't give you a regiment; I'm preparing the army for an attack. What enemy forces are there on Baćinac? The Forty-Second Division? Croats, you say? Yes, yes, our brothers. The Twenty-Fifth Home Guard Regiment. Ah yes, also our Croatian brothers. Why have they stuck fast to that slope as though Baćinac was in Zagorje? But then, it's easier for you when you're fighting against our brothers. I trust they haven't all decided to lay down their lives for Franz Josef on *my* Baćinac! You must finish the job on Baćinac on your own. But hurry, and take advantage of this fog. Drive them down into the stream, then don't stop until you get to Struganik. You must grasp the fact, Vasić, that today I haven't got one battalion to give you! Use enlisted men to make up your numbers. What do you mean, they've got no rifles? And how is it they're barefoot already? And why are their knapsacks empty? You'll get five hundred rifles by noon. That's all I have. I'll send you some grenades, too. Act decisively, and report to me as often as possible!"

He did not let go of the receiver, but kept hold of it on the cradle. Had he come to the point when officers were giving orders whose execution depended not on practical possibilities, but on the will of those officers? And what if just once such an order was not carried out? If only once the failure to carry out an order had no consequences for the person responsible, then it would be easy for subsequent orders to be ignored. What if Vasić did not carry out his order now? He let go of the receiver. The chief of staff entered the room, and gave him a tardy greeting:

"Any information about the enemy?" interrupted Mišić.

"None at all, sir. We didn't take a single prisoner last night. The High Command has forwarded a telegram from Pašić."

"I'm not interested in that now."

"But sir, there is something about the enemy in this telegram. This is what it says: 'The Italian newspapers are full of Austrian reports of victory over Serbia. General Potiorek has received the highest award, with a letter personally signed by Franz Josef. The Serbian army is in flight. Vienna is decorated with flags to celebrate the victory. Potiorek has invited foreign newspaper correspondents to come to western Serbia to witness the end of the country's existence. Pašić.' "

"Fine! Excellent!" Mišić jumped up from his chair, took his cap from the table, and began pacing about the room. "We're saved! Yes, Hadjić, we're saved. So those fools believe they've beaten us! Do you feel you've been beaten? The Serbian army, Vojvoda Putnik, and that fine fellow Dragutin? Who have they defeated? And what victory have they won? We're still here, and in two days we'll drive them across the Kolubara and Povlen. I was wondering why Field Marshal Oscar Potiorek was paddling about the Kolubara, and around Podgorina, after taking Valjevo. This man is reporting a victory over the Serbian army, ordering banquets, receiving decorations and congratulations, sending messages of thanks to the Emperor! Fine! Now we have to act wisely, but with determination. So Vienna is celebrating a victory! Field Marshal Oscar Potiorek has got a decoration!" He sat down at the table and dialed the number of the commander of the Danube Division, first levy.

"Mišić speaking. Good morning, Andjelković. What kind of a night did you have? Quiet? Then the men have had some sleep and feel rested. Today we must do what we can in this fog. Every platoon in your division must do something useful, something successful. There must be activity in all positions. Carry out small but carefully calculated attacks. See that you win some small victories—but your engagements *must* be successful. Every platoon, every battalion, every regiment must win a victory today—any victory. There must be some improvement in your positions. And some prisoners, of course. On the basis of those small victories, in two days—with God's help—we'll launch a big attack."

He spoke in the same vein to the other two division commanders. Then he called the High Command and told Vojvoda Putnik that Baćinac had been recovered, except for the left slope, and that he was waiting for news that it had been retaken, too. He reminded Putnik that he had promised him a division, with which he intended to strengthen his attack, and asked him to send ammunition for the artillery as soon as possible. Also some warm clothing and tents, as there were snowdrifts on Maljen and Suvobor.

Putnik answered peevishly, coughing as he spoke, and said that three batteries of Krupp cannon and some shells should arrive in three days; but he said nothing about reinforcements or Mišić's intention to launch an attack. He wasn't convinced; at the same time he wouldn't oppose him. He was an old fox who made his calculations on the basis of clearly established facts.

Dragutin brought him two cups of lime tea.

"Tell me, Dragutin, what are your buddies in the ranks worrying about this morning?"

"We're worried about the cattle, sir. A lot of them are dying. They're collapsing in the puddles and on the hillsides. The orderlies say that the ditches and roads are full of dead cattle. And the oxen are dying from the cannon's weight and the mud—their hearts can't take it. Next year, sir, there won't be any breeding cows. They've all gone sterile. And no calves, and no milk for the milk pails. Next year's going to be the worst there's ever been."

"And you can't see anything good anywhere, Dragutin?"

Dragutin said nothing as he stared at the fire in the stove.

3

"The students have arrived!" shouted Colonel Hadjić from the door.

His smile alarmed Mišić; the students' arrival was entirely eclipsed by Hadjić's smiles and rejoicing. He did not like this rejoicing, the occasion for which was not in fact so significant as people in their present state of hopelessness assumed. In any case he was not in favor of exaggerating the importance of their arrival, as the staff officers had been doing during the past few days. It reminded him of the proverb that a drowning man clutches at a straw. He lit a cigarette.

"Two platoons of them. I have distributed them among all three divisions." Hadjić's smile was replaced by a somewhat offended expression. "Don't you agree with what I have done, sir?"

"Yes, that's all right. Only you must tell all headquarters that the students are on no account to be kept there, among the staff officers. They must be with the soldiers. And see to it that no spoiled young man gets a clerical job through his father's influence."

"It would mean a great deal if you were to speak to them now, sir."

"I trust their fathers and teachers have told them all they need to know about duty. If you want, you yourself can say a few words to them on anything you consider necessary. Let them have a night's rest, then hurry them to their posts." He remembered Vukašin's son, Ivan. He really should see him, and at least greet him; after all, he had left his family in Vukašin's charge. "Please tell an orderly to bring Ivan Katić to see me. He's in the sixth student platoon."

He stood by the window looking at the top of the old apple tree, with raindrops dripping from its black branches. When they had parted, Vukašin had challenged the basic principles of his rights as a commanding officer. No one, he had said, has the right to sacrifice a nation's future, its children, for any cause whatsoever. The future, he said, lay with the intelligence and knowledge of its educated people— the pampered attitude of a politician with a European doctorate. Yes, my friend, a pampered and bookish point of view. But Vukašin Katić was the only politician who held such views irrespective of his personal advantage, and who would always express them plainly to everybody. He was that rare kind of person, a man who desired power yet dared to tell everyone the truth. He was a politician, but he loved truth more than power. Such a man was fated never to exercise power; that was why Mišić had chosen him as a friend. No, Vukašin, old man, a nation does not survive thanks to the intelligence and knowledge of its educated people; if this were so, we Serbs would have ceased to exist. We exist thanks to the knowledge we have acquired from laborious living and endurance, and the intelligence which is born under the plum trees and thornbushes and spreads throughout the entire nation like pollen in the orchards and vineyards. The intelligence needed for survival is attained by some higher law—but not in schools, not by reading books and discussing ideas. Nor does this life-saving intelligence originate in the houses of the wealthy—not in my house, Vukašin, nor in yours. For some time he had had no news of his sons Alexander and Radovan; their divisions had been heavily engaged every day. Well, they would meet whatever fate had been ordained for them. He had never asked their commanding officers anything about them; he would receive the same news about them as any other father. But that pallid, skinny boy of Vukašin's—nearsighted, too—wasn't made for the army and the front. It was a pity that he would perish. He was a volunteer, with a brave and honest heart. But he had told Hadjić that not a single student was to be kept at headquarters, so how could he remove Ivan?

He heard a knock; that would be Ivan. He turned toward the door.

"Come in, Ivan," he said. He was ill at ease, conscious of a vague anxiety: something soft inside himself, something warm and trembling.

Ivan Katić, wearing a wet, mud-stained overcoat, stood at attention and saluted; he could feel his cheeks burning with shame. Everybody had heard his summons to the commanding officer of the army: some had smiled contemptuously, others had made offensive comments. He had stopped in his tracks, undecided what to do. He didn't know what he would have done if Bogdan had not said firmly: "Why are you standing there, Ivan? You must go. The army commander has sent for you." In the stern presence of General Mišić, he felt his knees trembling. He remembered this sternness from the first time he had met him; he could never understand how a man could always be so stern, nor why a general had to be. The warmth of the room made his glasses misty, and he wasn't sure whether he had greeted "Uncle" Mišić—as he and Milena called him privately. Shame welled up in him once more; through his misted glasses he could just discern Mišić's outstretched hand. Well, if the war could cure him of feeling embarrassed, it was worth fighting. They shook hands. The general's handshake sent something heavy coursing through his veins: he began to tremble.

Mišić felt the sudden trembling of Ivan's hand. His feeling of awkwardness increased, and he was unable to hide it when he spoke:

"Sit down, Ivan. Did you see your father in Kragujevac?"

"Yes, I did."

Ivan remained standing. The general offered him his own chair and took another himself. Was this really Uncle Mišić, with his sandy mustache and white horse—his father's friend, whose visits to their house had given him prestige among his contemporaries? His curiosity aroused, Ivan had eavesdropped on Mišić's conversations with his father, which had always been conducted in a quiet and somehow conspiratorial voice. He had always been glad to give the general a message from his father, and so catch a glimpse of him in his room filled with acrid tobacco smoke, poring over large military maps stuck with pins, where surely, day and night, he was silently conducting campaigns against Turks, Bulgarians, and Austrians.

Mišić noticed Ivan's confusion, so out of his knapsack he took two of the apples from Struganik, and offered them to him:

"These are apples from my own orchard, Ivan. Have you marched from Kragujevac?"

"Yes, but I'm not tired."

"Have you had lunch?"

"We had something to eat. I'm not hungry." He took a hesitant bite, though he really didn't feel like eating an apple in front of the army commander. He put the other apple in his pocket for Bogdan. Through his misted glasses General Mišić now seemed to him even more blurred and unfamiliar. Mišić asked after his mother and Milena. He did not know what to reply. How could he chat with the commanding general as with an old family friend here at the front, with the sounds of battle dully audible behind the hills—a battle which he must join that very night? He wanted to thank him for his kindness, but tell him that there was now no point in trying to establish something from their previous peacetime life—something which for Ivan had perhaps been left behind forever when he kissed his father good-by at dawn, in front of the barrack gates at Kragujevac. He stopped eating his apple, but didn't know where to throw the uneaten half.

Mišić saw this: Ivan's face had softened when he spoke of his mother, and he felt sorry for him. How would he manage in fog and snowdrifts with those glasses? He remembered his own first battle. How could he brace Ivan a bit? There was nothing worthwhile that he could say to him, yet he dared not let this anxious and bewildered boy leave without some words of encouragement.

"Do you smoke, Ivan?"

"I haven't started yet, Uncle Mišić." He dropped his unfinished apple. "Forgive me, sir, please. My mind just wandered. You know, I am not used to the war yet." He pushed the uneaten apple toward a pile of logs.

"But why do you apologize? I like it that you've talked to me so calmly. Your father and I are real friends, and friendship is like a blood relationship—one which you choose according to some spiritual affinity. You look for something you like but don't have. You say you haven't got used to the war. This is my fifth war, Ivan, and I myself haven't got used to it, even though I'm a professional soldier. I always feel afraid when I hear the first shots—they startle me. One just doesn't have the strength to combat all the evil in the world—nor courage, in the face of all kinds of danger. Your father once said that a man who has never felt fear lacks the capacity for virtue. And he's right. So there's no reason to attribute special value to courage."

He believes I'm a coward, thought Ivan; that's why he's talking to me like this. He must cut short these patronizing justifications of cowardice:

"Excuse me, sir, but I can't agree with you."

A shadow of a smile flickered across the general's face, underneath his mustache singed by tobacco smoke.

"And why not, Ivan?"

"Because I consider that true courage is a matter of conviction—an expression of rational thought, and not of feeling or the external situation."

"That is more or less true. But we are not born with these convictions and this rationalism. All our good qualities are a matter of experience; that's how we acquire reasons for lasting convictions. This holds good for courage, too. But war always begins differently, Ivan.

Generally we have experience for the last phase of a war, but not for the beginning. I remember my first battle with the Turks in 1876. It was summer. Our firing line was up to the thighs in ripening wheat."

Ivan looked at the stove, wanting to cut short this moral tale full of compassion. He wanted to find some way of bringing this awkward meeting into harmony with the real feelings. He said:

"And what was your roughest experience in those five wars, sir?" The steam had gone from his glasses, and he could clearly see the general's cruel eyes. Unfamiliar eyes, as though he had never seen him before. This encouraged him and he added: "An experience that you wouldn't want your sons Alexander and Radovan to live through, and that you wouldn't relate to us students today, before we go to the front."

Mišić suddenly stared at Ivan.

"That's a lot you're asking of me, Ivan."

"A lot is being asked of everybody today, sir."

"Yes, that's true." Mišić began pacing about the room. "I don't know what my roughest experience was, I really don't. I'll tell you something that I remember very well from my first war. It was in 1876, when we were fighting the Turks near Deligrad. The battalion was drawn up in a field of stubble, because they had protested about some unbaked bread. For some days the soldiers had been getting just a dark, sticky mess, full of grass and dirt. Half the brigade was down with dysentery. General Horvatović, decorated with medals and accompanied by a Russian officer—General Chernayev was commanding the Serbian army then—this General Horvatović looked out over the hills, then stood in front of the lined-up battalion, and ordered every tenth man to step forward two paces. 'Load your guns!' he commanded. 'Now shoot at me! Shoot, when I tell you!' The soldiers' guns, already aimed, faltered. 'It's my fault that you're eating rotten bread. So shoot at the guilty man!' "

"That's magnificent!" cried Ivan, getting up from his chair.

" 'Shoot!' yelled General Horvatović, and thrust out his chest full of medals. The Russian in red trousers and a white shirt shouted 'Bravo!' at the top of his voice. The soldiers stared at the general, and their guns clattered to the ground. 'So you don't want to carry out an order!' shouted the general. The wretched men hung their heads. General Horvatović ordered their guns to be collected and told the battalion to form a square. Then that general—the worst that ever commanded a Serbian army—took out his pistol and one by one started to kill those men who had not dared to shoot at him."

"Frightful! Incredible!" muttered Ivan, staring at the general.

"And so, Ivan, the C.O. killed some of the soldiers, then ordered the battalion to shoot the rest. And that Russian officer in red trousers and a white shirt—the one who had shouted 'Bravo!'—ran off through the stubble."

Mišić stopped speaking: Hadjić came into the room with a telegram. "What has happened, Colonel? You can speak freely: this student is the son of Vukašin Katić, a friend of mine."

"The Commander in Chief is arriving this evening. That's the first thing."

Ivan withdrew to the wall and stood at ease, not wanting to hear the conversation. He could hardly wait to leave. He himself would have run off through the stubble, just like that Russian. Or would he have shot at the general? Yes, he would have. He stared hard at Mišić. Would he be able to shoot at him? Why had Mišić told him that story? Was it to justify some action of his own? He heard him give an exclamation:

"What? Milovac again? And what's the situation on Baćinac?"

"There's no news from Vasić."

The general took a step toward the window, then turned around and paused: "What platoon are you in, Ivan?"

"The sixth, sir."

"To which division is the sixth platoon going, Colonel?"

"The sixth student platoon has been assigned to the Danube Division, second levy, sir. We're sending the entire platoon there, because of their situation."

Ivan trembled. So that division was in a difficult situation! It was high time for him to take his leave of the general, thank him, and go out into the slush.

"Get me Vasić, please."

Mišić waited for Hadjić to go out. He couldn't finish the story about what happened near Deligrad. But why had he told such a story to this boy? So that he should know the truth? Or so that he might learn something from it? Perhaps he had some other reason: it was Ivan's first war. And his fifth.

"I think I should be going, sir, if I may."

"War is the very worst of all human activities, Ivan; it's always evil. But sometimes this terrible task can promote justice. And some people wage war just in order to live. We Serbians are fighting for our lives. See that you have the will to live, my boy, and go out to the battle with faith in your heart."

Ivan stood at attention and saluted, confused by the words he had just heard. Mišić gripped Ivan's limp fingers firmly with his cold hand. Ivan withdrew them quickly as though from a statue, and trembling, took his leave of this man who now seemed to him a stranger from another world.

General Mišić looked out the window at the black branches of the old apple tree in the dusk. He had not been able to postpone or change the path which that nearsighted, sensitive boy must follow; such was the law of justice. But why had this fact pierced him with sadness? And not only sadness but something else, too. He would write to Vukašin about the special rights of a commanding officer, which are regarded as rights only by those who do not know what price is paid for using them.

The student platoons assigned to the First Army stood lined up in the mud and rain in front of the staff headquarters. A lieutenant colonel, a veritable giant of a man, was talking to them in a damp, weary voice about their obligations to their fatherland, and explaining what the commander of the army expected of them at the front.

Danilo History-Book was standing in line behind Bora Jackpot; these patriotic words passed right over his head. The wet, mud-stained horses tethered to the acacia trees in front of the inn accompanied the high-pitched, level intonation with snorts as they stamped on the ground. Danilo looked at the huge inn, whose size bore no conceivable relation to that of the village, or to the importance of the road beside it, the muddiest road he had ever walked in his life. The heights above the village were swathed in cloud; the village itself lay scattered over the hillsides and along the streams in fear and wretchedness, and now seemed compressed into a muddy hollow under the rain and the muted rumble of gunfire.

From the steps of the inn the lieutenant colonel was talking about the shortage of artillery shells, and the Allies' promises to supply them in the shortest possible time. Danilo turned his eyes to the road that curved suddenly, compressing his sadness and the twilight. On the curve he caught sight of a white head scarf; it came gradually nearer and grew brighter, swaying with the rhythm of supple footsteps. His eyes went out hopefully to meet the wearer: a woman was approaching with short, light steps under a long skirt. She was dressed entirely in black, her face concealed by the white scarf; she had tightly wrapped, ample breasts, and shining eyes. She turned toward him full face and looked at him, slackened her pace, thrust our her full bosom, then lifted her eyes to meet his. His heart tightened under his overcoat, and fluttered under the strap of his knapsack. He could feel his blood coursing through his body, tormented by protracted desire. She paused and smiled at him. She looked pleased—as though she knew him well, as though she had been looking for him and found him, as though she had been coming through the rain and mud, in the dim half-light, straight to him. This completely confused him, and extinguished the smile with which he was looking at her expectantly, waiting for her to come completely into view.

Bora Jackpot warned him not to act so irresponsibly. Shouts of approval were echoing through the line at the lieutenant colonel's words, and cries of "Long live the High Command!" Then the officers gave a sharp command to stand at attention.

Danilo tried desperately to spread out his arms to show his powerlessness in face of this command, and looked at her with the full force of his longing. Before he turned away from her, a slight smile flickered from her lips, and a pale seriousness. Could such a woman actually be here, at this very moment?

The officers told them that they would leave for the front at half past six the next day, that they were to assemble outside the staff headquarters, and fend for themselves as regards supper and accommodation that night. Then at last Danilo turned around to look for her. She had disappeared. He rushed along the road to the end of the village, came back, turned into a blind alley on the hillside, hurried in the dusk to the last house and came back again, determined to look in every house until he found her. He couldn't go to the front, to his death, with this force unspent, the force which could be expended only in love, and given only to a woman. This longing to embrace a woman once more before going to battle was revealed to the entire platoon; it became a pretext for the feeblest and most pointless of jokes. Among his most intimate friends it aroused a sympathy founded on the suspicion, inherited from veteran soldiers, that those who run after women will perish from the first bullet. He could easily believe this, but fear did not quench his desire; on the contrary, it added fuel to the flames and made it more painful to bear, because of the apparent impossibility of ever gratifying it in their present situation.

Once more he rushed to the end of this mud village. On his way he ran into groups of his companions looking for somewhere to spend the night; they had no idea that he was looking for the girl in the white head scarf with laughing eyes, who had come swaying down the village with her full bosom thrust into the twilight, and that he was determined to look for her at the bottom of every well in Boljkovci! He turned in the opposite direction and went along another blind alley, then up the hillside, too, wading through the deep, sticky mud, while the gathering darkness was blotting out the white walls of the houses and the piled-up hay sheaves. He stopped in front of every gate, and peered into yards, sheds, and sheeppens. At last he came to the other end of the village, then in despair hurried back to the inn. He wanted to run, but suddenly stood transfixed: there she was, standing against a sheaf of hay, holding onto the fence and smiling at him, but with a wider, fuller smile than the first time:

"Where do you think you're off to, Corporal?"

Danilo trembled: she was beautiful—not a peasant girl.

"I asked you where you were going?" she said quietly, almost in a whisper.

"I was looking for you!" He moved toward the fence to take hold of her hands, but she stepped back and leaned against the haystack. Her body became tense, her breasts even more sharply outlined, and her smile flickered:

"I saw you hurrying through the village," she whispered, very serious. "I saw you. You looked as though someone was chasing you. I felt sorry."

"Who've you got at home?"

"My father-in-law and mother-in-law. My husband's a corporal in Stepa's army."

"What's your name?"

"What's yours?"

"Danilo."

"What were you doing before the war?"

"I was a student. I'm a volunteer."

"And now you've got your orders?"

"Yes. We're on our way now. Those fellows you saw in front of your inn are the student platoons."

"What a pity! I suppose you'll all be killed. And you're so handsome—really good-looking boys." Her head scarf was gray in the gathering dusk, which blotted out her eyes and rosy lips.

There was a sound of dogs barking up and down the village, and cannon booming behind the mountain.

"You haven't told me your name," stammered Danilo, overwhelmed by her sympathy.

"And what does that matter tonight?" she whispered. "Tomorrow you won't know the name of your own mother."

"You're so marvelously beautiful!" He stretched out his hands over the fence, and she straightened up, standing close against the haystack; perhaps a smile flashed across her face.

"You really think so? Or are you saying that because you're a student? What am I to you? But I'm really sorry that they're sending you all to your death."

"I mean it; you really are beautiful."

"And what were you thinking when you turned toward me? You were the only one that did."

"I was thinking that I must find you tonight. Even if I had to go to the bottom of every well in the village!"

"Would you really have looked for me in the wells?" She raised her voice, and leaned slightly toward him.

He couldn't see the color of her eyes. Were they gray or hazel? "Yes, I would. And I was thinking that if I wasn't on my way to the front, I'd stay forever in this one-eyed hole of a village!"

"And what else were you thinking about, while you were rushing to the last house in that lane? Go on lying to me, soldier, but not too much!"

"I'd decided I'd go from house to house looking for you, and that I wouldn't leave for the front until I found you."

"And if you hadn't found me?" Her sigh was more audible than her words.

"I can't hear you. Come a little nearer. I would have found you. I'd have looked in the wells, the haystacks, and the woodpiles. I'd have turned the whole village upside down!"

"What would you have done then?"

"Then I'd have taken you in my arms!" His voice choked, and he stepped into the water in the ditch beside the fence.

"Tell me some more. I don't care if you're lying!"

"I'm not, I swear. What can I do to convince you that I'm not?"

"All right, Danilo, you've found me, haven't you? So? Ah no! Don't jump over the fence!"

Danilo, despondent at this rebuff, jumped back from the fence into the water. Someone was calling the girl. She withdrew between the haystacks.

"My mother-in-law is calling me."

"But you mustn't go! You can't. I'll come into the house."

"Good luck to you, Danilo! If you were working at headquarters or somewhere nearby, I'd come see you every day. I like the way you look at me. And I like to listen to you telling lies!"

"Just a minute, please! I've got to spend the night somewhere. Couldn't I ask your mother-in-law if I could spend the night in your house?"

She came quickly up to the fence and whispered: "All right, if you've nowhere else to go. But you can't come by yourself. Bring a friend with you."

She disappeared behind the haystacks. Danilo's hand dropped from the fence; water flowed over his boots. And he didn't even know her name! "I'm in love!" he exclaimed aloud, wanting to hear his own voice. Then he ran to headquarters to find Bora Jackpot and another friend to spend the night with him.

He found a group of them standing under the eaves of a house opposite the inn, which was adorned with lanterns and surrounded by tethered horses.

"I've found a place for us to stay the night!" he said. "I'll take you to the house of a wonderful Serbian peasant—a real Šumadija peasant."

"I'd rather stay here," said Bora Jackpot.

"But why? Surely you don't want to spend the last night before we go to the front without sleep? Who knows what tomorrow will bring?"

Astonished and reproachful at his attitude, all four of his friends set upon Bora. At last, with great difficulty, they got him to follow Danilo, who dragged them off uphill through the darkness, not watching where he was going. Bora Jackpot came last, gloomy and unwilling, and entered the large house, the only one in the lane with any lights on. Reluctantly, without introducing himself, he greeted their host, who was obviously pleased by their arrival.

The girl greeted everybody except Danilo. She easily managed to avoid him, which confused and frightened him. Bora Jackpot, sitting beside the fireplace, whispered in his ear:

"Why, that's the girl in the white head scarf! Your doing again, Danilo! What makes you run after a petticoat like this? It's disgusting!"

Danilo blushed, sitting there on a three-legged stool, and only when Trička Macedonian and Saša Molecule were noisily talking to their host, did he sidle up to Bora and whisper:

"Isn't she a beauty?"

"She's just an ordinary peasant housewife. The villages are full of such busts and buttocks!"

"I find your cynicism disgusting!"

Offended, Danilo turned away from Bora and gazed rapturously at the girl, who was serving drinks around the spacious open hearth, moving sometimes briskly as though frightened, sometimes slowly as though very tired, and changing her expression with her manner of moving: an expression of sadness or joy constantly fluctuated on her face. But Danilo could never meet her glance head on, directed only at him; he kept his ears pricked to hear her mother-in-law pronounce her name:

"Stamena," called her mother-in-law, "the boys have wet feet! No one can be comfortable with wet feet. Bring them all some new wool socks, and a basin of hot water to wash their feet."

Bora Jackpot regretted that he had agreed to spend the night here. He felt weighed down by doubt and suspicion over this uncalled-for kindness, and had long been convinced that hospitality was at best the lowest human virtue. He looked carefully at their host Bogosav: a tall, thin, bewhiskered old man with a hangdog, melancholy expression and a melodious voice full of nuances. He listened to him expressing his pleasure—in carefully chosen words, ceremonially pronounced— that he had Serbian soldiers in his house on the eve of his patron saint's day, the feast of the Holy Archangel: the comrades and seniors, as it were, of his only son Miloje, who was a corporal in Stepa's army—God grant that he come back a sergeant! What Bora found most striking was that he should feel so pleased to have such guests when there were crowds of refugees pouring through the village, and sounds of battle from the other side of the mountain; and most of all, when in a few days' time there would be Austrians sitting around this hearth. Would he tell his daughter-in-law to bring new socks for them, and hot water to wash their feet?

Stamena brought in a basin, removed a large copper pot with hot water from the hearth, and picked up a pan to ladle out the water, holding a towel over her arm.

They had all washed their feet and put on the new socks, except for Bora; Stamena asked him to come over.

"Thank you. I washed my feet and put on clean socks before coming to your house," Bora lied.

"Still, you can do it again, young man. It'll keep you from getting tired. You'll sleep better," said their host.

"Thank you, there's no need."

His friends looked at him reproachfully, but he didn't care.

The host, Bogosav, took them into the guest room; Bora went in last, pausing at the threshold and observing everything around him: the blue trestle table and blue couches; the wide wooden bed, also painted blue, piled high with rugs and bedding; the walls decorated with photographs of a soldier, no doubt Corporal Miloje, with wreaths of dried grass and some kind of yellow flowers; and an icon of the Holy Archangel, with a censer burning underneath it. The host, speaking in a kindly voice, pressed him to sit down, and waited for him to take the seat at the head of the blue table, under the censer. But Bora sat down at the end of the table, opposite Danilo History-Book. Stamena and her mother-in-law brought them hot *rakija,* cheese, and scones.

Tričko Macedonian asked their host if he would flee in view of the rapid advance of the Austrians, but he replied firmly:

"This house and the meadow and the orchard—that's me. Where would I go, and what would I do without them? I've nothing I can save by running away. If they take me prisoner, I'll have to respect their law. And if they kill me because I'm a Serb, well, that's my fate, and I won't run away from it."

There'll always be wars as long as there are peasants and people who believe in fate, thought Bora, and wanted to say so; but he realized that this would have been more than discourteous.

"What do you think?" Danilo History-Book asked the old man. "Can we beat the Fritzies?" His eyes never left Stamena.

Bora warningly tapped the top of his boot and began to sip his hot *rakija.*

"I'm sure we will. We defeated them last summer at Cer, so why shouldn't we do the same on Suvobor? We're a tough people and we're used to suffering. We know how to endure. We can do a lot when we stick together, and when we're in a tight corner. And we don't set too high a price on our heads."

He fell silent. Bora liked the reasons and facts on which this peasant confidence was based; he found the last sentence particularly convincing. He began to eat his supper, but without the enjoyment which he could see on the faces of his companions, except Danilo. That infatuated ass was just gaping at Stamena, and scarcely touched his food.

"You've nothing to worry about, old timer, we'll certainly lick them," said Tričko Macedonian gaily. "We'll be a great nation—powerful and united. The greatest in the Balkans, victorious over Austria and Germany. And Bulgaria too, if she betrays the Slavs."

"Well, if you say so, boys, I'm sure God will make it so. But from what I know as a peasant, nobody has had any good from war, not even those on the winning side."

"Do you think that because so many of us will be killed? That we'll have to pay a high price for our freedom?"

"Some people's heads, my boy, have no more value than the head of a horse!"

Bora dropped his fork, and stopped chewing.

"There's many a human head in this God-forsaken country that has less value than oxen or fine fruit. That's how I see it. Some great evil has taken possession of the land. Evil begets evil. Apples don't grow on hawthorn bushes."

Danilo was not interested in what Stamena's father-in-law had to say. He was racking his brains as to where he could arrange a rendez-vous with her after supper. She served them with downcast eyes; perhaps her cheeks were a trifle flushed. Twice, from the shadow, she gave him a quick smile and an ardent glance. How could he shorten this supper, which his companions were enjoying so much? And where did she sleep? Everything he could think of seemed impossible, that night and in this place. As they were finishing supper he got up, as though to replenish the stove, and managed to whisper to her that he would wait for her in the haystack after supper; but she gave no sign of agreement. Anxious and despondent, he could not touch another bite, and refused to drink any more either. Was it possible that this peasant girl could deceive him, and deal him such a blow that night, just before he was off to the front and his death? Yes, he would surely be killed. What had he done to deserve such suffering tonight, such an unjust stroke of fate? He no longer looked at her. When they all fell asleep, he would sneak out and of his own free will go over the mountains, straight to the front—just as he had left home unknown to his mother, brothers, and sisters, afraid that he might burst into tears when they said good-by.

Tričko Macedonian began to sing, with Dušan Casanova and Saša Molecule accompanying him, while Danilo struggled to restrain himself from rushing out coatless and crossing the mountain in the darkness.

"When they've all gone to sleep, wait for me where I was waiting for you," she whispered down the back of his neck. He shrank back as though from a blow, then turned around and looked at her from his full height: her blue eyes were dilated and menacing.

Tričko Macedonian rose from the table, took out a handkerchief, and began to dance by himself.

Stamena came in with a pitcher of wine; she smiled at Danilo in a way he had never seen before, and nodded affirmatively. So began a night longer than his twenty-one years.

Bora Jackpot begged Dušan Casanova and Saša Molecule to put an end to this enjoyment of peasant hospitality, so they could play a last game of poker on the blue table under the light of the censer. He urged that they all wager every single thing they had, including such state property as their guns and ammunition, and so gain some inkling of the order and system of the universe that night, some idea of the direction in which the Great Wheel was turning.

Dušan Casanova and Saša Molecule agreed, but not to wager their ammunition; Bora Jackpot, however, had suddenly become excited at the thought of playing for bullets, too. Dancing, Tričko Macedonian bent over their quarreling heads, twirling his handkerchief.

For General Mišić the day had no morning: it simply sneaked in through his fitful dozing from the gloomy and ominous quiet of the night, during most of which he had sat up, kindling and poking the fire in the stove, and smoking. The apples which he had begun to roast lay burned and forgotten on the stove.

He heard laughter and raised voices. For the first time in the headquarters the orderlies were shouting gaily to one another. Couriers banged haughtily on the doors, and the operators were exchanging jokes with the division operators. He opened the door and asked the officers what had happened.

"We've won a victory on Baćinac, sir! A victory after our defeat—and on Baćinac, too!"

He could find no words to reply, and there was no change in the stern expression on his face as he went back to his room and stood beside the window, his gaze pausing on the top of the old apple tree.

The chief of staff, cordial and relaxed, called him to come drink a glass of hot *rakija* with the officers: "We must celebrate the first victory under your command!"

Mišić was pleased now to see the smile on Hadjić's face, and he liked hearing his words about the first victory, too; but for some reason he could not rejoice in the same way as Hadjić—he dared not. He passed into the inn where the chief of staff worked; the officers greeted him joyfully, vied in offering congratulations, and drank his health. Well, he thought, let them rejoice as much as possible, even if there is not much cause for rejoicing. It's better that way, and they'll be a bit ashamed to be downcast over a defeat tomorrow. Professor Zarija came up to him with his glass, absolutely delighted:

"Long live our general! Victory in war is the one human achievement that deserves to be celebrated—I'm convinced of it!"

"I don't think that's quite true, but let's believe it today, Professor," he whispered, then stood up with his glass full to touch glasses with all those present, talking as he did so about the attack to be launched by the First Army the next day. But with two or three exceptions, they wanted to talk only about the victory on Baćinac, and not to listen to him, as they were not convinced of the need to attack the next day. This worried him. They began to ply him with reasons which were stronger than their own belief; he didn't like this either.

Before he had drunk half his glass, the telephone rang; Hadjić lifted the receiver and his face clouded. The general merriment quickly subsided: all eyes were on Hadjić, who was saying crossly:

"There's no question of changing our positions. We're not retreating a single step! Do you want me to repeat this to the commanding officer?"

"What's happened now?" asked Mišić.

"The Morava Division and parts of the Danube have been savagely attacked—the entire right wing of the army."

"Tell them there's no change in last night's orders," he said, and went on explaining to the now quiet and chastened officers his plan for the following day's attack. The telephone had cut short their anxiety about the shortage of ammunition for the artillery. Hadjić put his hand over the receiver and said hoarsely:

"The Morava Division hasn't succeeded in repelling the attack on Milovac, sir. It is smashed up and scattered in flight."

"Repeat that we stand by last night's orders," said Mišić. He got up to go, somewhat embarrassed by such an ending to the celebration of the victory on Baćinac. Mist was drawing at his side through the orchards, over the black plum trees and the fences, and engulfing the hills in front of him.

"Milovac fell after a short battle. The Fourth Regiment has completely disintegrated, sir. Colonel Milić is in despair; he could hardly speak," Hadjić whispered to him.

"No matter. Tomorrow at seven o'clock the whole army will move to attack. We're going to attack, you understand? See that the dispositions of all the troops for an offensive are ready in an hour."

The grooms and orderlies also heard him. He wrapped his coat around him and went angrily to his room. He remained alone there, smoking and staring at the telephone. He could hear artillery, not his own. Against whom was he launching his attack? From what direction were they moving now? And what will happen tomorrow when they chase us onto Suvobor, and the snowdrifts pile up? And the next day, when we'll be weaker, still weaker? He dialed briskly and asked for the commander of the Morava Division:

"Tomorrow, the twenty-first, the army is launching an attack. You haven't forgotten that, Colonel Milić? Please don't explain to me how you ruined the right wing of the army. See that you recover Milovac before dark—do your best! That's all. What do you mean, night? You ran away in broad daylight, so now you can get together again—you and all your staff, up and down Milovac. That's all, Colonel. I shall wait for your report that my orders have been carried out."

He put down the receiver hesitantly, as though placing it on a wound. Somebody brought in wood and laid a fire in the stove. He didn't turn around. Did Potiorek intend to storm the rear of his army on the right wing? And what then? The ringing of the telephone startled him. He recovered himself and lifted the receiver.

"Miloš Vasić speaking, sir. There are long enemy columns approaching all parts of my division."

"Are they patrols or columns? Who could count the numbers of such big columns in this fog, Colonel? Because of the wisps of fog, your scouts probably think they can see a whole battalion of Austrians. Yes, yes. Thank you for telling me. And what's the situation on Maljen?"

"The snow's drifting there. Our sector is snowed in; we've heard nothing from them since morning."

"Drifting snow on Maljen, rain around the Ljig, thick fog covering the whole army. Yes, I'm completing your report. Continual engagements, from wing to wing, short and fierce. Field Marshal Oscar Potiorek obviously has a clear idea of his offensive. Yes, he's doing exactly what I would do in his place, attacking both wings. He wants to separate us from the Užice forces, then he'll rush down from Maljen, right at the heart of our army. Yes, that's Oscar Potiorek's intention. And now I must do what he doesn't imagine that I am capable of; but I can, and I must. Don't get excited, Colonel. The best decision is one that doesn't change. You'll get the orders for tomorrow's attack shortly."

He put down the receiver, went up to the window, and stared at the fog which was insinuating itself into the black tops of the apple and plum trees. Now he must think: he must think more quickly than Potiorek, but further ahead than Putnik. Fierce firing from the Austrian artillery began from the northwest, from Baćinac, on the left wing; he could not hear the battle being fought by his own infantry for the recovery of Milovac, on the army's right wing.

Prince Alexander, the Regent and Commander in Chief, passed through the staff headquarters with a gloomy expression on his face, listened anxiously to the reports from the divisions brought to him by Hadjić, then set off to inspect the positions. He did not invite Mišić to accompany him; Mišić did not offer to do so, nor say a word about the attack he intended to launch that day.

It was a day enveloped in thick fog and frost, the most difficult he had lived through since taking over the First Army. His plan for the army's offensive had been mistaken; his intention had not been consonant with practical possibilities, nor with the condition and position of his opponent. This plan had complicated and worsened his own positions even more, and had alarmed the division and regimental commanders. To Putnik he appeared simply ambitious, to the staff officers rash and imprudent, to the division commanders obstinate, while in the eyes of Oscar Potiorek he had shown the impatience characteristic of the weak and timid.

The telephone called out only defeats, and the strident appeals of the commanding officers for reinforcements and shells, clothes and footwear, bread and tobacco.

When he dozed off or sat staring at the wall, the entire army seemed spread out before him in the room, and all the positions extended on the table. He saw them, clearly and relentlessly: from the Ljig, and across Baćinac and Maljen, the thin and fragmented line of the First Army twisted and turned over heights and down streams through mist and snowdrifts. He saw its soldiers shivering in the rain and snow behind trees or in shallow ditches, without overcoats, standing in slush and freezing puddles with their disintegrating sandals; hungry, sleepless, deathly pale and thin, looking around them in despairing silence, trying to see where they could take cover when the enemy fire came even thicker and faster. Unit officers under beech trees heating *rakija* over a fire, afraid they'd have no time to drink it before the shrapnel caught them. Staff colonels in peasant houses, where they were at least protected from the cold and rain, quarreling among themselves, cursing Pašić and the Allies, criticizing the division commanders and threatening him, Mišić, because he so mercilessly pounded his troops. Division commanders, angry and scowling at everybody, standing beside their telephones, waiting for the reports—always the same—from the regiments, and his own increasingly impracticable orders; vexed with him because even after six days he couldn't see that the state of the troops was disastrous, and muttering to their staff chiefs that the First Army, tattered, torn, and bruised, was a severe casualty: if it didn't retreat immediately, in a couple of days it would have neither the wish nor the power to do so; if they didn't begin to withdraw to Rajac and the crown of Suvobor at dawn, the troops would perish in the forests, while the remnants of his silenced artillery would be smashed to bits in the ravines. The exhausted First Army would be devoured by its mountains, buried in the first snowdrifts. How immense would be that graveyard.

A report came in: Mednik was lost. He stretched out both his hands over the empty table and sat rigid: that meant that the deeply sagging center had been crushed. Both wings were now hanging, even more precariously exposed, attached to the center by weakened and divided battalions. Another report came in, very detailed this time, that Mednik was completely overwhelmed—reproaching him, in effect, for his directives about the offensive issued on the previous day, and warning him about those issued for the next day.

He understood and saw very clearly what the enemy was doing. First, annihilating with artillery fire—a typically Austrian tactic, characteristic of Potiorek. Then, pounding the demolished positions with infantry. The military doctrine of a wealthy nation but a poor army, deciding the battle not by superior wisdom and human action, but by ammunition and material resources. He was very familiar with this doctrine, conceived for a weak and timid army without spirit or morale. He had lectured on it in the military academy, and had made a vigorous attack on Austro-Hungarian military science. Would his former students recollect those words of his today, now that they were commanding platoons or battalions? What would they think now of their former teacher and present commander, when just such an army as he had criticized, acting according to principles which he despised, had crushed and destroyed all the positions it had attacked?

He gave orders for a counterattack to recover Mednik: it must be retaken without fail. No sooner had he replaced the receiver than a report came through that Orlovac was lost. Then he was cut off, and unable to give the order that it too must be recovered before dusk.

His adjutant brought in a letter. He recognized Louisa's handwriting on the envelope; it was the first letter he had received since they parted. He thrust it quickly into his trouser pocket; he dared not read it, and dull the edge of his great professional anxiety with family worries; in any case, he did not wish to read it to the sound of artillery. Had they repulsed his attacks on Mednik, or was his second line broken?

He turned away with a look Dragutin's invitation to lunch, just as he cut short any superfluous words from an officer or orderly.

The counterattack on Mednik had not even been attempted; Potiorek's new blows had bent and strained the left wing of the army to the breaking point. Nothing that he wanted to do was going well today. The enemy was outwitting him and paralyzing his action; everything that he had not wanted to happen today was in fact happening. Field Marshal Oscar Potiorek was by far his superior; he could see through his plans and understand them very well. Even without reports from prisoners, just by listening to the fighting—by following the fluctuations, length, and intensity of the engagements—it was clear to him that Oscar Potiorek had regrouped the Sixth Army and committed it to a decisive attack designed to conquer Serbia. This was the victory which he had already announced and celebrated in Vienna, and for which he himself had received the highest military award, and a letter personally signed by Franz Josef.

From noon on, in the ceaseless rain falling over the mountain, the student platoon split up, with hoarse farewells and feverish embraces, before going away into the forest or disappearing among the streams, moving ever nearer to the gunfire. It seemed to every one of them that they were parting forever. Hot tears were caught in their throats, and they were silent and confused as they looked into one another's eyes, now unfamiliar, different from those they had looked at in Skoplje. If someone at the moment of parting called out a nickname or repeated some barrack-room joke, it no longer sounded the same as before. Bent under their knapsacks, they hurried despondently forward behind the orderlies. And throughout the journey they were all troubled by the same anxiety, trying in a hundred different ways to figure out what could have happened to Bora Jackpot, Danilo History-Book, Tričko Macedonian, Dušan Casanova, and Saša Molecule—why they had not arrived at the assembly point from their sleeping quarters in Boljkovci, and so now lagged behind the rest of the platoon. That anxiety added to the uncertainty of parting: already five of them were missing.

In fact these young men were hurrying over the mountain, sweating and with their coats unbuttoned. They would have gladly thrown away their rifles and knapsacks, since they had to run downhill behind an orderly on horseback, who was carrying out the punishment for their tardy arrival at the assembly point by escorting them to the headquarters of the Ninth Regiment just below Maljen.

"Do you student gentlemen know that I've been in the saddle for three days and nights? I've had fresh horses so that they can rest, but there's been no replacement and no rest for me. And now I've got to ride all night again, and to Maljen, too!" He had said the same thing twice since they had set out, then put his horse to a gallop without waiting for their explanations and apologies.

They were silent as they hurried after him, sad at parting from their companions—perhaps forever—without having said good-by. When they had got up and realized they were late, they had been so upset that they were unaffected by the threats of the major from the staff, who shouted from the porch of the inn:

"You're at war now—not going off on an excursion! You'll be court-martialed for this!"

Then Prince Alexander appeared and sternly demanded an explanation for their lateness. They stood in line at attention, nudging each other longer than was seemly for decent Serbian corporals. Finally Dušan Casanova had cried out:

"Your Highness, we have no words with which to apologize. We can only say that we had the misfortune to spend the night with a peasant who was celebrating his patron saint's day—the Holy Archangel. So we were singing and talking, and didn't go to bed until daybreak. Then our host didn't want to wake us, so we're late. We're ready to take whatever punishment we deserve."

Prince Alexander had looked at each of them in turn, but absent-mindedly. Then, after a long look in the direction of the mountain from which the sounds of battle reverberated, as though thinking out a punishment, he said quietly:

"Let them go to Maljen!"

It seemed like a royal pardon and reward; Tričko Macedonian had cried out: "Long live Prince Alexander!" The Regent had seemed scared by this; he turned around and quickly went back into the inn, to staff headquarters. Immediately an orderly ran angrily down the steps, mounted his horse, and waved to them to follow him.

"Forward, guard of honor!" said Dušan Casanova, trying to make a joke—the last he attempted that day.

They had set off behind the orderly, passed quickly through the village, then immediately started uphill through the mud, each occupied with his own thoughts about the previous night, all of them sad for some personal reason.

Bora Jackpot had lost even his father's watch at cards; he had had to wager the watch, since diamonds and the red cards—which he played persistently like one possessed, but consumed at the same time with anxiety—had lost in practically every deal. He felt himself detached from the orderly motion and revolving chain of the Great Wheel, and falling into chaos and uncertainty, with no chance to defend himself.

For Dušan Casanova every combination had gone well; his heart was in the Great Beginning, Bora concluded. Every card worked out for him, even when he didn't want it; as the night drew to a close, he became frightened by his gambler's luck. However, Dušan had refused to wager his rifle and ammunition, although Bora, in despair and bitterness, with tears in his eyes had called him a cad—in spite of the fact that several times Dušan had lent him money from his winnings.

Saša Molecule, who had made superstitious efforts to lose at least some money, ended up much as he had started. He too had refused Bora's request to play odds-evens with their ammunition.

Finally they had put out the lamp, and the three of them had lain down on the wide blue bed, still wearing their boots and clothes. Tričko Macedonian had long been snoring on a straw mattress beside the stove. Then Casanova, moving quietly so that Molecule wouldn't hear, had tried to return his father's watch to Bora, who indignantly refused it. Bora was so humiliated, so reduced to penury, that he couldn't sleep a wink: during his very first night at war, he had broken both the solemn promises that he had made to his mother! What else would he do, if the Austrians didn't put a speedy end to him? It wasn't so much that he hadn't a penny in his pocket. He didn't really care about that—after all, he could do without tobacco; at least he would expend his feeble will power on some personal sacrifice.

Danilo History-Book had not even tried to sleep when Stamena left him, just before daybreak, in the straw in the shed. She had made him swear that he wouldn't forget her, and asked him to visit Boljkovci at least once during the summer, when the war was over. When he protested against this modest wish, assuring her in sincere and passionate whispers that he had fallen in love with her, and would certainly come back if he wasn't killed, she silenced him by burying his head in her breasts, saying she knew what men were like even in wartime; all she wanted from him was to look at him once more, but in the sunshine, from behind the ferns in her father's big fenced field, and to see his head framed by the sunlit leaves of the young beech tree. She whispered while he embraced her, and wept because it was growing light, and the war would take him away. Only when she had promised to come back—as soon as she had seen whether her father and mother-in-law were asleep—did he release her from his embrace, then watched her disappear forever, twisting through the gray light of dawn like a tuft of darkness, moving swiftly and making less noise than the rain. He jumped over the fence behind the haystack, and clinging to the twisted trunk of a birch tree, gazed into her yard; but she did not come back. He stayed there, waiting for his companions. It never entered his head to wake them; when Dušan and Saša reproached him, he said seriously:

"Forgive me, fellows, but I'm head over heels in love!"

No one responded to this, nor did they laugh, so afraid were they of being late at the assembly point. They tore across the mud to staff headquarters, accompanied by the barking of dogs. They felt like traitors as they were rushing headlong downhill, through woods or across open spaces, in rain and fog behind the orderly, who had only once in four hours turned around to look at them, and then just to scold and curse them again for being late. He forced his horse to a gallop. Out of a sense of guilt, and also of pride, they refused to ask him to slow down or give them a rest. They could hear the sounds of battle under the mountain as they stumbled and fell, but prevented one another from throwing everything out of their knapsacks, and getting rid of half their ammunition.

Suddenly Bora Jackpot, who from the beginning had walked at the head of the "guard of honor," stood still, as though transfixed by a bayonet: in the undergrowth behind the bushes he could see human eyes. It was a woman with two children, one in her arms, and the other trying to crouch behind her back. Why should they be so terrified of us, he wondered.

"We're Serbians! What are you hiding for?" he cried.

The woman remained rigid behind the thornbush, her eyes dilated. They stopped, and called to her to stand up. She looked at them mutely, and her eyes became even larger and more vacant. They leaped through the undergrowth, whereupon the little girl, barefoot and in rags, shrieked and buried her face in her mother's wet, mud-stained skirt, while the woman clutched the child still more tightly. Speaking in loud and agitated tones, they said that they were Serbian corporals, offered the little girl a lump of sugar, and begged the woman to stand up. She shook her head, and remained crouching; the little girl screamed, then was suddenly silent. Casanova took hold of the woman and lifted her up. She looked at them, silent and unbelieving: she was holding in her arms a dead child, wrapped in bloodstained napkins.

Bora turned his head away; Dušan and Saša asked in trembling tones where she had come from and where she was going. She continued to stare at them with the same mute, disbelieving gaze. Tričko took the little girl in his arms; she whimpered, then suddenly became quiet again. He caressed her.

The orderly turned to see what was happening, but did not dismount or say anything.

Dušan and Saša were listening dumbfounded to the woman as she related her story, word by word, with long pauses: the Austrians had killed her father-in-law and mother-in-law, and the male infant in the cradle; she and the female child had managed to hide behind a haystack; then, when it grew dark, she had taken the infant from the cradle, and had fled to the mountain with her little girl.

"Where are you going now?"

"I don't know."

"Where's your husband?"

She pointed to the black scarf on her head.

They unsheathed their bayonets and walked over to a wild pear tree in a clearing. They took off their caps, knelt down, swept away the fallen leaves from the tree, and started to dig a grave with their bayonets and hands. No one spoke. The woman stood beside the hedge, still holding the baby in her arms, with the little girl at her side; they stared at the young men kneeling down and scratching the earth under the pear tree with their nails. Danilo was resolved that the male infant from the cradle should be buried with military honors—a volley of gunfire.

Meanwhile Bora had jumped over the hedge and walked deep into the forest among the tall, bare beech trees. He leaned against the thickest trunk and looked at the trees. It just isn't true, he said to himself, that they don't see us humans, that they don't feel, don't pity us; it isn't true that the trees don't think.

Down under the mountain, battles were raging in the rain and mist; war was doing its job.

"Strong enemy forces are approaching my left flank. A blow in the most sensitive spot is imminent. Please send reinforcements, sir—quickly."

"You'll get as many men as I can manage, Vasić."

He said nothing further to the commander of the army's left wing. Evening engulfed the top of the apple tree beside his window, the adjoining plum orchard, and the fence. Dragutin lit his lamp for him, then left, his quick footsteps echoing through the staff headquarters in the inn. He gave orders to Colonel Milivoje Andjelković-Kajafa, the commander of the Danube Division, first levy, to give as much help as he could to Vasić on Baćinac in the course of the night. He could feel the night pouring over his body, coursing through it, and transforming him into something different from what he was by day. His cap, overcoat, and boots—everything that constituted his uniform—slipped from him. He felt he had become someone whom he could not see clearly and completely. There flitted through his mind, at random, moments spent with this or that person, from his childhood to his recent parting from his wife and little girl—some words spoken to somebody, and many spoken only to himself. He was alone, with the huge mountains in front of him hanging over Serbia—an undulating land borne away to eternity; a land offended by people to the point of icy indifference to their fate. Everything appeared different from what it was by day; the entire structure of values which prevailed by day quietly collapsed. Ever since he had been aware of himself, night had annihilated his ambitions, his desire for fame, any insults he had received, and extinguished all petty feelings, cut short unfinished thoughts. After the cares of the day there came to him a certain strength which was nourished by great fear—a fear from the depths of heaven and the very end of life, an end which he felt most deeply and saw most clearly at night. It was a fear of existence itself, before which he did not quail. Ever since he could remember, at night he had been stronger, freer, wiser. And now, quite clearly he felt a flicker of hope; but he would not immediately surrender himself to it.

He decided to write a report to the High Command, so that this distasteful task would remove from the forefront of his mind an unbidden idea which the night had brought to him: that he should immediately withdraw to the crest of Suvobor, and suddenly end this contact with the enemy. He must interpose at least some space of time between this leaping flame of an idea and a decision; he dared not follow it immediately. So he began his report to the High Command.

Miloš Vasić called again: "Baćinac is being attacked by strong forces."

"And what have you done about it?"

He could not hear him any more; they were cut off. He looked at his watch: a quarter past seven. They were attacking in mist and darkness; that was not the usual practice of the stronger force. He should have been the one to attack by night. Potiorek was taking over his tactics to confuse him, to paralyze his action, to force him to an irrational response. He would not decide anything now: first he would write his report to the High Command. He began to write: "I will defend Maljen, Rudo, and Baćinac to the end with the forces at my disposal; but in view of the importance of this sector, and the superiority of the enemy and their encircling movements, I consider that such army reserves as are available should be sent here."

He stopped writing. This was not a proper report; moreover, the arrival of a tired and depleted regiment would not save the situation. He pressed his temples with his thumbs, overcome with nausea from his aching head and too much tobacco.

Daylight was beginning to fade, and there were still eight of them left in the column. Ivan Katić and Bogdan Dragović were preoccupied by the same anxiety: where were they going? Their destination must be the worst of all. Ivan was worried lest he be separated from Bogdan; with him he felt less fear, and could stand the fatigue of two days' marching. As for Bogdan, the sadness of the day's partings, and the fear that there would be a battle that very night, pushed to the back of his mind his suffering over Natalia. He did not want a battle in the darkness, when people could not see him, and when he himself could not see them looking at him.

Wet and muddy, they slithered uphill and downhill, and pushed their way forward under their knapsacks containing one hundred and fifty bullets, and their long Russian rifles. Clouds leveled off the mountaintops, and a kind of solitary, empty quiet sank down among the bare, wet trees, notwithstanding the reverberation of gunfire at increasingly close quarters. They tried to walk side by side, as close together as possible, so that they would touch each other; if it had been dark, perhaps they would have held hands.

At dusk they reached a battalion headquarters, a dugout under an enormous hollow beech tree at the foot of a crag. Ivan was so tired that he toppled onto a rotten tree trunk, and sat staring up at the crag, from which guns were firing from two sides, one answering the other. He didn't care if the battle started at once, if only he didn't have to walk any further.

In order to conceal his fatigue, Bogdan stood behind Ivan's back. He peeped into the dugout: three officers were sitting around a fire, listening attentively to the report of the orderly who had brought them there—the last eight members of the sixth student platoon.

A handsome officer with a kindly smile came out of the dugout and stood in front of them, giving a relaxed greeting. He was tall, erect, with a carefully tended mustache and a small black goatee. He spoke to them in a mild, quiet voice:

"I'm very glad to see you. I'm Major Gavrilo Stanković, in command of the Fourth Battalion of the Eighth Regiment. I'm happy to welcome you as my comrades-in-arms, and will do all I can to make the hardships of war as easy to bear as possible. Come into the dugout and we'll celebrate your arrival."

"Who is this man? Did you hear him?" said Ivan to Bogdan in a whisper.

"A typical cultivated cynic," muttered Bogdan, but Ivan could not hear him because a machine gun had started firing from the crag above.

Silently and hesitantly they entered the dugout and were introduced to two captains; scowling, unshaven men in crumpled uniforms. Major Stanković told the orderly to prepare two glasses of hot *rakija* and invited the students to sit down, with apologies for the cramped space. Somehow they squeezed in and sat down: Ivan found himself sitting next to the major, but was still next to Bogdan, too. He felt more relaxed: if they had not been assigned to the same platoon, he would ask this unexpectedly benign major not to separate them. Such a handsome and refined man would certainly not refuse this request.

"Excuse me, sir, but where are we now, if that isn't a military secret?" asked Bogdan.

"We're just under Baćinac, young man; or if you prefer, under Elevation 620—a position which the commander of our army considers exceptionally important."

"That means we've come right into the lion's den," interrupted Cvijović, a law student. The other seven looked at him reproachfully.

Major Stanković continued, smiling slightly: "You've come when you're most needed. I'm expecting a serious Austrian attack tomorrow; they've been bringing up troops all day. It will soon be dark, but they haven't stopped shooting. Please take your coats off and dry your clothes a bit. I'd like to hear what some of you are studying," he said.

Ivan turned his eyes toward the fire: he saw no point in saying now what he had studied and where, so he nudged Bogdan to begin. Bogdan did so as briefly as possible, speaking almost in a whisper, and making no attempt to conceal his unwillingness to talk; he was listening to the machine-gun fire from up above. If only the battle could be staved off tonight; he wanted the slaughter to begin in the morning, when people could see.

Although Ivan found it very pleasant by the fire after seven hours of slogging over the mountains in rain, he could hardly wait to hear their assignment. But he was still filled with amazement at this major who was talking like a professor:

"Like you, I too perhaps know the most important things about our fatherland. You will see for yourselves this very night that at times this knowledge is deceptive and illusory. Believe me, one can understand the fatherland only in time of war, and one can love it only in time of defeat. Then the mask of government, and all the sordidness of human affairs and institutions, are torn from its face. In time of defeat and suffering, our country is raised above us like a mother, pointing the way to goodness and justice. During the next few days you young men will be filled with new sensations. Believe me, you have no concept of what our soul—the soul of all of us—is really like." He paused and listened attentively to his battalion in its position.

"But isn't defeat humiliating, Major?" asked Ivan. Bogdan frowned.

"No, young man, it isn't. In time of defeat, the victor is humiliated far more often than the vanquished. I have never felt more pride in being a Serb than in these days of defeat. Now that the whole of Europe is at war, just tell me who can rightly say virtue and justice are on our side! What army dares believe this now? Only ours. And no other. All of them have their own sordid interests and some evil aims. Even the Russians, because they're striving to enlarge their empire. They're fighting this war in the interests of their own greatness."

"Forgive me, sir, but in order to achieve this victory, must we not start to win some battles?" said Siniša, a philosophy student.

"Indeed we must. Of course it is necessary to win engagements in time of war. And this will happen. But for our ultimate destiny, it is of no significance who will emerge the victor here on Baćinac tomorrow— or in some other place near the Ljig, or Belgrade. The ultimate issue will not be affected by the temporary possession of Suvobor and Maljen, Belgrade and Kragujevac. Of this I am firmly convinced. We have simply to hold out until the fateful hour, when all human affairs and aspirations will be arranged according to a higher law. Until then we must continue to exist, as a country that has freedom and strives toward justice. This will surely happen, my boys, no doubt about it."

"And do you think, sir, that the soldiers, the peasants, can believe today that justice is on our side? Do you think that they're really upheld by this belief?"

"Forgive me, young man, but I didn't hear what you studied?"

"I was at the Sorbonne. I began philosophy, but I was there for only one year," Ivan replied.

"Very good! You'll see for yourself this very night that only this great and holy faith upholds our soldiers. As a result of experience, I have come to believe that faith, and love of justice and freedom, are inherited human qualities and not acquired convictions. We are born with the desire for justice and freedom; we are born either with good qualities or without them. A man comes into this world either virtuous or wicked, and nothing taught in school can help him—you'll see that I am right. I ask you, what teachers have taught the Serbian peasants to fight so tenaciously for freedom and justice against one of the Great Powers of Europe? We are a people who love freedom and justice; that is the nature of our minds and souls. How else can we understand the fact that the Serbian soldiers—naked and barefoot, without artillery protection, and often without enough food for days on end—are giving their lives for every hillock and meadow from the Drina to the Kolubara, and that they're still fighting? Do you think it's fear and court-martials that prevent them all from running off home?"

Wounded men were being carried slowly past the dugout. The students looked at each other. Ivan was seized by a desire to challenge the major's views. He listened to him and to the shooting from the heights, while his exhausted feet grew numb and his wet shoulders cold. Just before the terror and uncertainty which would begin that night, he wanted this fantasy world to go on forever. Perhaps it was the last illusion of all: the mild commanding officer carried away by his faith in things of the spirit, and in the sacredness of justice. Bogdan held his head in his hands, and only half-listened to this unusual major, who continued to talk in the same didactic manner about some higher, metaphysical justice which would regulate this unjust world, and maintain an equilibrium between good and evil, life and death. The other students also found it hard to listen, and were eagerly accepting the hot *rakija*, into which Major Stanković was pouring a generous helping of sugar. Ivan and Bogdan gazed out: it was snowing lightly in the dusk. The shooting continued; the machine-gun fire died down.

Major Stanković stood up and said quietly:

"It's time for you youngsters to be going to your platoons. Most of you will be in charge of sections. Karalić, you arrange where they're to go, and take them to their platoons. And all of you, please don't hesitate to come to me at any time, if you think there is anything I can do for you."

"He's not a cynic, after all," Ivan whispered to Bogdan as they left the dugout.

"He's got some trouble of his own," answered Bogdan, then added in a louder voice: "Tonight we're going to get stuck in a snowdrift."

Ivan would have liked to challenge this opinion of Bogdan's, but at that moment one of the scowling captains was reading out the assignments to platoons. When he heard that he would be in the same platoon as Bogdan, the most courageous and loyal person he had ever known, he shouted joyfully:

"That's wonderful! Thank you, sir!"

They all looked at him in surprise, except Bogdan, who stood staring at the crag above, from which came the sound of shooting.

The last eight members of the sixth platoon of the Student Battalion quietly embraced one another and set off behind the orderlies over Baćinac, on their way to their positions.

Ivan and Bogdan walked through a wood of felled trees, among which a few fires were burning feebly; soldiers were clustered around them. Low clouds dragged across the heights.

"I've broken with Natalia," Bogdan said.

"When?"

They stopped between two tall, dark tree stumps.

"I sent her a letter from Boljkovci. I've been turning it over in my mind ever since we left Kragujevac. I carried the letter in my pocket as though it were a knife. But at Boljkovci, while you were with the general, I sent the letter."

Ivan saw tears in Bogdan's eyes, and he turned his head away: could Bogdan really be crying?

Bogdan did not want to conceal his pain; moveover he could not rid himself of the foreboding that he would be killed that same night: in the dark, in their first battle.

The orderly turned around and shouted to them to start moving. They hurried on in silence toward the first big fire, around which some soldiers were crouching.

Ivan stopped a few paces from them, astounded by their appearance. They were ragged, mud-stained, unshaven; not one of them had a complete uniform: they looked like captured slaves. Were these the men he was to command? Those who had overcoats had no breeches, and those wearing jackets had tent flaps wrapped around them. Only a few of them had boots, and the peasant bags on their shoulders were empty. They were gazing at the fire with dulled eyes.

"Good evening," stammered Bogdan. He too was surprised at the poverty-stricken appearance of the soldiers; their wretchedness aroused his compassion, and made them seem closer to him. But Ivan didn't know how to greet them; he just looked at them, petrified. Did they believe in the major's sacred higher justice? Were they exalted by their suffering? Lies, nothing but lies, everywhere.

A smallish man got up from the fire, a stocky second lieutenant wrapped in an overcoat, who with a forceful movement revealed a number of medals on his chest:

"Are these the students?" he asked the orderly in a challenging tone.

"Yes. Katić and Dragović, assigned to your platoon, the second, as corporals."

"I'm glad to see them. Let me introduce myself, gentlemen. I shall be delighted to see how you'll defeat the Austrians. War is what we want—war with Austria. Long live Greater Serbia! Have you forgotten how you raised hell after the annexation of Bosnia and Hercegovina?"

"No, sir, we haven't forgotten," said Bogdan firmly. As he looked toward the fire he could see the contemptuous smiles of the soldiers.

"Fine, Corporal! Tonight you will have a chance to show me just how you students will defeat Austria. Let me have a look at you spoiled darlings!"

Aleksa Dačić, who was sitting by the fire, laughed aloud. Ivan and Bogdan looked at each other, struck by the same feeling. In the clouds up above, a machine gun started firing, and the revolver shots intensified.

"May I ask, sir, what is your function here?" asked Bogdan.

"My name is Luka Bog. You can see my rank, and you can also see from my chest what sort of a soldier I am. I got the Obilić Gold Medal for bravery at Kumanovo, and the other one at Mačkov Kamen. You'll hear about the others under more favorable circumstances. Now let me tell you how things stand here: for cowards and weaklings I'm a hundred times worse than Potiorek. To heroes I'm a mother, and for the platoon, God Almighty. So adjust yourselves to this state of affairs. You, the cheeky fellow—the tall one with the mustache—go to the first section, where I can keep an eye on you. And you, the nearsighted one, go to the second, where you won't see me, but I'll watch you."

Ivan and Bogdan stood still: they did not know what to say, or what was going to become of them.

Bogdan Dragović, corporal of the first section of the second platoon, sat down on a tree trunk and forgot even to smoke, though he was holding a lighted cigarette; he was alone on Baćinac, on Suvobor—in the entire land of Serbia. He was now alone. Ever since he had first been aware of his own existence, he had never felt so alone: the two fires in the darkness beneath him were burning beyond the boundary of the world; and those dark-faced, speechless, despairing men whom he would order to give their lives for this Baćinac seemed no closer to him than the tree trunks lit by the flames of the fire; as for Baćinac, this forest of felled trees, was it really the fatherland for which they must now die? He had been ready to die on the barricades in the cause of revolution, to be shot for trying to assassinate the King, to be hanged as a revolutionary leader, looking the enemy and hangman straight in the face—stubborn like Robespierre, or with a smile on his face like Dimitrije Lizogub—leaving behind him an imperishable memory, an inspiration to others. He was ready to die with his comrades, but not with these men sunk in despair, commanded by a saber-rattling thug. He had always been ready to die for his ideals—he had demonstrated this clearly enough. When had he ever been afraid of the police? Had he ever on any occasion been frightened during a demonstration or a strike? But to die in the dark, with people whose very names he didn't know; to experience death at the hands of those who killed only in order to be killed themselves—an unknown, unseen death—what was the point of that, and for whom would he be dying? His whole body trembled. In the clouds far above his head, the battle erupted, while the wounded were being dragged down the mountainside in the darkness, groaning and cursing at the clumsy stretcher-bearers. For him the beginning of the war was Luka Bog and these wounded. From the dead there was no sound; they had paid their debt to Baćinac, and would be left to rot in the rain, along with the tree trunks.

Up above him, behind the fire, there was a terrific blast; weird black shapes lit up by flares of light flew upward, then disappeared into the blackness of the crags and the roaring of the stream. He was sprawled beside a tree trunk. When had he fallen down? And what had caused him to fall?

"Mortar! Put out the fires!" shouted Luka Bog.

Sitting by the fire, Ivan Katić felt something pouring over his head and his knapsack. Was it earth, sand, or shrapnel? It didn't matter;

whatever it was, it was over, and he was alive. But why did he feel no pain? They said that you felt the pain of a wound later, when it cooled. He waited for the pain to begin, and looked at the soldiers around the fire who were staring at him dumbly, as though nothing had happened. Perhaps nothing had happened. He felt to see if his glasses were still there: it was all right, they were. Fine: he hadn't moved under fire. He smiled at the soldiers, but they did not understand him. He seized a fire brand to revive the fire and thus demonstrate that nothing had happened. He would write down in his True Observations: danger illuminates, or irradiates life and gives it its true meaning; he would send them to Milena or perhaps to his father.

"Put out those fires, I tell you!" shouted Luka Bog.

"Get up, Corporal," a sergeant said to him. The sergeant, the one man present who was shaved and tidy, was looking at him closely. Ivan had noticed him as soon as he had sat down by the fire.

"How shall we put it out?" asked Ivan, getting up with great difficulty, as his legs felt numb.

"Lighting a fire in this rain is hard work, but putting one out is the easiest thing in the world."

His voice was calm, his manner serious, and he was unshaken under attack, though only a sergeant.

"What's your job, Sergeant?" Ivan asked in a whisper.

"My name is Sava Marić, and I'm a peasant from Pranjano, near Čačak. Unfortunately for me, I've had to be leader of the second section for over a month. Now that you've arrived, I'm thankful to say, I won't have to lead anyone but myself through this mess."

"But won't you still be in charge of the section? Why should I do it? I could be your assistant, if you need one."

"That wouldn't be right. You haven't studied and been to school for nothing, and it's not just a matter of chance that I'm a peasant. You do your duty, but I'll be here when we have to attack, or when there's something difficult to do."

Another shell burst; Ivan thought it was lower than the first. This time he was not spattered with earth, nor did he feel frightened. In the light from the explosion he had a quick glimpse of Sava Marić, then everything was drowned in darkness and thunderous rumbling. He did not see when and how the fires had been extinguished.

"Platoon, assemble! Bugler, sóund the assembly!" shouted Luka Bog.

The bugle shrilled in the darkness and the soldiers stumbled along, their tin cans jostling. Under no circumstances would I want to lose sight of Sava Marić; he checked that his glasses were in his pocket, and the spare pair in his knapsack.

"Here! You new corporals, I mean you students, tell your men to form a firing line and move up to the position. There's hell let loose up there—they've pushed us out of our trenches!"

"Sava, where are you?" asked Ivan imploringly.

"I'm here, sir. I'll be beside you tonight."

Ivan couldn't see him, but he wanted to embrace this man because of what he had said, and the way in which he had said it. After Bogdan he'd found another man—a real man, and a peasant, too. Nearby he could hear moaning and groaning.

"Who's that groaning, Sava?"

"It's the wounded, sir. When the reserves come up, they always meet the wounded first—either them or the prisoners. But for a long time now we've only met the wounded."

"That's terrible—I mean, it's unpleasant. You go forward to charge, and you see wounded men—your comrades—coming back." He realized that he was talking nonsense, but he couldn't help it.

"Well, that's how it is. In another engagement you'll envy them because they're coming back."

He couldn't hear Sava because of the tremors caused by the explosion. In front of him, where the fires had been, earth was falling and there was a sound of clattering stones; had they stayed there just a few moments longer, the shell would have blown them sky high. The next one would get them. They must move about—every single moment. But where? He took a step forward, stood still, then a step to the left. The soldiers would see him. Sava was standing up. When was the moment of real danger? And if there was danger all the time, when did one move away, stand up, or move forward? His teeth were chattering—this was impossible, it must be from cold and fatigue. One must believe in God or fate or chance; one must do this for psychological reasons—one must find some means of deceiving oneself. From such deception, courage was born. No, this was all rubbish! One must know, and know with certainty, that there was no pain in death.

Luka Bog ordered the platoon to move forward to the position with fixed bayonets.

"Sava, do we really have to use our bayonets?"

"Yes, we must."

Bogdan found himself in thick, whirling, broken darkness. The hillside rose steeply, barring his way: he stumbled over the tree stumps and bushes, and couldn't hurry. His feet became entangled with the undergrowth, his knapsack pressed hard on his back, and he was bent under his rifle. He wanted to throw something away, but didn't know what. He was alone amid this shrieking and banging, quite alone; this was death.

"Dragović, where are you? I tell you, Dragović, I see better by night than by day!"

"I don't care!" he had wanted to yell, but could only stammer these words; Luka Bog didn't hear him. "Don't shout at me!" he tried to call out. He could hear Luka Bog again—right on his back, as if sitting on top of his knapsack:

"Forward, forward! The Austrians are in sight! Now a river of blood has to flow!"

The first thing was to kill this loathsome creature. "Yes, that's the first thing," he whispered, unable to hurry because the slope was steep. His legs turned to water; he staggered forward in the darkness, which seemed to be bursting asunder. Fragments of fire and clotted lumps of darkness flew above his head. He fell down into the thornbushes, onto the mud and stones. Above him shells whined and exploded. Burning jets of greenish light whipped at him; he felt that he would burst from this shooting, from the din up above, and the groaning all around him—not a single man, arm, eye, no one to see him die. Someone called him—Luka Bog. He hid behind a stone and placed another over his head, so that he was practically buried by stones. He would have liked to get right inside the face of the rock.

Suffocated by heat, Ivan Katić ran here and there alongside the quarry, intent only on keeping his glasses on his nose, and on not losing sight of Sava Marić or lagging behind him. Soldiers moved past him, then disappeared, pushing against one another, calling out names; there was shooting everywhere, from the earth and from the sky. He ran into groans, then curses, stumbled against something soft, then fell over a wet, soft body. He ran on, deafened by explosions and blinded by flames, then collided with a few men who were also running: were they chasing him or running away? He fired, lunged his rifle, and dug into something with his bayonet. A piece of wood? A man? He moved back, jumped up, and plunged his bayonet into the darkness. Someone grabbed his shoulder:

"Lie down, Corporal! We've driven them back!"

"Is that you, Sava?"

"Yes, it's me. Lie down, for God's sake!"

He lay down on something hard. The shooting suddenly stopped.

"What do we do now?"

"We've driven them off. And you did everything just right."

"When did we drive them off? And what did I do right?"

"We forced them out of our trenches with our bayonets."

"But how did we do that? I didn't use my bayonet! Or perhaps I did." He realized that he was trembling, and gripped his rifle with all the strength he could muster.

"People can't always do it right off."

"Well, I think I did. Did you?"

"Yes, I did. When we get all mixed up in the dark like that, and we are at each other's throats, that's when it's best to use a bayonet."

"How?"

"I caught one man by the belt. Then I gored him, like I was sticking a knife in a pumpkin."

"I didn't see anything. I'm nearsighted, you know. What happened to the first section? My friend Bogdan is with them."

"They're on our left, lying in the trenches."

"Was anyone killed?"

"Must have been. We lost two men, and four are wounded."

"Who?" He tried to recollect the faces of the soldiers with whom he had sat around the fire. He stumbled against something soft; perhaps it was those two—the men who had been killed. He smelled the moist palm of his left hand: blood! He thrust his hand into the earth and struck a stone, on which he rubbed his hand: he would rub the skin off his fingers. Indeed, blood smelled sweet; the heavy, acrid smell was from the explosive. The sudden silence clouded his brain.

Around him soldiers were breathing heavily and panting. He wanted to see their faces, and he wanted them to see that he was there. Had they seen him running in front of them? He had never once bent over since they had moved to attack; he had never once lain down under that heavy fire, he was sure. He felt that he was trembling now from some other cause—was it happiness? Could it really be true that he was happy? Yes, indeed, he was. As soon as it was light, he would write down his thoughts for Milena: after his first battle, a man feels happy. I feel happy, for the first time in my life.

"Sava, we really haven't lost many men—only two, after so much shooting. But what about Bogdan? What's happened to him?"

He jumped out of the shallow trench and moved hurriedly to the left, calling out Bogdan's name.

"The corporal isn't here," someone said.

"Where is he? When did you last see him?"

"He disappeared somewhere in front of the rock face."

"But that's impossible!" Ivan ran down the quarry, still calling Bogdan's name.

"Where are you off to? Get back!" shouted Luka Bog from the darkness. "This is no picnic, you silly student! Get back to your trench!"

Ivan burst into tears and moved off to the right, into the darkness and silence.

Bogdan Dragović, packed inside the stones with his chin resting on one of them, breathing the acrid smell of limestone, heard Ivan calling his name, and grasped the full horror of his situation: he had hidden, he had run away! He was a coward—a loathsome coward!

It was the darkness, perhaps, and his suffering over Natalia—but what on earth had happened to him? During the apprentices' strike in Valjevo, he had been beaten and trampled all night long, but he had not betrayed his comrades from Belgrade. And at Čukarica he had seized guards by their bayonets! So what could have happened here? He would never be able to look anyone in the face again, never be able to tell anyone the truth—and what would he say to Ivan? My God, he thought, I'll kill myself! He rolled away the stone from his head, and raised himself to an upright position; his eyes were filled with smoke from tracer bullets, and his nostrils with the smell of powder; a burning spasm rose from the pit of his stomach. The roar of the shells was intolerable; he grasped a stone with both hands and began to vomit. Groaning and vomiting, he seemed to lose consciousness. I may have suffered a concussion, he thought; this notion, flashing through his mind, brought some hope of salvation. He could hear the sound of his vomiting, and his hoarse, repulsive moaning. Yes, I must be concussed, he thought.

"So that's where you are, you spoiled baby of a student! Why are you bellowing like that?"

Above him he heard the voice of Luka Bog, and fell flat on a stone in his own vomit.

"I've suffered a concussion," he whispered after a while. Then he caught sight of a spark of light above his head.

"That can happen the first time, at the beginning of the war. The explosion shakes you up—it goes right to your heart."

"I have a concussion, I tell you," he whispered. Now there was no way out; he would have to kill himself. He would not let Luka Bog—that loathsome, barrack-yard saber-rattler—humiliate him.

"All the same, you've been lucky, you wretched little pen-pusher. It's not a bad concussion. There are folks that shit the first time things get hot. I've seen them with my own eyes. They fill their pants with it—you can't stand being near such a casualty."

Bogdan jumped up and stood in front of the glowing cigarette. "I'll kill you!" he said. "Do you hear?"

"Now you're talking more like a man! Get out of my way; you stink of your own shit."

"You're a bastard, a loathsome bastard! I'll kill you with my bare teeth!"

"Don't make such a noise, young man, or the Fritzies will turn their machine guns on you. Then you really will shit. It would be a pity with those new trousers."

Bogdan leaped to throttle him, but Luka Bog jumped sideways and hissed:

"Stand at attention, Corporal!"

Bogdan lurched around in the darkness: he would make an end of everything, immediately, while it was still dark.

"Nobody need ever know about this first concussion of yours, not a soul. I give you my word of honor as an officer. It will be our military secret. Why don't you say something? Like a cigarette?"

Bogdan fumbled for the cigarette, but immediately threw it away. Then he walked behind Luka Bog, resolved that in such a state he would not wait to see the morning.

Ivan heard Luka Bog's voice while he was lying in the trench, in despair because he didn't know what had happened to Bogdan.

"Sava," cried Luka Bog, "where is that half-blind corporal of yours?"

"He's right here in front of you, sir."

"Where are you, young man? Still in one piece? That lanky pal of yours with the whiskers was hit on the head."

"Is he badly hurt?" asked Ivan, jumping up.

"No, not really. The shell burst quite a ways from him. Knocked him out and filled him with smoke from the explosive. But he threw up and got rid of it. Now he's all right, he's lit a cigarette. As soon as a casualty takes a cigarette, you know he's over the worst."

"You're sure there's really nothing wrong with him? Can I go and see him?"

"This is no picnic, and you're not to sit around. I tell you, he had better luck than he deserved."

Ivan ran over to Bogdan:

"Are you badly wounded?"

"No, I'm not."

Ivan embraced him in the dark. Bogdan pulled away and stammered:

"I'm a coward, Ivan."

"Don't be afraid. Luka Bog said that a shell exploded a long way from you, and the smoke poisoned you and made you sick." Ivan spoke in a gay and joyful tone, and stretched out his hands to place them on Bogdan's shoulders.

"How did Luka Bog know that?" muttered Bogdan.

"He came and told me. I was looking for you as soon as we had recovered our trenches."

"No, Ivan. Luka Bog was not telling the truth. I was so frightened that I never even got to the trenches—that's how scared I was!"

"Don't talk nonsense! Your mind's still confused."

Bogdan said nothing, struggling to accept the fact of his initial shameful behavior.

"How will you remember our first battle, Bogdan?"

"I don't want to remember it. I want to start my war experience all over again. But that's impossible!"

Above them the loud noise turned into singing.

"And we believed that we were brothers, that we were fighting for unity. Do you hear what our Croatian brothers are singing?"

> "Forward, brave sons of Croatia,
> Forward through the rain and mud;
> Onward in our task of vengeance
> For Ferdinand and Sophia's blood!"

"They're just barbarians. You find such people everywhere. They're traitors! Not Croatian people!"

"And are Serbian people in my section?"

From the stream, Luka Bog called out: "Corporals, count your men! If anyone deserts tonight you'll pay for it with your own heads."

Colonel Miloš Vasić, commander of the Danube Division, second levy, was giving some information by telephone to General Mišić; he spoke without any greeting or preamble.

"Yesterday evening, between seven and eight o'clock, the enemy took Baćinac by assault."

"Well?"

"I ordered a counterattack, but had no troops with which to carry it out. The Eighth Regiment is completely scattered. The situation here is terrible!"

Mišić turned his face to the shadow, and slumped down in his chair. His plan of attack was demolished. Once more he had taken a licking on Baćinac. He raised his voice:

"Have you anything more to tell me?"

"If we go on defending these positions, my division will disintegrate completely in a couple of days. This is also the opinion of all the regimental commanders."

"Have you and your regimental C.O.s no other idea about the future of the troops under your command?"

"That is the true state of affairs, and it is my duty to tell you so."

"It is also your duty, Colonel, to have faith, even in times of great difficulty. You must have faith, even when no one else does."

"Forgive me, sir, but there is no need to instruct me in human virtues. I am informing you in no uncertain terms that we are on the verge of catastrophe; in fact, it is already here."

"But even in catastrophic circumstances, Vasić, people want to continue their existence, to live. You and I have the right to give orders to a large number of people, and to require them to endure great hardships, and to give their lives, only in order that our people might not experience what you describe as catastrophe. That is the only justification for our actions. Do you hear me, Colonel?"

"Sir, I cannot listen to interminable lectures on patriotism, based on your authority over me."

"And I cannot forever go on convincing my colonels that they are not sergeants major. Is there anything else you wish to tell me?"

"If you intend to accomplish something, give us fresh troops. And ammunition for our artillery. That above all, General!"

"Yes, Colonel, I understand. But during the past two days you have already received all the men in Serbia who can be called up and sent to the battlefield."

"But we have received men without weapons, without rifles. What can I do with such men? They've disrupted the troops even more."

"I'll send you some rifles. You'll get the rest when you take up your positions. Have the students arrived?"

"Yes, they have. It really is terrible, tragic, that they have to come."

"That is their fate and their duty. And please note that not a single one of them is to stay with the staff. Just a minute, what shall we do about Baćinac?"

"We must immediately withdraw to the main defense line. I am firmly convinced of this."

"If you withdraw, what will happen to the crest of Suvobor, Vasić? Our entire defense will be shattered."

"Our defenses will be shattered tomorrow, whatever we try to do. That's the state we're in now. We're on the verge of collapse."

"You're absolutely convinced of this?"

"I am no less unhappy about it than you are, or Vojvoda Putnik."

"I'll get in touch with you again in half an hour."

"I can't wait that long. I must withdraw. At any moment my staff may be taken prisoner. Even as we talk, I'm not sure that anyone's defending me!"

"I told you, I'll get in touch with you in half an hour."

He put down the receiver. He would have liked to trample on that well-known, odious self-confidence which had its origin in the ministerial post which the colonel had once held, rather than in the courage of a commanding officer who was ready for anything. But he dared not destroy it—by no means. Just now he needed such an opponent, now more than ever.

Was that the flame blazing up in the stove, or the rumble of the Austrian artillery? It didn't matter; there was no other way out. They must move from under the brandished ax; they would have to concentrate and tighten up. There was already snow and frost on the mountain; the roads were impassable. But all this was also awaiting the army of Oscar Potiorek, although it was much stronger and better equipped. He is determined to defeat me here, but it is here that I must save the situation. Two separate fates must be broken on the same lance. A man who is trying to save his very existence will venture more and can endure longer than one who is fighting for victory. This is the one lesson of history in which we can believe tonight. We must believe in it; it is the only one that prevails over all others. All the unfavorable factors—the mountainous terrain, the snow, cold, hunger —must now be on my side; they must not be subservient to Potiorek's will and his plans. When the morning reveals that I no longer occupy the positions I held today and tonight, let Oscar Potiorek try to guess what I'm planning to do. Let him at least make his way up the heights of Suvobor and Rudnik with fear in his heart, let him get stuck in the mud and snowdrifts. Let him look for the Serbian First Army. Yesterday and today he aimed his shells as though at a dummy.

He dialed the High Command. He could not withdraw the army to the crest of Suvobor without Putnik's agreement. And what if Putnik did not agree? What if he opposed the withdrawal by arguing that it would threaten the flanks of the Užice Brigade and the Third Army, expose the Second Army to attack on a wide front, and undermine the defense of Belgrade? He knew all these reasons, these obvious facts which would carry conviction with any sergeant; but he must save the First Army: this was more important than any unfavorable consequences. While he waited for Putnik to come to the telephone, he thought out how he would present his case. He put the receiver down on its side: he didn't have a single reason or a single fact which Putnik did not already know! Putnik would say to him exactly what he himself had said a while back to Miloš Vasić; and Putnik would be right, just as he had been right. If Putnik was not right, then neither had he been right in the eyes of Miloš Vasić. And what if Miloš Vasić was right? Outside in the darkness, someone was playing a flute. Who could be doing that now? Was there really someone who could play his flute in Serbia on this night? Where had he heard this song and this flute quite recently? On the bridge at Ribnica! Could it be Dragutin? Yes, it was Dragutin, playing to him from a shed. When he had brought in wood and lit the fire, he had heard that Baćinac had fallen. Mišić's voice was trembling:

"Mišić speaking. Good evening, Vojvoda!"

Putnik coughed; his voice was barely audible. "What good news have you got for me?"

"I haven't heard any good news from my positions today."

"Well, go on."

"I've lost Mednik, Orlovac, and Baćinac. The enemy is still attacking tonight. They've concentrated three corps, mostly on the left wing of my army."

"And what have you decided to do?"

Putnik's voice was suddenly free from coughing, and rang out clear and metallic. This made him hesitate; he said nothing while he reflected. Dragutin went on playing in the darkness. There was a tinkling sound in the distance.

"I'm asking you, Mišić, what you have decided to do?"

"'I've decided to pull back the center and the left wing to the Suvobor ridge, and to take up our position on the line Suvobor-Rajac-Prostruga. I'm concentrating my forces, and resting the troops for at least one night. I want the army to get one night's sleep, if nothing more."

Putnik began to cough again, wrinkling up the wires and the distance. Mišić waited for his voice and words to become disentangled from the hills, streams, and forests. Then you're abandoning Maljen, he would say.

"Go on, Mišić."

"Maljen is an open wound, sir. You must give me one division to reinforce it. My front line is thin and extended, and not protected by snow. The end stretches over three mountains."

"Yes, Maljen." Putnik fell silent. A smothered cough rumbled in the distance. "I'll call you again in a quarter of an hour."

"Vojvoda Putnik, this is the last possible moment for me to send instructions to the divisions."

The operators were shouting to each other. Mišić replaced the receiver. Behind his back the chief of staff sneezed.

"Sir, the enemy are taking advantage of the fog to launch sudden attacks and sallies. And a sudden attack is fatal to an army with wavering morale."

"A surprise attack is unpleasant for any army. There is no reason why it should be any worse for us than for others."

"They say that the troops are terribly anxious and frightened today. And the number of deserters has grown rapidly since noon. I think we must set up court-martials. Yesterday evening the High Command asked what our court-martials were doing."

"While I am in command of a Serbian army, and while that army is defending its hearths and homes, there will be no court-martials in my regiments. I'll call you in twenty minutes."

Hadjić withdrew quietly, walking backward. Dragutin was playing a flute in the darkness; tonight the orderly was instilling courage into his commanding officer. A shudder ran through his body. If they had been playing flutes in the regiments, or if others like Dragutin had been playing a flute in the platoons, he would not be writing an order for withdrawal onto Suvobor. As long as there was no singing or flute playing in the platoons, no dancing, no bawdy jokes among the soldiers—while they still cursed Pašić, and not Franz Josef and the Austrians—it was useless to talk of an offensive. Now it was not necessary to defend land or positions, but to work for the soul of the army, to strengthen its spirit and set it on its feet. That was the one strategic principle that would save it. Tomorrow he would lecture on strategy to his students, and explain victories and defeats in a different way. If there was a tomorrow!

The telephone rang. Would that be Vasić or Putnik? He would not answer immediately. Yes, he must give the army one night's rest. And they must have one cooked dinner, a dinner cooked in pots. One day on which no one would be killed. He must give the soldiers a little respite.

He lifted the receiver, and heard the sound of coughing and wind blowing.

"I'm here, Vojvoda."

"Go ahead with what you've planned. And do your level best to keep Maljen. I'll send you the Drina Division as reinforcements. Good-by, Mišić."

"And shells! Please, for God's sake, send shells. My army has only five field cannon!"

The telephone crackled, and the operators called to each other from the end of the world. For a long time he did not remove the receiver from his ear. Vasić was right, Putnik was right, and he himself was right. What if Oscar Potiorek knows that we're wrong? What if he believes that we have made a mistake? But he'll not find that out tonight.

He wrote instructions to the divisions that at the crack of dawn they were to abandon their positions and withdraw to the crest of Suvobor. But as soon as he had signed the order and given it, with a brief explanation, to the chief of staff for further elaboration and dispatch, he was seized by an acute anxiety: by taking possession of the crest of Suvobor, not only would he fail to shorten his front, but his army would be regrouped into three distinct parts only tenuously connected, incapable of concerted action or the use of field artillery if the shells arrived. He could no longer hear Dragutin playing.

He got up, moved over to the window, grasped the wooden shutters, and looked through the glass at the glowing butt of his cigarette in the darkness. His head ached, and he felt a pain in his stomach; he could no longer think clearly. That glowing cigarette, that fleck of fire in the darkness was somehow ominous. He moved away from the window and walked slowly and wearily up and down the room. Until daybreak he would not think about the withdrawal. He put more wood on the fire and breathed in the scent of fresh beechwood. He liked the scent of sapwood, and the sap of a healthy tree trunk, better than that of grass and flowers. Every tree had its own characteristic fragrance, which varied with the season of the year, a fragrance redolent of strength which never destroyed anything or committed any evil: a strength from which came leaves, flowers, and fruit. A miracle, something perfect in itself. From the depths of the earth it climbed up to the heights by way of invisible tubes, answering the challenge of the sun, and then burgeoned in its full glory. And all this from invisible beginnings—everything sprang from invisible beginnings. The Creator could see the flower in the stone, the fruit in the mud, the leaf in the refuse. Such was the vision of the Creator. No, he would not summon the commanding officers again that night. They must not feel him hanging around their necks. He poked the fire and looked at the flames and the embers, but couldn't settle down. Then he remembered Professor Zarija. He might be a great chatterbox, but he was the only man on the staff who always had a smile on his face and a pleasant word on his lips. He opened the door and told the orderly to summon him.

The professor soon arrived without a smile, and with a strained expression. He began to wonder if his faith too had died.

"What's going on in your mind tonight, Professor?" He received him standing up. "Sit down and have some apples."

"I'm thinking, sir, about the greatest injustice in recent history: the injustice of the Allies toward Serbia. It really is unheard of! At Valjevo we gave our lives for Paris and the French; on the Kolubara we defended the Dardenelles for the English; at Milovac we shed our blood for the Russians and the Ukraine. And on Baćinac we've perished at the hands of our Croatian brothers, giving our lives for their freedom. It's incredible, sir! And that whore Rumania just keeps silent. It doesn't matter if Belgrade falls, as long as Bucharest is safe! As for the Greeks . . ."

"Let's not talk about that tonight. Have you got a book, Professor? Don't be cross! Give me something that will outlive both our Allies and our enemies. And us, too, and our suffering in this muck, with no overcoats and boots, and nothing inside us but a bit of frozen hardtack. Something that will last forever—if you have such a book."

"I've got Njegoš's *Mountain Wreath*, General."

"Isn't there plenty in it about our sufferings?"

"Would you like *War and Peace*?"

"Haven't you something about ordinary people, real people?"

"You want something about the people? Well, I've got Victor Hugo's poems, in French, and Goethe's *Faust*."

"No, not poetry. My life has passed it by, somehow. Let's have something by one of our Allies, anyway. I like those thick, boring books with close-set type. My little bit of technical know-how makes you smile?" He sat down on the stool by the stove and poked the fire. "You've forgotten that I was illegally retired after our victories over the Turks and Bulgarians. In order to educate my children, I took out a loan from the bank on a bill of exchange which Vukašin Katić signed for me, and then, together with some business associates, I founded a publishing house. So I began to learn a bit about the printer's trade and learned the different kinds of letters, and about type and page makeup. Well, that's it, Professor. You never know what you might have to do. So bring along *War and Peace*."

Zarija was soon back. As he handed Mišić two leather-bound volumes, he asked in a whisper:

"And what about the Montenegrins, General?"

"They're doing their best. You know, Professor, if we had two full armies of Montenegrins, we'd be spending Christmas in Vienna, or . . . That's a nice binding. If I'm still alive after the war, I'll learn the bookbinder's trade and bind books for myself and my friends. I've got a few ideas of my own about this. Professor, have you ever taught dumb students?"

"Of course I have, General. If it weren't for dumb students, I'd never have finished high school or gone to the university in Berlin. In a small country there aren't many scholarships available."

"Well, I'm a dumb student when it comes to good literature. You can take that for granted, so read me something you like. And I'll pay you for this midnight lesson given just before our withdrawal to the crest of Suvobor—I'll pay you when we've driven Field Marshal Oscar Potiorek over the Drina and the Sava." Mišić handed him the book.

Zarija tried to smile. But now Mišić didn't want to test his faith. Anyway, battles for survival were not won by the sort of faith you found in pen-pushers; as a rule, you could make use of that faith when it was a question of freedom.

"I find it difficult to think of any part of *War and Peace* that I don't like, General."

"That's hard to believe, Professor. People don't manage to say much that is good or wise, very little in fact. But when it comes to action, even less."

"Do you think this is true of great men? Napoleon, for example?"

"I think it exactly fits Napoleon, whom I esteem above all others as a military leader. Napoleon, genius that he was, really only won one battle with his head. For the others his opponents deserve at least some of the credit. It's always like that when men are fighting for victory and glory. Actually, the way I interpret history, it often happens that the defeated are more deserving than the victors in the case of a particular victory. And with regard to military history, I've come to the conclusion that it's those who have not fought for victory that deserve the greatest respect."

"Forgive me, General, I don't quite follow you."

"I mean those who have fought for survival, Professor, those who have fought to defend the very existence of their nation. In wars of this type, knowledge of military science isn't worth much; such wars have their own strategy and tactics, and they're always different. Nobody has studied this kind of knowledge and skill. You couldn't even teach it to your sons. So don't read me anything about war, battles, or military staffs. Read me something about peace, something rooted in peace."

"You don't want to hear about Kutuzov? That bit about when he was at Borodino . . ."

"No. Kutuzov believed that war was won by patience, by time. But it isn't so. In our present war, the only need for patience is when you're dealing with the High Command, and perhaps with the Allies. As for time, if you think of life and history, time always works against the small and the weak. Among those Serbs who have any sense, Vukašin Katić has grasped this better than anybody."

"And do you think time is against us? Against Serbia?"

"Of course it is! Read me that bit about old Prince Bolkonsky, about how he saw his son off when he went away to the war."

About noon the student "guard of honor," in frozen overcoats and breeches, stood at attention between a red-hot stove and a large dining table with a military map and a telephone; behind it sat the regimental commander and his chief of staff, who paid no attention to their arrival and presence in the room. The commander, with a piece of tile in his jaw, shouted into the telephone:

"Colonel Vasić has ordered that Rior and Maljen be defended to the last man! And I've no shells, not even a trace of one. Yes, I know. Wait for them with fixed bayonets! Nonsense! I can see that everything's freezing—let it freeze!"

He banged down the receiver. Only after he had twisted the piece of warm tile and settled it against his jaw, did he look at each of them in turn, with an uneasy and irritable expression on his face. They stood more stiffly at attention, their frozen collars thawing and the melted ice trickling down their necks like raindrops.

"Well, what am I supposed to do with you university gentlemen? Just tell me, please, what I am to do with you?"

"Distribute us among the troops. We've come here to fight," said Danilo. He was the one who found this reception by the regimental staff hardest to bear.

"But what use are you to me? Why didn't the High Command send us shells, instead of you young men? Why hasn't the government sent us overcoats, boots, and tents instead of students?" The commander stood up, stretched out his hands, and without thinking let the warm tile drop from his jaw. This infuriated him and he shouted: "Give that to me!" He glared at Bora Jackpot as though he would like to crush him flat.

Bora hesitated, trembling, uncertain whether to obey. One of his comrades nudged him, so he slowly bent down to pick up the commander's remedy against toothache. He said:

"I suppose Vojvoda Putnik would know why we're here, sir."

Danilo History-Book struck his thigh with his fist to shut him up. Then he was sorry he had done so; that was what he had done at every inspection at Golgotha, in Skoplje.

"Don't speak until spoken to!"

The commander stamped angrily toward the window and looked outside. His shoulders were trembling.

Saša Molecule whispered something to Danilo.

The commander turned around and glared: "How can I replace the officers that have been killed with idiots like you? Tell me that!" He looked at each of them in turn, then at his chief of staff, who was smoking and making marks on the map with a pencil. "Please go outside and wait under the eaves until I tell you where to go."

Reluctantly, they saluted and went out into the wind, which was blowing up the snow and freezing the sodden earth.

"Let's go in the shed. We won't stand under the eaves, just to spite him," said Dušan Casanova. They followed him. Then Bora Jackpot said:

"I'll never be able to understand—not if the war lasts a hundred years—why these representatives of the fatherland, and the other so-called leading lights of the nation, are practically always stupid and cruel! Just why should this idiot of a lieutenant colonel treat us like criminals?"

"Because he's got a toothache," said Tričko Macedonian. "Just put yourself in his skin for a minute: you're losing battles, you've no shells, everything's freezing up, and you've got a toothache! Now how could you be refined and gentle?"

Bora Jackpot leaned against the shed; from habit, he thrust his hand into his pocket where he kept his pack of cards, as though feeling for a cigarette. A sweet tremor ran through his fingers. No, he wouldn't throw them away, as he had resolved to in the hut last night. In a game of cards—in the world of signs, numbers, and colors—there were no underlings, for everything happened in accordance with the law of the Great Wheel; it was the same for everybody: changeable, just, incomprehensible. Only at cards could men achieve equality in this world. If he had had a single dinar in his pocket, he would have immediately dealt the cards for a hand of poker with Dušan and Saša. But he felt ashamed to borrow money now. Meanwhile he could hear the sounds of battle, both concentrated and far-ranging.

The others were listening to this, too, and watching the men in the supply train mercilessly beating with stakes the oxen whose carts had got stuck in the ditch.

"I just can't understand how the peasants can beat their oxen like that when they get their livelihood from them, and perhaps love them as much as their wives," said Danilo.

"That's our national trait. We're cruel to those we love," said Dušan.

"We're not cruel, we're only unlucky," said Tričko.

"Enough of these mental gymnastics! Whoever survives Rior and Maljen can start thinking about things then," said Saša.

"Come here, you students!" shouted the regimental chief of staff from the doorstep.

They walked up to him; only Tričko Macedonian stood at attention.

"You're to go to the lines immediately, and then you'll be assigned to your platoons. Sergeant Lukić will take you there. I hope you know your duty." He raised his hand to his cap, but did not complete the salute.

They felt somewhat relaxed: they would be together for at least a few more hours. The snowdrifts were getting deeper. Sergeant Lukić, with a fixed smile on his face, led them onto the road on his horse. As soon as they had left the village and were moving toward the forest, he got off his horse and began to tell them in great detail how in a battle only one bullet in a hundred found its mark, and how they should behave responsibly and considerately to the soldiers, who were already veterans. Somewhere up above them, in the forest toward which they were going, they could hear the rattle of guns exchanging fire: a dry sound, more bewildering than alarming. The wind blew more strongly and the snow became thicker. The trees whitened where their branches forked, and the snow powdered the bushes and lumps of earth.

When they entered the wood Dušan Casanova, who was now at the head of the "guard of honor," stopped in the first clearing and turned around:

"You know, I'm enjoying this—I really am! What a marvelous forest! And this light snowfall, and a bit of wind from the north—it's like something in a story by Turgenev. And that shooting: it's as though a crowd of volunteer workers were gathering dry branches in the wood. By God, it's glorious!"

At this the smiling Sergeant Lukić grew serious and passed him by in silence. The others looked at him sadly and fearfully, but this made no impression on Dušan. He bent down, made a snowball, threw it, and hit Trička in the back; Trička did not turn around. Dušan then sobered up and moved on behind the others, keeping to the rear.

Suddenly the sounds of battle stopped, as though the gatherers of dry branches had come to the end of the wood. The wind roared thickly through the young beech trees interspersed with firs, and powdered them with dry snow. They walked in silence, slowly. As they climbed up through the wood, the white cover of snow became thicker and cleaner; they spread themselves out so as to leave the impressions of their own footsteps, looking at one another in silence, and taking care not to tread on one another's tracks. Each wanted to have his own, knowing that before dusk they would disappear.

Bora Jackpot asked the sergeant if they could have a short rest; he at once agreed, happy to have an opportunity to talk to them about the Allies, who were not giving Serbia the help she deserved and had a right to expect.

Bora then tramped into the wood in search of a tree trunk, so he could write a letter to his mother before his first night in the trenches. Dušan Casanova ran after him, and found him behind the young firs. He handed him the watch he had won from him at cards in Boljkovci:

"Please take it, Bora. Be a pal."

"I can't! It's not a question of honor, not that at all. No, I can't!"

"I gave my watch back to my father in Niš, honestly. I can't stand listening to the time passing by. I couldn't sleep a wink in the hut because of the ticking of your watch."

Bora looked at his father's watch in the palm of Dušan's hand; he couldn't hear its ticking for the wind. Then he thought of his mother's promise: "You could ransom your life with your dead father's watch."

"We've been playing cards together for two months, and you must have seen that I don't play for money. Only the cards can give me back what they've taken away."

"Stop talking nonsense! We're right under Maljen. Maybe we'll go into battle this very evening. Can't you hear how quiet it is in this great wood?"

"I can hear the wind. And that's why I can't take the watch."

"If you don't take it, I'll throw it into the forest right now—right under your nose!"

Bora took the watch without looking at it, and dejectedly walked further into the forest; then he sat down on a felled beech tree, took a notebook and pencil from his pocket, and began to write rapidly:

Dearest Mother,

I am sending you my last thoughts from Maljen, just before we go into battle.

If I'm killed, I'll know that the bullet was fated to get me, from the very moment they cut the cord which bound me to your navel. All my life I've been convinced that I've been loved beyond measure by the tenderest of mothers. And I believe that at this time I'll give my life for the most unfortunate of nations.

I am extremely agitated by this completely new feeling which has possessed me on the way to the front.

Now I am playing for Infinity.

I shall fight the good fight, whether in victory or defeat.

And really, Mother, what more can a man do than sacrifice his life? (He carefully crossed out these words.)

If you feel sad, then play a game of patience. I'm the jack of diamonds.

On a clear night you can look for me among the Pleiades. (He angrily crossed out this sentence, right to the last word.)

The bearer of this letter will bring you my father's watch.

I hug you till my last breath.

Bora

In the fir tree a bird chirped above his head. He would have liked to see it. The wind whistled through the wood.

TO PAŠIĆ, PREMIER OF THE ROYAL GOVERNMENT OF SERBIA, NIŠ:
SINCE THE STATE OF THE TROOPS IS TERRIBLE AND THEY NO LONGER OFFER ANY RESISTANCE WE CONSIDER THE SITUATION MOST CRITICAL STOP ALEXANDER FIRST ARMY

TO SPALAJKOVIĆ MINISTER OF THE KINGDOM OF SERBIA TO ST. PETERS-
BURG:
AGAIN IMPLORE THE RUSSIAN GOVERNMENT TO SEND 50-60 THOUSAND
MEN DOWN THE DANUBE WHILE IT IS STILL NAVIGABLE AND BEFORE IT IS
TOO LATE STOP PAŠIĆ

TO BOJOVIĆ, MILITARY ATTACHE TO THE SERBIAN ARMY, LONDON:
BUY MUNITIONS WHEREVER YOU CAN AND WITH ALL POSSIBLE SPEED STOP
PAŠIĆ

TO PAŠIĆ, PREMIER OF THE ROYAL GOVERNMENT OF SERBIA, NIŠ:
THE ENGLISH GOVERNMENT REFUSES TO HURRY STOP I HAVE WAITED
SEVERAL DAYS FOR THE MINISTER TO RECEIVE ME STOP I HAVE TO WAIT
SEVERAL WEEKS FOR AN ANSWER STOP IN GENERAL THE ENGLISH ARE VERY
DIFFICULT TO WORK WITH STOP FOR ALL OF THEM THE IMPORTANT THING
IS TO RAISE MONEY AND THEY ARE NOT AT ALL CONCERNED ABOUT US
STOP BOJOVIĆ LONDON

TO BOŠKOVIĆ, MINISTER OF THE KINGDOM OF SERBIA TO LONDON:
DO YOUR UTMOST TO MAKE THE ENGLISH HELP US BY PUTTING PRESSURE
ON THE FRENCH TO FULFILL THEIR OBLIGATIONS REGARDING MUNITIONS
STOP WE ARE NOT ASKING FOR SHELLS TO USE AGAINST THE ENEMIES OF
OUR ALLIES FOR NOTHING STOP THE MUNITIONS HAVE BEEN PAID FOR BY
A PREVIOUS LOAN STOP IF SERBIA DOES NOT RECEIVE MUNITIONS AT ONCE
SHE WILL NOT BE ABLE TO HOLD OUT TWO WEEKS STOP MR GREY AND
LORD KITCHENER KNOW VERY WELL HOW MANY DAYS AUSTRIA AND
GERMANY REQUIRE TO REACH SALONIKA AND THE BOSPHORUS STOP PAŠIĆ

TO BALUGDŽIĆ, MINISTER OF THE KINGDOM OF SERBIA TO ATHENS:
COMPLAIN TO VENIZELOS THAT GREECE HAS LOANED US 20,000 SHELLS
WHICH WE WILL RETURN IN 1915 STOP TELL THE GREEKS THAT IF THE
BULGARIANS ENTER MACEDONIA AND CROSS THE VARDAR AND TAKE BITOLJ
FROM US THE GREEKS CAN SAY GOOD-BY TO SALONIKA STOP THE BUL-
GARIANS WILL NOT STOP AT BITOLJ AND OHRID STOP THEY NEED THESE IN
ORDER TO TAKE SALONIKA AND KAVALLA LATER STOP OUR GREEK FRIENDS
MUST REALIZE THAT SERBIA'S MISFORTUNE MEANS THE BEGINNING OF
THE COLLAPSE OF GREECE STOP PAŠIĆ

TO RISTIĆ MINISTER OF THE KINGDOM OF SERBIA TO BUCHAREST:
TELL THE RUMANIANS MOST FIRMLY THAT IT IS HIGH TIME THEY
ENTERED THE WAR STOP IF SERBIA FALLS RUMANIA FACES DIFFICULT

TIMES STOP IF THE BULGARIANS TAKE MACEDONIA FROM SERBIA RU-
MANIA WILL LOSE THE DOBRUDJA STOP AND THE BULGARIANS WILL NOT
STOP THERE STOP SO IT IS IN THEIR INTEREST NOT TO HESITATE FURTHER
BUT AT LEAST TO GIVE PERMISSION IMMEDIATELY FOR THE PASSAGE OF
MUNITIONS FROM RUSSIA STOP THESE MUNITIONS WILL DEFEND THE
SERBIAN ARMY AND RUMANIA STOP PAŠIĆ

At dusk, amid whirling snow, the Austrians dislodged Luka Bog's
platoon from its position for the second time that day, first with
shrapnel and then by assault; this platoon was part of Major Gavrilo
Stanković's battalion, and after the loss of Baćinac the last to retreat in
any battle.

Luka Bog was running through the forest heading off and stopping
his men, waving his revolver, shooting into the air, threatening, im-
ploring, shouting:

"Where have you soldiers got to, damn your eyes? Don't you students let these cowards get into the stream! The Austrians are up there
on the hill, you fucking bastards!"

Ivan Katić sank deep into the snow as he ran after his men in the fog.
Bullets struck around him; his men stumbled and fell. He called them
by name—he had learned all their names in the last three days—but no
one stopped. He was alone among the beech trees and the sputtering
bullets. He turned around and fired at random into the air and fog, in
the direction from which men were shooting at him—men who had
appeared momentarily as blue shapes in the snow, yelling wildly.

"Why are you standing there, Corporal? Come on after us!"

It was Sava Marić calling to him from up above, through the fog;
higher up on the slope, the firing was slacking off.

"The C.O. is ordering us back to the position," Ivan said weakly.

"Let him go back, then, and you follow me, sir."

"Why do you have to call me 'sir'?" said Ivan sharply. "Enough of
this farce! When you address me like that, it's as though you were
slapping my face!" He stumbled among the beech trees, sinking into
the snow above his knees. In four nights and three days of fighting,
this Sava Marić had taught him more about goodness than anyone he
could remember; but his insistent respect for Ivan's rank in all circumstances was beginning to irritate him.

"Why on earth should it upset you that someone respects you?"

"For you I'm not a corporal. I'm not here to lord it over anybody. I
hate this exaggerated hierarchy!" Then he regretted using the word
"hierarchy" when talking to a peasant. "Call me Ivan, or if that's too

familiar, then Katić." He caught up with Marić and they walked side by side toward the stream and the murky fog.

"But sir, it gives me pleasure to respect a man, great pleasure. I know nothing finer than respecting a man."

Ivan stood still and looked at him, reflecting on what he had just heard; Sava Marić stood still, too. Where had he read this, or from whom had he learned it? He stared hard at this lean, wide face, with its large, deep-set eyes of indeterminate color. It was his mustache and hands that proclaimed him a peasant; from his words and principles, he seemed a well-read man. What sort of a person was he? Only a few Austrian guns were firing from their position, and a solitary Serbian one from the forest. Perhaps it was Luka Bog conducting the fight by himself; who else would be so pigheaded as to go on fighting in vain?

"But Sava, there must be the right conditions for people to be respected. That means they must deserve it."

He sat down in the snow; Sava Marić sat down next to him.

"As I see it, both sides should deserve it, sir, the one who pays respect just as much as the one who receives it."

"How do you figure that?"

"Well, I think like a peasant. Winning respect is real hard work—that's what I think. You can't inherit it like land. Can't buy it either, like rank or contentment. There's no way you can force a man to be respected, you can't even ask for it. And the worst thing of all about respect, sir, is that it's so difficult to keep. People take it away from you, and time devours it. Few people go to their graves respected."

"Who did you learn this from, Sava? And what have you been reading?"

"Well, I've read Vuk's *Poems,* and *Hajduk Stanko.* But I learned about respect from mý grandfather, Avram. He used to point people out to me as they walked down the lane past our house. 'You see that man, my boy? You should always kiss his hand. The road exists so that he can walk on it, and we are here in order to see him. But when you meet *that* man, then look down at the ground. If you've got a bunch of twigs, wipe away his footsteps. The road he walks on is no good, and it's better for us if we don't meet him.' "

"And what kind of people were those whose hand you were supposed to kiss? Were they honest, rich, or brave?"

"They were wise, sir. And if a man has human wisdom, he can't be either a coward or a scoundrel. He won't be poor either."

Preoccupied with his thoughts, Ivan said nothing. The sound of gunfire on his right prevented him from understanding Sava properly.

"I don't know whether that's the whole truth, Sava."

"What does it matter if it isn't, sir?"

Bogdan Dragović knelt down beside a beech tree and fired at random into the fog, from which men were firing at him just as aimlessly. He was perfectly aware of his irrational behavior: that made it all the more painful. Although for three days he had not stirred a step from the ranks of his squad, had remained absolutely motionless under the impact of shrapnel, and Luka Bog had looked at him with a smile, he could neither blot out nor alleviate the shame and torment of that first battle in the darkness on Baćinac. He recognized the "military secret" in every glance from Luka Bog. He even avoided Ivan, and shunned encounters with the student-corporals from other platoons. In his squad he behaved like an orderly and not like a corporal, a "gentleman from the university," as that sly and insolent Aleksa Dačić termed him. He kept the fires going through the night, dragged wood from the forest, and covered sleeping soldiers with his coat; he also shared with the soldiers all the underwear, socks, and food that he had. The previous day he had shared his remaining cigarettes with his squad. He felt ashamed to talk like a socialist. When the soldiers blamed the government, or cursed Pašić and the Allies, he said nothing. During the lulls he examined himself right from the beginning, from the time of his father's death, and tried to find his sins, faults, and weaknesses throughout all of his life he could remember. Perhaps he lacked the character, will power, and strength needed for the aims he had set himself. He would never soar to the height of ideals and achievement. If he was killed, perhaps he would at least leave behind him the illusion that he had been something and could have done something. He could at least be a victim of the war.

They were no longer firing at him out of the fog from above; still, he fired three more bullets. He didn't even have any reason for running away. Alone, he descended through the murky silence into even deeper gloom, into the murmuring of the defeated army, the groans of the wounded crying out to be carried to the dressing station. He did not go down as far as the noise of the soldiers, but leaned against a beech tree and stuck his rifle in the snow. Luka Bog came up to him with a flask of *rakija* and offered him some to wash away the smoke from the gunpowder. Luka Bog took a swig from the flask; today he had been drinking continually. He sat down between Bogdan's feet and his gun:

"So they've settled our hash today as well. This is the thirty-sixth time I've been beaten since we left the Drina. Do you realize, young man, what that means for a Serbian officer—thirty-six lost battles? Just think of it, damn your cowardly eyes! I can't go on like this. Tomorrow we're *not* going to show our backs to the blue coats and Franz Josef's crown."

Bogdan started to walk away in order not to listen to him, but Luka Bog stopped him:

"Sit down awhile in the platoon headquarters, young man. What were you studying?"

"I was studying law."

"You want to be a lawyer?"

"No, I want to be a judge."

"Well, sit down. I order you. That's not such a bad job. People are dreadful thieves and scoundrels. You've got to beat them a lot harder than oxen. You'll never go wrong if you just hit a bit harder. You're a fool not to drink some *rakija*. No women around, and if there wasn't even any *rakija*, who could put up with all this?"

"Perhaps you're right."

"What a skinny, bony fellow you are! You've got decent eyes, and those whiskers—you seem like a real man. Yes, you do look like a man. All right. Now, young man, do you know where Eden is?"

"No, sir, I don't."

"And the river Fisau, that flows around the whole land of Evilska?"

"No, I don't."

"And do you know where the river Geon is, that flows around the land of Huska?"

"I'm afraid I have no idea. I've never heard of those rivers or those countries."

"Well, never mind about that, young man. Nobody in this country knows what they ought to know—except to make use of the fog when things are all fouled up."

This was silenced by the sounds of battle, which were blazing up in the darkness somewhere to the right. The shells reverberated in the streams. A crowd of soldiers came up, shouting:

"Look here, when are we going to get our rations? For the last two days we've had nothing but half a piece of hardtack. I'm hungry, I can't get out of this bottomless pit! Why can't you at least give us some cigarettes? How long are we going to go on like this, for God's sake?"

"As long as you keep deserting."

"We're not going to die on an empty stomach!"

"All right, I'll tell my orderly to open my stores—you can take everything except the *rakija*. Sredoje, give them everything there is to eat!"

Bogdan got up and began to descend the slope in the gathering dusk and freezing fog. The beech trees were barely visible. He listened to the grumbling and cursing of the soldiers; their rebelliousness cheered him.

"That you, Mustachios?"

"What's happened with you, Cvijović?"

"Ciga and Drakče have been killed. And Nenad's wounded. Our bunch are dying like flies—it's terrible!" whispered Cvijović, who then disappeared into the gloom.

"Drakče and Ciga," he whispered. Ciga had made some joking remark when they parted; he hadn't even said good-by to Drakče. That was the end of their two months' companionship. The dead would freeze, and the snow would drift over them; then the beasts of the forest would come, and the birds and the ants. By the time a shepherd boy stubbed his foot against their skulls, the war would be over and won. He swallowed his burning saliva. They had both been students of engineering, one at Munich and the other at Zürich; in the barracks they had wrangled till daybreak about iron constructions with huge arches.

"Ivan!" he cried. He had been sitting next to Luka Bog and listening to his nonsense, and he hadn't asked about Ivan. His squad had been under fierce fire.

"I'm here, Bogdan!"

Bogdan made his way through the discontented and hungry soldiers, who were muttering among themselves. He called Ivan's name again, then sat down beside him; he could hardly see his face.

"Ciga and Drakče have been killed. And Nenad is wounded. An awful lot of our bunch are getting it."

Ivan said nothing, but recalled the two men who had died beside him that day: one had had his stomach torn by shrapnel; his hands had scratched convulsively at the snow and his face had been distorted, as he died an agonizing death with the snow reddening under him. The other was a conscript whom he had had to warn about not shooting; he lay motionless, looking down his gun: his death had been painless and dignified. Pallor had spread rapidly over his youthful face like a shadow, making it look serious, and at the same time older.

"Ivan, do you remember Don Quixote?" asked Bogdan.

"Don Quixote, Don Quixote," stammered Ivan to himself.

"Platoon, assemble!" shouted Luka Bog.

"So there'll be no sleep tonight, either," whispered Ivan. He checked that his glasses were in his pocket, then set off behind the groups of soldiers. How he would have liked to stretch out in the snow, fall asleep, and never get up again. He hadn't slept for more than two or three hours a night since they had arrived at the front, and then usually sitting up. He repeated the words of command, determined to lie down in the snow and sleep as soon as they moved away from the Austrians and got themselves out of the stream.

But there was no getting out of the stream. The frost gripped his feet and plucked at his ears; he scraped his leg against something blunt and bruised his knees; the freezing darkness thickened. Every step taken by the column broke the surface of the snow; the crackling, squeaking sounds of men marching God knows where reverberated through the forest. How long would it continue? Ivan staggered. Sava Marić was behind him; he never stopped talking to him, asking him questions and pushing him along. Ivan couldn't understand him and had no strength to reply, but one thing he was sure of: as long as Sava Marić was alive, *he* would go on fighting. Uphill, then downhill. His knee knocked against a log, his arms encountered a tree trunk. Sava pushed a lump of sugar into his mouth. Sweetness is not sweetness. But sleeplessness hurt, it hurt intolerably. It would be good to die, to sleep—to fall asleep forever, no more books or people. What bliss! What was the purpose of seeking after truth? He fell down in the snow; it was warm and soft, even cosier than his mother's bed. If I could only freeze to death. Sava, let me freeze to death! Daddy, there's no greater torment in the world than sleeplessness. No need to talk about hunger, Bogdan. Revolution is a dream, that's true. War, too. But now people are fighting. Just to sleep, to sleep for a hundred years. Leave me alone, Sava, I want to freeze, then I can sleep. The beech trees are cracking from the frost. No they aren't, Sava, they're asleep. Lucky beech trees! What was this silence? And how important was freedom? Ah, that was the peace they talked about. Sava pushed him against something hard and told him to go to sleep. Salvation at last.

The platoon had arrived at their new position. They lit fires and lay down beside them. But Bogdan Dragović could not sleep because of the terrible cold. The beech trees cracked from the frost, and the sound of their cracking echoed through the deathly silence of the forest. Bogdan gathered dry branches in the gloom, and struggled for some time to roll a felled tree trunk over the snow; he was happy to exhaust himself in this way, to do some good to somebody that night.

He lit a fire, and covered up the soldiers. There were two conscripts, dressed like young men from Šumadija, who were hugging each other to keep warm; he covered them with his overcoat. The experienced soldiers lay peacefully on branches by the fire; now and again someone would fidget because of lice and scratch himself in his sleep. The conscripts and the new soldiers started in their sleep, pronounced the names of women, sobbed, charged in battle, fled. If Bogdan could have fallen asleep and dreamed, he would surely have dreamed of Luka Bog, and how he himself had vomited. What was his mother dreaming about tonight? She dreamed about him every night he was away from home, and when he came home she related all her dreams to him. What was happening to her and his sister in Valjevo now, under enemy occupation? For whom were they now weaving carpets and rugs? The ladies had fled from Valjevo, and the Austrians had no need of their carpets and rugs. For them occupation would bring hunger and silence. The looms would no longer be working. Was Natalia asleep? He had never seen her sleeping. She had once told him in a chance remark that she slept on her stomach, without a pillow, using her folded arms as a cushion. How many times had he imagined her lying stretched out on her bed in her nightdress—he could see only a single white knee! And how gently, softly, tenderly she breathed! When he was doing sentry duty at night in Skoplje, if there was no wind he could hear Natalia breathing. He had heard her and seen her, but he would never do so again. Never. He got up from the fire and went away into the forest, plunged into the icy gloom and looked for dry branches. The film of ice under the fresh snow cracked under his footsteps, muffling the sound of his chattering teeth.

At dawn the Austrian cannon opened fire in answer to the grenades with which the Eighth Regiment was peppering the slopes and heights. Beside the fires of Luka Bog's platoon, which today constituted the battalion reserve, the conscripts moved around, gazing in astonishment at the older soldiers too weary for fear, and staring at the heights above the scattered beech trees, from which the icy wind had dispersed the fog, thus revealing the Serbian positions to the cannon, while the Serbian rifles remained silent.

Bogdan Dragović was much more disturbed by the pathetic innocence and childlike terror of the conscripts, than by the cannon. Their movements, unrestricted by discipline or vanity; the freedom of their fears. This was the fear of a victim, not that of a warrior: a fear born of weakness and innocence. Meanwhile the cannon fired their shells onto the bare hill slopes; the mountain reverberated and drowned in their thunder, while the wind drifted and dispersed the fog among the bare beech trees. These village boys, with their empty multicolored bags, some of them without guns, were not just frightened; Bogdan saw sadness in their eyes, which now always looked the same. For the first time since he came to the front, fear was not the strongest emotion Bogdan felt; some different, hitherto unknown sensation seemed to dominate his feelings as a soldier, and he got up to comfort the conscripts. At least he tried to, but he himself was full of foreboding that something terrible would happen that day. This was his fourth or fifth morning at the front; it was the first time so many cannon were firing, and so early—the first time that he had seen something different and unexpected in the beech trees, the snow, and the people.

Major Stanković's orderly summoned him and Ivan Katić to battalion headquarters. They were disturbed by this summons, and scarcely breathed as they walked through the scattered beech trees; the very air seemed thick from frost and the explosions of shells. They walked in silence. Blackbirds and bullfinches flew around them, fleeing from the hillside toward the streams before the oncoming shells. The thought passed through Ivan's mind: I suppose they'll kill our birds too, but he didn't utter the words.

The previous day and night the two of them had not spoken a single word; it was as though a bullet had shot through their compelling need to tell each other all their experiences and thoughts. Now this day and night of silence seemed to both of them a kind of desertion, a betrayal of their friendly affection. Bogdan blamed himself for it, and the wounding of his self-esteem on Baćinac, while Ivan felt sorry that during the past few days Sava Marić had become more necessary and significant to him than Bogdan Dragović. Just to break the silence, he said:

"Last night a piece of bacon and some sugar which I had left over from my mother's parcel were stolen from my knapsack. They took some socks and underwear, too. But my glasses and notebooks are still there. Perhaps it's not a bad thing. Now we're all just about on a level. I can hardly wait to wear out my clothes and boots—then I'll look just like them."

"As far as that goes, I already do. I gave my shirt and scarf to a wounded man, and I've given out my tobacco. Now I'll have to buy some from that Aleksa Dačić from Prerovo, the place your folks come from."

"Have you got any lice?"

"Yes, but they don't bother me."

"I find them an awful nuisance. I can't kill them—I find it revolting. I just won't kill a louse, even if it eats up my brains."

"But you've got to kill lice."

"Even so, I don't think I will."

They reached a shepherd's hut. Inside, Major Stanković's orderly was shaving him beside a fire.

"Excuse me, gentlemen, do come in. In a few minutes I shall be ready to begin a day at war. Some frost, isn't it?"

They saluted him and entered the hut, marveling at this shaving in the freezing weather under the Austrian bombardment.

"Sit down on those logs. Did you manage to get some sleep last night? We're going to have a hard day today, have you heard? Our regiment is to defend Babina Glava."

"Babina Glava!" The words escaped from Ivan in ironic amazement.

"Yes, Babina Glava. An exceptionally important position. The regimental C.O. has sent me a personal directive from the division commander. But first let's have a few drops of *rakija*," he said, smiling.

This smiling face covered with soap reminded Ivan of a clown; there was no possible occasion for smiling in the present circumstances. The longer he observed him, the more this major's confidence and hail-fellow-well-met manner appeared as a pose, a deliberate act to create a good impression. He would have liked to ask the major whether he was tormented by lack of sleep.

"Are you a reserve officer, sir?" asked Bogdan, in whom the major's behavior inspired respect.

"No, I'm a regular officer. I attended the military academy in St. Petersburg. Why does this surprise you? You were training to be a lawyer."

"Yes, I was studying law. My name's Dragović."

"You know, Dragović, when I had to choose my life's vocation, I believed that my generation had a mission: the liberation and unification of the Serbs, for which our people have yearned for five centuries."

He wiped his face with a towel and combed his elegant black beard. Ivan thought to himself: if I survive the war, I'll wear a beard like that. Meanwhile Bogdan was asking himself: could this man order his soldiers to fire on strikers, demonstrators, or socialists? Perhaps he might become the Serbian Krapotkin.

The corporals Cvijović, Siniša, and Mitić came into the room. Ivan and Bogdan jumped up and hugged them; then they looked at one another. The joy of reunion was suddenly extinguished: in the course of four days they had all aged, and of the eight members of their group, three were already missing.

"Is Nenad badly wounded?" Bogdan asked.

"They say his arm's broken."

Major Stanković shook hands with them all in turn, and told his orderly to prepare two well-sweetened portions of hot *rakija*.

"Well, young men, how have you been received in your platoons?"

"At first with suspicion and distrust," said Cvijović. " 'What do we want with these young sprigs of gentry coming to be in command over us?' But yesterday three of the men said to me: 'We're really grateful that you've come, boys!'."

Major Stanković filled his pipe—an ornate pipe edged with gold—and lit it. Ivan and Bogdan could not remember him smoking a pipe the first time they saw him in the dusk on Baćinac. Siniša whispered to Bogdan:

"Tolstoy's Captain Tushin smoked a pipe, remember, but it was a cheap little cherrywood pipe. That was all right. But look at this guy!"

"You can be a bastard and a scoundrel with a cherrywood pipe, too," Bogdan retorted in a whisper.

Ivan also thought this pipe unsuitable for the time and place; it would have been all right for some German baron sitting by an open fireplace under his hunting trophies, but not for the commander of the Fourth Battalion of the Eighth Serbian Regiment, here at the foot of Babina Glava.

Still smoking his ornate pipe, Major Stanković turned to them and said:

"Well, I share the feelings of my soldiers. I must tell you something very important: it's quite true, you're not just ordinary soldiers. You have a mission, you thousand students . . ."

"One thousand three hundred of us arrived at the front," Cvijović corrected him.

"Very well, one thousand three hundred. Now you won't make any real difference to our numerical strength. It has always been the fate of us Serbs to fight against a stronger opponent. But you will instill into our exhausted soldiers a belief in the justice of our cause, the justice of our country's cause. A country without a just cause does not deserve great sacrifices, and its freedom has no real significance for its people. You know, my boys, I am deeply convinced that our nation values justice above liberty. Liberty is frequently sordid, false, and deceptive. It can even be misused. And its methods of operation are arbitrary and change easily. Whereas justice is pure, true, and consistent. It is either given equally to all, or does not exist for anyone. Do you agree?"

"But justice can be cruel, sir," interrupted Cvijović.

"Yes, indeed it can. It demands a great deal. But courage in the cause of justice is the highest of human attributes, the most honorable. At least, that's how I feel about it."

One of the glowering captains came into the hut; when he saw the students around the fire with Major Stanković, his face grew even darker.

"Everything all right, Paligorić?"

"Yes, sir. I've put him in the best place. The observer should be on that big old beech tree—exposed to the fire."

"Good. Sit down, we're going to have some hot *rakija*. Now, Corporals, I have some good news for you. Last night we received a Danglis cannon and quite a few shells. You'll see how pleased the soldiers will be."

An orderly ran up to him: "Sir, the Austrians have moved to the attack with four firing lines!"

Cvijović winked at Bogdan. Major Stanković looked at the breathless orderly without a trace of excitement or agitation. The student-corporals looked unblinkingly at the officer, whose self-confident tone remained unchanged.

"Run up the slope and say that on no account must any ground be yielded. Now our cannon will have work to do! Milan, heat that *rakija*. Oh, it's ready, is it? Paligorić, go to the cannon; I'll go with the ranks. Have we got a field telephone to the beech tree?"

"Yes, I've done that. Only I haven't picked an observer."

The student-corporals watched the orderly clumsily pouring their *rakija* into mugs. For which of them would this be the last pleasant occasion, the last kindness of Major Gavrilo Stanković, Ivan wondered, looking at each of his companions in turn. Savo Marić had told him that he always knew in the morning which soldier would be killed that day.

"Now, which of you boys would like to act as observer for our battery today? I need someone who won't be driven off the beech tree by bullets and shrapnel, someone with good eyesight, who can judge distances."

"I'm half-blind, unfortunately," whispered Ivan, but his voice was inaudible because of a shell exploding nearby.

The student-corporals said nothing and kept their eyes on their mugs as they sipped their hot *rakija*. Bogdan looked Major Stanković straight in the eyes: his heart was pounding. Now everything would be decided; he would either redeem himself or die.

"I need someone calm and steady. An observer has to have strong nerves—and will power," went on Major Stanković, meeting Bogdan's glance, and continuing to talk about the qualities necessary in an observer.

They all had the same feeling: that as soon as the major concluded, one of them would have to volunteer to climb the old beech tree, which was raked by machine-gun fire and shrapnel; one of them would have to carry out this order, initiated by an act of kindness and developed in the name of justice. Bogdan could feel inside himself that excitement of having courage for anything done in the eyes of his fellow men, which he had always experienced until that night on Baćinac; it was this quality which had made people love him at the university, in the barracks, and wherever he had lived up till now. He first smiled, then laughed aloud. His companions looked at him in astonishment; Major Stanković shook out his pipe, and observed him closely.

"I'll be the observer," he said quietly, still smiling.

"You're sure, Dragović?"

"Yes, Major, I'm quite sure. Let's go there now."

"Good. The rest of you young men, get back to your sections. In the evening, when the Austrians begin to tire, come see me, and we'll drink some *rakija* and have a chat. Dragović, you come along with me."

As they left the hut, Ivan managed to squeeze Bogdan's hand: a gesture not of admiration but love.

"Don't worry," said Bogdan firmly, and set off behind Major Stanković through the scattered beech trees in the forest, where exploding shells were producing bursts of earth and snow. Bogdan hurried to catch up with the major, then walked at his side in step with him, in the direction of the explosions. The snow in the immediate vicinity was blackened by powder, and burning fragments of metal made them catch their breath and halt as they shrieked by. Major Stanković placed his hands on Bogdan's shoulders:

"I too like to undertake something that is a challenge to fate, an action performed without hatred, or prolonged physical exertion. Something pure and noble, which a man confronts face to face."

"Yes, indeed," said Bogdan, feeling a sudden desire to confess to this man, as to a father, what had happened in the darkness on Bačinac. But then, in a small clearing on the slope, he saw the old beech tree, sawed by wind and thunderstorms. They hurried toward it in silence.

Ivan Katić was standing next to Luka Bog in front of the lined-up platoon, behind which rose the smoke of the still smoldering fires.

"So that colleague of yours volunteered to climb up in the beech tree, did he? He volunteered to act as observer?" asked Luka Bog for the second time.

"Yes, he did. Why does that surprise you? I think Bogdan Dragović is the bravest man in the entire Student Battalion."

"And you believe that he would dare to sit in the beech tree right in front of the Austrian lines?"

"That's what I said. Anyway, you can go see for yourself."

Ivan moved away a few steps to the left, in order to end the conversation. He wanted to be with his soldiers, to be no different in any respect from those men who had their caps pulled over their ears and their coat collars turned up, who were stamping about in the snow with their teeth chattering as they listened to the battle.

"What's going to happen, sir?" Ivan asked the second lieutenant somewhat impatiently. On the second day at the front, he had come to believe that the worst moments for a soldier were those just before a battle: that feverish period of waiting in which not a single thought or feeling lasts; that state of uncertainty in which the immediate surroundings lose their familiar appearance and time its normal flow, in which the past is annihilated and the present becomes nonexistent.

"I'm waiting for the hardtack. Soldiers can't fight on an empty stomach!" replied Luka Bog, and threw away the butt of his cigarette in front of the ranks.

Three of the soldiers flung themselves on the cigarette butt, pushing one another aside as they did so. One of the soldiers picked it up from the snow and squeezed it; when the other two walked dejectedly back to the ranks, he opened his fist, only to be disappointed; the butt had been ground almost to powder. But he didn't throw it away; he returned to his place holding it in the palm of his hand, so that he could separate the strands of tobacco from the snow.

Luka Bog looked at him in silence and lit another cigarette. Ivan watched him: how could there be two such men as Major Stanković and Luka Bog in the same battalion?

Luka Bog threw away the second cigarette, but toward the front of the platoon. This time several men rushed to pick it up, and Ivan didn't see who got it; the others returned to the ranks, gloomily silent. Luka Bog drank up the *rakija* in his flask; his orderly ran up and handed him another full one.

An orderly from battalion headquarters came running through the forest, shouting, "Get to your positions! What are you waiting for?"

"We're waiting for hardtack—you needn't shout," answered Luka Bog. "It's going to be a long day, and some of us are going to get killed!"

"The battalion commander's orders are that you must immediately close the breach in the position of the first platoon—to the left of the juniper tree!"

Luka Bog threw away the cigarette which he had only just lit, this time toward the rear of the platoon. One of the men jumped out and stamped on it, grinding it into the snow; then he returned silently to his place and spat audibly.

"You'll get your hardtack when we close that breach. It's better that way; here you'd only get half a ration, but over by the beech tree some will get a whole one and two onions each as well. Ah, there goes our cannon! Hear it?"

The soldiers turned toward the forest: they didn't believe that it was the Serbian cannon firing; they hadn't heard it for days.

"That's our Danglis. So no more running away from now on. Here, young man, here's four cigarettes for each of the two squads. But don't give them out until we've closed that breach. Now listen to what I have to say, all of you: when I give the order 'Charge!' you shout, 'Hurrah!' so the Austrians will think we're a whole regiment! Got that? Now form a firing line and follow me! A river of blood is going to flow!"

The soldiers crossed themselves, then moved off. Ivan started to cross himself, then stayed his hand: what was the point now of this symbolic gesture in which he didn't believe? Sava Marić crossed himself twice, with slow, wide movements of his hand.

He's lucky, he believes in God, thought Ivan, and made sure that he had his spare glasses in his pocket. He walked along the ranks to give out the cigarettes.

Sava stopped him and whispered in his ear: "Everything that people do which is not dishonorable and doesn't harm anybody should be done. You shouldn't be too different from other people, even in your honesty."

"You're saying this because I didn't cross myself?"

"What does it cost to have a little faith? No one knows where a man's salvation may come from."

Ivan followed despondently behind Luka Bog, who remained erect under a hail of bullets. "Charge, Serbians, charge! Stick them with your bayonets! Kill them with your teeth! Make a river of blood flow!" he shouted.

Ivan bent down and made a jerking movement, then stopped as though he wished to cross himself. But he felt that it was shameful and dishonorable to pray now, and hurried on up the slope. Medics were carrying down wounded men, dragging them through the snow. They moved toward a clearing which was being raked by shellfire. He would not be able to run past those black holes and bubbles of fire. Something hot choked his throat. Luka Bog was waving his hand to hurry them on. Ivan repeated the words to his soldiers, trying to recollect the rules for a charge which he had learned and practiced in Skoplje. He shouted to them, then whispered some orders. He made an effort to run, but the snow caught his knees, his legs got tangled up, and his feet stuck fast; he fell down into a black shell hole, momentarily blinded. His brain whirled, his eardrums felt as though they were bursting; he felt for his glasses and saw arms waving aimlessly, and a bleeding, headless torso with entrails spilling out. He blinked. That's how he would be the very next moment. He dug himself into the snow and stones. Oh God, Thou art! His mouth was full of earth and snow; his head seemed to be bursting into a thousand pieces. Somewhere far away through the shrieking and tumult, he just managed to hear Luka Bog shouting "Charge!"

He must move on. He got up staggering, then looked around him to see who was left from the platoon and where they were. In front of him, sprawled in the snow, soldiers were firing; a blue wave of Austrians was coming down the slope. A bugle sounded, then two bugles; they sounded different. A burning sensation, a roaring noise, and some firebrands threw him onto the soft, warm whiteness. Luka Bog shouted to him, calling him a sister-fucker; Ivan jumped up and began to look for him among the soldiers who were falling down, throwing away their guns, and running along the steep white hillside. The wave of blue overcoats advanced like smoke, waving their bayonets. Now was the time to drop down and shoot, he remembered. He knelt down and began to fire. Beside him Staniša, the best looking man in the platoon, gave a groan, dropped his gun, and thrust his head into the snow. Those still alive fired, stood up, and shouted "Hurrah!" Someone called out for his mother. Yes, mother again—his mother: she was standing on the station platform, but not waving; she couldn't even raise her hand as he receded into the distance. But why didn't those bluecoats fall? They were advancing in a crouching position; they felt no fear. Why not? Hatred forced Ivan to his feet and coursed through his entire body, because *they* were not afraid. He straightened up and ran in front of his men toward the blue overcoats, which were not bending down or firing. He felt only hate—not fear but hate—because they had no fear. The blue mass thinned out, halted, moved uncertainly, and fell down under the shellfire, then quickly rose and rushed away up the slope. One of them stayed behind—a tall, erect soldier, firing from a standing position. Ivan halted, amazed and frightened. "Coward!" shouted someone. The tall, erect Austrian in the blue overcoat stood firm while taking aim, and fired. Ivan knelt down, aimed at his chest, fired. The tall man dropped his gun and fell slowly into the snow. I've killed him! Ivan ran up to have a look at this man, the bravest of them all; blood-flecked foam trickled from his lips, his large, long-lashed gray eyes looked at Ivan without hatred and without fear, simply indifferent. Was death really like this? Ivan looked at him with conscious superiority, while the red trickle meandered over his full, sculptured lips and sank under the collar of his overcoat. Blood outlives thought. Ivan leaned over him: perhaps he was still alive. He put his hand on his forehead; the warm touch startled him, he groaned and thrust his hand into the snow, staring unblinkingly into the large gray eyes with long lashes, like a girl's. A young man! And I killed him! I killed him because he was the bravest of them all! Why didn't he run away? Was it because he felt hatred, too? Ivan sank deep into the peace of that gray look, and felt that in some way he had died, too. Soldiers were running forward past him; he heard someone call his name, but he stood motionless, caught in the light of those gray eyeballs, sunk deep in their eternity; in those gray-blue orbs he saw a reflection of someone wearing glasses, a distorted, terrified face: someone who had once existed.

"Has he got anything in his bag, Corporal?" someone shouted. "Let's share it!"

Ivan turned around. His men were lying down in front of him and shooting. One of them smiled—a repulsive sort of smile. That was the man who had mentioned the dead soldier's bag.

"Get up! Into the Austrian trenches!" He heard Luka Bog's voice but didn't see him. Ivan got up and set off up the steep, white slope; he felt no fear, and perhaps no longer any hate either.

In the crown of the old beech tree, Bogdan Dragović was clinging to its trunk like a lizard, and watching the counterattack of the Serbian battalion through his field glasses; but for the frightful shooting, the scene of the battle would have been amusing to watch through the round lens: a mixture and interchange of comical and panic-stricken movements, like a moving picture on a screen. He felt like that just now because, thanks to him, Paligorić's gunners had silenced two Austrian cannon and blown up a machine-gun nest. At that time Major Stanković was standing under the beech tree, and after every shell fired by the Danglis he shouted: "Where are we now? Very good, my boy. We must have lunch together today. I have some roast sheep's head."

Then the major ran off to help repel the three-pronged Austrian attack. Bogdan watched through his field glasses to see how his courage functioned in battle, and saw him under shrapnel and annihilating shellfire, only sometimes stooping slightly; he even stepped back from the firing line and filled his fancy pipe, though he didn't light it. Then he disappeared among the soldiers behind the juniper trees. The thought flitted through Bogdan's mind: courage in battle has its origin in either intense hatred or extreme pride. Major Gavrilo Stanković showed only pride, pride which must be connected in some way with the sacred justice he talked about. In St. Petersburg he must have had at least a whiff of revolutionary faith; this emerged in his talk about justice and his love for the students. If this good man had been his commanding officer on Baćinac instead of Luka Bog, he would never have vomited out there in the darkness.

As he brought the bare, snow-covered heights into his field glasses, with the dark woods on either side, he focused his lens on a pair of horses without riders, standing motionless as though frozen still in the snow. A sudden idea arrested his thoughts: a great deed has significance and beauty only if performed among people. What sort of courage is it that no one sees or knows about? And was this really such a great deed—his being in the beech tree, as yet unperceived in the lens of some Austrian field glasses, as he watched two firing lines attacking each other in the snow, or subsiding onto the white slope with awkward, unfamiliar movements? No, he could not really redeem himself in this way; this was not really a great deed worthy of esteem and admiration. His teeth chattered with cold as he breathed in the scent of the bark. A skein of blue smoke hovered over the snow-covered slope dotted with corpses. Two armies, speaking two different languages, were yelling and moving toward each other. Where was Ivan?

He looked for him through his field glasses, but the smoke and shrapnel made it impossible to recognize any of the soldiers. He could not even see Major Stanković. Violent firing erupted from the Austrian artillery; it seemed that those two cannon silenced by Paligorić's Danglis had been stunned only temporarily.

"Where are those big guns firing from?" shouted Captain Paligorić over the field telephone.

"I don't know."

"What do you mean, you don't know? Find them!"

Bogdan looked for them in the forest. He looked for a long time at the small grove in which the two recently silenced cannon had been firing. He could see nothing but smoke. Then he saw them—first one, then the other. Shells roared over his head and fell behind his back.

"Take the first position! Go back to where we hit them the first time!" Stanković said into the field telephone.

"That's just where those two are hitting at us," said Bogdan.

Three shells churned up the grove. Bogdan felt angry; the Austrian shells were flying just above the branches—they would split him open like a sparrow—but only one in five of their own found its mark.

"Hit the same place again!" he shouted, filled with a bittersweet sensation.

The branches cracked over his head, sprinkling him with twigs and bark; he clung yet more closely to the tree trunk. They had found him: machine-gun fire was peppering the crown of the beech tree. Now the real thing was about to start! He heard Paligorić's voice through the receiver:

"Now we're going to pound those Austrian trenches! See that we don't miss!"

He trained his field glasses on the slope where the battle was thundering, raising clouds of dust in which it was impossible to distinguish the two opposing sides, or the dead from the living, since all alike were hidden under smoke and shrapnel. A little lower down, in the direction of the forest, the medics were dragging away the wounded.

"The machine gun's spotted me! The bullets are raking the branches all around me!" he shouted into the receiver.

"Never mind that! You're not the only one who's catching their fire," answered Paligorić.

Yes, he was right, it was worse for them. He scraped off the old bark with his forehead, and noticed a dead or frozen beetle. Its shining, rigid feeler spilled over the pupil of its solitary eye. It was cowardly—

despicable—to envy an insect. He took up his field glasses to see the position: Major Stanković was walking toward him with his orderly, shouting something and waving his arms. He couldn't hear him because of the shooting, but was filled with joy, a joy which he had never experienced before. Around him, bark splintered and branches snapped. He didn't care if a shell got him, he wasn't going to move.

"Don't worry!" he shouted as loudly as he possibly could to Major Stanković, convinced that in his presence he would dare do anything of which a human being was capable.

Paligorić asked where the bullets were falling. He felt something sting his thigh, and clung even more tightly to the tree, making himself smaller and thinner. Was he wounded? He was not aware that blood was flowing down his leg. His cap fell off. The beetle drove its feeler right into his eyeball. There was no escape; he dared not even blink. Something stung the calf of his leg. He was finished. If he jumped, he would be cut to pieces in flight.

"Look out, Dragović! Look out! Above you!"

He heard Major Stanković's voice, and moved sideways to see him: when a shell hit you, you flew up into the air and split in two, and one part went into the black smoke and the other plunged into the white snow and subsided there, making a red stain on its white surface. The feeler of the beetle poked right into his eyeball.

"Gavrilo!" he yelled, dropping his field glasses and falling into the snow; he could not breathe, and felt a dull pain in his ribs. Was he wounded, or had he broken some ribs? But Gavrilo had been killed! He jumped up and ran toward the shell hole, and stood in front of it transfixed: blood was spurting from naked, loose ribs. He groaned, burst into tears, and covered his face with his hands.

"Dragović! Dragović!" Someone was calling him, groaning at the same time. He lifted up his head, and a few paces away he saw Major Stanković lying in the snow with a torn, bloodstained jacket, his mouth wide open. He realized that the shell had blown the orderly to bits. He shouted:

"Stretcher-bearers!"

A hot blast flung him into the shell hole. As he fell he saw his old beech tree slowly collapse, its trunk shattered, and break into pieces as it rolled down the white slope.

4

The First Army had withdrawn to the crest of Suvobor, but General Mišić did not feel that this had made any essential change in the situation of his forces or the opportunities for future action. His army remained overextended and split up into three sections, with the left wing on Maljen trembling in expectation of a powerful blow which could cut it off. From early morning detailed reports had come in from all the divisions that the enemy were forming three corps to strike at the First Army.

Mišić sat at the table, ceaselessly poring over the reports: Field Marshal Oscar Potiorek must utterly despise him, since he was so persistently pushing his offensive over trackless mountains—the most difficult terrain for artillery and extended columns—instead of taking Belgrade and plunging into the heart of Serbia through the valley of the Great Morava, over level country with roads and railways. That meant that Oscar Potiorek knew that the First Army was the weakest of the Serbian forces, that it was exhausted and battered; all that was necessary was to go on battering until it was broken. So in spite of the mountains, the absence of roads, and the frost and snow, he was striking persistently at the First Army in order to crush it and reach the Western Morava valley over its dead body. In this way he would shatter the entire Serbian defense irretrievably—a victory indeed worthy of the decoration he had already received, and which had already been celebrated in Vienna for several days. Oscar Potiorek was behaving like a victor, making for Salonika and the Dardenelles by the most important route. All his decisions as an army commander sprang from his own will; he controlled the time, conditions, and direction of all movements. He gave no indication at all that he took into account any plans of the Serbian command, or that he had any regard for the thoughts and intentions of his immediate opponent, Živojin Mišić.

Above Mišić hovered the large, heavy face of his chief of staff, Hadjić, who stood blinking and silent, holding a sheet of paper in his hand.

"We have received one more report on the Austrian forces concentrated against our army. They have three corps—that is, six divisions—with the full complement of artillery, sir."

He then fell silent, looking down at Mišić from above. Mišić could not endure it; he called Vojvoda Putnik on the telephone.

"I am obliged to inform you that the state of the First Army is extremely critical. And the enemy is concentrating fresh troops."

Putnik interrupted him: "The state of the First Army is much worse than you realize, in your usual optimistic way. Much worse."

"Tomorrow the situation will be still worse, if the other armies remain as passive as they are at present, and if the High Command takes no action."

"I will order the Third Army and the Užice Brigade to make a decisive attack as soon as possible."

"Someone is responsible for the First Army's being reduced to the state it's now in."

"Mišić, this is not a suitable occasion for you to display your customary malice and contempt for other commanders."

"Tomorrow I will be attacked by six divisions of fresh men at full strength. Six of them against three of mine—three divisions at half strength, without cannon and shells, without bandages and bread!"

"Yes, I know. And I'll do all I can. What more do you want?"

Mišić banged down the receiver. How long would he have that old wheezer around his neck? Ever since he passed his captain's examination, Putnik had been above him. How much longer would it last?

There was that manikin—Putnik's "élitist officer" and favorite, and an expert bureaucrat—swaying again in front of him:

"Maljen has been attacked by strong forces, sir. The Fir Grove has already been lost after a violent struggle."

The Fir Grove? That was the lovely wood of newly planted trees, with bountiful springs. He got up, put on his cap, buttoned his jacket, and threw his unfinished cigarette in the stove.

"Colonel, will you please summon all the chiefs of staff and section heads. Also, send for all officers above the rank of lieutenant."

Could he perhaps outwit Potiorek? Attack him before he formed his corps, surprise them in the process of formation? Hadjić returned with a crowd of officers who filled the entire room.

"Sit down, gentlemen. I have requested you to come here to ask your opinion about what we should do. Not to discuss our present situation, but to suggest how we should change it, because the time has come when we dare not make a single mistaken decision. Any decision we take now will decide our fate."

He looked at them all in turn, squeezed into the café owner's small guest room, all of them anxious, some of them calm and impassive. They should join the fighting men at the first opportunity; let them earn their officer's pay and rank there. One of them began to speak:

"I am convinced, sir, that without fresh troops to make good the losses in the regiments, we cannot possibly change the situation for the better."

"And if there are no fresh troops? If there is no one else we can mobilize?"

"Then we'll all be killed. Forgive me for speaking so frankly."

"Have you any other suggestion, Lieutenant Colonel Djokić?"

"No, sir, I haven't."

"Well, how would it be if you handed over your duties to Major Milosavljević, and joined the staff of the Danube Division under the command of Miloš Vasić?"

"I am ready to do so, sir."

"Then take your things and go there as soon as we finish this discussion. Now I would like to hear the opinions of the rest of you."

"I would venture to suggest, General, that it is lack of artillery and shells which has got us into our desperate position. We should send the government an ultimatum!"

"We should send the Allies an ultimatum! We can't go on like this for a single day longer, sir!"

"We should send the High Command an ultimatum, too!"

Nothing but indignation, shouts and threats, and censure of the staff and the High Command. Such feelings were totally useless. They were seated higher up than he was, and he could not see all their faces. He raised his voice:

"Have you any other suggestions, gentlemen, apart from ultimatums?"

No one spoke. They looked at him insolently, then at one another. He felt that they too were opposed to him.

"At least send the soldiers some tobacco. They haven't had any for ten days in the front line."

"Yes, tobacco," whispered Mišić. "And what else?"

"We need tents and boots—boots above all; they're much more important than tobacco!"

"What else, gentlemen?"

"We've used up all our medical supplies. We've no more bandages."

"If only the shells would arrive, sir, I wouldn't be afraid of even six of Potiorek's corps!"

"Well, that's enough of these administrative requirements. Now I want to hear your suggestions regarding strategy and tactics."

"Do we have to discuss these with you, sir?"

"Yes, Milosavljević, I think you should."

They were silent; some of them whispered among themselves.

"I hope you won't take it amiss, sir, if I say it would be right for the deputies and ministers to come to the front and fight. Yes, fight. Our soldiers will go on fighting only if they see that none of the gentry and members of the government are going to stay alive while they die."

"We've scraped the barrel to send men to the front: we've brought in the students and conscripts, but we still have the deputies of the Assembly and the members of the government. Have you any further suggestions, Panto?"

"Yes, I have. I demand—or rather request—to be sent to join the fighting forces immediately. You can put a sick or wounded officer in my place."

"Then get ready to move to the Fourth Auxiliary Regiment of the Morava Division, as second in command of the regiment."

"Thank you, sir."

"I too would like to join the fighting men, sir. I should like to have the command of a battalion; I do not wish to be a staff officer."

He looked at the major, a handsome, clean-shaven man with a well-tended mustache, who as a division commander had twice been punished for café brawls and for a scandalous association with the wife of a local mayor. But he had passed his major's examination—a surprise attack—without criticism. Mišić smiled as he thanked him:

"You will get your battalion, Djulaković. Do any more of you wish to join the fighting men?"

"I am ready to do so, sir."

"I am, too."

"You can send me, too, if necessary."

"I will send you, Savić. Thank you. You can get ready to join the troops. The rest of you can now get on with your work. I am grateful for your advice. Hadjić and Milosavljević, would you stay behind, please?"

While the officers slowly and silently filed out of the room, he thought: I have to make the wrong decisions entirely by myself; I can share with them only success. Hadjić and his assistant Milosavljević stood by the window, waiting for him to speak.

"What are we going to do with Potiorek's three corps?" he asked.

"We must at all costs hang on to the positions we have taken today," said Hadjić.

"We must wage a decisive battle on the Suvobor ridge, then move to the offensive—as you have already planned," said Milosavljević.

"Ever since we left the Drina we have been holding at all costs positions which we have taken by night, and then withdrawn from them the following morning or evening. We are constantly fighting decisive battles, and losing time. Now we're on Rudnik and Suvobor. We need new ideas on strategy and tactics. We've got to act differently."

They were all silent.

"I understand you. Now you can go back to your work. Please ask someone to bring me some lime tea—a whole pot."

Mišić felt that he was deceived in some way, that he had deceived himself. Napoleon was right: a good commander does not need military advisers; he needs only as many facts as possible about his own troops, and precise information concerning the enemy. No, he must not wait for Potiorek to strike; salvation lay in taking the initiative away from him, in not allowing him to form his corps. He must go out to meet him and destroy his plans. He must put Field Marshal Oscar Potiorek in a state of confusion.

As he drank his lime tea, he decided to form a Suvobor striking force from the two Danube Divisions. He would put Miloš Vasić in command, a man who always knew his own mind. He began to write his orders: "I have decided to attack the enemy before he attacks. Please do not give in to the prevailing mood and situation. The soldiers must now have faith that the commander can and must do the things he requires of them. Act intelligently, as intelligently as possible, think out plans of action, and take into consideration as much as possible the unknown factors in the enemy's plans. Have solutions ready for the maximum number of battle contingencies. I have complete confidence in you."

Lost in thought, he drank his lime tea, then drowsed beside the stove. He roasted some apples, which burned. He savored their fragrance for a moment, redolent of times long ago—gone beyond recall—then forgot it. He stretched out on the bed and fell asleep immediately. His sleep was broken by the crowing of the café owner's rooster. What a fine voice he had! There was no response to his crowing; everything was quiet. Well, Serbia would continue to exist, even without roosters. Today I attack! The troops have already moved into action. He threw back the bedclothes, and put on his boots and jacket. He lit the stove. If they could win a great victory today, the First Army would be resurrected.

But there was no sign of daybreak; the dawn light was blotted out by mist. He could not even see the top of the apple tree by the window. Why was it such a sooty fog? He was gripped by fear at the sight of such a morning, at a lack of visibility so great that it pressed down upon the earth and swathed his army and battleground in a thick, cold immobility. It was seven o'clock and still dark.

He was startled by the telephone. Miloš Vasić, commander of the Suvobor striking force formed the previous evening, was speaking in a hoarse voice, as though from the bottom of a deep well:

"I don't ever remember such a fog, sir. I've never seen anything like it in my life. It's rolling up from the ground and the trees, it's pouring down from the sky. You can't see even a few paces ahead."

"Yes, I see it, Vasić. But I'm not interested in this meteorological information."

"It's out of the question to make any troop movements from the positions we occupied last night. The troops would be scattered and lost in the fog."

"And have the Austrians two pairs of eyes? What if Potiorek's troops got lost in the fog?"

"I can't say, sir. But I wouldn't be willing to risk any movement."

"Perhaps such a risk could save the First Army, Vasić."

"If you ordered me to move, I wouldn't be able to carry out the order."

"You mean you cannot, or you won't?"

"I simply can't see anything, sir."

"Then postpone the attack. Postpone it until . . . Get in touch with me as soon as the fog disperses a little."

He left the telephone and opened the window. The fog rolled into the room, filling it, pressing down, swirling. He could not see the table with the telephone, nor the bed or the stove. He groped toward the window; the fog smelled of the rotting tree stumps.

He could see it as though on the palm of his hand: from Maljen to Rudnik across the crest of Suvobor and Rajac, in fog and snowdrifts—there was his army, mute, frozen, their teeth chattering, lying in shallow, torn trenches. Today he must be seen by the whole army; everyone must be aware of his presence. He must visit every headquarters and every position, be at the side of every soldier. He must share their anxiety and sufferings. First of all he rode to the army staff headquarters.

"Hadjić, I don't believe the situation is just what is being reported from the divisions, and I will not believe this while I am in command of the army. Our people want to survive, by God they do. They want to exist on their own land and in their own way. The centuries bear witness to this, Major Milosavljević. Why should they agree to cease to exist because of their present misfortunes? Because of their extraordinary, their immeasurable sufferings? Gentlemen, we have suffered ever since we existed as a nation, because we are determined to exist as Serbs, as men. Not only because of our freedom, our faith, and our government, Professor. But out of spite too. Yes, we're a stubborn people; you can bend us, but you can't break us. And we are able to endure much wrongdoing, Colonel. I would stake my life that we could bear much greater sufferings than those we're enduring today. No one is so wise as to know what man can and will do in order to survive. You'll see. Now let's go to the lines. Dragutin, get me a handful of walnuts, soft ones, please."

He rode forward through the fog and the raw dampness which cut into the mountain side, through the thick, snow-flaked mud; he rode in silence for hours, all the way to the headquarters of the Morava Division:

"Milić, don't talk to me first about withdrawal, and then right after that about not having cannon and shells. Will you officers please tell me where your division slept last night? Why didn't more battalions sleep somewhere dry? Today the army that has had a good night's sleep will beat the one that didn't; I know that very well. Have you cooked some prunes for the soldiers? Serbia may not have canned food, but she's got prunes. I insist that every morning the soldiers receive a ration of stewed prunes cooked over a fire. And I don't want to see any more officers who haven't shaved!"

On he rode, through the thick, muted gunfire and the whine of bullets, across the heights; he would not go on foot or take cover. Let him be seen by those who were running away in droves from the Austrians!

"Why have you abandoned your position, Captain Perić? What sort of a rabble is that running away down the streams? And who ordered you to withdraw the battalion? A bit of machine-gun fire, two pieces of shrapnel, and a grenade or shell—and you show your backside! How have you got the army into such a deplorable state that the men run away at the mere sight of an Austrian? So you were decorated for bravery, were you? When? You no longer deserve that medal, Captain. You have disgraced yourself today on Drenik. I know, but remember this: a young girl and a soldier lose their honor only once. They alone cannot expiate their shame. Collect your battalion at once, and in an hour's time I want to hear your answer to the first question from the major's examination which you've failed."

He made his way past exploding shells through deep valleys, shallow trenches and logs behind which stood silent soldiers, unwilling to meet his glance.

"God bless you, soldiers! Now why don't you mend those shoes a bit? And how come you burned those jackets and blankets? Are you bothered much with lice? To tell the truth, it's cold for them, too. Now, boys, do you think it's harder for us than for the Austrians in this bad weather, this murk, this trackless land of ours? Now soldiers, don't give the answer off pat. Just imagine that this stream isn't called Dragobiljski, but Tanedelski Gorge, let's say. You haven't the faintest idea what lies behind that hill. You don't know where you're going to spend the night, or where you'll see the next day's dawn. And everything you see hates you, from the trees to the dogs. Everything is strange, and everything is against you. There's an officer at your back with a revolver. You've got to go on. And you don't know what you're killing people for, or why they have to kill you. Corporals, wars aren't won only with cannon and shells. A war can be lost inside us, in our hearts. That's where it's won first, too. Now, man, tell me what you've had to wet your whistle on! You're right, my boy, we must be ready for things even worse. Do you know who it depends on when we'll get back to Valjevo and Šabac? That's right, Whiskers. It depends on how many of us in the First Army really want to get back to the Drina, and are determined to! If we really want this with all our hearts, then in ten days' time we'll be back at our frontiers. Now for God's sake, isn't it better that we fire at their backs? But if things go on as they are, they'll always be firing at *our* backs, and by the time we get to the Morava, there won't be one of us left!"

He rode through the undergrowth, shaking the snow from the mountain pines; in front of him the battle raged in the dense fir groves. He caught up with a short, slow-moving column:

"Now Sergeant, speak to me as if I was your father: who are the soldiers swearing at? You don't mean to say they're not swearing at anybody? Not even at Pašić, or the government, or the Allies? And what about me? If you can't speak the truth, don't say anything. No, don't do that, it's not good when soldiers don't say anything. Never mind if they're always cross and bad-tempered. It's better if they're angry with the Austrians than with us, but if they won't curse Potiorek, then at least let them swear at me! And has this strong fear got into your soldiers too, Sergeant? How could they not be frightened? Then why do they run away so easily? If you gave your squad the order 'Forward with bayonets,' would they obey? That's not good, then. But do you think the Austrians are afraid of us? That's what we've got to work on—they must always be more afraid. You must scare them all the time, by every means you can think of. Come a little nearer, please, Lieutenant. Do the soldiers want women? You were at the military academy, I remember you; you can tell me the truth—I'm not the bishop. I don't like that: when men don't want their wives, they don't want freedom either. It's your job, Lieutenant, to remind them of their duty both to their fatherland, and to their wives who've been waiting for them since the middle of the summer to the first snowfall, without anybody so much as touching them. Wife and fatherland are separated not in love but in time."

Shells drove them all into a stream, including Mišić's staff, then into a regimental dressing station:

"God bless you, heroes! Are you all properly bandaged? How come there aren't any bandages? For God's sake, Doctor, how is it that your dressing station has no bandages? We've no hospitals, no beds, no clean blankets, and we know why. But we must have bandages! Listen, Doctor, if a government can't provide bandages to wrap up the wounds of its defenders, then the liberty of that country doesn't mean anything. You'll get some this very night; yes, you'll get plenty—all you need!"

The wind sprinkled his eyes with snow; he could hardly keep in the saddle, or feel his toes inside his boots, and his stomach ached. But he had to get to the heavy firing behind the beechwood, then make his way over the rocky ground to the dugout of the battalion head-quarters, where there were Austrian prisoners.

"Lieutenant, please ask the Austrians what they have eaten the last few days. Good. Are any of them sick? Is it from the cold, the rain, or the frost? We haven't left them a barracks or a hotel on Govedje Hill! Ask them, my boy, if the soldiers are coughing much. The Austrians aren't telling the truth. Did that man surrender, or did he have no means of escape? Look, all three of them have holes in their boots. That's a good sign. Their overcoats aren't worth much either. Have a look at what's in their bags. You've already done that? And what did you find? Well, well, a bit of stale hardtack! I'd like that Mr. Feldbebel to answer one more question. Is he a Czech or a German? And let that brave Hungarian tell you how they dragged their cannon through this mud and snow. Of course they stopped in their tracks. Excellent. Now they're going to stop and stay put!"

From Maljen came the booming of artillery—a short, fierce burst of firing; he bent over in his saddle. On his way back to the staff headquarters he encountered a supply train bogged down in a stream.

"Don't beat your animals to death like that, man—stop it! Call your companions and give the cart a push. Can't you see it's stuck! You need four oxen. How can you look at that ox with blood pouring from its nostrils like that? And what'll we do when they collapse? There aren't any more oxen in Serbia. What are we going to use for plowing in the spring? You mustn't do things like that!"

At dusk he reached the staff headquarters in a blizzard; he could scarcely stumble to his room with its warm stove. He summoned the professor to keep him company until the report came in from Maljen.

"You're just the man, Professor. You can forget about those pupils of Napoleon—Kutuzov and Clausewitz. More than anything, my army needs laughter and jokes. If I could just hear that, I'd make a bet with you when we'll get back to the Sava and the Drina. If only these wretched soldiers could laugh, make a few jokes! Laughter and jokes, which a worn-out, exhausted man needs more than anything, aren't included in the army rations. If only someone could provide them, Professor. I'll propose you for the Karageorge Star if you can bring a smile to those gloomy faces on the staff—I'm quite serious. What is the most difficult task for a commander? I suppose it's to think up plans better than his opponent's; he's got to think more deeply, and look further ahead. Yes, I'm quite sure of that. Courage, that's always the most important thing in war. Most people have the courage necessary for both living and dying. In fact, sometimes they have more courage than is sensible or useful. One's got to use one's head, Professor. That's what decides the issue in war, as you yourself know. But it's a weary business thinking so intensely! One must think, and be able to think, in every situation. And who can always do that?

"Call the High Command; ask what's being done about the vojvoda's promise that our neighboring armies would start to attack. Also tell them that our right wing is under violent attack, and we've had to abandon some important positions. The High Command doesn't need supernatural wisdom to grasp Potiorek's intentions. He's going to smash our front in the direction of Gornji Milanovac. And that's the end of Kragujevac.

"Dragutin, I've no more apples. Try to get me some, but small ones, that's the kind I like."

He started writing: "Dearest Louisa, I hope you're well. Until now I haven't had a moment to write to you. I'm wearing warm clothes and I haven't yet caught a cold. I can't sleep much, but that doesn't bother me. If only my restless little Andja could sit in my lap tonight, I'd be as strong as a horse tomorrow. I'd see everything across Maljen, Baćinac, and the Ljig."

He stopped: he couldn't find the words to write. That day he had completely exhausted his supply in talking to the soldiers; he had scattered them over the Morava Division's lines. He read over what he had written, and felt ashamed; he crumpled up the paper and threw it in the stove. He took a fresh sheet and leaned over its white surface: a broken, abandoned line of trenches meandered from the Ljig to Maljen.

From the time he had come to the combat zone, Adam Katić had never felt so frightened as at the present moment, as he was waiting for his cavalry squadron to go into battle on the slopes of Dićka Glavica. Had his ears detected any oasis of quiet on the mountain, he would have yearned to leap into Dragan's saddle and ride there. It was already dusk; the infantry regiments were beginning their third counterattack since noon to dislodge the Austrians from Dićka Glavica. Mist enveloped the hills and streams, so that not even the treetops were visible; you couldn't see a horse or a soldier more than a few paces ahead. The wind swirled up the fog, bringing with it snow and the smell of gunpowder. Shells were falling around the cavalrymen waiting in the bitter-oak wood. It was as though the wind was shaking shells from the trees; one couldn't even hear their flight, because the wind was howling through the branches. Adam watched a shell rend the darkness, flash past a bare tree, with a repulsive smell. He stroked his horse between the eyes, wiped away the snow from his neck, and babbled to him, shuddering as he did so.

Medics were carrying wounded men past the squadron lined up for the attack; the battle suddenly swept down behind them. Buckshot scattered among the bitter-oaks, and groans echoed the sound of horses neighing in the wood. The wind was blowing more strongly than ever; the darkness deepened. Adam asked the men around him:

"What are we waiting here for? Why don't we get away?"

No one answered him; he clung to a tree trunk, the horses near him sank into the fog. Dragan followed his movements with his head, and never stopped sniffing at him and licking him. Spurts of fire in the treetops momentarily burned up the fog and stopped the howling of the wind in the branches. A bugle sounded. He couldn't tell if it was the signal for a charge or a retreat. He hugged Dragan's head, kissing the cold, darkening flower between his eyes. People were shouting something. He felt for the stirrup and mounted with difficulty. Dragan shook himself under him; this trembling completely unnerved Adam. Should he turn Dragan around and rush into the stream and the pathless forest? Above him was rugged ground and gunfire; branches were falling on him. He felt sick of it all: he was going to fall from the saddle. But Dragan was trotting through the forest, up the slope, through the fog, into the thick of the battle, into the crowds fleeing down the mountain side. Around his head, bullets were spattering the trees like hailstones; flaming branches were extinguished in the darkness.

"Dismount! Fix bayonets! Forward!"

He did not dismount; he dared not separate himself from Dragan, who was trembling violently. He tightened the reins with a convulsive movement; they raced into the stream at a gallop. For a long time the leafy treetops threw flames up in the sky. Should he desert and go back to Prerovo? Never, Dragan, never! He pressed in his spurs and pulled Dragan over to the right, into the shelter of a hill, or so it seemed to him. He jumped from the saddle, tied Dragan to a small bitter-oak, and began to stroke his forehead:

"We're going to get killed tonight!" he said aloud, more in anger than despair. He kissed his horse, then ran off into the darkness of the forest, and up the hill to the crag where the battle was raging. He came across some men who were standing against tree trunks and firing into the fog, through which machine-gun fire and grenades came hurtling toward them. Through the brushwood and the fog he could faintly discern the spurts of fire from the Austrian weapons.

Uroš Babović came up to him: "We won't get out of this alive! Let's make a bolt for it, Adam!"

"Perhaps we won't get out alive. But I'm not going to break my horse's legs jumping over ravines."

"They won't even give us a decent burial, you idiot!"

"I don't care!"

"Get your grenades ready! Don't anyone move a step until the order!" shouted the commander.

As he prepared his grenade, he thought: how will I find Dragan in this blackness? He trembled against the lichen-covered tree trunk; he did not want to lie down on the wet snow. Suddenly the Austrians stopped firing, and the Serbians, too. He could hear the groans of the wounded, and the stretcher-bearers calling to one another through the forest. From up above, where the Austrians were, waves of heavy fog descended, soaked with the smell of gunpowder.

"Don't shoot until you hear the command!"

The threatening whisper passed from tree trunk to tree trunk. Adam turned around and looked hard at the tops of the trees, trying with their help to fix the position of the hillock beside which he had left Dragan. He would run back to him as soon as he had thrown his grenade. The forest roared as the wind and the Austrians advanced. Danger had the voice of a wind—of all the winds he had ever heard, from all the dark nights he had ever lived through. He wanted to know which member of his section was next to him at that moment.

"My name's Katić. What's yours? Why don't you say something?" he whispered, but no one replied.

The roar of the icy wind and the murmuring of the bitter-oaks rose higher and higher to the invisible stars. Dragan would run away from this infernal roaring of the wind, and from the soft footsteps of the Austrians through the snow and the clods of earth.

Volleys of gunfire from either side and from above, from the side where Dragan was, broke through the darkness and the roaring wind in the forest. The man next to him gave a groan:

"Katić, my leg has gone! Don't leave me! I'm asking you like a brother!"

Bullets whistled around his head, grenades burst everywhere, but he didn't take cover: should he rush toward that ring of fire, toward Dragan?

"Get back! To the left! After me!"

But he couldn't move; Dragan was on his right, and lower down. He stood against the tree trunk, trembling, and tightened his grip on his grenade and his rifle; he had no idea where he would go.

"Katić, save me! Don't leave me!"

He recognized the voice of Corporal Jakov, but dared not speak to him: if he tried to save him, it meant leaving Dragan. Increasingly they were hemmed in by rifle fire from above, from the side where he had left Dragan. He ran a few steps downhill, then a shell blast knocked him flat; he didn't know how long he had lain there, spitting out snow, leaves, and the stink of gunpowder. He crawled back toward the groaning corporal. He felt for him with his fingers as he bent down:

"Get on my back! But where can I go without Dragan?" he sobbed.

Still moaning, Jakov embraced him, hanging round his neck, then with his sound leg climbed on his back. Adam pulled him up by his wounded leg and set off to the left, behind his section.

"Where can I go without Dragan?" he muttered deliriously, as he carried his wounded corporal through the undergrowth. He didn't hurry; he didn't want to go too far from Dragan. As soon as they stopped firing in that direction, he'd go back. He descended to the stream, where there was shelter from the bullets. He listened. The firing receded as the roar of the wind rose.

"I'll have to leave you here, Jakov. Don't swear at me—I must. I'm going to get Dragan."

"Would you really leave a comrade for the sake of a horse?"

"You know I'm not a traitor, damn you! But I can't leave Dragan. Crawl downhill to the stream. I'll come back for you."

"That dumdum smashed my thighbone. I'd finished my ammunition. Just carry me a bit further. I'm worth more than your horse, for God's sake!" He groaned aloud.

"Don't swear at me, I'm not leaving you. I'll come back with Dragan."

He rushed back through the forest toward the dwindling gunfire which was coming down the stream. He ran, slithered, fell. He looked at the tops of the trees: he had no idea where he was. He dared not go any further. Dragan used to come to him from the meadow when he whistled; he put his bent finger to his mouth and whistled. He repeated it several times. He pricked up his ears: if Dragan had heard him, he would neigh. But all he could hear was the Austrians calling to each other, and their bugle, in the stream. He concluded that the battle was over: they were assembling. Had they killed or captured Dragan? He burst into tears, and walked through the forest—back, then forward, to the right, to the left, whistling as hard as he could. But there was no hillock anywhere. He whistled again. The wind howled in the leafy crowns of the bitter-oaks.

He went from tree trunk to tree trunk, feeling with his hands, but unable to see them in the darkness; the forest roared, and gusts of icy wind and fog swirled round him. He felt as though he was choking, and whistling became increasingly difficult. Still, he didn't stop whistling. He dared not go any further. Uphill and down, from tree to tree: his hands were damp from the lichen. But he couldn't find the hillock anywhere, nor could he hear the sound of neighing. Besides the wind, he could hear two abandoned wounded men moaning further up the stream. He dared not go to them. He would have to carry Corporal Jakov somewhere, but where? Afterward he would not know how to get back to where he had left Dragan. Yet how could he possibly look anyone in the face tomorrow if he left a wounded man in the stream tonight?

"Jakov!" he shouted angrily.

He heard a gun firing from the stream; because of the wind, it was impossible to tell from which army. He called Jakov's name again, this time louder.

"Adam." He was startled to hear Jakov's voice just behind him.

"Why didn't you speak right away, for God's sake?"

"I didn't recognize your voice at first—I can hardly hear you. I'm bleeding to death."

"Where are you?"

"It's too late now. Go look for your horse. I won't live to see the day."

"Don't talk like that!" Adam bent down and felt for him with his hands. "Put your arms around my neck and hold tight. You haven't heard a horse neighing?" Jakov did not reply.

Adam carried him through the roaring blackness of the forest, in the direction where the battle had taken place. He fell down several times. Jakov moaned and breathed down his neck, but his breathing became increasingly faint. Adam also found he was holding him less securely, and had to take hold of both of his legs. Than Jakov fell off, and didn't even utter a sound when Adam tried to catch his wounded leg. Adam's hand was wet and sticky. Jakov sank into the snow, no longer moaning. Was he speechless from pain, or had he lost consciousness? He pulled Jakov over his shoulder like a sack; he had better carry him to the squadron as quickly as possible, and then come back. He strained to remember the direction, and began to count his steps, to calculate how many paces he had walked while carrying Jakov. Adam's windpipe ached from the effort, and he could hardly breathe; he would have to rest a little. He struck a match to light a cigarette and caught sight of the corporal's wide open eyes and parted lips. He was dead! He shook him, and pressed his head to Jakov's chest; he was no longer breathing. He folded Jakov's arms on his chest.

"He's dead!" said Adam aloud and put the cigarette back in his pocket. He was trembling.

Then Adam jumped up and ran back through the forest toward Dragan. He remembered that he should count his footsteps; he had run about fifteen paces. He managed to whistle. The forest roared. He continued through the murky night and howling wind, counting his steps aloud. Then he stopped, whistled to Dragan, listened, then continued counting his footsteps aloud between the trunks of the bitter-oaks, forward, then backward. He whistled again.

As soon as darkness fell, the regiment withdrew from the shallow trenches, away from the frost and blizzard, into the streams where there was shelter from the wind; there it waited for morning by the fires. Danilo History-Book and Bora Jackpot's platoon remained at its post and kept watch. The commander gave the men permission to light a fire in the grove of fir trees beneath the trenches; they could get warm there, but only ten at a time. They lit the fire in a hole made by a fir tree which a storm had torn up by the roots.

Bora refused to accept this act of compassion on the part of the commander, and did not leave the trench: he nestled on a heap of fern leaves and squeezed himself against the wall of the trench. He felt drowsy, not having slept for two nights. He listened to the whistling of the wind above his head along the edge of the trench, and to the sound of a broken branch moaning like a living thing in the frost and snow nearby. Anyway, he liked the night; one didn't have to look at the misery of war.

Danilo History-Book sat on the branch of a fir tree beside the fire with the soldiers. The wind blew the snow along, curled up the smoke, bent and twisted the flames, and scattered the soldiers from its path, sprinkling them with snow. He was watching them: their caps were turned down to cover their ears; some had tied pieces of tent flap around themselves with bits of string; many had sandals that had fallen to bits and wore only socks, covering the soles of their feet with bags or caps tied on with string. Those caps had been taken from men who had been killed, thought Danilo, and some had been stolen from another platoon. He chewed the frozen remnants of his hardtack, staring at his boots and overcoat. This inequality, which he was power-less to change, was extremely distasteful to him.

"Hey, you student! Would you like some prunes, Corporal?" A soldier behind him handed him a helping of prunes.

Surprised and delighted, he took two prunes: "Thank you very much!" he said excitedly.

"Five for a penny. Take as many as you want."

Danilo stared at him, disappointed. He could not see the man's eyes under his cap, and there was snow on his shoulders, mustache, and cap, but Danilo recognized him: that very day the C.O. had picked on him in front of the lined-up battalion, because of a torn blanket. He had won a medal for bravery: single-handed, while cut off from his platoon and surrounded, he had captured seven enemy soldiers, plus a machine gun and a crate of ammunition; he had also performed other notable actions. Danilo took two more prunes, and gave the heroic salesman a penny.

"Paun, give the fellow what he paid for," said Corporal Zdravko, whom Danilo found irritating on account of his kindness, and his desire to comfort with words such as, "Don't be frightened—they don't all hit."

"It's all right, thank you."

"No, you must take them, Corporal." said Zdravko. "If a man's going to buy and sell, let him do it honestly."

"Take what you've paid for!" said the salesman-hero angrily.

"I don't want your prunes! Get out of my way!" said Danilo, also angrily.

"Could I take your other prune, Corporal?" asked a soldier with caps wrapped around the soles of his feet; a bare heel peeped through his torn sock.

"Take all five!" said Danilo.

They began to quarrel violently over a single prune. Danilo got up and walked off through the blizzard and the darkness to the trenches; he sought out Bora Jackpot and sat down beside him.

"Are 'heroes' really so greedy and pitiful, Bora?"

"You'd better whisper your big discovery, or they'll hear you."

"But can people with such base feelings really be fighting for such exalted and sacred aims as the liberation and unification of all the Serbs?" Danilo raised his voice and trembled as he spoke.

"Danilo, old man, you didn't have to see this to know why heroes are poverty-stricken and greedy, and that people with base feelings—to use your words—are fighting for high ideals."

"Do you really find it normal that people in general—and our soldiers in particular—should be like that?"

"Yes, I do. It's as simple as that—people are poor and greedy. The only thing I find strange is that they're fighting for those sacred aims at all. The real question, old man, is why they are heroes, and why they are giving their lives. Why don't they kill their C.O.s and their pigheaded corporals and all go home? There they are, at it again. Hear that shouting? Just listen, and you'll hear what they're shouting from the stream."

"Look here, men, who are we freezing for here? Run away home to your villages. You're dying barefoot and hungry for Pašić and those yellow officers!"

The blizzard cut off the shouts and threats, scattering them through the deep valleys, the darkness, and the roaring forest.

"Are those our soldiers, Bora?"

"They're deserters—from another regiment, probably. Ever since it got dark they've been wading across the streams and fleeing over the mountain toward the Morava. Just listen to that man grumbling!"

"Run off home!" the voice said. "I tell you, Serbia's done for!"

"It's dreadful, Bora."

"It's simple reality, Danilo, reality without any high-flown lies."

"I'm not going to freeze on Maljen. I want to die in battle like a man—in a charge!"

"Your wish will be granted tomorrow. Lean against me and turn up your coat collar, if you haven't already done so. Your chest will be full of snow. Why have you suddenly shut up?"

"Does our vow still hold good, Bora?"

"Yes, it does. I'm no hero, but I won't abandon you if you're wounded."

"I won't leave you either."

"And it really matters to me that the Austrians shouldn't take my father's watch."

"You needn't worry. Let's not talk about it any more."

"It's only by talking about such things that I can keep awake. The effort to keep awake is unbearable. But if we fall asleep, we'll freeze to death."

"They say it's an easy and pleasant way to die."

"I don't believe that. Danilo, talk about something. About women."

"Perhaps Serbia really is done for, Bora."

"It's not our problem whether we get killed in a victory or a defeat. In fact, I think it would be more exciting to get killed in a defeat. No one will ever mention your name if you get killed fighting for victory. Just listen to that dry branch groaning!"

"What's that deserter shouting?"

"Listen to that poor tortured tree and its branch!"

"There's nothing that has astonished me so much here at the front as the groaning and complaining of the wounded. That's horrible!"

"They say that shrapnel wounds are awfully painful, especially when there's a frost."

"I know that. But still they are men, and soldiers. To hear Serbians crying out like that! I don't remember anything like that from *War and Peace*."

"Do you really believe that Bolkonsky was deeply moved by the endless blue sky and the white clouds when he lay mortally wounded?"

"Yes, I do. I really can't stand listening to that dry branch."

"Well, what do you think went on in the mind of our friend Dušan Casanova when the shrapnel burst in his chest?"

"He didn't have time to think of anything. Tričko said he died on the spot."

"I don't believe one can die absolutely without thought or pain, without being aware that one is dying."

"It's easiest if one dies in the first battle, like Casanova."

"In the whole Student Battalion, he was the one who took the greatest chances at poker. We had agreed to play a game after our baptism of fire. Tell me about that peasant girl in Boljkovci. What was she like?"

"Oh, she was marvelous, absolutely wonderful!"

"Yes, she was your last!"

"No, not because of that, honestly."

"Tell me everything that happened. I just can't keep awake. We'll soon get snowed in. Poke me with your fist when you no longer hear me talking. Lean your back right up against mine. That's right. Love, any kind of love, is at bottom a matter of warmth and touching, and I mean warmth, not temperature. Go on talking, Danilo."

"You'd better do the talking, since you're so sleepy. Let's put my knapsack over our heads. The snow's blowing down my neck."

"Sit on the fern leaves, and put it where you want. That's fine. As our late friend Casanova used to say, one doesn't need much to be happy. I haven't managed to fall in love yet, fortunately for my mother. After the wars with the Turks and Bulgarians, there was a whole division of widows in Belgrade; enough of them for anything you can think of, and for everything in trousers. After we had avenged Kossovo and liberated southern Serbia, we made it clear that we hadn't grown up just to join the army. And we did manage to raise the women's skirts. Pity the victory was so short-lived. Pity that Gavrilo Princip was determined to get himself into the history books."

"Don't talk like that! If there's anything else worth fighting for, apart from the fatherland, it's a woman."

"Right! But I prefer that war aim in the plural. Now tell me what happened with that wonderful peasant girl."

"I'll remember to the end of my life those two or three hours on the straw in the shed between the first and third cockcrows."

"I don't believe you. But go on talking, I'm falling asleep."

"Corporal Luković, we're beginning to freeze. Shall we light another fire?"

"You can light two. Light five. Set all Maljen on fire."

"What time is it, Bora?"

"My watch has stopped. I haven't wound it up since Dušan Casanova was killed. I can't stand listening to it beating the time away next to my heart. Tell me something about the Hungarians, Danilo."

"I really don't have anything to say about them. When I went to Budapest last autumn I fell in love with another student, a girl called Nevena from Novi Sad."

"And you've never once been in a whorehouse in Budapest?"

"If you only knew, Bora, how much I suffered!"

"That's something I'll regret. I'm going to be killed, and I've never been in a real whorehouse. Hit me so I don't fall asleep. Hit me, be a buddy. And after midnight I'll see that you don't fall asleep."

"Get up and run a bit. Come on!"

"I couldn't get up now even to dodge a shell. The drifting snow has wrapped me up so nicely. I don't feel the wind at all. Only hit me, that's right, but harder. And tell me more about Nevena."

"Well, I fell in love with her in the train on the way to Budapest, when we were both going to the university. That was the first time I felt like that, although we'd been to high school together. You know—Romeo, Werther, all that sort of nonsense. We loved each other that one autumn and the whole winter. But when the pear trees bloomed, she ditched me."

"Why then?"

"That was the first time I saw her walking with this other guy. As long as I live, I'll remember them walking past the pear trees in bloom."

"What next? Speak a bit louder, I can't hear you over the wind."

"Well, when we both went home for the vacation, I used to hide among her father's beehives every evening at dusk. I used to lie under the beehives so I could see her pass between the box hedges on her way from the well to the house, and watch her stop at the gate and talk with him. I did this every evening in July—the whole month—until Princip assassinated Franz Ferdinand."

"Please tell me more about that summer and the honey. And speak louder—let the soldiers hear it, too. I adore honey. It's the most wonderful food in our entire Galaxy. Hit me on the neck, Danilo. The honey must have had a marvelous fragrance at dusk in July."

"Yes, the wax had a thick, heady scent. And the hives had a marvelous smell."

"Bees are the most wonderful of all creatures. In fact, they're the only creatures in our Galaxy that have a fragrant scent. How many hives did Nevena's father have?"

"Probably about thirty."

"The evening must have hummed. The whole summer must have hummed."

"Yes, they were like huge cities. The most perfectly organized cities in the world."

"In the entire Galaxy, in fact."

"Yes, they have a perfect system of justice and duties."

"But bees are cruel."

"They sure are. I saw one of them lynch some bugs that had got into a hive."

"That means they wage war. And they kill other bees."

"Yes, they do, but only with just cause."

"They don't have any sexual urge, so they're absolutely pure. And so industrious! Hit me harder, or talk louder. Besides the wax and the honey, you haven't said anything about the special scent of the pollen from the flowers."

"It was kind of sweetish and intoxicating. Bora, don't go to sleep. Let's both move about a bit and get some air."

"I told you not even a shell would get me up. You moved suddenly, and now the snow's blowing over me again. Hit me on the neck, and I'll do the same for you after midnight. That's right, just right."

"Do you like mulberry trees, Bora?"

"No, but I know what they look like."

"My grandfather—my mother's father—has a path bordered with huge mulberry trees on his estate in Kamenica. The sun sets among them. You wouldn't believe it, but when the wind moves through their tops, it makes a murmuring sound. Can you hear me? I loved listening to the wind shaking the mulberries, and to the soft thudding noise as they fell. Like water dripping. Can you imagine what it was like?"

"Yes, a sort of rotting sound."

"Then flights of white geese would come."

"Yes, they're stupid creatures."

"And my grandfather Nikola used to say, with tears in his eyes, 'Ah, my boy, I have just one wish: to stand among my mulberry trees and see the Serbians, liberated from the rule of foreigners, riding on white horses!' I wrote in my farewell letter to him: 'Grandfather, I'm going to Serbia, and I'm coming back to you on a white horse.' "

"I've never seen a white horse."

"There are some. I've seen them."

"I only know them from fairy tales."

"If I do get back home on a white horse, would you like to come stay with my family in Novi Sad?"

"I sure would. I like to travel."

"Be sure to tell them I was a hero. That would mean a great deal to them. Just lie if it isn't true."

"I don't care whether it's true or not."

"My mother will give you a little wooden horse. For your son. You won't find a prettier little horse in all Bačka. A lovely little dappled horse. My grandfather gave it to me."

"Hey, Danilo, you aren't sleepy at all! Why don't you wake me up?"

"Did you hear what I just said?"

"Yes, I did. I adore horses. That's the one creature in our Galaxy that I wouldn't be able to kill."

"Hit me harder, Bora, go on, harder still."

"*You* hit *me* for a change! And talk loud—about horses, geese, bees, just go on talking!"

"Maljen is in an uproar, Bora."

"So is our entire Galaxy, Danilo. The Great Wheel is whirling round."

"Don't mourn for me!"

"And don't you mourn for me, either."

General Mišić was speaking over the telephone from the First Army headquarters in Boljkovci: "We've lost Maljen, Vojvoda. The enemy is now on the Suvobor ridge."

Vojvoda Putnik, speaking from the High Command in Kragujevac: "And what steps have you taken?"

"I haven't been able to take any steps. Maljen was taken about four o'clock yesterday afternoon, but I only heard the news around noon today."

"And where are we now?"

"We've lost more than eight hundred men killed or missing. About four hundred have passed through the field dressing station. Some platoons have been entirely wiped out—not a single soldier or officer left."

"I'm asking you about the positions, Mišić."

"My left wing is almost completely broken. The gap on the western crest of Suvobor has opened up. I'm cut off from the Užice Brigade."

"I was expecting Maljen to fall. It's a good thing it didn't happen a week ago."

"The Austrian thrust at the army's rear is irresistible. In two days we'll be driven back as far as Čačak. And I ask you to examine the critical state of the First Army most closely. It's worse than ever."

"Have you anything to tell me which will not be included in your regular report?"

"Events overtake our regular reports, Vojvoda. The position of the First Army changes hourly. It's worsening rapidly."

"I can hear you."

"Our central positions are sagging, too. The Austrians have taken the flanks and the heights—all the best positions for an attack on Suvobor. They've got control of all the mountain paths; they now have the conditions required for large-scale movements and maneuvers, while we no longer have any possibility of attack."

"I had no faith in that attack, even when you self-confidently announced it two days ago."

"But I believed in it, Vojvoda. I had to believe in it."

"You should believe in things as far as the facts allow, Mišić."

"I had to believe even when the facts were against me. I must still believe now, in spite of the facts."

"On such an extended front as you have, something should have happened to our advantage in the course of last night and today. War always has its own iniquitous justice, a kind of infernal equilibrium. Can you hear me?"

"Today the First and Sixth Regiments used grenades and bayonets, and quite successfully. Hatred has flared up. They've summoned the strength to look the Austrians in the face. That's the only good thing I can report about my army today."

"Have you praised these regiments for fighting with such enthusiasm?"

"Yes, I've sent a message of commendation, and I'll recommend them for decoration."

"I'm listening, Mišić."

"I'm not absolutely sure that tomorrow we'll be able to defend the positions we hold this evening. For this reason I've given orders today to all divisions regarding directions for a possible withdrawal."

"You must rescind these instructions immediately! You must continue to hold the positions where you are this evening."

"That is impossible, Vojvoda. I have reports from all the divisions that under the cover of the fog—all day today, and last night, too—the enemy have been constantly grouping their forces for an attack tomorrow. Three corps."

"That doesn't matter. Stay where you are!"

"But I haven't a single reserve battalion to send to Maljen, to slow down the encirclement of the army from the southern spurs of Suvobor. My army is exhuasted by fighting day and night, by the broken terrain, by the snow and frost. The mountain has chewed it up."

"The mountain is chewing up Potiorek's army, too. His forces are also exhausted by the rugged terrain and the blizzards."

"Potiorek may have the power to win victories, but I haven't the strength to defend the ground I'm standing on."

"Do I really have to convince you tonight what the withdrawal of the First Army would mean for the entire defense system? The result would be catastrophic! Isn't that clear to you, Mišić?"

"And I am asking you, Vojvoda, what will happen to Belgrade and all the Serbian front if I inform you tomorrow that two of my divisions have been wiped out? That the First Army—"

"Just a minute, I haven't finished. I will immediately order all the armies to attack fiercely and ease the pressure on you. But you must at all costs defend the positions you hold today. I repeat: the fate of the Serbian front is in your hands. Stay where you are!"

"And artillery? And shells? Can you hear me, Vojvoda?"

"Pašić has told me that a ship with fifty thousand shells arrived at Salonika today. They're being sent on to Kragujevac by train tonight. Provided the Bulgarians don't cut the rail line. Inform all headquarters and troops of this. Every soldier must hear that ammunition is on the way. And stay where you are!"

"I'll do it. To the farthest possible limits."

General Mišić, from the headquarters of the First Army: "Yes, I can hear you all right. Is the snow drifting where you are?"

Colonel Milivoje Andjelković-Kajafa, commander of the Danube Division, first levy, from the front line: "It's pitch-black. Last night the Austrians revealed their intention to break through my front today. They've been massing their forces in front of our positions all night; the movement of supply trains and batteries has never stopped. Just before daybreak they pounded my infantry and artillery with fierce gunfire. Well aimed, too. They've taken Slavkovac."

Mišić: "You must get back everything they've taken. You must do so immediately. Kajafa, it's better not to fight two battles for the same position."

"I've ordered an attack for the recovery of Slavkovac, but without success. They're pressing us even harder."

"Then *you* attack harder, too! There must be no giving ground today."

"Is that the Drina Division? Mišić speaking. I can hear you."

Colonel Krsta Smiljanić, commander of the Drina Division, from the position: "The enemy is approaching along the entire front of my division. My troops are having difficulty resisting. Assistance is essential, sir, and most urgent!"

Mišić: "I require the maximum effort in defense. You must be calm and steadfast, Smiljanić. You must use bayonets and grenades as you did yesterday. You must look the Austrians straight in the face. I cannot offer you any further help—I haven't got anything. And don't forget that today we dare not lose a stream or a hill!"

"Hello, Morava Division! Get me the division commander. Mišić speaking. What do I need to know about you, Milić?"

Colonel Ljuba Milić, commander of the Morava Division, second levy: "I've got my finger on the trigger, sir. We're waiting. We're prepared for a general attack, but it seems too early for them to move. There's a thick fog. You can't see anything."

Mišić: "It's not that they can't see anything, but they've struck at the weakest point first. Can you hear the racket from the Danube Division's lines? They're not having an easy time. You must help them at once with your cannon."

"I have very few shells, sir. If our Danglis guns are used today, they'll have to be silent tomorrow."

"Then use them today. Let me know how your gunners do."

Krsta Smiljanić, commander of the Drina Division, first levy: "I have to shout, sir. The plaster's falling because of the cannon. The Slavkovac slope has fallen, and there's a fierce battle now for Gradjenik."

Mišić: "For Gradjenik?"

"Yes, Gradjenik. I'm suffering severe losses. Their artillery has mowed us down. We're fighting desperately. No more can be expected from my troops."

"Gradjenik must be defended. Its fall would have fearful consequences for the central positions of the army. The Danube first levy would be placed in an extremely difficult situation. Can you hear me, Smiljanić?"

"We can all get killed, but we're powerless to halt the enemy's advance."

"You must *not* all die, and you must halt the enemy's advance!"

"But how? And with whom? In my division there won't be a regiment left by nightfall. Do you realize that, sir?"

"Yes, I do. And you must realize that Gradjenik and Elevation 801 must be saved. I have no other instructions."

"Please send at least one battalion to assist me. I'm begging you to send one battalion!"

"I can't even send you a platoon."

"Transfer some men to me from some other unit—just for today!"

"What's the point of taking from the weaker to give to the weak? Hello, Smiljanić! Hello, Drina! Lieutenant, get me the Drina Division."

The commander of the Drina Division: "Elevation 801 has fallen, and Gradjenik has been taken, sir."

Mišić: "And what's going to happen on the Gukoš positions now?"

"They're offering desperate resistance, but it can't last long."

"Surely you could have done a bit more today, Colonel!"

"I have to inform you that the Fourth Auxiliary Regiment has been mowed down by artillery—massacred!"

"Gradjenik and Elevation 801 must be recovered."

"But how, sir? Tell me that!"

"Put all members of the staff, including your own, in the firing line. Can you hear me? Now get down to work, Colonel. I'll order the Danube Division to help you."

"Give me the commander of the Danube Division, first levy. Mišić speaking. Hello! Do you realize what's happened, Kajafa?"

The commander of the Danube Division, first levy: "The situation is frightful. I'm under attack from Gradjenik on the Šiljkova slope."

"What? The Šiljkova slope?"

"The Ninth Infantry Regiment is in disarray—they've withdrawn toward Little Suvobor."

"Gather up your men and do your utmost to recover Gradjenik and Elevation 801 before nightfall. Yes, they must be recovered before nightfall. Now we needn't waste more time talking."

Vojvoda Putnik: "I've received your report. The situation cannot remain as it is, Mišić. In view of the state of both armies and the Užice Brigade, it is essential that you recover yesterday's positions. You must get back everything you've lost today!"

Mišić: "I'm carrying out your orders, and doing what I said I'd do in yesterday's report. But as I'm neither God nor the Devil, I can't do the impossible. The troops are fighting with their last ounce of strength. I've ordered even the staff into the firing line!"

"Serbia has always had to defend herself with the last ounce of strength, and always will. That is our fate."

"I have no wish to enter into historical explanations. Particularly today, on Suvobor."

"But you have to explain yourself to the High Command."

"Yes, that is my fate."

"Then please listen to me carefully. The loss of yesterday's positions will necessitate the withdrawal of the Third Army. This will undermine the Second Army and break up our entire central front—our entire defense system. Then the fall of Belgrade becomes inevitable!"

"The only solution is for the Second and Third Armies to attack."

"Do everything you possibly can, as I told you yesterday. Do your very utmost to recover and hold your positions. Good-by!"

"I have something more to say."

"There's no need to say anything further; we have agreed on what is to be done."

The commander of the Drina Division: "If hell exists, it's here on Glavica. We're being pounded from all sides, and from behind, too."

Mišić: "What is the Morava artillery doing?"

"They're doing fine. Couldn't do more. They're grinding them to powder, but the Austrian command doesn't mind losses. They're advancing in waves all the time. The Third Regiment is meeting them with grenades and bayonets. My orderly tells me that blood is flowing like water. My regiment is reduced by half. It can't hold out for long, under attack from twelve fresh battalions."

"I can only ask one thing: hold on! Hold on until nightfall!"

The commander of the Danube Division, first levy: "I wish to inform you that we have recovered Elevation 801. I have completely smashed an entire Austrian regiment!"

Mišić: "And where was that, Kajafa?"

"I wiped them out on Bezimeno Brdo. They'll have cause to remember that Serbian hill without a name!*"

"Yes—Bezimeno Brdo, covered with mountain pines, scrub, and dogwood. But the top is quite bare. Good for you, Kajafa! That's the way to do things! And what's happening now?"

"I've continued the attack in the direction of Dobro Polje."

"Can you drive them back? Down the ravines! Try to capture the edges of the elm wood!"

"Just a short time ago, by the Devil's own luck, a fog rose up and hid the advancing columns from my view. The Austrians were firing furiously from Dobro Polje. And they have pinned down the Second Regiment. I have moved in the Ninth Regiment from the Šiljkova slope to help them, but so far without success. I shall succeed tonight, sir."

"That's right, Kajafa! We must work by night, damn them! In our country the night is ours. We can see our own folks even in the darkness and fog."

"Who knows what we can do, with God's help? I'll certainly do my best."

* Bezimeno Brdo means "Nameless Hill."—Trans.

"What are your priests doing, Kajafa? Yes, I said your priests. Hello! Let them get on with their work!"

"Get me the Danube Division, second levy. I want the division commander. Mišić speaking. What are you doing, Vasić? Why aren't you reporting?"

The commander of the Danube Division, second levy: "I'm defending Babina Glava, sir!"

"And what have you done?"

"We've carried out your orders, but with great difficulty. I'm told that the Austrians are regrouping for a new attack. If we have a repetition of today's attacks, I'm not in a position . . . I can hear by the movement of the firing that my right flank is in flames. You can't see anything for fog and snow."

"We must recover Gradjenik and Dobro Polje by nightfall! And by your intervention! I'm returning the Second Infantry Regiment to you. Get the Eighth Regiment going at once."

"The transfer of regiments from one position to another over these slopes and ravines, with so much snow and frost, is a wasteful use of our forces, sir."

"I can't hear you well!"

"It's robbing Peter to pay Paul."

"Exactly, Colonel. That's just how I command the army. I take from the weak to give to the still weaker. Then from the very weakest point I transfer to a stronger one on the verge of collapse. From any position not under attack, I send help to one being destroyed. And I order that one to resist, whatever the circumstances. When an attack has failed, I order it to be repeated. Where men are running away, I order a counterattack. Is that clear, Vasić?"

"There are reports of a fresh attack on Babina Glava."

"Maybe so. Now act according to my orders: rob Peter!"

The commander of the Drina Division, first levy: "I wish to report to the army staff that we have held the Gukoš positions, but by a final, desperate effort. The Third Regiment has repelled an enemy force three times its size, using grenades and bayonets in the dark. Battalions are being reduced to platoons. A number of officers and students have been killed. There are many men wounded. All seriously. We have covered slopes and heights with blood."

Mišić: "Give the soldiers my warmest thanks for their splendid work and the unforgettable deeds they have performed today for the survival of our people. They all deserve our gratitude and praise."

"What should I do with seriously wounded men in this frost and snow? The wind is blowing up again, sir."

"I don't know, Smiljanić."

"Mišić speaking, from the First Army. Get me Vojvoda Putnik, please. I want you to listen to me very carefully. Can you hear me well?"

Vojvoda Putnik: "Have you had a difficult day?"

"The hardest part has been the end, Vojvoda. With the fall of Gradjenik and Elevation 801, the central positions of the army have eroded considerably. On Suvobor they have been broken, and are bending sharply in the direction of the Suvobor ridge. There are deep inroads into the left wing, which is all but cut off. Today the right wing has been threatened as well."

"That was to be expected. That was exactly what Potiorek had in mind, to attack the army's main line of communications. Go on."

"For the first time since crossing the Kolubara, the enemy is attacking frontally regardless of terrain, adverse weather conditions and natural obstacles. He's pressing forward without regard to losses."

"What does it matter to Potiorek that his Czechs, Croats, and Bosnians are being killed? What does he care about the Hungarians? Or in general about his losses? He's moving toward the Dardanelles!"

"He's initiating a decisive battle, beginning with night attacks in darkness and snowdrifts."

"He's in a great hurry, and the days are short. That haste does not indicate strength. If things were going well, he wouldn't have changed his tactics."

"I'm not convinced of that, Vojvoda. The enemy is stronger than us in all respects. It's dangerous for us to remain in our present positions. And impossible, too."

"I told you yesterday what I think of your strategy."

"I remember what you said. But I must repeat: your attitude is devoid of initiative, Vojvoda. It is passive, and contains no element of military risk. It does not stimulate the will. It kills the spirit of the soldiers."

"That attitude is an expression of all the various needs of our defense. It takes into account the entire Serbian front, not just one section of it. It's not the First Army that will defend Serbia, but her entire armed forces."

"That's what one learns at the military academy. But in wartime, a single infantryman can win the war."

"Ever since I knew you—since you took your captain's examination—you've always considered your own affairs the most important. That's how you're thinking about your front today."

"But it's against my positions that Potiorek has directed his strongest forces. If he manages to break through there, he can expect to win his greatest victory. Potiorek isn't Napoleon. Nevertheless—"

"Potiorek is a German idiot. Soon every old woman in Serbia will know that. Go on."

"I'm warning the High Command that my army is dispersed among a tangle of slopes, streams, and heights. It's lost in the mountains. We no longer have a line or a strategic plan. The directions of movement overlap, and this creates disorder and panic. The soldiers see this. They think the command has lost its head. Chaos and hopelessness are apparent both in the staffs and the troops."

"That simply means that you have to think out your maneuvers carefully, Mišić. Go on, tell me all you have to say."

"The continued struggle in the present positions, to hold the Suvobor ridge, is bringing the army to the last stages of exhaustion. The troops will be utterly exhausted by tomorrow, if the enemy continues to attack like today. It's not only that the First Army has no strength left to fight for victory; it hasn't even the breath to take a step in that direction. The First Army no longer has the power to defend itself."

"Živojin Mišić, let me ask you what you would do if you were in the High Command tonight, and Bojović was in your place, saying what you're saying?"

"I would have respect for Bojović's opinion."

"Then Stepa, Šturm, and Božanović would telephone you, call you a weathercock, and resign."

"In that case I would accept the resignations."

"To which positions do you wish to withdraw your army?"

"I propose that at dawn tomorrow we abandon the mountain chain Suvobor-Rajac-Prostruga and withdraw to positions in front of Gornji Milanovac."

"I am just asking you once more—as a man, a soldier, and a Serbian—to think of the entire front and its defense, to think about the Second and Third Armies. Their flanks will be very seriously threatened by your withdrawal. They will be completely unprotected. All the efforts and sacrifices we have made so far would become meaningless. And what would happen to the Užice Brigade? Potiorek would reach Čačak in two days on its back, and the next day we would have to abandon Belgrade. What sort of a backbreaking strategy is that, Mišić? Where's the logic of it? Tell me that!"

"According to my strategical reasoning, Vojvoda, events would not develop as you forecast. Why should the neighboring armies be obliged to withdraw? Why should we abandon Belgrade?"

"Then what would happen, Mišić?"

"We would acquire a firm and secure front for the First Army, capable of resisting any attack, and of moving forward at a favorable moment. Meanwhile the enemy would be spread out over mountains where there are no roads to bring up artillery. The snow and frost would destroy their offensive power. They would fall into our trap, and their strength would be fatally dissipated. Their striking power would be exhausted, and a crisis of morale would ensue."

"Go on, please."

"Moreover, it's clear that this could only help the other sections of the front. The other armies would be more secure, and could attack the enemy's weak and extended flank. Potiorek would not be able to withstand this attack; his collapse would be inevitable."

"Everything you suggest is completely unrealistic—a junior officer's pipe dream! A dangerously optimistic plan, Mišić. God Himself would have to lend a hand in that strategic plan, with the help of all possible goddesses—and circumstances."

"I can't understand you at all!"

"You certainly don't. Only gamblers and desperate men dare to hope without justification, relying on chance and luck as their allies. I am neither a gambler nor a desperate man, and therefore do not count on luck and chance."

"Do you really see me, Vojvoda, as a desperate man and a gambler?"

"You're an old soldier, Mišić—just forget about your vanity in these difficult times. That's all right for lieutenants . . . Just a minute, I haven't finished. Please collect your thoughts and think sensibly, as you know how to do very well. We've got to take account of the time. We've got to work on the basis of the enemy becoming exhausted and putting off a decisive blow. The Austrians have a fire burning under their feet. The Russians are pushing forward from the Carpathians. The offensive of the Imperial Balkan Army is finished. Now time is working for us. We must make good use of it."

"Time never works for the small and the weak. They have to work for themselves, and for time."

"Sleep well, Mišić! Good night."

All night long there had been a sound of pigs grunting, goats bleating, and cows mooing from the positions which the Serbians had just abandoned without a fight. Many members of Luka Bog's platoon believed that the animals had got lost in the mountains in their flight from the approaching Austrians; they suggested going after them, so that after ten days of living from hand to mouth on hardtack and prunes, they could eat some cooked meat. However, Luka Bog, who had established himself with his orderly in an abandoned log cabin, would not allow them to leave the new positions—not even to sleep around a fire. They were expecting a big Austrian attack along the ridge of Suvobor in the morning, and the Fourth Battalion was digging in to meet it. The previous night Luka Bog, in a state of particularly frenetic anger, had warned Ivan Katić and Bogdan Dragović that, alive or dead, they would not withdraw from Previja.

It was a dark, murky night, with snow falling. They could hear the scraping of spades; the men were digging trenches, then snatching a little sleep in a sitting position; Bogdan Dragović and Ivan Katić woke up those who fell asleep, hurried on those who were digging, and talked about Major Gavrilo Stanković, who had been seriously wounded: if people like him lost their lives, what would victory mean to Serbia? Ivan affirmed that the defeat of Serbia was inevitable; Bogdan had reached a similar conclusion, but said nothing.

Just before dawn they again heard the sound of pigs grunting, and also the crowing of roosters, this time from the Austrian side. Sava Marić cried out aloud in a happy voice:

"Wonderful! We've won a victory on Suvobor!"

The soldiers said nothing; Ivan went up to him: "What has happened, Sava?"

"The Austrians are hungry, sir."

"How do you know that?"

"Can't you hear the pigs and the roosters? Just listen to that goat bleating in German!"

"Yes, I can hear it. But what does that prove?"

"That proves that there are no pigs grunting, no roosters crowing, and no kids bleating. Nor were there any last night, and no cows mooing either. That was the hungry Austrians, sir! Their supply train got stuck in the snow, their bags are empty, so they're grunting and bleating in the dark to try to get the animals up there. They want to find some and slaughter them. Just listen! You think that's a pig or a goat? No, that's a sign that God is with us! And I can't remember such heavy snow before Saint Nicholas' Day. How come we're up to our waists in it at this time of the year?"

Ivan said nothing: the grunting and bleating were not very clear, but then he didn't really know what sort of sounds pigs and goats ought to make.

Exhausted by lack of sleep, hunger, and the labor of digging trenches, the soldiers attached no significance to the observations of Sava Marić. By dawn they had dug their holes, in which they crouched and dozed. Ivan settled himself in the trench beside Sava, covered himself with a tent flap, and fell asleep, listening to the snow falling.

At dawn a blue wave of Austrians flowed over Previja in a dense, close-packed firing line, but they did not shoot; they were clearly convinced that the Serbians had withdrawn further the previous night. They had in fact started too early and set off without proper fighting order to capture one more slope, and thus confirm their imminent conquest of Suvobor. Sava Marić spotted them first: they were advancing slowly and softly, sprinkled with snow and talking among themselves.

"The Austrians, Corporal!" he said, giving Ivan a poke.

Ivan thrust his head out of the tent flap and tried to stand up. "Where are they?"

"There they are! Wake up the soldiers! Let's give them a taste of fire!"

Ivan discerned the blue phantoms through his misted glasses: they were slipping as they advanced, and coughing. He climbed out of the trench and crawled over the snow, going from one soldier to another, waking them up, and saying in an ominous voice:

"The Austrians! Can you see them? Take aim, but don't shoot until I give the word of command. Pass this order on!"

He went back to Sava Marić's trench and began to aim at the phantoms: at blue phantoms, not at men. The Austrians stopped, as though listening to the wind. Either they were discussing something among themselves, or they were not set for combat. They kept turning around and asking questions, as if waiting for someone. Ivan trembled from the awareness that he would kill them as though at target practice; he could now kill anyone he wanted, whomever he chose. Under his command at least twenty men would be killed—Austrians. They were people—*people!* It was terrible. But he could do it. And the power to do so excited him. Another sensation excited him, too: it was hideous. He looked at Sava Marić: he had pressed his cheek against the butt of his rifle, an expression of peace concentrated on the left side of his face. That is conviction, not hatred, thought Ivan, and he felt surer of himself, more capable of giving those words of command which he must pronounce in a few moments. He must do this, and he could. Behind the Austrians, who were still standing crowded together, an officer shouted:

"Forward! Don't be afraid of the wind!"

Ivan understood that much German; he couldn't see the man, but he wanted to see him and to aim at him. The Austrians came forward in the same disorderly line, again moving slowly and hesitantly.

"Don't shoot without the word of command!" said Ivan quietly. Then he leaned over the butt of his rifle and with the top of his gun sought out the officer, the one who was not afraid of the wind, or the bare whiteness of Previja. The snow stuck to his glasses; he couldn't see the man, but he wanted to aim at him—a brave man. He saw the Austrian ranks, quietly advancing in a series of blue and white fragments; they seemed less and less like men. He must wait for that brave man, the one who was not afraid of the wind.

"Don't shoot until you hear the command!" he repeated in a self-confident voice.

Bogdan Dragović was stunned at the thought that whenever he wanted to he could kill, without danger to himself, one of those men who were walking slowly over the slope of Previja, sinking up to their knees in snow. He was afraid he might kill someone who would not defend himself, and who was not threatening him. The sight of his rifle moved from one Austrian to another; he did not know at whom to aim, whom he wanted to kill. He could see neither their faces nor their rank: how could he pick out a real bastard, one of those who killed old men and village children, who hanged peasants and raped women? How could he recognize a man who went after loot, bent on conquest—a filthy Hun? Or the man who had wounded Major Gavrilo Stanković. In that black shell hole where he had burst into tears from a profound pain for Gavrilo a different war had started for him; it had acquired a significance broader and more inevitable than any ideas, and deeper than any known rational arguments. His gun sight stopped, trembling, on a huge, fat Austrian wrapped in a black peasant's shawl, a shawl which he had surely stolen. He would kill that fat man; he was one who went after loot, a disgusting bastard; he must be, since he was so large and fat, and had the effrontery to wrap himself in a shawl stolen from a poor old woman.

A volley of fire from Ivan's section thinned out the dense Austrian firing line. Those who were not hit stood about in confusion, not knowing from which direction the gunfire was striking them; only a small number fell down in the snow among the dead and wounded.

The fat Austrian wrapped in the black shawl turned around to run away, but Bogdan fired before he could turn his back, and brought him down in his tracks. Then he fired a second bullet into the black heap on the snow. At Ivan's command another volley felled those who were stuck in the snow and attempting to take aim from a standing position; those who had not been hit turned and tried to run away through the deep snow, struggling through it as though their feet were bound. Bogdan finally hit one of them, then dropped his gun; if it had been night he would have run away and flung himself into the snow, so as not to look at the black patches on the whiteness that were his two victims. His teeth chattered.

Luka Bog ran up out of breath, without his overcoat, crying:

"Charge! Charge those goddamn Huns! Get your teeth into them! Make their blood flow like water!"

The platoon got up. Without much haste they set off, wading heavily through the deep snow, to kill the remaining Austrians.

"See how easy it is to make holes in them? They're softer than us, didn't I tell you?" he said as he walked down the firing line, brandishing his revolver. "If every Serbian platoon made mincemeat of as many Huns today, Potiorek would be out of Valjevo in three days! Come on, forward to the bend and that hill!"

Aleksa Dačić paid no attention to Luka Bog. He ran from one dead man to another, and shook out their bags. They were empty; no food. Only at his fourth attempt did he find a small packet of biscuits, and some coffee and tobacco.

The soldiers halted at the bend, and from a standing position began shooting at a supply train.

"Don't kill the horses! Keep your fire for the men!" shouted Luka Bog.

Ivan and Bogdan met each other among the dead Austrians, black protuberances on the whiteness of Previja. As they looked at each other, their eyes said: did you kill anybody? Neither of them spoke.

They were afraid to speak of what they had done. Bogdan handed Ivan half a cigarette; Ivan took it, lit it from Bogdan's half, and for the first time inhaled the smoke avidly, from the very depths of his being. They smoked in silence, watching their soldiers hurriedly searching the dead Austrians and removing their overcoats and boots. It was very quiet; the snow was falling ever more thickly, drifting slantwise.

General Mišić: "How have you spent the night, Kajafa?"

The commander of the Danube Division, first levy: "In continuous infantry attacks; they never stopped the whole night, sir."

"Did at least one of the battalions manage to sleep somewhere dry?"

"Only if they found some hut or sheepfold in the firing line. At least it's good to know that the Austrians didn't sleep either."

"The soldiers must have some cooked food for breakfast. And don't forget my order of yesterday: you must have a stronger faith than the enemy!"

"Drina Division, please!"

The commander of the Drina Division, first levy: "I am reporting that I have not carried out the planned attack. At dawn the Third Regiment abandoned Zabran in disorder. At six o'clock the enemy launched an all-out attack on the entire front of the Drina Division, against all positions. I'm sorry my voice is hoarse. I have a cold."

Mišić: "Be careful about your communications and co-operation with the Morava and Timok Divisions. Drink hot lime tea, well sweetened. And don't forget: our only reserve force today is our faith in ourselves."

"Give me the Danube Division, second levy."

The commander of the Danube Division, second levy: "We moved at dawn. The situation is frightful. Their intentions are clear enough —we don't need prisoners, there's nothing we have to guess at. We won't be able to hold Babina Glava for long. That's all for the present."

Mišić: "All our positions were attacked at dawn, throughout the whole army. Can't you hear the roaring and crackling over Suvobor? Potiorek is determined to drive us off the Suvobor ridge. Do your utmost to hold Babina Glava till nightfall, Vasić. And you must have faith in your soldiers, more than you have now. That's an order!"

"Hello, Morava Division!"

The commander of the Morava Division: "The Austrian infantry are advancing in close-packed waves. Their artillery is working accurately, and it's quite terrifying. Our counterattacks are not succeeding. I am unable to carry out the orders given yesterday and last night."

Mišić: "You simply must hold your positions. Your entire duty is contained in the word: you *must*."

"I do not understand your order."

"I hate this order more than you do. But you must. And you must have faith, too. I command you to have faith in yourself, and in God. The fate of the left wing of the Third Army depends on you."

The commander of the Danube Division, first levy: "I've been thrown back in the direction of Little Suvobor and Šiljkova slope."

Mišić: "Then stay where you are! You are not to yield a single beech tree, not even a bush, in front of Šiljkova slope!"

"They have attacked with three columns and are making a massive penetration. We can do nothing to resist them."

"They're mortal. Put bullet holes in them! You can do that, Kajafa."

"We're under deadly artillery fire from Gradjenik and the Black Summit."

"Let them get as close as possible, then use bayonets and grenades. They won't keep up the attack for long. I'm sending you a unit of Danglis mountain cannon. And you will receive help immediately from the Danube second levy."

"Vasić, please! How are things with you?"

The commander of the Danube Division, second levy: "I'm just managing to resist the hammering on my left wing. It's extremely difficult, and we won't be able to keep it up for long."

Mišić: "You must attack immediately to assist the Danube first levy. Kajafa is in difficulties. You must help him!"

The commander of the Drina Division, first levy: "My Sixth Regiment has been wiped out. I can do nothing with them. There are only six hundred rifles left—six hundred, I tell you! The artillery from

Lisina is destroying us. They're pounding us with cross fire. The Third Regiment is in a bad way, too. I have ordered a withdrawal."

Mišić: "And is that really all you've been able to do?"

"Absolutely!"

The commander of the Danube Division, first levy: "They've re-taken Elevation 801. The troops on Rajac are hardly strong enough to provide a lateral wing and guarantee our withdrawal along the Pro-struga heights. I can't meet a blow from Rajac; I must inform you that this is quite impossible!"

Mišić: "Then what are you going to do? Can you hear me? Suvobor is collapsing!"

"Let the Morava Division take the hammering from Rajac."

"The Morava Division has been pushed back onto Lisina and Retke Bukve. They cannot possibly get to Prostruga. You and Vasić are personally responsible for the defense of Suvobor and Rajac. Just the two of you—I've no one else to send! That's all I have to say."

Vasić: "Podovi has been attacked, too. They're pushing through between Babina Glava and Ravna Gora. My division is in terrible shape!"

Mišić: "And what are you doing, Vasić?"

"I've ordered the Eighth and Eighteenth Regiments to close the breech on Ravna Gora. And I've attacked them on the Dičina."

"And what happened? Hello, Vasić! What happened?"

"What did you say, Kajafa?"

"I haven't been able to hold Šiljkova slope. I just couldn't, sir. My right wing was ground to powder."

"Kajafa, I do not wish to hear from the lips of my commanding officer the words *ground to powder, crushed, frightful, desperate, cata-strophic!* Hello! A people and an army are not wiped out in this way—neither man nor God permits it. Can you hear me, Kajafa?"

"But what if the armies are unequal, and man is powerless to defend himself?"

"In a fight for survival the forces are always equal. A man always has the power to defend himself. Can you hear me, Kajafa? For that, a man always has the power."

"Everything's shaking around me. I no longer know what I'm doing."

"You must stop further penetration. They're enclosing us in a vise-like grip. We have only one line of retreat. As I told you before, you two are responsible. I have no one else! Can you hear me, Kajafa?"

"I'll do all I can. I dare not do any more, sir."

"You must do what you think impossible, Colonel."

"Yes, Vasić, I can hear you."

"We're still on Molitve."

"What do you mean, you're *still* on Molitve? You'll stay there until I give orders to the contrary. Regroup your forces there."

"What with ridges, then these chasms and slopes, my divisions are completely split up. No two battalions can keep together as a single unit."

"It seems like that to you because you're looking at a map. But we don't defend our lives by looking at maps, Vasić. A map does not show either our fatherland or our freedom. Even when you took your staff examination you had to know your country the same way you know your house and your wife."

"Thank you for the geography lesson, sir. But it's not that my division has got lost on Suvobor—between them, the mountain and the enemy have cut them to ribbons. I've got an entire corps against me."

"Now listen to me! If our position doesn't improve immediately, and the enemy remains on the Suvobor watershed, then we're surrounded and gripped by the throat! There's a gaping hole between us and the Užice Brigade. The Austrians are going to pass through it in marching columns, do you realize that? So you must defend Suvobor today, Vasić."

"But how, I ask you? And who with? Can you hear me? Who am I going to defend it with?"

"With your own head, Colonel!"

"I can't defend Suvobor with my head, sir!"

"Well, you have to, Vasić! I'll say the rest of what's on my mind when I hang up!"

Kajafa: "You realize that I do not go back on my statements, sir, nor do I fear the results of my decisions."

Mišić: "I'm not obliged to listen to everything you say, Colonel."

"But I am obliged to report everything, sir. And if I defend Rajac today, I'll have to abandon it tomorrow. That's all."

"We are fighting today among ourselves. Listen to me. Village constables and road menders are doing their duty for their fatherland. We all get paid for doing our duty. Can you hear me?"

"I carry out my oath as a soldier from honor—not for pay, sir."

"A soldier does not give his oath only in the barracks and in peacetime, Colonel. We soldiers have given our oath for a single day, a single hour. For a single moment which awaits us. Only a woman requires perpetual fidelity. Our fatherland requires us to give this promise only once, but once and for all. Such a time has now arrived. Can you hear me, Kajafa?"

"As army commander, have you really no other orders for the defense of Suvobor? You appeal to me through my oath, but how am I to appeal to my soldiers?"

"I have no reserves to give you for Rajac. I am making use of my ultimate right as a commander in appealing to you through your oath. You can use this right, too. And let me know as soon as you have done something to our advantage."

Hadjić, chief of staff: "Two telegrams have arrived from the High Command. We have suffered heavy losses in attacks made this morning through noon by the Obrenovac Brigade and the Second Army. The attacks were unsuccessful. Moreover the Third Army has not been able to resist the blows received today. The left wing has retreated suddenly in disarray. They are asking us for immediate help."

Mišić: "Tell them that I can send them the orderlies, my own included. What about the attacks of the Užice Brigade? Are they going to help us, to prevent our left wing from being surrounded?"

"They haven't reported at all, sir. I don't think we dare count on their attack."

"Could the Montenegrins try to do something?"

"The High Command has forwarded a telegram to us from General Janković in Cetinje. He says that yesterday the enemy attacked throughout the entire day. In four days the Austrians have suffered about six hundred casualties, dead and wounded. The Montenegrins do not have adequate forces for an offensive."

"I have no further orders until nightfall. I have already threatened the division commanders and called on them to fulfill their oath. They will do the same to the regimental commanders, and they in their turn to the battalion commanders. But the battalion commanders will not dare to threaten the platoon commanders. And that is the limit of my power as army commander. All that remains is to use court-martials."

"Even the regimental commanders dare not use threats. Today in some regiments it has come to blows and fisticuffs between the officers and the soldiers. There are reports from Milanovac and Čačak of a mob of deserters coming down the mountain. And a lot of men have given themselves up to the Austrians—a whole battalion and six officers."

"There are no deserters, and no one has surrendered in the First Army, Hadjić. Anyway, those who desert and surrender do so because they are unhappy and desperate men. Don't reproach me, I'm not shouting at you. Please tell the division staffs immediately to ask the prisoners taken today whether they are tired and hungry, and whether they are short of ammunition. Also whether they have reserves behind the firing line."

Ljuba Milić: "The position of the Morava Division can no longer be maintained, sir. The defenses are collapsing."

Mišić: "And do you think that the position of the First Army, which as you know is under my command, is any better? Do you think that the position of the entire Serbian armed forces is any better than that of your division, Colonel?"

"I am responsible for Morava Division, second levy, and not for the First Army or the entire armed forces, sir. I am speaking and acting within the limits of my own competence and duty—and my own capacity, too, believe me."

"You are responsible for your division while it is in the barracks or on parade. But when the survival of our people is at stake, then, Ljuba Milić, you are responsible for everything that has happened since the fall of Kossovo, in the year 1389, until this moment. You are responsible for everything until the fall of the final curtain. Can you hear me? Yes, that's right. And when it gets dark and the Austrians can no longer see you in their gun sights, then withdraw your forces to the line Ploče-Sastavci-Česte Bukve."

"What about the cannon? How am I to get them to Česte Bukve? I don't see any path marked on the map: the terrain is impassable there."

"Don't talk to me about maps! Our country is like that, you have to go on your hands and knees. You can get through everywhere, and drag along everything you want. No place is impassable—do you hear me? If a man hasn't passed, then the farm animals have; and where they haven't been, the wild beasts have. Now we must follow their tracks. We must defend everything we possess, every plant, every creature of the forest, every footstep!"

Miloš Vasić: "All my efforts have failed. My division is falling to pieces. The remains of one regiment already disintegrating have charged against Parloge and Ravni Gaj."

Mišić: "Well, what of it? Do you expect me to sympathize? What about your next efforts?"

"I expected more understanding from my commanding officer, sir. Meanwhile my efforts are continuing, but they are the efforts of a cripple. The dying men are scratching at the ground, that is, the snow."

"It's not the snow they should scratch, but the man responsible for their plight. So try at least to do that. Scratch him!"

"I have ordered a withdrawal, which is now proceeding. I had no other alternative."

"And why the hell must you save your own ass at all costs? You can't forget that you were once a minister. So now you have to piss on the army command, you bastard!"

Mišić: "Now, Hadjić, is there any more bad news you haven't told me? Why are you crying?"

Hadjić: "The worst possible thing has happened, sir! Just ten minutes ago Živko Pavlović reported from the High Command that shells have arrived which cannot be used in our cannon!"

"But why can't they be used? Good God, they know the caliber of our cannon!"

"Yes, that's true. But these shells have come from France, and they are two and a half millimeters longer than the caliber of our cannon. So we can't use them. It must be sabotage, which we couldn't possibly foresee. It's disgraceful! The Allies have written us off. They've simply sacrificed Serbia. Come into my room, sir, and see how the officers are sobbing! Strong men are weeping, and the operators, too."

"Hadjić, come with me into your office. God help us, heroes!" Mišić said to the officers. "Stand at ease. Now look me straight in the eye. There's nothing I can do for you, and no one else can either!"

All day long not a single wounded man had been carried down from Previja; two or three attempts to do so had met deadly accurate fire from the Austrian machine gun on the hill. The soldiers prayed for fog, for drifting snow, and for darkness. Fog did gather at the bottom of the valleys, but the heights remained clear. Previja was an expanse of whiteness dotted with corpses and the wounded, who were still being constantly raked by machine-gun fire.

Only when darkness fell did the platoon collect the wounded and withdraw to the trenches on the upper rim of Previja; two more men had been wounded by the machine gun from the hill, then Ivan and Bogdan went down to the log cabin to report to Luka Bog that they had lost fifteen men that day.

"But we've beaten them, young men! We've won! Just a short time ago an orderly brought me a message of commendation from the commander of the Eighth Regiment. He's going to recommend us for a decoration, and the commendation of our platoon will be read in front of the entire regiment—in fact, in front of the division. Mišić will know about our victory!" Luka Bog was in high spirits; it was the first time he had been drunk on account of a victory.

"Where are we going to spend the night?" snapped Ivan, who could not grasp the fact of the victory and its significance; he was angry and offended by his commander's high spirits.

"We'll spend it where we've spent the day. I'd have you know that the Austrians are on Previja, young man. The wounded can be carried to the regimental dressing station. And tomorrow we'll make mince-meat of yet another Austrian battalion. You have the honor of being entrusted by the regimental commander with the defense of Previja until tomorrow evening. The fate of the division hangs on the defense of Previja, and the fate of the First Army and the Užice Brigade depends on our division. The defense of Šumadija, Pomoravlje—the whole of Serbia—depends on Previja! You see, Katić, Austria and our fatherland are on Previja. We've got to kill them with our teeth! There's going to be a river of blood!"

"Do you mean that we're going to be under fire from that machine gun on the hill until tomorrow evening?" cried Ivan indignantly.

"You bet we are! But perhaps you'd rather hide under your granny's skirts, you spoiled brat? Back to the trenches! Dragović, we've received a sack of hardtack, and half a bag of onions. Send for the soldiers and hand it out for supper."

They left the cabin in silence and climbed up the slope. Bogdan was thinking about Major Stanković with sadness in his heart; Ivan comforted himself with the thought that there was still Sava Marić. The machine gun on the hill fired short bursts at long intervals. When it was not firing there was silence on Suvobor—an ominous silence.

"Where on earth have you been, Corporal? Have you decided that we're going to collapse and die in this frost?" Aleksa Dačić welcomed Bogdan in front of the trenches.

"We haven't decided anything. We're only carrying out orders, Dačić!" said Bogdan uncertainly; he could not see Dačić's face.

A few men jumped out of the trench: "Why don't we withdraw? The whole battalion has withdrawn; you can't hear a human voice or the firing of a gun anywhere. We're alone in this wilderness! What's going to happen to us when it gets light?"

Their shouting frightened Bogdan. Were the soldiers actually revolting against him? And what should he do?

"The rations have arrived," he said, speaking as loudly as they had. "Dačić, go to the log hut and bring the sack of hardtack."

"But he'll steal it, boy!"

"Just a minute—*you* go, Lazić. And the rest of you, listen while I explain things: we have orders from the regiment to defend Previja. We're acting as the defense force for the regiment and the division. Previja is a very important position."

"Let that bastard Luka Bog defend the division. And you corporals! When it's daylight, that machine gun will bore holes in our heads. Can't you hear it? And we'll freeze tonight in this snow."

"Well, I'll be here with you."

"I don't give a damn about you."

"What did you say, Dačić?"

"You heard me!"

"Get back to the trench! Off with you, Dačić! Get back to the trench when I order you, you bastard!" said Bogdan, choking with anger.

The soldiers slowly returned to their holes in the snow, grumbling and cursing. Bogdan felt ashamed of the way he had shouted; plunged in despair, he sat down and lit a cigarette. If anyone had told him two days ago that he would have shouted at his soldiers like that and called them bastards, he would have boxed his ears. What had made him so angry with those unfortunate men and their petty revolt? If he didn't get killed during the next few weeks, what would be left of his convictions and ideas?

The machine gun whipped them with tracer bullets from the hill.

Aleksa Dačić trudged through the snow from one soldier to another, talking to them:

"Look here, men, let's go to the hut and raise hell with that son of a bitch. The students are pigheaded idiots. No good asking them to do anything. They've got paper in their heads instead of brains. They've been clobbered on the bean, and want us all to get killed. Let's take Luka Bog by the throat!"

"Who's going to do that? He's a bastard, all right. Let's just get out of here—what else can we do?"

"I don't want to run away. We've got to go on fighting."

"For what? And who with? In another three days our platoon will be finished."

"Don't shout, you fool, the corporal will hear you. The Fritzies can't last long. They've frozen their asses on Suvobor. Their bags are empty. You've seen that. And their supply train's stuck in the snow."

"Ours got stuck at Valjevo! Their supplies will be all right, you needn't worry. They've got an empire behind them."

"Then why were they grunting like pigs and bleating like goats last night? Come on Sreten, let's the two of us go raise hell with the almighty Luka Bog!"

"And what if the darkness were to swallow him up tonight?"

"I'm all for it. Let's swear on oath, then it's on all our heads. It's best that he should go. He doesn't have a soul in the world. And we've all got homes that'll be destroyed."

"You're right, Vlajko. We'll be in a hell of a fix if we stay here till daylight."

"Let *him* be in a fix! But let's swear first that no one will give the show away."

Aleksa listened, and after some hesitation refused to agree.

"No, boys, I can't go along with that. He's a swine, but he's also a Serbian officer."

"My ass aches for him! But our houses will still be empty, and our children will be orphans."

"Come on, don't let's get at each other's throats. He's a son of a bitch, all right, but a Serb. Let's just go raise hell with him, and threaten him a bit."

"I'm really scared you'll frighten him, you idiot."

"Now just a minute, men, there's something else we can do. Corporal Katić is a good man, and refined, too. Let's get him to go see the C.O. He's the son of Vukašin Katić; Luka Bog won't dare do anything to him."

Bogdan Dragović noticed the unrest among the soldiers and felt that they were right. It was only on their side that he was prepared to die; he must always support them. He went down to the log hut to try to convince Luka Bog that the platoon must be withdrawn from Previja;

or at least that he should let them come down to the stream and light a fire.

Wrapped up in his overcoat, Luka Bog was sitting beside a fire, taking swigs from his flask and making jokes with his orderly, who was preparing some cornmeal mush for his supper. He received Bogdan cheerfully:

"Nice to see you, young man. Sit down, I feel like having a chat. Take a swig!"

"No thank you, I don't drink."

"What, you still don't drink? Never mind, in a week from now you'll be a real drinker. I'll bet my life."

"I don't think so. I've come to tell you something."

"You know, you did a good job as observer in that beech tree. I wouldn't have climbed to the top of that tree, not for anything. I give you my word of honor as an officer!"

"You're most generous, sir; I appreciate it." Bogdan could see that Luka Bog was smiling. He would try to get a little closer to him first, instead of immediately urging a withdrawal from Previja. Meanwhile the machine gun on the hill gave a short, warning burst of fire.

"Where do you come from, sir?"

"I suppose I came from my mother's belly."

"Well, that's a pleasant place."

"Yes, it is, provided your mother isn't a whore."

"Are you a regular officer, sir?"

"Young man, I was born an officer. I began to chew a saber as soon as I was weaned. A bit later I put on the uniform." There was no smile on his face as he said this, but he winked at Bogdan and nodded his head affirmatively.

"Which do you like best, your saber or freedom?" asked Bogdan, smiling. He was trying to joke, but his legs and back were numb with cold.

Luka Bog frowned: "What's all this nonsense about freedom? Why should an officer love freedom? Anyone that loves freedom should go to the barracks and the ranks, to curse and be cursed!"

The orderly mixed the cornmeal mush in a mess tin—seriously, as though performing the most important task in the world. Fog and darkness pressed down on the doorless hut; the machine gun cut through the silence in its own arbitrary fashion. Bogdan struggled to find the strongest possible reasons for withdrawal, and behaved as though he were listening with the closest attention to Luka Bog's sudden burst of enthusiasm.

"You know, young man, I like to win, to be victorious. In the barracks or in the officers' mess, I bend everybody to my will: wise people and the rich, the handsome, the corrupt—everybody! Everybody under my command is mastered by me whenever I feel like it. And in wartime I lord it over generals, emperors, governments! You know what? I've already conquered Turkey and Bulgaria! Yes, *I* did that—that was *my* work! What more have Putnik and Stepa done for victory than me? While we're fighting and dying, we're all rendering equal service. And just think what it will mean now to conquer the Austrian and the German Empires! What a day it will be when we dance the kolo on German flags in Terazije!"

"Can you hear that machine gun from the hill, sir? Do you realize that when it gets light, it'll finish off the platoon?"

"To hell with the machine gun! Now young man, are you aware, or did you read somewhere, what happened to Adam when he took a bite from Eve's apple, blast her eyes? What came over him to make him lose God's trust for the sake of a worm-eaten apple? What a fine time we would now be having in Eden . . . ! No Fritzies, nobody hungry, no lice, no snow—spring and autumn all the time! Now somebody should be sorry for us because we have to suffer and fight. But just think of it: we've lost eternal paradise because of a rotten apple! Would a louse or a fly—or any creature but man—have done such a thing on this earth?"

Bogdan listened carefully; Luka Bog was a bit drunk, but he was talking with enthusiasm and conviction: man was indeed justly condemned to eternal suffering, and did not even deserve pity.

Ivan Katić stood at the opening of the hut, and spoke without any attempt to conceal his indignation:

"You're sitting here keeping warm, while the soldiers are freezing up there! They're getting mutinous, and they'll all run away. They're right, too!"

"Just tie up those mutineers and bring them to me at once! What are you waiting for? Tie them up and bring them here immediately!" said Luka Bog sternly.

"You can tie them up yourself. I'm not going to."

"What's that you said, young man? So you're mutinous, too, are you?" Luka Bog threw off his overcoat and stood up with a threatening gesture.

Bogdan felt ashamed at being caught by Ivan in an unofficial conversation with the commander; but he was also afraid that Luka

Bog might slap Ivan's face. He jumped over the fire toward Ivan and stood in front of him protectively. He cried:

"Ivan is right! You don't know what the soldiers are saying, sir! There's no sense in sacrificing what's left of our platoon!"

"Get out of here! Get out at once, blast your eyes!"

Humiliated and offended, the two young men went out into the freezing darkness and set off toward the summit of Previja, trudging slowly through the deep snow. When the machine gun on the hill fell silent and the darkness thickened, Bogdan spoke to Ivan in a hoarse, trembling voice:

"Stop a minute, Ivan. There's something I want to tell you. You know, I used to think I knew something about war, and about people. I used to think they fell into two main groups, the unhappy and the wicked. Well, you know my ideas. But now they're all mixed up, and I feel I don't know anything about people. Especially after tonight's conversation. I don't even know what kind of a man Luka Bog is. I don't know what kind of a person I am myself, or what I'll be like tomorrow."

"I feel I'm beginning to understand people, and the war too," said Ivan in a sharp, vindictive tone. "If I go on fighting for one year, I'll be a wise man."

Neither could see the face of the other, but both wanted to; they had a premonition that each would see the real face of the other, unknown until now. Without a word they set off each in the direction of his own squad, drawing farther and farther apart in the darkness, listening to their echoing footsteps on the freezing snow.

Before Bogdan could find his hole, some bullets whistled over his head: that machine gun on the hill offended and humiliated him as though it had struck him or spat in his face. That was not a weapon; it was some kind of monstrous force set above humankind. The will behind this punishment and humiliation was Austria. If there was a truly brave and proud man among the Serbs on Previja, he would destroy this monster on the hill that very night. He squeezed himself into the narrow trench, crouched down, and snuggled his head into the collar of his overcoat, but couldn't close his eyes. He watched the spinning darkness and listened to the complaining and coughing of the soldiers around him.

"Corporal? Where are you, Corporal?"

"Who's that? What do you want?" said Bogdan, straightening his cramped, frozen legs with great difficulty.

"It's me, Milovan, the lieutenant's orderly. Someone has killed Luka Bog!"

Bogdan jumped out of his hole: "What did you say? Who killed him!"

"While I was in the forest gathering wood, a gun went off in the hut. I thought it was him firing his gun, like just for the fun of it. I brought in the wood, and what a sight met my eyes: he was stretched out beside the fire with his forehead smashed by a bullet! And not a soul to be seen!"

Bogdan trembled, unable to believe or grasp what the man had said. "Who have you told about this?"

"Only you. You'd better come have a look."

Bogdan hurried down the slope of Previja in a dazed state, amid short bursts of fire from the hill. In the hut he beheld the outstretched body of Luka Bog, with his forehead shattered, his lips wide open and covered with blood, as if shouting: Get out of here! A little book peeped out of the pocket of his overcoat; he could not see the flask of *rakija*. Bogdan bent down and took the book from his pocket; it was a torn, wet, crumpled copy of the Old Testament. So he had fallen asleep in his Eden, on the banks of one of those rivers of whose whereabouts Bogdan had been unable to tell him. He put the book back in the pocket. It was Aleksa Dačić who had killed him; he was the only one capable of such a deed, thought Bogdan, and felt even more afraid.

"How is it you didn't see anyone when you heard the shot?" he stammered.

"I didn't see anything, sir, really I didn't!"

Almost collapsing from fear and shuddering, Bogdan leaned against the doorpost of the hut. What would happen now? What should he do? He must report to headquarters.

"Where is the battalion headquarters, Milovan?"

"I don't know, sir. *He* knew. And the orderly hasn't come back yet."

Bogdan left the hut and hurried back to the position to tell Ivan what had happened. He was a wicked man, a criminal, to do that, he kept repeating to himself, even if it was Luka Bog. He found Ivan and breathlessly related to him what had happened.

"Now the two of us are responsible for the platoon. And for the murder of Luka Bog," he concluded.

"You're the corporal of the first squad, so you inherit the command unless there's someone of senior rank, which there isn't." Ivan's calmness astonished Bogdan.

"To hell with all that chain-of-command nonsense! The C.O.'s been killed. A man has been murdered—even if it was Luka Bog. This is our army, our people. We can't take such a superior and cynical attitude."

"Do you want to set up a military tribunal? And pass sentence on Luka Bog's murderers in this icy wilderness? At dawn the murderers will be shot, and then we'll make our final charge against the machine gun on the hill. A fitting end for a platoon on Suvobor!" Ivan stopped, realizing that there was no sense in continuing in this tone, which might estrange him from Bogdan; so he added in a more concerned voice: "I'll agree to anything you suggest."

"I don't know where the battalion headquarters is, so we can't inform anybody until the orderly returns. I don't know what we should tell the platoon—what we should tell them officially, I mean, because they knew about this before we did. Perhaps we should interrogate anyone who seems suspicious?" Bogdan fell silent; the machine gun on the hill spattered Previja with a long, wavering stream of bullets. Dare he proclaim Aleksa Dačić the murderer? What if he accused him unjustly?

"Let's ask Sava Marić's advice. I have more confidence in his common sense than in anything else now. Sava, come here, please."

Even in the darkness Sava Marić did not forget the service rules, and saluted them correctly. Bogdan related what had happened, mentioning that he suspected Aleksa Dačić. The machine gun interrupted the recital with two short bursts of fire.

"When that shot was fired in the hut—I heard it very clearly— Aleksa Dačić and Spasoje Božić were haggling with Sreten about the price of a flask of *rakija*. Then they were auctioning cigarettes. So I'm sure it wasn't them," said Sava calmly.

Bogdan was doubtful about this evidence. The more persistently Sava indicated that Aleksa Dačić had nothing to do with Luka Bog's death, the more obvious it appeared to him that Sava had resolved to protect someone in the platoon. Perhaps Sava was a party to the crime himself. According to his peasant's reasoning, there would be nothing wrong in killing Luka Bog. If the whole platoon had agreed on it, what could be done now? The orderly could have done it.

"Why don't you say something, Ivan?"

"If Sava's way of thinking isn't in accordance with justice, just now it's certainly useful."

"But if the two of us agree with him—that is, with the rest of them—then we become accomplices."

"Well, he certainly was a swine, Bogdan. He was cruel and heartless."

"That's true. But he was cruel and heartless on behalf of the fatherland, not from personal motives. And he was an unhappy man. I realized that this evening. I can't pass judgment on an unhappy man."

"You decide whatever you wish. I'll agree to everything you suggest—everything," said Ivan. He sat down in the snow. "Anyway, no knowledge, no principle has any value here on a night like this."

"But we must have some moral principles even tonight, on Previja. We must salvage something, Ivan."

"But I don't know what, I really don't. When everybody in Europe is behaving like criminals, what can we do tonight, in this snow and ice—one wretched, mangled Serbian platoon? It makes no sense, none at all!"

"If by any chance I survive this war, Ivan, I'd have to report to the first available civil court that I was privy to a premeditated murder."

"And do you think anyone will have any conscience left in the future, in peacetime? And you're a socialist, a revolutionary! You're—well, anyway, I've told you I'll agree to anything you decide."

"Are you suggesting we should keep quiet about the murder, and behave as though Luka Bog was killed in battle? As though he sacrificed his life on Previja? Is that what you want?"

"Why not? We're all sacrificing our lives—either today or tomorrow, it isn't important which. Don't you agree, Sava?"

"If I may say so, sir, I wouldn't decide anything now. Wait until the morning. When it's daylight, you'll see everything better. And perhaps the problem will solve itself. I would suggest to you, Corporal Dragović, since you're now the commanding officer, that we withdraw from Previja into the fir grove."

"We're not going to withdraw before dawn! There's to be no withdrawal from Previja without orders," he said, turning to go. Then he paused: "Ivan, you know that we're the main defense of the regiment and of the division. You know how important Previja is."

"Yes, anything is possible. The issue of the war might be decided on Previja."

The machine gun on the hill pierced the gloom with short bursts of fire; Bogdan walked toward it through the snow, returning to his squad with despair in his heart. It should be destroyed with grenades—that hideous monster, that Austria; that would save the lives of two or perhaps three hundred people. It should be done now, while it was still dark, by Aleksa and Spasoje. Should he go with them? Perhaps that machine gun would settle everything. He stopped in his tracks: perhaps some principle of justice would be satisfied, some injustice redeemed. He would make it impossible for himself to perform any act of injustice. He would save the platoon. Major Stanković would surely have approved of that. Bogdan walked toward his squad, and summoned Aleksa Dačić and Spasoje Božić.

"We'll freeze here, Corporal. And that last recruit from yesterday's draft got nicked by the machine gun while he was darting along beside the trench. His arm's broken."

"How many grenades each have you got? Follow me!"

"Where are we going, Corporal?"

"We're going to wipe out that bastard on the hill," said Bogdan. Luka Bog too had spoken of the machine-gun as "that bastard on the hill."

"Are you in your right mind, Corporal?" protested Aleksa Dačić loudly. "How are we going to hit that machine gun when you can't see a thing? And how are we going to get up to it when the ice is cracking, and you can even hear footsteps on the next slope?"

"Follow me, I said!" Bogdan felt a certain sweet delight in subjugating Aleksa Dačić; it was as though the encounter with the machine gun would settle all their accounts since Baćinac. "Stop grumbling! Aleksa, you keep to the right and Spasoje to the left!"

Excited and confused as he was by many feelings, he felt no fear. The icy surface of the snow splintered under their feet, and their legs often sank into the snow to their knees. Bogdan did not slacken his pace, even though Spasoje and Aleksa warned him. He hurried so that this would in fact happen. He felt somehow satisfied with himself. He found he had reached the mountain pines, and that the ascent was continually steeper; he began climbing the hill. But the machine gun was silent. Since he had resolved to go in search of it, it had made no sound in the murky darkness. He stood still and waited for it to fire and reveal its lair. But the gun was silent. Previja was silent. The whole of Suvobor was silent. His nostrils crackled from the cold air. Spasoje and Aleksa were sniffing and talking in whispers.

"Will it soon be dawn?" he asked them, also in a whisper.

"Yes, soon."

"Then we must hurry. Are we going in the right direction?"

"Yes. But it isn't far now."

"What do you mean by not far?"

"When you begin the steep part, it's less than fifty paces. We should crawl now, sir."

Aleksa was challenging him. Even now he felt no fear. Or perhaps that thievish peasant was able to conceal his fear. He must ask him.

"Do you think we should start to crawl immediately?"

"It depends on where your heart is."

"Then we won't crawl!"

Bogdan set off without even bothering to move quietly. He stumbled against the mountain pines, fell into the snow more and more often, and waited for the machine-gun bullets. But the machine gun remained silent. Bogdan's heart beat louder, its thumping became increasingly audible. The traitor! He stopped and crouched down. The thumping of his heart resounded throughout Previja, through the whole of Suvobor. Not from fear—from something more significant, more terrifying, more fateful. But he didn't want to think about all that. Presumably this was the moment that Major Stanković had described as "face to face": face to face with death. He felt a desire to sit down, to lie among the mountain pines and prolong this time of unseeing quiet, with the machine gun silent above his head, to think about himself and his life—his long, long life—to the uttermost limits of thought. He wanted to think about his distant past, and his utter insignificance in relation to that vast expanse of space and time which coursed through his body, his head, his arms—united with this expectation of something infinite, beyond the confines of thought, for which he felt no fear. But he could see himself clearly enough: a fire burning in the darkness, a heart thumping in the silence.

"What are we waiting for, Corporal?" whispered Spasoje.

"We're waiting to hear it. I don't know where it is."

"Once you do hear it, then you've defeated Austria."

"Come on, Aleksa! Let me see you!" He unscrewed two grenades and began to crawl through the pines; the icy surface of the snow crackled and snapped as though a whole battalion was on the march, but still the machine gun was silent. He felt hot, and was sweating all over. He crawled along, panting; still no sound from the machine gun. It was tormenting him, humiliating him. He could bear it no longer. His head bumped against a stone; the darkness was suddenly filled with flashes and pain.

"Where are we, Aleksa?" he said, groaning aloud.

Behind the stone right above his head, the machine gun spewed out fire and dust, which made him jump up to take a look: it was a huge black mass outlined against the sky, enclosed in a clump of its own fire. He hurled both of his grenades at it, then fell down into its soft, burning beastliness, into nothingness.

Aleksa Dačić threw another grenade, and shouted: "Spasoje, what are you waiting for?"

The machine gun was suddenly silent. The Austrians groaned. Spasoje didn't throw his grenade.

"Hit it, Spasoje!"

No sound but the groaning of the Austrians, and someone running over the hill toward the stream on the other side. He ignited a grenade and threw it in the direction of the groans. He could hear only a single hoarse moan, increasingly quiet.

"Where are you, Corporal? Spasoje! We've settled them!" Aleksa got up with his gun at the ready, moved toward the rock, and began to climb over it. The smoke and the foul smell of the explosive made him cough. He fired a bullet into the dark, groaning, tangled mass of bodies. He felt for the machine gun; its barrel scorched his hand, but he jerked it with all his strength and pulled it down over the rock into the snow.

"Now you're mine, you German brat!" he cried aloud. "Corporal! Spasoje! Where are you, damn you? Ah, there he is!" He climbed over the rock, banging his knees, and walked among the corpses and cases of ammunition. He pricked up his ears: someone was running down the hill. He fired a bullet after him, then again called out to the corporal and Spasoje in exultation. He crouched down and lit a match: four dead men, a pile of knapsacks, blankets, packing cases. He didn't know what to pick up first to see what it might contain. He found two pocket watches, both working, then collected everything from the inside pockets of the jackets; he would look at his finds when it grew light. He shook out the knapsacks: there was no bread any-where, but he found two cans of food and some kind of jam. So they're starving just like us, he said with satisfaction—aloud, so Dragović and Spasoje would hear him; but he no longer called their names until he had finished collecting everything of value. He loaded the knapsacks and blankets on his back, and slithered down the icy surface of the rock toward his companions. He called their names. I suppose they're not dead, he thought quickly, then lit a match: there was Spasoje, with his head blown open, in a pool of blood. The bullets had cut him to ribbons. "Poor devil!" he said aloud. He lit another match: the cor-poral had rolled against a pine tree and lay on his side. He went up to him and pressed his head against Bogdan's back; he could hear his breathing.

"Didn't I tell you to crawl, you silly ass of a student? Now what am I to do, Corporal? We need you, we need the blankets, we need the machine gun. We need every goddamn thing!"

He put down the knapsacks and the blankets, hoisted Bogdan onto his back, and ran with him to the clearing and the gentle slope of Previja. He left him there and went back; took the machine gun, the knapsacks, and blankets; and dragged them down the hill to where Bogdan lay unconscious. Then he carried him toward the trenches, calling for help as he went. The soldiers didn't come to him, though he called out that he was carrying the wounded corporal. He set him down beside the first trench and called Ivan Katić. But he didn't wait for him: you get a medal for bringing in a machine gun, so he ran back toward the hill for his booty.

Ivan came up slowly; when he grasped that Bogdan had been wounded, he burst into tears and knelt down beside him. The soldiers finally realized what had happened, and carried Bogdan down Previja to Luka Bog's hut.

When Ivan had summoned up strength to go down there, he stood transfixed in front of the hut: on one side of the fire, which the soldiers had rekindled, Luka Bog lay stretched on his back, his face covered with blood; on the other, Bogdan Dragović lay with his eyes closed, and his face shrunken and faded, with its enormous black mustache. A soldier quickly and silently unbuttoned his bloodstained jacket. In order not to see the wound, Ivan turned toward the darkness and the forest. What was there for him to go on fighting for now?

General Mišić: "Please work out the details of my confidential instructions of the twenty-sixth at once. You don't approve of them, Hadjić?"

Hadjić: "You mean the instructions about withdrawing the army to positions in front of Gornji Milanovac?"

"Yes. You're not sure about this? Tell me what's on your mind; I need to hear everything now. At a time like this we should not be divided by rank, but only in our attitudes and arguments. We should differ as much as possible while we're making decisions, so that afterward we'll be in agreement in both action and command."

"The danger is very great."

"But don't be in a hurry with the instructions. The actual order is the last stage in the process of command. But you haven't told me everything."

"The instructions of the twenty-sixth will have considerable consequences for the neighboring armies. We must first secure the agreement of the High Command for such a withdrawal, sir."

"And if the High Command does not agree? What then?"

"I think it is now impossible to act otherwise than in accordance with the decision of the High Command."

"And what if we're not convinced that it's right? If there are other facts, not immediately apparent, which are on our side?"

"Those facts are also known to the High Command, sir. And you can see further from the hilltop, as the old saying goes."

"That's if the people on the hilltop aren't blind, and have better eyes than those on the hillside or at the bottom. But on many occasions I have doubted the clairvoyance of those who look down from the top of the hill. The clouds are nearer, but the people appear smaller. Have you any other facts against withdrawal?"

"Imagine what our position will be if the High Command does not agree!"

"That's my headache. So hurry up with the arrangements for the divisions. We must send out orders by nine o'clock."

"Give me the division commander, Drina. Mišić speaking. What have you got to tell me, Smiljanić?"

Smiljanić: "My division has withdrawn from Dička Glovica to the line Golubac-Klače.

"Send me a written report about that immediately. And now please tell me the things you would not include in your reports to the army staff."

"I don't understand you, sir. I hope that my reports are exhaustive, and that the staff is aware of the state of the Drina Division."

"Your reports are the kind that should be sent to the High Command. But I'd like you to tell me the things you would relate tonight to a friend, or a schoolmate whom you happened to meet at headquarters."

"Well, to speak in confidence, our situation could hardly be worse. There's a gloomy silence in our headquarters, like after a funeral. And all around, a sort of ominous murmuring and muttering in the dark. The snow is blowing over; it's dry and hard. Are you listening?"

"Yes, I understand. There's darkness and confusion in the soldiers' hearts. They're afraid of the new day that's coming. They have only one brief thought."

"How could it be otherwise, sir, when the battalions have been reduced to platoons? We just can't count the losses, not to mention those killed this afternoon. The dressing stations are full. There have been casualties among the medics, too, and there are no longer people available to carry the wounded."

"That's why we must move the entire army out of the range of fire before dawn. Move your division over Lalinac and Boljkovci in the direction of Nakučani, to a position at Tripovac, then spread out to the right and bend back to the Gornji Ljig, toward the village of Mutanj. Can you hear me, Smiljanić? As soon as you have occupied the new positions, the soldiers must have a really good meal, then a good sleep. That's the most important thing for tomorrow. But the staff must get on with their work and make preparations for an attack. As soon as the army is rested, assembled, and drawn up, and as soon as the shells arrive and ammunition for the infantry, we must advance immediately—toward the Kolubara and Valjevo. Good-by! Hello! I've forgotten something important: they're altering those shells in Kragujevac, the two-and-a-half-millimeter shells."

"Give me the Morava Division, please! I want to speak to the commander personally. Mišić speaking. Have you any suggestions to make to me, Milić, or any requests?"

Milić: "I should like the Second Regiment and that battalion of the Third which you transferred to the Danube Division to be returned. It's going to be difficult to hold out tomorrow with the forces I have."

"What's your greatest worry at this moment, Milić?"

"I'm most worried about the officers and the ammunition. I'm losing a lot of officers—there's never been a war in which so many officers have been killed. I've got schoolteachers commanding battalions now, and students and peasants in command of platoons. I already have to turn the platoons over to students. And they're getting killed, too, like bees in a fire."

"Are you satisfied with those boys who haven't even finished school?"

"Yes, they're doing well, but many of them are getting killed, as I told you—far too many. As for artillery, my cannon will have to be silent tomorrow."

"Perhaps they won't. They're altering those shells from France in the cannon foundry in Kragujevac."

"I've still got a few shells left which the soldiers hid from their officers. Just to be on the safe side!"

"I know all about the cannon. Tell me something more about the men."

"We're tormented by hunger. The rations haven't arrived, and the looting is terrible."

"Even if the command can't win every battle, they must always manage to feed the army. Looting by the soldiers is a misfortune of which only the command need feel ashamed. Can you hear me, Ljuba? Are you convinced that it is now time to act according to the instructions I sent two days ago? Or do you consider that tomorrow we should remain in the positions we hold this evening?"

"Only you know whether as many people must be killed tomorrow as have lost their lives today."

"What would you decide if you were in command of the army?"

"If we're attacked tomorrow as we have been today, my division won't be able to hold out."

"Then act according to the orders you've been given. At four in the morning, move along the watershed between the Lalinac and Slav-kovac rivers, and you know where to proceed after that. Then the first priority is to feed and rest the army and the animals. The battle for Suvobor will be won by the side that's slept longest, the one that's had just one hour more of sleep. Then tomorrow evening send me a detailed report about the morale of your troops. I want to know as much as possible about how the men feel, and about their will to fight. Good-by, Colonel!"

"Give me the commander of the Danube Division, first levy. Mišić speaking. Good evening! What must we remember this day for, Kajafa?"

"Anyone who survives this day won't want to talk about it, won't be able to. At any rate, I won't."

"That's just why we'll talk about it to our grandchildren, God willing. I'm listening, so talk and we can share our troubles."

"I'm ashamed to try to do that."

"There's nothing to divide us now; we're on the same level, Kajafa. Why are you whispering? Have you been wounded?"

"I don't dare speak aloud. The fact is, I feel ashamed."

"But why, for God's sake? You've done your duty honorably and heroically."

"I don't know how one commands a division heroically. But I haven't commanded it honorably—I'm still alive."

"How are things with the division at the moment?"

"I no longer have a division, sir. I have seven wretched and exhausted battalions on Rajac; that's all I know now. The other battalions are scattered over the ravines and swallowed up by the fog. It's like dough. I don't know how I'm going to get them together."

"And what's happening on Rajac?"

"Until dusk they pounded us on all sides with shrapnel and murderous shellfire from Elevation 801. They've made mincemeat of my division. Nearly two thousand soldiers have passed through the dressing station during the last three days. Then there's the dead, the prisoners of war, the deserters."

"I authorize you to make your own decision for tomorrow. Only keep me informed what you intend to do with the division."

"I don't know what to do in this fog. I have so few senior officers that I can't be sure any of my orders will be carried out. My troops are suddenly scattered. They've been hungry for two days; only those who take from others have anything to eat."

"We can't go on like this. Can you hear me, Kajafa? We can't go on like this a single day longer. If we have no ammunition to defend our freedom, or artillery to fight for our unity, our soldiers must at least have bread to survive. At least that! Please carry out my instruction of the twenty-sixth. Billet the troops in villages, then get the pots going. Cook some veal and roast some lamb; see that the men have fresh baked bread and *rakija*. I'll see that you get some tobacco, too. And they must shake the lice out of their clothes and get cleaned up."

"I didn't hear you. Are you giving orders for a withdrawal? Why have we to get cleaned up, sir?"

"I'm giving orders for the troops to get rested and refreshed for an advance. In a few days we must again rush over the crest of Suvobor. So see that the soldiers get rid of their lice. They sap a man's sleep and his pride in himself. Lice-ridden men aren't concerned about freedom or their fatherland. I'll call you tomorrow evening from Gornji Milanovac."

"Get me the Danube Division, second levy. Mišić speaking. Give me the commanding officer, please. Then send for him, I'm waiting. What are you doing tonight, Vasić?"

Vasić: "I'm quelling a riot among the staff, sir. My officers are saying that the army staff and the High Command have abandoned us on Suvobor. That even if we avoid the shells and bullets, we'll collapse from hunger in the frost. The officers at least have the possibility of dying an honorable death. A few minutes ago my orderly, a second lieutenant, shot himself in the eye—committed suicide in the clean snow. And the blizzard is still raging here."

"What do your soldiers think when the officers commit suicide?"

"Those who are still alive are in no state to think, because of fatigue and sickness and hunger. They're simply waiting for something to happen, they don't care what, to bring them release from their sufferings."

"And what is your opinion? What were you thinking of doing tomorrow, Vasić?"

"We cannot and dare not spend the night here. This is absolutely definite. We can just barely get out of this inferno tonight, but by tomorrow we won't have the strength even for that. No one will even want to save his life. A few more hours of this, and no one will be able to bother about anything."

"Oh yes they will, Vasić. A man wants to go on a bit longer—even just to see a snowflake, or give one more groan. Even death is not the end of hope, Vasić."

"There's darkness in the men's hearts. Hope and pride have been extinguished, and even hate has died."

"But you and I are commanders just because people believe that our will can outlast any defeat, and that our spirit rises above every victory. Can you hear me, Vasić?"

"What do you wish me to do tonight, sir? Please tell me!"

"Tell me something that's not a commonplace fact of war, something not apparent to everybody. The sort of thing that we can sense only when there's nothing to be seen around us."

"I am frightened, sir. There's mounting panic here; you hear it in every word. I can feel it in the overcoat I'm wearing. And that coughing from the kitchen—perhaps you can hear it?"

"Then get down from Suvobor at once and move toward Teočin and Brezna. Hadjić will explain to you the dispositions of the whole army."

The brick floor, walls, and ceiling of the café in Vrčanin smelled intolerably of *rakija*. It was here in this overheated, musty room that the staff headquarters had been established that day; at Boljkovci it had been impossible to hear oneself speak because of the gunfire from Rajac.

He left the room and went into a shed. The snow was drifting past. He told Dragutin to light a fire, so that he could watch it while he collected his thoughts.

In silence he roasted some ears of corn. The snow continued to drift in dazed, iridescent flakes. At Ravna Gora and Mujov Grob, the mountain side reverberated with gunfire. From time to time dry, blinding powder from rifles and machine guns blew in with the wind: the commander's orders of the day were coming to an end. Not his orders, or those of his commanders; it was Potiorek's men who were tramping over Suvobor, seizing the last heights in preparation for tomorrow. All the time they were looking at maps: they were conquering these maps with their black arrows, and making circles around the areas they would attack. At this very moment Field Marshal Oscar Potiorek was making a circle with the handle of his riding whip around Rajac and Suvobor on the large map hanging in his headquarters: where among the Serbian beech trees was he warming himself over a fire? With the same whip he would indicate the direction of the next day's attack.

It was all unnecessary. The next day Oscar Potiorek would fight against the mountain, the snow, the mud, the steep slopes, and the streams; he would advance in silence, for a sudden quiet would descend on Suvobor, Ravna Gora, and Rajac. Not a single gun would be fired from the Serbian First Army. Not a single soldier would be visible from Kačara to the river Dičina. It would be silent and empty. Nothing but beech trees, their trunks powdered with drifting snow, and frozen streams. Over the hillsides he would see the tracks of the Serbian columns, the marks of their footprints in the virgin snow. Next day at noon, instead of receiving reports of victories, Oscar Potiorek would read telegrams announcing that there were no Serbians on the crest of Suvobor. Such news would have confused and alarmed even Napoleon, let alone this Austrian. Yes, it certainly would have upset Napoleon; but would it have the same effect on Potiorek? Just how could one alarm and confuse him? It was no use thinking like this. An army commander must always fight first against himself; he must vanquish the man who acts as he thinks that his opponent thinks and plans to act.

A feeling of horror, and the thick, beautiful flames made him shudder; he stared into the darkness beyond the large irridescent snowflakes; some orderlies and junior staff officers were standing under the eaves of the inn, moving about and whispering among themselves, watching him roast the ears of corn and waiting for him to speak and do something. Then Dragutin brought in some firewood and put it down, gently and quietly.

"Tell me, Dragutin," he whispered, "what are the soldiers hoping for now—I mean your comrades, the orderlies and grooms, those who work with the staff?"

"What's the use of the soldiers thinking, sir? They do what they have to do, as far as they can."

"But can they still do it, Dragutin? Can they go on doing what they have to do?"

"They must."

"But how long will they be able to?"

Dragutin wrinkled his eyebrows and hunched his shoulders; holding himself rigidly in this position, he stared at the embers. Then he moved softly outside, into the darkness, and his voice sank to a whisper.

"What did he ask you?" Professor Zarija asked Dragutin.

"The wood is damp, so the fire's smoking. You can see how he's frowning," said Dragutin.

"You know, gentlemen," said Zarija, "every peasant plays the role of a sage in the presence of a townsman who isn't a tax officer, a police clerk, or a merchant—even though he's never heard of Tolstoy's Platon Karatev, and doesn't know the alphabet. But we aren't like Count Bezukov. We know each other through and through, Dragutin."

"Yes, sir, that's your business."

"How *could* they make that mistake over the caliber of the shells? After all, they know the caliber of our cannon; we bought them from France. Cannon aren't like peasants' shoes, and the French aren't illiterate. Two and a half millimeters, for God's sake! The Judases! We've paid for them in gold and blood, and they destroy our hopes by this trick. That's Europe for you! All right, why doesn't the general ask for those botched shells to be sent to the positions anyway? At least the soldiers would see them, even if they're no use. Our gunners would shove them into the cannon somehow; what does it matter to them that they're two and a half millimeters? At least the cannon would fire something; if only we could hear *our* guns going! Never mind, we'll gnaw at those two and a half millimeters with our teeth—what is that to us?"

Tola Dačić, who had not wished to return to Prerovo, was now walking around the headquarters and dressing stations of the First Army; he waited for Dragutin in the shed of the staff headquarters and spoke to him in a whisper:

"Why is the commander in such a flurry?"

"What have his worries got to do with you?"

"A great deal, let me tell you. The lives of my sons depend on his worries. What's he asking you through those whiskers of his?"

"He asked me if I would surrender to the Fritzies tonight."

"I suppose you didn't tell him?"

"I told him I'd give his Austrian opposite number a bad time!"

"Why did you say that?"

"I don't know. But that's how you have to talk to him."

"He was leaning over the fire a long time. He'll scorch his whiskers. It's not good to look at a fire such a long time."

"He's getting warm. What's better than warming yourself in a shed, with the snow drifting in?"

"People who stare at a fire and say nothing either have big accounts to settle with the Almighty, or they're planning mischief for somebody."

"And why are you hanging around the headquarters, you old fusspot?"

"I want to see how you work on the staff, and what the commander's doing in bad times like these. I have three sons in the First Army, they're all much the same age, and I've got a right to go into the headquarters and see what's going on there!"

"You'd have no right to do that if you had thirty-three sons in the First Army! Živojin Mišić isn't your hired man."

"I know better than you what he is and what he isn't. But I don't know whether he's a lucky man. What do you think? You're close to him—you can see whether he's the kind of man that things turn out well for. Do you think he's going to have luck on his side?"

"How should I know? What's that got to do with you anyway?"

"But it does concern me, young man. If he doesn't have luck on his side, then we've had it. Only a man who has more luck than strength and wisdom can master a disaster of the kind we're facing now."

But the First Army could not have done more than it had actually done, thought Mišić as he poked the fire. It had lacked the strength to maintain a single success and then exploit it the next day. Everything that had been gained one day, dearly bought with blood, had been lost the next day with even greater bloodshed. Success in one position had lost significance because of failure in another. What had been held at all costs for two days was lightly abandoned on the third day because of the general breakdown. The fall of important positions had caused the collapse of secondary ones. The army had been reduced to an unorganized mass of corpses, deserters, and traitors; it had been crucified and bled white by a fighting force of far greater strength.

Time too had disintegrated and crumbled, washed away by rains and blown apart by blizzards. Night undermined day. Then day came crushing in with the ebb of dawn. Time had become fluid like water, wandering like a stream, and finally everything had rushed into one headlong torrent directed against him. From the moment he had taken over the command of the army, nothing had been simple or lasting, neither in space nor in time, in movement nor in thought. Time and the course of events had played havoc with ideas, annihilated decisions, forcibly interrupted orders transmitted over the field telephones, and instructions in the logbook of the army staff. All his attacks had ended in defeats. He had attacked a stronger enemy; he had tried to defend more than could be defended. Was it his fault that the losses had been so heavy, that the army was now so exhausted? Where had he gone wrong, and when?

He huddled into his overcoat and poked the fire, then stared into it.

"Good evening, General," said Tola Dačić quietly. He was carrying a bag on his back with some strips of painted blue wood tied to it.

Mišić looked at him in puzzlement, then saw that it was the old man whom he had met on the highway when he took Dragutin as his orderly—the old man who had cried out, "You see, folks, he looks just like any Serbian soldier!"

"Can I get warm by your fire?" he whispered.

"Yes, come sit down. What are you going to do with those blue strips of wood?"

"They're to make crosses for my sons. Unless, God forbid, they cannot escape the fate of the last one."

"And where are your sons?"

"All three of them are in your army. The fourth was in Stepa's army, and he stayed at Cer. No sign that he even trod this earth. I wanted to ask you—I hope you won't mind—what was on your mind all evening while you were looking at the fire?"

Mišić started with an awkward movement and lifted up his cap; he had been surprised and caught in a state of fear. He leaned forward to catch the old man's whispers:

"Please don't reproach me. It's my right as a citizen. I have nothing else to give you."

"I believe you. But first take that blue wood off your back, and throw it in the fire. Go on, throw it in! Don't think the worst will happen!"

"And why should it bother you if I do? Faith has an upper limit and a lower one."

"And what do you think the lower limit is?"

"It's in your heart. You can never express it in words. I'll take my bag off if it hurts your eyes."

Mišić listened: from the darkness he could hear Dragutin playing his flute. He began to tremble.

"Sit down so we can talk."

"Tell me, General, how long can things go on like this?"

"You think we can't go on much longer?"

Tola Dačić did not reply immediately. He looked at the fire. "A man by himself can stand a lot, but the people all together can stand everything. That's how I see our misfortunes."

"Do you put your trust in God?"

"Even God can't do much for really great suffering and misfortune. It seems as though even He doesn't know quite what He's doing, and can't fix the beginning and the end of things."

"Are you saying this seriously, or just for something to say?"

"With me it's all the same. But it seems you've decided not to give in to the Fritzies?"

"I've made up my mind that we'll drive them out of Serbia, God willing. And that as soon as possible, within a few days, my man."

"And where are your children, General?"

"Two of my sons are in the army. My elder daughter is a nurse, and I have a little girl with her mother in Kragujevac."

"Are your sons officers, or ordinary soldiers?"

"They're ordinary soldiers. In the front line. Like your sons."

"Thank you. Now I believe what you say about your sons, too, and what you plan to do with the Fritzies."

Tola Dačić loosened the blue wood from his bag and threw it into the fire. He was silent for a while, until the flames caught it, then turned to Mišić and asked:

"If, God forbid, I should ever need something, may I come to you?"

"By all means."

"Now I guess you want to be alone with your worries for a while?"

"Yes, I must."

"Well, God grant that your sons may outlive you. Thank you for letting me get warm by this nice fire."

"Thank you for talking to me. And good luck!"

His eyes followed the old man as he departed. Dragutin was playing the flute. The flames leaped upward, roaring and yielding themselves to the darkness. A burst of flame, then nothing. First the wood, then the glowing embers, then ashes, then nothing. He made a pattern among the ashes with a stick. A trail among the ashes. Then nothing. To win, or to survive. All the second lieutenants know about that, or think they do: he had taught them how battles are won, and how to wage war victoriously. He knew how all the great battles in history had been won, how battles should be waged for victory. Oscar Potiorek knew this, too. Both his junior officers and mine know it. But how do you fight battles for survival? How do you win that one saving victory, a victory for one's very life? That is a battle which is not a victory, about which nothing is written in the history books, or in any other kind of learned works. A battle in which victory has no value or glory. A flame, then darkness. Ashes, then nothing.

He would tell Putnik immediately what he had decided, without a moment's delay. Let him replace him by someone else. Let him summon him before a court-martial.

He got up and hurried to the telephone.

Mišić: "I wish to inform you that I have been defending Suvobor for three days, to the point that both the fighting men and the command are completely exhausted. We've made great sacrifices to take Maljen and Suvobor, which I hoped would serve as support for an offensive."

Vojvoda Putnik: "The High Command is well aware of this. The First Army has acted according to the plan of the High Command, Mišić."

"I don't dispute that, Vojvoda. But your strategic plan is finished, played out. Its success required human strength, and the activity of the other armies, which was lacking. I assure you, I'm not thinking only of shells and artillery. The First Army has worked to the utmost limits of its strength. It is not possible for any purpose on this earth to demand greater sacrifice, or greater effort and suffering."

"So now you're asking that we give the First Army official leave. After we've given out decorations and promotions. Tell me the outcome of today's fighting, Mišić."

"The enemy is firmly established on the ridge of Suvobor. All that remains is for him to rush down toward Boljkovci by way of Prostruga, and then it's all over with the First Army. Are you listening?"

"You haven't been smitten by the faintheartedness characteristic of great optimists such as yourself?"

"I'm still an optimist, Vojvoda. I have faith, and I know why, and what I have faith in. Whereas you people in the High Command are optimists on paper and at the start, and fainthearted on the ground and at the end."

"You can discuss all that in your memoirs. But now, Mišić, please tell me why you called me. I have urgent work to see to."

"I want to explain my reasons for issuing an order to withdraw the army to positions west of Gornji Milanovac."

"What order? When did you give this order?"

"Just half an hour ago, I gave orders that at dawn tomorrow morning the army should withdraw to new positions."

"Are you crazy? Who gave you the right to gamble with the fate of the Serbian armed forces, and with Serbia itself?"

"It was my conscience that authorized me to do what I have done, Vojvoda, my sense of responsibility for Serbia and her armed forces. My convictions."

"And what about *my* convictions, and *my* sense of responsibility? And those of the other army commanders? They have no less to endure than you have. They're not fighting Viennese ladies with fans, but divisions of brave and determined villains. What's going to happen to the Second and Third Armies, after your disastrous decision?"

"It won't be any worse for them than it is today. And in a few days they'll find the situation much easier."

"And what about Belgrade? We will have to abandon Belgrade immediately. Do you realize, you optimistic fool, what the loss of the capital means to a people and their government?"

"I take no responsibility for the fact that Serbia has her capital in a place where there should be only frontier guards."

"Here is the Commander in Chief, Mišić. Please tell His Highness the Regent, Prince Alexander, what you plan to do."

Mišić: "There's nothing I wish to say to any prince. I don't wish to talk to a Russian cadet about the army command. He's fighting for his crown, and I am defending the Serbian people."

The Commander in Chief, Prince Alexander: "I can hear you very well, General, and I won't forget a single word you've said. Yes, this is the Commander in Chief, and your future King."

"You'll be King only if I save the First Army!"

"You won't be able to save anything by your pigheadedness. It's your job to do your duty and submit yourself to my command."

"Only within the limits of my conscience."

"Within the terms of your oath, Mišić!"

"Within the limits of my convictions as a commander, Your Highness!"

"I order you to carry out the instructions of the High Command. You are not to retreat one single step!"

"Only emperors can issue such commands. I will neither accept nor issue them."

"The command to retreat must no longer be given in the Serbian army. Otherwise Serbia is finished. Do you understand what I have said?"

"Serbia will be finished only when her commanders lose their wits, and her soldiers no longer have faith."

"I have spoken my last word."

"Then I will no longer command the First Army, and I do not wish to carry out your instructions. That is my last word. What was that you said, Your Highness?"

Putnik: "Putnik speaking. Hello, Mišić! Hello! Did a hornet sting you on Suvobor, that you've got such a swelled head? You are talking nonsense, Mišić! Nonsense! Only you are capable of saving the Serbian armed forces? And only you have been called to that task? Is that what you're saying? And what about the rest of us? We are just twiddling our thumbs, I suppose!"

"Either you accept my decisions, or I'll hand in my resignation immediately. I'll resign, do you hear? Hello! Don't cut us off! Can you hear me, Vojvoda?"

"Now listen, Mišić. The two of us can't challenge each other to a duel because of curses and insults. Let the clerks and operators talk about how Putnik and Mišić are just like their baggage men when it comes to using the Serbian language. We dare not be annoyed or offended by anything tonight. Vanity and other feelings of that kind belong to peacetime."

"All kinds of feelings belong to war!"

"Let's leave this luxury for after the victory. Now let's take one more look at what you intend to do. Let's look at it calmly, as if we were considering the strategy of Frederick the Great. Otherwise we'll find ourselves rubbing down the horse of some Austrian sergeant. Are you listening, Mišić?"

"Yes, I'm listening. Go on."

"If the First Army does not go on defending the watershed between the Kolubara and the western Morava, the following consequences are inevitable: the Second and Third Armies and the Obrenovac Brigade will have to retreat, since they won't be able to defend their thin, extended flanks. If—as would be unavoidable—the Užice Brigade is pushed towards Čačak, then, I repeat, Belgrade will have to be abandoned. The fall of Belgrade will threaten the front throughout the Danube basin and lead to the encirclement of the Great Morava valley from the eastern side, where the Bulgarians are likely to attack at any moment. Yes, I said the Bulgarians. And then, Mišić, what if Potiorek presses you harder, and pushes you from the slopes of Suvobor and Rudnik toward Kragujevac? Will we be able to hold Kragujevac, with the Austrians in Čačak? And how much of Serbia will we be able to defend, when there are armies massing around Kragujevac? Be logical, for God's sake!"

"All these strategical theories of yours are precise and logical. If anyone answered differently in an examination, I wouldn't appoint him to the General Staff."

"Then what is the problem?"

"It's the strategy of maps and staff officers, and of history books. But we've got to act differently here and now, on Suvobor. We can act only once; there can be no repetition, no learning from past mistakes. Can you hear me?"

"Go on."

"The First Army is not in a position to make a choice of strategic theories. It simply must abandon the Suvobor watershed. It must avoid the blow which would fall tomorrow, because it would be absolutely unable to withstand it. You must grasp this and have confidence in what I say: I am here in the lines, and know the state of the troops and the general circumstances better than you and the entire High Command!"

"And what about Potiorek? What do you think he's going to do?"

"I don't think Potiorek will be able to dislodge me from the new positions. He won't be able to do much at all. Suvobor will break him."

"But battles and indeed a war can be lost even with the deepest convictions, and the best knowledge of one's troops and one's situation in general, Mišić."

"Battles are won by the man who has his own overruling idea, and who can dominate space and time—a man who never loses the initiative. That was my answer to you when I took my examinations. Tomorrow Potiorek won't know what I want to do, and what I can do, I can assure you of that. If he can remember anything at all from military history, he'll be in a state of confusion because he won't know what is happening. Are you listening?"

"Yes, go on."

"Let our soldiers not see the Austrians, or hear them either, for at least twenty-four hours! Let them have a proper night's sleep in peace and quiet, a good meal, get warm, and restore their energy. Then they'll be able to run uphill!"

"But I want more *facts*, Mišić."

"I give my solemn oath that victory will go now to the side that is less hungry, sleeps longer, can run up faster to the hilltops, keep on marching for more hours, and remain longer in the snow."

"I'm listening. Have you any further facts?"

"The side that has faith in its commander, and believes that he's looking after his men and is concerned about them. It's the soldiers not in a state of despair who'll hold their own and come out on top. Those who can sing a bit and make jokes, and take a look at a woman. It's our duty to make these things possible for our soldiers. Can you hear me, Vojvoda?"

"Yes, go on. I'm listening carefully."

"I have one more thing to say: victory will go to the side which has the stronger positions for attack, the one which is more densely concentrated and has less to defend. The side that is ready to attack decisively, and as quickly as possible. And that's going to be the First Army."

"So these are the facts on which you've based your fateful decision?"

"I haven't made this decision solely on the basis of facts."

"Then on what else, General?"

"On unseen factors, Vojvoda—factors involving faith and risk."

"But what are we going to do if Potiorek forces you to retreat, as he has done on Suvobor and Gukoš? Did you hear me?"

"If he does force me to do that—which I by no means believe that he will—if through some unforeseen circumstances he compels me to withdraw, he still can't force me to flee toward Kragujevac. On the contrary, I shall remain on the defensive long enough to allow the other armies in turn to withdraw to a new defense line."

"That is a risk which could be followed by surrender—a very great risk, Mišić. Only military leaders who set their own aims above those of their people and their state have the right to take such risks. Those who are commanding a foreign army in a foreign land."

"It's only by taking risks that a commander can affirm his wisdom and power."

"That wisdom is for the birds. You are overlooking one essential factor. How would this sudden withdrawal of the First Army affect the vacillating and indeed shattered morale of the entire Serbian armed forces? Evidently it hasn't occurred to you that in twenty-four hours all three armies could crack up, nor have you thought about how your decision will be received by the other army commanders. Mišić, it's still not too late, you must countermand your instructions for withdrawal."

"I cannot do that. I can't, and I won't. I've told you what I'm able to say now."

"And I have told you what it's my duty to tell you."

"Then please accept my resignation from the command of the First Army."

"Is your resignation really an argument in favor of withdrawal?"

"My resignation is my last means of affirming my responsibility as a commander in the eyes of the troops and the High Command. I can do nothing further."

"You're blackmailing me tonight, Mišić. Blackmailing me without mercy. You're tendering your resignation because you're sure I don't dare accept it."

"You know me well enough to know that I don't resort to blackmail, and still less to blackmail of my fatherland. My resignation would mean withdrawing my oath. Can you hear me?"

"I require you to submit with the utmost speed a written statement of your decision to withdraw the First Army from the Suvobor watershed. I'm waiting for it!"

Mišić: "Give me Vojvoda Putnik, please! I have decided to carry out your order. I'll read to you a written statement concerning my decision to withdraw the First Army to the positions Nakučani-Takovo-Semedrež."

Putnik: "You're surely not going to withdraw all the way to Semedrež from the Suvobor ridge? Why, that's near Čačak!"

"I intend to withdraw all the way to Semedrež because a halt near Suvobor would have no tactical advantage. Only by a deep withdrawal can I achieve my aim, Vojvoda!"

"Do you see any sense in withdrawing close to Čačak and the approaches to the Morava? Is it an original idea?"

"Yes, Vojvoda, it is. Only by having ideas which the enemy cannot foresee can we avoid losing the war, since we're unequally matched in all other known factors. Can you hear me?"

"Yes, I'm listening. Just a minute, will you repeat those positions near the Morava? Yes, go on, please. Is that all?"

"That is what I've written down. If my opinion is not accepted, then I'll take no responsibility for the consequences. Did you hear what I said, Vojvoda? I'm asking if you heard me? Hello! Hello! Who's cut us off? Would you please connect me; I want to speak to the head of the High Command. Hello! The High Command, please! Why doesn't someone answer? Hello! Why doesn't he answer? I want to speak to Vojvoda Putnik. How is it that he doesn't answer? Why? He doesn't want to come to the phone? The stupid old wheezer!"

Živko Pavlović, Vojvoda Putnik's assistant: "I want to speak to the commander of the First Army."

Mišić: "And what more do you want from me?"

"I wish to inform you that Vojvoda Putnik has approved the withdrawal of the First Army to positions northwest of Gornji Milanovac. But your line on the left wing is changed. Your liaison with Užice Brigade is poor. In a short time I'll tell you of the alteration required by the High Command."

"Long live the High Command!"

At night the Austrians came up quietly and entrenched themselves about a hundred paces from the trenches of Bora Jackpot and Danilo History-Book's platoon; they entrenched themselves at the other end of the clearing, at the edge of the forest, just as the Serbians had done. In the dark night made turgid by the fog, Bora felt that there was something furtive and senseless in this sneaking, stealthy movement of the soldiers, this secretive digging of trenches, and he did not allow his squad to fire a single bullet. Danilo had suggested they should charge, and quarreled with Bora over this, but the platoon commander had not considered his proposal a sensible one; for if they came out of the trenches, the platoon would be scattered—the platoon which was supposed to form the rear guard of the regiment, perhaps even of the division, in the large-scale withdrawal scheduled to begin at dawn.

"What's this about a withdrawal? How far are we going to withdraw?" asked Danilo rebelliously, trying to relieve his feelings.

"I don't know; no point in asking me. At dawn our whole army is going to withdraw from the mountains," answered Second Lieutenant Zakić, sipping hot tea in the darkness behind the trenches.

"That's good strategy. General Mišić is an expert at having large masses of men floundering about," said Bora, speaking a little more quietly. Then he jumped into the trench next to the biggest fire and dozed off beside it while listening to the soldiers talking about the frost.

As soon as there was enough light to see a few paces ahead through the icy mist, and to distinguish between a man and a beech tree, Second Lieutenant Zakić emerged out of the forest and summoned Bora and Danilo:

"The regimental commander has given orders that at least two Austrians be brought to him by noon at the latest. Officers, if possible. If we send soldiers out on that job, they won't come back." He looked first at one, then at the other.

Bora was amused at the way the lieutenant's words dissolved in the warmth of his breath, as though the frost was pouring them out, then annihilating them. It simply didn't enter Bora's head to play hide and seek with the Austrians in this frost and fog, and hunt men as though they were animals. Danilo thought to himself: is this a chance to perform a heroic deed, or just a stupid, risky adventure? People were getting killed—Saša Molecule had been seriously wounded the previous day—yet here they were acting as some sort of reserve, meandering about the mountain to the rear of the big battles, pursued by artillery, retreating after a few rounds of machine-gun fire, never going into a real battle or taking part in an assault or counterassault. If they didn't engage in real battle today, before this withdrawal from the mountain, tomorrow he would be a coward.

"There's a chance to win a medal, Corporals."

"Also a chance to avoid being frozen stiff, sir. I'll take three soldiers and go out hunting," said Danilo decisively.

Bora saw on his face a pallor not due to the whiteness of the frost. Looking at Danilo, he said:

"For hunting these sophisticated Germans, I'd take experienced hunters: Corporal Zdravko, Paun, and that Damnjan who can't even hear his own footsteps when he walks."

"No, I'll take Paun and two others."

"Then get going at once," said the lieutenant. "Keep to the left, alongside the stream. Only pick out one of the officers. And don't manhandle him; please behave like gentlemen!" The lieutenant then plunged back into the forest and the mist.

"A very refined way of giving an order! Now I'd like to hear someone saying that we're an army of peasants!" said Bora caustically. He was frightened for Danilo, who, without a word, but with a long, warning look, moved off into the mist and crunched through the silence and the frozen snow.

Bora returned slowly to his place in the trench, trying to make as little noise as possible as he broke the film of ice; he remembered that a few nights ago Danilo had given him his little colored wooden horse to give to Bora's son. How pointless it all was!

The frost compelled both armies to come out of their trenches, which they did at the same time. The Serbians did not realize that the sniffing and coughing, and the crunching of the snow under the feet of men firing their rifles, did not come only from them. It was the Austrians who first realized the difference between their own heavy movements in their boots, and the lighter tread of the Serbians, most of whom were wearing peasant shoes; it was even easier to distinguish the sniffing and coughing of the Serbians, louder and deeper than their own; in alarm, they opened fire. The Serbians, surprised and frightened, dropped back into their trenches and answered with a rapid volley.

Bora Jackpot tried hard to believe that this was the great, fateful battle that so much obsessed Danilo. But there was no real military reason for it, there was no hatred. Fear and anger had come into collision. The motivation was psychological, a matter of character. Habit and inertia. It was men—not soldiers—fighting. He began to fire into the fog: that's how he would begin, by killing the fog and the hoarfrost. He raised the barrel of his rifle a little, so that the bullet would hit the forest; he wanted the hoarfrost to fall from his bullet. He turned around toward the forest: Austrian bullets were peppering the undergrowth and scattering the hoarfrost. It was beautiful in a way. There was a buzzing, hissing sound over his head. His forehead was above the surface of the snow; he arched his back and fired. This bullet whistled above the tops of the beech trees, white in the darkness.

The firing suddenly stopped. Bora did not know who stopped first; perhaps both sides stopped at the same time. Obviously the great, decisive battle had not taken place. There was no reason why it should. He stared into the fog, then peeped above the snow-covered rim of the trench. There was a sharp smell of gunpowder; his nostrils were crackling. His ears, nose, toes, and fingers ached from the frost as though gripped by pincers; his bones were beginning to crack. He walked along the trench to see what damage the firing had done. The soldiers looked comical, with hoarfrost on their eyebrows and mustaches; they didn't look like soldiers. If a bullet hit one of these soldiers now, it would cause the death of a frozen, helpless, wretched man, not a Serb, an enemy of Austria-Hungary and Germany. Speaking in a whisper, he warned them not to cough. They pulled their caps over their ears, and crouching down in the trench, coughed in spurts. The hoarfrost dripped down from the trees in the silence. It was as though he could hear the streaming, whirling movement of the fog. He came back from the middle of the trench still more quietly, holding his breath, and returned to his own place.

From some distance away, the Austrians began to sniff in the fog; they stifled their coughing after someone warned them with a threatening hiss. Who is my opposite number on the other side of the clearing, and what does he look like? But he's more afraid than I am! He's cruder, and hates me more than I hate him. He's ambitious; he's in the war to get promotion and a medal, the poor bastard! Now if we were men of honor, like the knights and real heroes of the good old days, instead of nationalists in this modern age of machines and airplanes, we'd agree not to shoot at this coughing and sniffing. It's not honorable to take advantage of unfavorable natural conditions, and to kill the opponents of one's King and country with the help of the frost—to kill sick men who are coughing and sniffing.

The effort to make no noise did not last long: the frost compelled them to move about, and made their teeth chatter; they opened their bags and chewed frozen hardtack and ate onions. Beyond him in the fog, Bora could hear the light thumping of mess kits; so *they* were having breakfast, too, but eating with spoons. They were subjects of a wealthy empire. Conquerors! But now a sense of equality and solidarity was being established. Fine! The Serbians were chewing normally and sniffing normally, though their coughing was somewhat subdued, in accordance with the strength of their nation and their army. The Austrians were conversing quietly as they ate their breakfast; that was the right of the stronger, the privilege of the victor. It was a pity Danilo wasn't here to listen to the two armies eating, so he could see what they were really like now, and understand that they were acting as they did through faith in their common humanity, a humanity going beyond hatred and deeper than fear: a humanity that surpassed flags, badges, and uniforms. This discovery excited him. There was hope. Or just folly, traditional stupidity. Perhaps that was it.

He came out of the trench and walked beside his squad's trenches, between the two armies breakfasting in the snow on the mountain; between two masses of frozen, sleepless, hungry men, eating what their governments decided they should eat while at war. Now that would really be heroic, if they were to share their breakfast and eat together on this white clearing, then take leave of one another like ordinary human beings and go back to their trenches and their job. He walked freely over the frozen snow, dotted here and there with cartridge cases, and cracked the film of ice. The Austrians must certainly hear him. Well, let them realize that he had some faith in them. His soldiers looked at him in amazement. They stopped chewing, and their movements became more subdued. They could not believe their eyes. He continued walking back and forth on the crisp snow, torn between two fears. He was not afraid for himself—indeed not, mother dear, the only mother in the world! I'm only afraid that some bastard, some idiot, will kill this hope, this trust, this human solidarity in a time of suffering in the bitter winter. Then the war will be lost for both sides, for everybody, and forever. What folly! Where was Danilo now? Bora sniffed, coughed, and began to walk normally. The fog rolled across the clearing, from the direction of the Austrians. The soldiers looked at him in alarm.

"Are you drunk or crazy, Corporal?" whispered one of them from the trench.

Bora smiled in response, though he could not see the man in the fog. I know that game played for gain, for filthy lucre, he thought. But this is something different, men. The sniffing and coughing spread through the trench; he could hear sounds of disturbance from the Austrian trenches, too. One of the Serbians suddenly stopped coughing, struck dumb by fear. Bora stopped and listened; all was quiet except for the sound of labored breathing in the frost, the fog streaming through the mountain pines and the scrub, and the rustling of the hoarfrost as it fell in the forest. He could not stand the silence; he fell prostrate on the snow in front of the trenches; his heart was pounding. Helpless, he waited for a machine gun, a grenade, a shot. The waiting grated in his ears. He strained his eyes into the fog, toward the Austrians, unable to tear himself away. He had no idea how long this lasted.

Then he turned around toward his own soldiers; they were standing motionless, staring into the fog, their rifles cocked. A shot rent the silence of Suvobor. Bora's body went limp and he could see nothing. From the other side a rifle answered; the bullet whistled sharply.

"Who fired that gun? Why did you fire? You mustn't fire!" he cried.

The soldiers said nothing, gripping their rifles and clinging to the snow-covered edge of the trench.

Once more silence spread through the fog between the two armies. Bora got up; his knees were trembling. He stood still, unable to take a step forward. Now really frightened, he was testing human solidarity here in the frost; if he was killed, it would be a man that killed him, not an Austrian; he would shoot not in the name of Austria-Hungary and Franz Josef, but in his own name and for his own sake. It would be the criminal in man firing at the naiveté and folly in man. If he was killed now, it would please the pessimists: his death would prove that war was older than men and would outlast them. His soldiers waved to him to come lie down in the trench; they whispered and threatened. But he would not.

"Don't be afraid," he said in his usual voice. How stupid! He should say something quite different, but they wouldn't understand him. "No, I won't!" he said, expressing obstinacy in both his voice and his eyes. That was something they must understand and approve of. One leg sank a bit deeper in the snow, but he was still standing, carried away by temptation, uncertainty, gambling on everything. Yet he felt no fear. Let them kill me if they wish; but I want to make sure that they're bastards, criminals. He answered his soldiers with his eyes, feeling as though he was floating away in the fog, as though it was bearing him away like a wisp. His chattering teeth were floating away, too, and the frost stopped his very breathing. Can they see me? To them I'm nothing but a wisp of fog, floating in the fog. If my soldiers are again the first to open fire, if they cannot restrain themselves, then there is no hope for humanity: while we exist, we will kill each other; we will even kill each other after death. He felt that a puff of wind would knock him over. He was done for, if the wind blew.

"Stop being a fool, Corporal! They'll put a hole in you as if you were a bag!"

These words made him fall flat in the snow, and rolled him into the trench.

The Austrians opened fire, first with a machine gun and then with rifles, shattering the impenetrable mist. The Serbians, who had no machine gun, returned the fire with their rifles, but with a rapid volley.

Bora pulled himself together and began to fire in the direction of the shooting, toward the people who had not maintained the solidarity; he fired at them because their fear was greater than their humanity and reason. He looked sadly down his own trench: the soldiers whom he could see looked grave, or else just as they usually did; their movements were free and businesslike, and they sniffed loudly and coughed with all their might. The firing slackened more and more— from fatigue, perhaps, or common sense or cunning? The Austrians also fired at longer intervals. Perhaps they could all see there was no sense in it. Only a few rifles were firing from both trenches, then only two.

Bora walked down the trench to see which of his soldiers were still firing and to ask them why. Anyway, they were absolute cowards! Now there was only one rifle firing from each side. They could be clearly distinguished by their sound: the Austrian one had a double sound, as though emphasizing the hyphen in the name of the mighty empire. By the time he reached the end of the trench, even that last rifle was silent.

Suddenly it was quiet in the trench once more: the men moved about with little steps, coughed in their caps, restrained their sniffing. Moving as inconspicuously as possible through the narrow trench, Bora returned to his own place, walking on tiptoe so as to make little noise; then he stared into the fog, the quietness, the unknown. The frost gripped his fingers and the joints in his arms and legs, and cut at the soles of his feet, his ears, his nose. What had happened to Danilo? He had an uncontrollable desire to smoke. After that game of poker in Boljkovci, he had sworn that he would not light another cigarette while the war lasted. But now he felt he must have one. What did the pledged word, the oath, the vow mean now? People were getting killed. Or they were sleeping. The soldier next to him had smoked one cigarette after another the previous night, as though his bag was full of them; he would ask him for one.

"Say, pal, would you give me a cigarette? I'll pay you back," he said, poking the soldier who was now sleeping with his head reclining, settled well down in the trench, while his gun lay in the snow on the edge.

He fell over, revealing a jet of frozen blood on his face and a bullet hole in his forehead.

Bora gave a start: "This man's been killed!"

"So it seems," whispered another soldier, hopping about as his teeth chattered.

"When did it happen?" Bora asked aloud.

"It makes no difference, Corporal. At least he isn't cold any more."

Out there in the fog one of the Austrians also said something in a loud voice.

"Take him away." Bora shouted.

"Where can I take him? Anyway, we'll be getting out of here in a few hours. This trench can be his grave; let him rest here."

Bora clung to the snow-covered edge of the trench, staring into the fog and gripping the butt of his rifle. Out there the Austrian was saying something, speaking sternly, but in a muffled voice. The soldier Bora had been talking to nudged him, and offered him a cigarette.

Bora took the cigarette, lit it, and climbed out of the trench. He smoked as he walked beside the beech and fir trees, and fired his rifle provocatively at the frozen snow. The soldiers turned toward him in amazement; some of them smiled. He understood them. If he had started shooting, he would not now jump back into the trench. The cigarette was distasteful to him, but he would not throw it away. He stopped and listened intently: over there in the fog one of the Austrians, probably an officer like himself, was pacing slowly on the frozen snow. Had one of his men been killed, too? How disgusting! Why should I want someone over there to be killed, too? What good would it do Serbia, my fatherland, that a man wearing the Austrian uniform should be killed in this shooting match which was triggered in the basest and stupidest manner? He continued pacing up and down.

The soldiers came out of the trench in proportion to their courage, indifference, and shivering; the bravest and least prudent walked about near the beech trees, while the more cautious and timid fired from the trench. No one spoke a word.

Bora leaned against a beech tree and listened to *them,* over there in the fog; he could hear the reverberation of their heavy, crunching footsteps and their shooting. On their side too, not a word was spoken; they simply sniffed and coughed like the Serbians. So again we can see to what extent we're all just people—that is, in this situation, how damn cold we are. What can have happened to Danilo? We should have agreed that our oath is not valid in cases of reconnaissance and hunting for prisoners. But that guy certainly led us all by the nose! Which one of us in the barracks at Skoplje would have said that Danilo Protić wasn't nuts on history at all, but just a sentimental, lovesick guy with the prettiest little wooden horse in Bačka? A passionate lover who's suffering because his girl friend left him, and dreaming of fulfilling his promise to his grandfather that he would come back riding a white horse through the geese and the mulberry trees.

"What are you jumping about for? Get back into the trenches!" shouted Second Lieutenant Zakić, the platoon commander, from the mist-laden forest.

"Please sir, the men will be frozen stiff," said Bora, but the silence drove him back into the trench, where the soldiers were already descending.

From deep in the fog and the forest, there came the sound of a bugle.

"Fix bayonets!" ordered Zakić.

The Austrian machine gun sprinkled the fog and the forest; the rifles kept it company.

"Don't shoot until you can see them!" cried Zakić.

Bora stared into the fog: surely those despairing men were not going to charge? How could one use a bayonet on a frozen fellow creature? He looked at the dead soldier: he had stiffened and was now a rigid corpse. At least he didn't smell.

The Austrians stopped firing: had they been shooting in order to warm themselves up a bit, or had they stopped because they were cold? Silence reigned once more. The hoarfrost rustled in the fog; the soldiers sniffed and coughed louder and louder. And those men over there in the fog were coughing and sniffing, too. Who would come out of the trenches first? Who had the greatest trust in his fellow man, who felt less fear, who was the biggest fool?

From over there in the fog came the sound of boots stamping on the ground and crunching snow. Loud coughing. Feet moving quickly, close together, as though making a charge or dancing the kolo. They're braver than we are. They believe that we're human beings. Or do they despise us and think we're cowards? A lot of questions for one answer; many points of view, but only one solution. As long as none of the Serbians fires; if only we don't show ourselves to be crude bastards—swine!

"Don't shoot until I give the order!" Bora said, speaking loudly so that the men at the end of the trench could hear.

The Austrians heard him, too: there was a sudden silence. Behind them, all was quiet; a blackbird chirped in the fog. The chirping of the blackbird taunted the silence: the hoarfrost fell from the trees, the sound of breathing in the trench became more concentrated. The bird's chirping became shorter and quieter, and finally ceased. The silence had destroyed it. One of the Serbians fired—he couldn't stand it any longer! The sound of the shot reverberated through the entire mountain, the whole country, the Galaxy, to death itself.

"Idiot! Swine! Why are you shooting?" shouted Bora angrily.

The Austrians rushed back into their trenches. So they've lost faith in our having any sense: now they're convinced that we're cowards and bastards. It's stupid to rely on intelligence and virtue. War is eternal. Bora leaped out of the trench and moved about on the spot. With small steps. The very silence froze and became rigid. The fog pressed down upon him, suffocating him; it crept under his overcoat, seeped through to his skin, under his shirt, penetrated to his bones, and streamed through his veins: thick, damp, gray, and freezing. Some-where nearby the blackbird chirped. He listened to it, expectantly, longingly. How did it get food? It must peck at cartridge cases and bullets. Then he heard it no more. The bullets, the fog, the silence had engulfed it.

To the left a bullet whistled past, high up; behind him someone fired. Now it was some wretched Austrian who couldn't restrain him-self. But he wouldn't go back into the trench until the machine gun started in. There was silence again, the same sort of silence. Over there in the fog, the sniffing, coughing, and stamping of feet grew louder. The Serbians too began to come out of the trench, sniffing, blowing on their hands, moving around. If the grip of the frost became harder, and the fog denser, there would be an armistice. And when the Ice Age began, there would be peace. Perhaps. Some sort of vague sadness, indeterminate like the mist, drove him back into the trench. He sat down and curled up on his little pile of fern leaves beside the rigid corpse of the soldier. Had the blood frozen in his veins? Red ice. Perhaps his heart was already frozen, too. A frozen pear of red ice.

Danilo History-Book jumped into the trench; Bora was frightened, and unable to show his pleasure at seeing him.

"How can you sit beside a dead man?" asked Danilo.

"He's frozen stiff."

Danilo turned his back toward the dead soldier, crouched down, and lit a cigarette.

"What did you manage to do?" whispered Bora.

"It was awful. We caught two of them shitting. Hungarians. One of them sat down in his filth, when Paun lunged his bayonet from behind a beech tree. He smelled so horribly when we were bringing him in that I couldn't take it. And suddenly I felt so wretched and ashamed that I couldn't speak a word of Hungarian."

"Anyway, you've certainly earned a medal."

Danilo smoked in silence. Bora took the cigarette from his lips, took two puffs, then returned it. A bugle sounded.

"What's going to happen now?" whispered Danilo.

"Nothing special. A charge, perhaps. The game continues," said Bora, almost indifferently.

TO PAŠIĆ, PREMIER OF THE ROYAL GOVERNMENT OF SERBIA, NIŠ:
SAZONOV AGAIN EXERTING PRESSURE STOP ONLY IF WE GIVE BULGARIA MACEDONIA ACCORDING TO 1912 AGREEMENT RUSSIA WILL GUARANTEE NOT ONLY BULGARIAN NEUTRALITY BUT HER IMMEDIATE ENTRY INTO

THE WAR STOP RUSSIAN GOVERNMENT REQUIRES THAT SERBIA AUTHORIZE
CONDITIONAL PROMISE OF MACEDONIA TO BULGARIA STOP SPALAJKOVIĆ
ST. PETERSBURG

TO SPALAJKOVIĆ, MINISTER OF THE KINGDOM OF SERBIA TO ST. PETERS-
BURG:
PLEASE GIVE MY MESSAGE TO SAZONOV PERSONALLY STOP BULGARIA MUST
NOT BE REWARDED WITH SERBIAN TERRITORY HAVING BEEN PROVED A
TRAITOR TO THE SLAV CAUSE STOP MOTHER RUSSIA SHOULD NOT BREAK
SERBIA WHEN SHE IS FIGHTING WITH HER VERY SOUL STOP REWARD OF
BETRAYAL CAN NEVER BE JUSTIFIED WHEN SERBIA IS AT HER LAST GASP IN
HER STRUGGLE FOR FAITH RUSSIA AND SLAV UNITY STOP PAŠIĆ NIŠ

TO PAŠIĆ, PREMIER OF THE ROYAL GOVERNMENT OF SERBIA NIŠ:
YESTERDAY SAZONOV INFORMED ME THAT FOR MILITARY REASONS RUSSIA
CANNOT SEND US ONE CORPS AS SHE IS FIGHTING ON THREE FRONTS STOP
THERE IS NOW A DECISIVE ENCOUNTER BETWEEN HER AND GERMANY STOP
RUSSIA FEELS THE GREATEST DISGUST FOR RUMANIA STOP BEGS YOU NOT TO
LET THE ARMY LOSE HEART STOP THE END OF OUR SUFFERING IS NEAR STOP
IMPORTANT AND DECISIVE VICTORY IS SURE STOP SPALAJKOVIĆ ST.
PETERSBURG

TO BOJOVIĆ, MILITARY ATTACHE OF THE SERBIAN HIGH COMMAND TO
LONDON:
BUY SHELLS IN AMERICA STOP BEG FOR THEM AND PAY WHATEVER THEY
ASK STOP PAŠIĆ NIŠ

TO PAŠIĆ, PREMIER OF THE ROYAL GOVERNMENT OF SERBIA, NIŠ:
NOT EVEN THE SMALLEST QUANTITY OF AMMUNITION AVAILABLE FROM
AMERICA STOP EXPORT FORBIDDEN STOP BOJOVIĆ LONDON

TO SPALAJKOVIĆ, MINISTER OF THE KINGDOM OF SERBIA TO ST.
PETERSBURG:
PLEASE AGAIN IMPLORE THE CZAR OUR SAVIOR STOP AND SAY AGAIN THAT
SERBIA IS AT DEATH'S DOOR STOP PAŠIĆ NIŠ

TO PAŠIĆ, PREMIER OF THE ROYAL GOVERNMENT OF SERBIA, NIŠ:
GRAND DUKE NIKOLAI NIKOLAEVIĆ IN HIS CAPACITY AS COMMANDER IN
CHIEF OF RUSSIAN ARMED FORCES INSISTENTLY REQUIRES SERBIA TO
STRENGTHEN RESISTANCE TO AUSTRIA AND IMMEDIATELY SURRENDER

MACEDONIA TO BULGARIA SINCE IT IS SERBIA'S DEFENSE LED TO THE WAR AND THE PRESENT CRISIS STOP SPALAJKOVIĆ ST. PETERSBURG

TO SPALAJKOVIĆ, MINISTER OF THE KINGDOM OF SERBIA TO ST. PETERSBURG: IF THE RUSSIAN GENERAL STAFF ARE COUNTING ON SERBIA AND BULGARIA FIGHTING TOGETHER AGAINST AUSTRIA THEN YOU MUST TELL RUSSIA BLUNTLY THAT THIS CO-OPERATION IN WAR IS QUITE IMPOSSIBLE STOP SUCH AN ALLIANCE AT THE PRICE OF OUR SURRENDERING MACEDONIA WOULD END IN OUR MUTUAL EXTERMINATION BEFORE THE EYES OF THE ENEMY STOP BULGARIA CAN BE USED ONLY AGAINST TURKEY STOP SO LET HER HAVE PART OF THRACE IN RETURN FOR THIS SMALL SERVICE AND SOME OF OUR TERRITORY UP TO THE VARDAR STOP THAT IS IN PROPORTION TO HER ROLE AND IMPORTANCE STOP PAŠIĆ NIŠ

5

The great withdrawal of the First Army began at the crack of dawn. A front thirty kilometers long hurriedly broke up, then reformed into irregular columns which poured down the rocks and slopes of Ravna Gora, Rajac, and Suvobor toward their new positions. All this took place in the half-light, quietly and despondently: the pain of numerous and constant defeats had hardened in the hearts of the soldiers, and they were weighted down with the uncertainty as to how long this retreating could go on. And what then? But down below, at the foot of the mountain were warm houses, bread, dry socks; also old men with tobacco, and women ready to speak human words and anxious to do things that only they could do. Meanwhile the Sixth Austro-Hungarian Army did not fire a single shot at the First Serbian Army, which had left only a few platoons on the crest of Suvobor, not so much to defend it as to show that the army still existed.

In the retreating columns of the First Army only the baggage men in their carts raised their voices; they shouted and beat their horses and oxen even more fiercely than usual. Only one song was heard in Serbia that dawn of November 29, 1914, and only one flute was played: the flute of Tola Dačić. The soldiers could not believe their ears. Yes, Tola Dačić was following the carts of the wounded and playing all the time. The baggage men shouted at him and threatened him with their bundles of sticks; the lightly wounded cursed him; but the seriously wounded begged him to play. And Doctor Kustudić, who was riding sometimes in front of the oxcarts full of wounded and sometimes at the rear, shouted at the top of his lungs:

"Go on playing, man! Go on playing!"

He was slithering down the icy slopes of Rajac, stumbling over the bumps in the dim light of dawn, playing his flute to the accompaniment of the heaving, grinding, and rattling of an oxcart, playing whatever came into his head; he mixed up bits of songs and dances, interweaving them with one another, and never finished any of them. Suddenly everything was confused in his head: Serbia was being broken to pieces, sliding into an abyss. Whoever was master of the mountains was master of Serbia; but she could not be defended in the plain between the Morava rivers. He would personally tell Živojin Mišić that, and ask him what he had in mind.

As soon as it was fully light, and the column of wounded halted in front of Gornji Milanovac, he thrust his flute into his empty bag and disappeared down the road to town; he was going to seek out the army headquarters and General Mišić.

Riding slowly along the frozen, bumpy path, Mišić and his staff reached the slope above Gornji Milanovac at dawn. He tightened the reins and slackened his pace even more, feeling a sudden desire to pause for a moment. A mist hung low over the little town, which he knew was crammed with refugees, wounded, and supplies.

He saluted everyone whom he met on the road or caught sight of in the yards; no one except the soldiers returned his greeting. A shudder ran through him when he encountered the look of mute fear and apprehension in the eyes of all those he met as he went down the lane toward the largest building in the center of the town. After they had passed by, a feeling of uneasiness surged up along the road, in the yards filled with carts of refugees, and among the women and children at the doors and windows.

He halted in front of the large two-story building of the district town hall; he refused Dragutin's help to dismount, and quickly escaped from the eyes of the refugees and local people into a cold, empty corridor, leaving his officers and team of horses in front of the entrance. The officers were at once surrounded by civilians who wanted to find out what was happening: up on the mountains all was silent; but why were General Mišić and his staff coming into Gornji Milanovac? A guard was interposed to ward off the prominent citizens who were trying to push their way into the headquarters to see the general.

Spasić, Mišić's adjutant, took him to a well-heated room on the first floor, with windows looking out onto Rudnik and Vujan. He told the chief of staff that not a single report was to be brought to him until the next morning, and no one was to be allowed to see him; he was to be called to the telephone only to speak to Vojvoda Putnik. The soldiers carried a cast-iron army cot and a pile of beechwood into his office, while Dragutin brought a bag of apples. He took off his boots and walked about the large room, then lay on his bed and ate an apple.

He stared at the ceiling: what was the utmost Field Marshal Oscar Potiorek could do, the utmost he would dare to do, now that the First Army had come down from the Kolubara watershed to the foot of the mountain? If he was waging war by force alone, he would most probably act as Vojvoda Putnik had foreseen. But if in addition to his seven corps Potiorek also had nine strategic theories, it was possible that he would not choose the line of action which his opponents most feared. History shows that few great battles have been decided only in accordance with the logical decisions made by commanders. Victory goes to the commander who can feel and see those things which his opponent does not take into account, if that opponent thinks and acts only logically at all times.

As he reflected about this commander who would not fight as he would have fought against the Serbian army if he were in that commander's shoes, but who was out to break him and vanquish him, he struggled to perceive the nature of this opponent. He would like to have known where he was born, what sort of person his mother was, whether his wife loved him, and whether he had children. A man who has had a gentle and tender mother, who has grown up with a good grandmother and a just grandfather, cannot kill innocent and vanquished people even in war, even in a foreign land. Is that really so? Who knows what a man is *not* like who is in command of armies, and who in wartime has the right to give any kind of order? When they had talked together just before they parted, in front of his wife and children, Vukašin Katić had challenged this unlimited right possessed by a commander, a right exercised in the name of the fatherland and freedom. What had happened to that unhappy son of his, Ivan? He must ask in the division tomorrow. He would also ask about his own sons, Radovan and Alexander. He must write a few lines to Louisa. What was he thinking about? Today he could have talked only to his mother. No one else. He would like to sit beside the hearth, look into her moist blue eyes, and ask: what should I do? He felt numb all over his body, his eyes began to close.

What would he do today and tomorrow if he were in Potiorek's place? Without a second thought, he would pursue the First Army: he would pursue it without mercy toward Čačak and the western Morava valley. And in a few days the Serbian front would collapse, exactly as Vojvoda Putnik had predicted when he opposed his plan to withdraw from the crest of Suvobor.

He heard himself sigh, and was afraid someone else might have heard, too; he coughed, got up from the bed, lit a cigarette, and began to walk about the large, empty room. He could hear people making noise, and women shouting outside the headquarters, but he preferred not to take a look.

If he and Vojvoda Putnik could now see only the favorable strategic opportunities open to the enemy, why should Field Marshal Oscar Potiorek not see these also? How dare he, Živojin Mišić, reckon on this general, who for two months had won every battle in Serbia, proving to be an incompetent? And how, in the present military circumstances, could he fail to respect the opinion of Vojvoda Putnik, a commander who in three wars had never made a mistake which an opponent could discern and take advantage of? Putnik, who never believed that there was only one means of achieving one's end, who knew how to ponder longest over the shortest conclusion, and be the first to find a way out of the most complicated situation. A man who always acted so that he had time enough and to spare for everything. So how could he, now at his weakest, oppose both Putnik and Potiorek at one and the same time? Only once, perhaps, dare a soldier oppose both his senior officer and his enemy in order to fight a battle which would be lost or won once and for all. Was it just on Suvobor that he had not been able to escape this temptation?

His head ached and his temples pounded. He threw away his cigarette and walked over to the window: in the distance, from the positions occupied by the Third Army, came the dry, infrequent sound of cannon being fired; to the west, along his own army's lines, all was silent. For how long? The road to Čačak was crowded with refugees. He pressed his forehead against the cold windowpane. Within the range of his vision there was nothing but empty space.

Perhaps statesmen could decide questions relating to the progress, liberty, and rights of a people; military leaders could defend or conquer lands and cities. But neither of them could decide the fate or survival of a nation. No, this was decided by some other force, some power that lay below the surface of all visible facts, and above all measurable strength. Something stronger than any material factor, and more potent than logic or numbers; something that would outlast the will to win, something deeper than hatred. Something by which a man and a nation survived and endured, even though a time of death prevailed throughout the world. Only by means of this force was it possible to resist Potiorek and drive him across the Drina. When he had tried to explain this to Vojvoda Putnik, Putnik had been convinced he was mistaken; when he spoke of it to his subordinates, only the toadies and the irresponsible would allow that he was right.

"May I speak to you, sir?" said Hadjić urgently. "The High Command reports that the alteration of the shells to fit the caliber of our cannon is making good progress in the munitions factory in Kragujevac. The cartridge cases are being cut down two millimeters and remounted. The shells should begin to arrive in two days at the latest—that is, the day after tomorrow. Several thousand of them, sir."

"At last, thank God! Thank you, Hadjić. Have you anything else out of the ordinary to tell me?"

"Bulgarian guerrillas have destroyed the bridge on the Vardar and cut the railway line at Djevdjelija."

"That's to be expected. All right, Colonel. Just a minute!" Hadjić stood beside the door: he was radiant with joy, and his fleshy, often bloated face with dark pouches under the eyes had an unusually gentle, good-humored expression, quite unfamiliar to Mišić. Perhaps he had judged the man unfairly.

"Did you want something, sir?"

"Do you agree that we should summon the division commanders for a discussion?

"I think that is absolutely essential, sir."

"In that case, see that they are all here the day after tomorrow."

As soon as the squadron came down into Takovo and was given orders to rest, mend their clothes, and get rid of their lice, Adam Katić gave a dinar to his friend Uroš Babović and asked him to feed and water Kljusina, as he called the horse he had received after Dragan's disappearance and his own flight through the Austrian lines. Then he took half a piece of hardtack and a few hard-boiled eggs, and withdrew to the cowshed, to sleep, and suffer.

He was perhaps the only soldier in the First Army who was unhappy and angry because the army had withdrawn from Suvobor and Rajac to the foothills. If we couldn't do anything to them when we were up there and shooting at the top of their heads, he thought, we're now absolutely done for when we're under their heels; in a few days they'll chase us down the Morava like hares. They'll wipe Serbia off the map before Christmas. Dragan will remain in captivity, they'll take him away to Austria, and some potbellied Austrian coward will ride him. But no, he won't ride him—Dragan won't let him. So he'll use him to plow, to carry wood and manure. He'll drag himself around some wretched German village as long as he has any teeth, then they'll force-feed him and take him to the butcher. Those swine eat horseflesh; they'll make him into sausages and eat him. It would be best if he was killed—in a charge by a cavalry regiment. But it was terrible, really awful, that he wouldn't be able to die in Serbia. We're running away from the infantry, from a few shells, there's no more need for a cavalry charge, none at all; so Dragan won't be able to die in Serbia. One hope remained: when they finished with Serbia, they might send him to the Russian front. There, fighting against the Russians, he could perish in a fitting manner, in a charge against the Cossacks. If he could at least meet his death from a real man. He should have continued to look for him. He must have gone toward Valjevo, Mionica, and Ljig; that's where the division staffs were. Dragan had not been kept at the front on Suvobor. If he had not been killed for obstinacy, he must still be in that bitter-oak wood. Perhaps Dragan had run away at the first volley, when the Austrians had fallen on the squadron in the darkness. He must have galloped off into the stream or up the hillside. But in that case I would surely have met him by now, damn him.

For two days and three nights he had sneaked around the Austrian supply trains and staff headquarters, dressed in a uniform he had taken from a dead Austrian. They had chased him like a mad dog around the enormous empty sheep pen in which he had taken refuge, keeping an eye on the route along which the Austrian army was passing. He had put his head right in the lion's mouth! What more could he have done? He pulled the blanket over his head and sank into the darkness, rigid in the shivering cold.

"Adam, your uncle's looking for you," said Uroš Babović, waking him up.

"What do you mean, my uncle? I haven't got an uncle. Go to hell."

"Adam, my boy! It's me, Tola. Why have you hidden yourself in the manger, for God's sake?"

Yes, it was Tola. He did not uncover himself, he would not get up from the manger, ashamed to be caught by someone from Prerovo—and Tola Dačić, at that—in a situation in which people from Prerovo might laugh at him.

"Get up, Adam, and let me have a look at you!"

Adam threw off the blanket and sat up in the manger.

"Why are you playing hide and seek with the army? I've heard that Aleksa and Blaža were alive two days ago. Since then there hasn't been much shooting. We're running away, as you see."

"No, my boy, you're not running away. General Mišić isn't running away. You'll be back on Suvobor in a few days, and then you'll be making for the Drina. General Mišić personally gave me his solemn word that the Austrians will be out of Serbia before Christmas."

"Stop throwing General Mišić at me! Tell me what's going on in Prerovo."

"All the women sent you their greetings."

"Stop lying to me, I don't want to listen to you. I've lost Dragan." He got up, trembling.

"What can you do about it, Adam? It's the times we live in. People are losing crowns and empires. They're being left without their estates and their honor. Without a grave, or any sign of their existence. Look after yourself as best you can." Tola put his hand on Adam's shoulder.

Adam moved away. "Don't worry about me. But there is something you could do for me. Go to Prerovo, and ask my father to buy me a decent horse wherever he can find one—the best horse in the district—and to bring it to me at once. I can't do anything with this nag, and even in wartime I'm not going to ride just any old horse. Please do this for me!"

He looked into the old man's tearful eyes.

"Yes, I'll do anything you want. But first I must see Aleksa and Blaža. They're somewhere with the troops, near the villages of Leusić and Brajić."

"You go look for them. If you get to Prerovo, tell my father what I said. And remember me to everybody who sent me their greetings."

He got back into the manger and again covered his head with the blanket.

"Wake up, Corporal, wake up! There's nothing more frightening than a dream!"

Ivan Katić pulled himself together: Sava Marić was waking him up, and before he opened his eyes his hand flew to his inside pocket: his glasses were there! He broke into a cold sweat; that was the spare pair his father had given him in Kragujevac when they said good-by. His last pair. During the withdrawal the previous night, under some place called Nameless Crag, a branch had swept off his glasses while he was jumping over a stream, and he had not been able to find them. That was the most terrible thing that had happened since he came to the front.

"You cried out in your sleep. What were you dreaming about, sir?"

Ivan opened his eyes, got up, and put on his glasses; soldiers were sleeping around a hearth with a big fire.

"I was dreaming about something absolutely frightful; my glasses flew off," he muttered. "What time is it?"

"Nearly midnight."

"I've slept for fifteen hours! What are the latest orders?"

"We're to rest, mend our clothes, and get rid of lice. I've left you some supper. Come up to the fire, you're shivering. Here's your supper. Now I'll lie down in your place."

"Thank you, Sava. Yes, you lie down. I won't sleep again before dawn." He felt his glasses again, and wiped away the sweat on his forehead.

He took a tin plate with a piece of roast meat, an onion, and some black bread, then sat down on a three-legged stool near the fire and began to eat. Sava lay down in his place on the straw which Ivan had brought in.

Although he could not remember when he had last eaten meat, he could scarcely chew it: in his dream his mother's hand had removed his glasses. What did this dream mean? His mother's hand, stretching from the sky. Yes, his mother's hand had taken off his glasses and thrown them away. He stopped eating and felt the frames and side pieces of his glasses. Should he tie them to his ears with a piece of string? No, wire would be better. But where could he find a piece of wire? Sava would surely know the best way to tie his glasses on, so he could never take them off. In his dream they had flown like butterflies, hovered above him like birds, and burned up in the sun.

He held on to his glasses with the fingers of both hands and stared at the fire: his entire body—all his bones and muscles—had one thought, one feeling, one presentiment.

Tola Dačić stepped across the threshold and caught sight of Aleksa among a group of about ten soldiers sleeping around the fire. He remained in the open doorway. Yes, Aleksa was the biggest of the bunch here, too. But he'd got very thin, poor boy. Tola's eyes filled with tears. Who was this fellow with those enormous glasses, God help him, writing something in a book on his knees? He noticed his rank, and greeted him quietly:

"God bless you, Corporal."

"Good evening. God bless you, too."

"My name's Tola Dačić, from Prerovo. Aleksa's father," he said, a bit more loudly, looking hard at his son: he wasn't so very thin, not like those other poor wretches.

"You're Aleksa's father? Do you really come from Prerovo?"

"Yes, I do, and right proud of it!"

"Do you know the Katić family? Aćim Katić? He's my grandfather. My name's Ivan Katić."

"Are you Vukašin Katić's son? And my Aleksa is under you?"

"Yes, Vukašin Katić is my father, and I'm Aleksa's corporal."

Tola stared at him. He'd never seen anybody wearing glasses like these: you couldn't see his eyes through the lens. He was half blind—and Aleksa's corporal! A skinny, stooping creature without a mustache, who looked as though a puff of wind would blow him away, and he commanded men—real men! His Aleksa. Such was life, no help for it; whatever horse you started riding, you wouldn't get another till it fell in its tracks. Do those Katići really have to be on top of us Dačići, even in war? He went into the house, took off his bag, and said:

"Well, Katić, God is almighty, but I would say that war is even mightier. How nicely it's worked out that in this mess Aćim's grandson should be my Aleksa's officer, so now you'll both be pleased to see me. You Katići and we Dačići are nourished by the same soil and neighbors, alive and dead. I'm right glad, my boy, I really am, that you're Aleksa's officer!"

"Take this stool and sit down. What's my grandfather doing?"

"I'll sit on the floor, you stay where you are. That's how things have to be, and always will be. No, I won't sit on the stool, I like sitting on the ground. Well, your grandfather Aćim's all right. He's very worried about Adam; he worries about his grandsons."

Tola fell silent and stared at Aleksa: they were all lying on their sides, but Aleksa had spread himself out, and you could hear him dreaming even out in the lane. But he was thin! Only his whiskers were thicker, and his bristly beard, like a second crop of hay. Who did he get that bristly beard from, blast him? He was wearing Austrian top boots, they'd keep his feet dry. Anyone whose feet were all right during a war would stay alive. Still, it wasn't right, really, taking boots from a dead man. He should throw them away. He's got an Austrian overcoat, too. But his cap is ours, thank God, and his jacket and breeches are Serbian. I can't see if he has any medals or stars. Four months of risking his skin for the government, and they haven't even made him a corporal. Well, if there's no justice in peacetime, can you expect any in war? At least he's alive. Better a live swineherd than a dead captain.

"Why don't you wake up your son? It'll be nicer for him if you do it rather than me."

"Leave him alone, let him sleep a bit longer," said Tola, his eyes still on his son: there were plenty of good dowries in Prerovo, with one house in three having no sons to carry on. Aleksa wouldn't be the servant and hired man of the Katići after the war, not for any wicked law, or any injustice in Prerovo either! What's this horrible dream you're having, my boy? Surely they're rushing at him, the villains, surrounding him. The veins are sticking out on his forehead. He's broken out in a sweat. And how he's groaning, poor thing. If it's like this when he's asleep, what's it going to be when he's awake?

Tola got up, jumped over two soldiers, put his hand on his son's chest, and whispered: "Aleksa, my boy, wake up!"

Ivan Katić rose quickly with his notebook.

"When you two have had a good talk, I'll come hear what you have to say about my grandfather," he said, and went out.

Taking hold of his jacket, Tola nudged Aleksa gently. Aleksa squinted and turned over on his side.

"Aleksa, my boy, I've been looking for you for the last three weeks. I've brought you a change of clothes, some socks, and something to put in your gullet."

"And so you've found me here," mumbled Aleksa, his eyes still closed.

"The good Lord told me you were here."

"It was General Mišić. He's our god."

"And he's a man, too, and none to touch him. Just before you came down from Suvobor, he told me things will soon be all right in Serbia."

"General Mišić told you that?" said Aleksa, still not opening his eyes or turning over.

"He did indeed! Told me personally, Aleksa. We talked together three times, the two of us, man to man, as though we were neighbors, or relatives even."

"One of the soldiers will hear you, and then I'll be a laughingstock till the end of the war."

"Come on, get up, so the two of us can have a little talk, and you can have a bite."

Aleksa remained lying down with his eyes shut, and didn't answer.

Tola sighed deeply, sunk in gloom: since he was a baby Aleksa had been wrong side out when he woke up. Such disaster in the country, with half of Serbia perishing, but that didn't change Aleksa. He got up and sat on the stool previously occupied by Ivan Katić.

Aleksa stretched, rubbed his eyes, and sat up on his elbows. "Are the folks at home still alive?"

"Yes, they're all alive and well. Only we're all worried sick about you. Let's greet each other properly, my boy!" Tola's eyes filled with tears and his voice trembled as he stretched out his hand.

Aleksa rose slowly, greeted his father with a sullen frown, and sat down beside him, stretching his hands toward the fire. Tola gave him two packets of tobacco and began to take the other things out of his bag—socks, underwear, bacon, and bread.

"First of all, Aleksa, tell me when you last saw your brothers? Or heard anything about them?"

"Blaža was alive when we were at Molitve on Little Suvobor. Since then I've been told his battalion had a bad time on Anateme, or some such place. I haven't heard anything about Miloje since we left Pecka. Now tell me how many men from Prerovo have been killed."

Aleksa began to break up the bread. Tola passed him a flask of *rakija*.

Wrapped in his overcoat, Mišić stood at the window, and felt excited as he looked at the highway where oxcarts laden with shells were passing. The windowpanes rattled and the room shook from the heavy loads. The lanterns in front of the staff headquarters cast their light over the road.

Mišić wanted to open the window and call out to those baggage men and their oxen: he wanted to tell them that no more valuable load than theirs had ever been carried over the highways of Serbia; that in their life span no harvest would ever make their axles creak more loudly than they were creaking this evening, and had been doing throughout the day, along the road from Kragujevac to Suvobor; he would have liked to say to them: Listen, my good men, the sweat of your beasts and your own weariness will never reap a nobler reward than the work you are doing tonight, under Suvobor. If he had not been expecting the division commanders, he would have told them to halt, offered them *rakija,* and wished them a safe journey up to the cannon; he would have asked them to strike up a song that the people and the army might hear: the shells have arrived!

Speaking sternly and in a whisper, Dragutin ordered the soldiers where and how to place the tables and chairs they were carrying in. Mišić turned around and said:

"Have you heard that the shells are on the way?"

"Yes, sir, we have. The ground is shaking. Now everything is in God's hands and yours, sir."

Each of them spoke one sentence; Dragutin remained mute, standing a little apart from them near the stove, looking dejected.

"Do you believe the time has come for us to move toward Valjevo and Šabac?"

"Indeed we do. That's what we all think, sir. The army is waiting for your orders. We're not giving in, sir!"

Again all four of them replied separately; meanwhile, for some reason Dragutin was frowning.

"Well, keep on hoping. Soon we'll be moving up the mountain." He saluted, and watched them moving slowly out of the room. They had not shut the door.

The division commanders and section chiefs entered, halted, and saluted; he returned their greeting in silence. The room reverberated with the creaking and rattling of the carts. He wanted them to listen to it for a few moments, to soak in that strained, crunching sound, that heavy rattling reminiscent of a summer thunderstorm. Can you hear it? his eyes asked them. He could see fatigue and sternness written on their faces; Vasić looked the weariest, and Kajafa had the gloomiest expression, quite glowering. He shook hands with the commanders. He waited until they were all seated, a bit disappointed and at the same time puzzled, because none of them expressed pleasure at the rumbling sound from the road, as though shells for the Serbian cannon were dragged along there every day.

"Is everything quiet in the lines?" he asked, speaking softly and at the same time provocatively, as he shut the window.

"There's a bit of shooting in the rear guard. Just to let them know we're still at war," said Miloš Vasić; the other commanders reported briefly in the same way.

"But it's not so quiet where we are now, as you can hear," he said, looking at them in turn, waiting for them to say something about the shells, and apprehensive about the purpose for which he had summoned them. "The orderlies assure me that they've seen singing and dancing among the troops today."

Miloš Vasić smiled at him: a thin, sarcastic smile. Mišić looked hard at him, trying to guess what he was feeling. Among all the division commanders, none had such bold ideas as Vasić, and no one opposed

Mišić more firmly. The smile still lingered on the edge of his lips, under his thick black mustache.

"The first thing I wish to say is that this evening we're not making a decision about victory, but about survival. Sometimes a single commander can make a decision leading to victory. When it's a question of survival, we must all decide what is to be done." Kajafa raised his eyebrows, as though in surprise. "Yesterday I sent you the report of the commander of the Third Army, General Šturm, concerning the state of the enemy. We have no reason to disbelieve the statements of soldiers who have deserted from the other side. The enemy is quite exhausted, their losses have been enormous. Their supply situation is desperate, their artillery is stuck in the mud and snow. Their morale is very low. The time has come when we can beat them with branches from the trees." He stopped: this conclusion was overhasty and too strongly worded. The same smile flitted over Vasić's face once more, this time even more sarcastic. "Now is the moment, gentlemen, for us to drive the enemy from our land." He stopped again: could it be that his hands were trembling? He hid them under the table. "The shells are on the way, the men are rested and eager to fight. But we know from times long past that every battle must first be won in the heart and in the head; and in an army, this means in the staff." He stopped speaking. Perhaps he should have left them to say all that had to be said. For his part, he didn't have the faintest shadow of doubt, none whatever.

"We're also getting reinforcements tonight, sir," said Hadjić. "Six thousand draftees and some police and frontier guards. The government is sending us its last reserve. We will make up the strength of those regiments which have suffered most."

"Now I am waiting for you to give me any facts which are not in harmony with my beliefs; please do not hesitate to tell me."

Milivoje Andjelković-Kajafa, commander of the Danube Division, first levy, spoke. "I don't wish, sir, to bring up any facts which would militate against an offensive, because I'm in favor of an offensive, not for military reasons, but because of sheer human necessity."

"I would very much like to hear those military facts which would be arguments against an offensive, Kajafa." Mišić spoke in a challenging tone; he was pleased with Kajafa's attitude.

"For obvious reasons, sir, we should have accepted the Austrian ultimatum last summer. But we didn't. We were bound to refuse as a people, as Serbs. So now we have to act according to the same principle which impelled us then, and we should act as speedily as possible. Otherwise, our collapse is imminent and inevitable."

"Do you think we could attack in two days?"

"The best thing, sir, would be for us to attack tomorrow. Time is racing on; the old clocks can't keep up with it. It's toppling down on us from Suvobor and Rajac."

Mišić felt a kind of fear in face of this firmness even more passionate than his own, this conviction for which this bold man did not even wish to expound his reasons—a man in whom, ever since Mišić had known him, pride stood above any kind of calculation.

"I too am of the opinion that we must make a decisive attack as soon as possible," said Ljuba Milić, commander of the Morava Division, second levy. "The enemy has not taken advantage of our withdrawal from the Suvobor crest. They are acting without a proper strategic plan. Now we can assume the initiative." Milić spoke slowly, word by word, looking straight in front of him.

"And how long would the army need to prepare for an attack, in your opinion?" Mišić wanted to meet the eyes of this strange man.

"At such a very critical time I think we dare not act more quickly than we are really able to do. We must do everything we can to achieve success. It never has been the most difficult thing to act quickly," answered Ljuba Milić after lengthy reflection; he looked briefly at Mišić, then again straight ahead.

Mišić waited for Kajafa to answer Milić. But Kajafa was staring at the window, lost in thought; there was not a tremor on his face, his lips were compressed, and he was again fidgeting in his chair.

"And what do you think, Krsta? The Drina Division has suffered heavy losses."

"It is my belief, sir, that the army has successfully passed through a crisis of morale. You only have to go through the lines, and look at the soldiers and listen to them today. The men are again ready for the greatest sacrifices and deeds of heroism."

Such an attitude pleased Mišić; the battle was easily won with officers for whom this kind of faith was the strongest of all reasons to attack.

"And can your division be ready to attack in two days?"

"As far as timing is concerned, it seems to me that we have to reconcile Kajafa and Ljuba."

"So, gentlemen, the cup has come round to me," said Miloš Vasić, commander of the Danube Division, second levy; his voice was hoarse, and he still had a sarcastic smile on his face. He cast his eyes on everybody seated at the table. "Well, I'll drain it to the dregs!" He raised his voice, as though proposing a toast; his smile faded and his brow wrinkled. "Unfortunately I cannot see why you are so enthusiastic about an offensive, although I'm as keen on victory as you are. I hope no one would dispute that." He looked hard at Mišić with his large wide-open eyes.

Mišić felt obliged to say, "Of course not. No question of it."

"You see, I am deeply convinced that we haven't the resources or the general strategic conditions for a big offensive. Yes, gentlemen, that's my view. We're soldiers, not poets, and our wishes must not exceed our capacities. Our aim—the expulsion of the Austrians from Serbia—is not in dispute. The only thing on which we're not agreed is when and how this is to be accomplished."

"We learned those things in the junior officers' course, Vasić," interrupted Mišić; he could not stand Vasić's rhetorical self-confidence.

"Oh yes, sir, I know that these are very banal truths. But what can we do about that? They're banal just because they have lasted longest, and most frequently proved valid. It was just two days ago, gentlemen, that we barely managed to extricate the army from total disintegration in the face of frightful pressure from the enemy—that is, if you can regard one third of our normal strength as constituting the army. In actual fact, to speak precisely, we fled from Suvobor, Rajac, and Ravna Gora. And now, apart from those shells and a few hundred men, has anything new or significant happened which would increase our striking power? With what are we going to move to an attack? Where are the necessary resources coming from?" He stopped speaking, and drummed on the edge of the table with his fingertips, while at the same time casting his eyes over the whole company.

Mišić waited for Kajafa to oppose Vasić; but Kajafa remained staring raptly at the window, with his head turned away a little, in order to hear better the shouting of the baggage men from the road, and the creaking of the carts. Krsta Smiljanić was straining his fingers, so that his knuckles cracked; Ljuba Milić was scratching the table top and looking at his knees; Hadjić coughed, frowned, and shifted in his chair. The rest of the section chiefs were looking at Mišić, hoping that he would silence Vasić, whose voice in fact rose in volume:

"And today we've abandoned Belgrade! The enemy is successful on all fronts. Vojvoda Putnik is again demanding court-martials and extraordinary measures to prevent the wholesale dissolution of the army. So what sort of 'general facts' can we reckon with, when we want to launch an attack?"

"I have put before you the most important general reasons," said Mišić. "I will also add others. But for all your clever talk, I don't see what you consider a suitable solution."

"I will immediately make a proposal, sir. We should first prepare ourselves as well as possible, and wait for the enemy in strong, well-fortified positions. Then we should engage in a large-scale battle, destroy his striking power, and after that go over to the offensive until our foe is annihilated." Vasić stopped speaking, but both his facial expression and his bearing indicated that he had not said all he wanted to say.

All those present except Kajafa looked straight at Mišić, who lit a cigarette in order to steady himself, so that his voice would not betray his feelings.

"Your estimate of the general situation is not accurate, Vasić. You have overlooked the most important factor: the exhaustion of Potiorek's army, and the severe crisis which it is now experiencing. But in a short time, two or three days, they will have left this crisis behind them. At the present moment their power is at a low ebb, while ours is increasing. If we don't take advantage of their momentary weakness, it will be lost to us forever. Your belief that our attack would have better prospects of success if we parry one more strong blow from our enemy —a strengthened and reinforced enemy—represents a strategic principle which would cause a candidate to fail his major's examination."

"Are you seeking from me, your subordinate, formal agreement to a decision already taken, or an expression of opinion to be treated with respect in making a decision?"

"If you want a completely frank answer, I want to see whether you gentlemen, capable and sensible men, can produce any arguments strong enough to shake my faith in my own convictions. Our decision will be a fateful one, and should not be taken on the basis of the convictions or the legal right of one man."

"And what does this mean, sir?"

"Decisions of this sort have a deeper basis than our grasp of the facts and arguments relating to the present situation. To take decisions at such times as these, we must respect some arguments inherited from our ancestors, and also some which will be contributed by our descendants."

Vasić smiled at him: "I must admit that I hadn't the slightest thought of such strategy. Neither you nor any other of these gentlemen have repudiated my facts. I'm sorry to say so, but you haven't," he said, stretching out his hands and shaking his head. "But over one thing we are in agreement: the fate of our offensive will decide the fate of Serbia. And what if we don't succeed?"

"In that case we will simply continue the struggle as we have done till now," interrupted Hadjić.

"The trouble is, Hadjić, after an unsuccessful attack we wouldn't have the resources to go on fighting as we have fought from the Kolubara to the crest of Suvobor. Who would dare to take such a risk today? Would you, General?"

"Of course I would!" replied Mišić. He was still waiting for the other commanders to oppose Vasić, who was deliberately challenging them. It was well known that he had no respect for some of them.

"Look here, Miloš," said Krsta Smiljanić, "you may take it from me that although Potiorek is master of Suvobor, Prostruga, and Rajac, he has nevertheless lost the battle."

"An army on the move and making an attack is always stronger than an opponent of the same strength—we've always known that," said Ljuba Milić.

"We dare not leave it to the stronger side to choose the time and the place to strike!" said Major Tisa Milosavljević in agitated tones. "If we make it possible for our opponent to do this, I must admit—with despair—that Serbia would lose the war within ten days."

These last words alarmed Mišić; it boded no good when Serbian commanders spoke aloud of the possibility of losing the war. He got up and went to the window, leaving them to wrangle among themselves. Two oxcarts full of shells were moving into the light of the lanterns in front of the headquarters. Ljuba Milić was saying something about the weather; Mišić turned his head so that he could hear him.

"It's the weather that decides all human affairs. There's no sense in acting against it. Anything you do contrary to the weather is bound to fail."

"Look here, gentlemen," said Major Tisa Milosavljević, "everything that the Serbian land can produce has been pitted against the Austrians. First of all, bad roads. Then mountains, rain, and snow. And poverty, our dire Serbian poverty. Empty barns and sheeppens. The hatred of the women and the old men. Everywhere they are met and surrounded by this terrible hatred. They can't see where they are in the fog." Mišić liked Milosavljević best of all the staff officers, even though he talked like Professor Zarija.

"But let me tell you, gentlemen," said Vasić, "all these facts of yours are half wishful thinking, half unreasonable risk."

"In two months our army has not won a single major victory. We dare not launch an offensive unless we are absolutely convinced that we'll win. It would be a foolish risk otherwise." Mišić returned quickly to the table, prepared to hear what Vasić had to say. He was speaking with a sense of conviction proportionate to his consciousness of his superiority over the others.

"Vasić, let me say something now about the spirit of the army. Everything that I know about men leads me to conclude that in a healthy individual, nothing is so easily or quickly renewed as hope. Or faith, gentlemen. Even in the most desperate situation, man yearns for hope. In their hearts, minds, and will, the Serbian soldiers are sound and healthy men. Very much so. I feel this to be so, I know it—our people want to live, to endure! So make the best of that, Miloš Vasić!"

"Still, defeats are not easily forgotten, sir. And suffering is remembered for a long time, too. We know this from poems, songs, and books. For us Serbs, Kossovo is not of the greatest importance as an historical event; it's our very being, our destiny, the expression of what we are," said Vasić. He spoke in a whisper, and for the first time seemed really moved, and to be speaking exactly as he thought.

"No, you're wrong, Colonel," said Mišić. "A man can hardly wait to forget suffering and defeat. It's part of our human nature, one of the laws of our biological health which has enabled nations to survive under all sorts of conditions in every period of history. A nation does not remember suffering because it wants to remember pain and defeat, but for the sake of revenge, to acquire the hatred which will provide the strength needed for victory. A man must be able to hate, Vasić, if he is to survive. So a nation remembers its suffering in order to have the strength to hate."

He fell silent, regretting the words he had just spoken; they seemed quite inappropriate to the present occasion. "Forgive me, gentlemen, for exceeding the limits of my competence. What I wish to say is that I am convinced that the strongest reason for our moving to the offensive as quickly as possible . . ." He paused to light a cigarette, waiting for a train of wagons to pass, so he could speak in silence. "We are a peasant army, that means a defensive army: one that doesn't fight for victory and glory, but for homes and children, meadows and sheepfolds. People will fight for their own name and their own grave. Such an army can do everything, but only when it is fighting for survival, when it sees and knows for what it must die. The morale of our army is wavering not because the Austrians have been winning battles, but because we have had to abandon the very things for which our nation entered the war. The soldiers have lost sight of the purpose of their struggle and sacrifices. We must now give it back to them. We must summon them to rush forward and reclaim what is theirs—their homes, and peace for their children. Tomorrow or the day after, we must launch a decisive attack, or we will cease to exist as an army."

His glance rested on Vasić: instead of a shallow and sarcastic grin, his face now showed a deep, painful smile; sadness had frozen on his face and hands. This was not the expression of a defeated man, he felt. But this evening he had no more time for the errors of Miloš Vasić. "I wish to thank you, gentlemen, for your support," he concluded, "you most of all, Colonel Vasić. And now let us have supper; and while we're having supper, we'll only tell jokes. Milosavljević, ask them to bring in supper."

"May I venture to ask, sir, what kind of wine the staff has?" asked Kajafa, speaking at last, and resting his folded arms on the table.

"We'll have Župsko wine, Milosavljević. Did you want to say anything further, Kajafa?"

"No sir. I've said all I wish to say. Now I'm interested only in the wine—in the absence of those fascinating feminine creatures, the most wonderful thing in the world!"

Mišić smiled, and the thought crossed his mind: was this the first time he had smiled since he had taken command of the First Army?

Dearest Mother,

A century has passed since we said good-by in Niš station. Not a century of time, but a century of life—a hundred of my lives. Happenings, people, and deaths. Time doesn't exist for a soldier; war kills time, too. There is danger, and physical exertion, inconceivable to anyone who hasn't been in the war. Lack of sleep. Cold. Hunger. Fear of death is not the worst thing by any means.

When we parted you were a real Mother of the Jugovići.* No, that's nonsense—you were yourself! Now I can't even feel wonder or gratitude to the person who gave birth to me.

Since yesterday morning we have been somewhere south of Suvobor; I don't know how long we'll be here. I don't know either why it's still so quiet on the second day we're here. Orderlies are passing through on their way to Milanovac; I suppose there is a post office there.

Mother dear, the one thing I want in the world is a bed. My own

* The wife of a Serbian noble in the fourteenth century, celebrated in Serbian heroic poetry as the mother of nine sons who fought the Turks.—Trans.

bed. A nice, clean bed prepared by you. You have no idea, Mother, how wretched and dirty our people are. I've been racking my brains to understand why they're so wretched.

I want to snuggle down into my bed and fall asleep—to sleep for at least several years. I'd like you to come sit at the head of the bed sometimes, but not to take off my glasses, as you used to do when I was reading in bed and fell asleep with them on! Please, mother: while I'm alive, don't take off my glasses while I'm asleep! To dream in my own bed, with you putting my glasses on me when I had taken them off, that would be for me victory, freedom, and peace in this war.

I remember how we sometimes used to argue about human virtues. The war has convinced me that you were absolutely right. Goodness is the greatest and rarest of human qualities. I've met two or three men who have this power for goodness; perhaps the world might be saved at least a little by this gift. I've written more about this in the True Observations I've prepared for you.

I'm just not capable of such heroic and national hypocrisy as to tell you that you've no cause to worry about me. Please *do* worry, Mother! Worry a lot! I want very much for you to do this. I don't know what else your love for me could mean right now.

With love and kisses,

Ivan

Dear Milena,

We've fled from the Austrians, and are now resting in peace and quiet. But the killing still goes on: we kill lice, poultry, and cattle. Milena, have you any idea what misery is?

I used to believe that grief for a loved one was the greatest suffering. Now I know that the cold in the trenches at night is harder to bear than any spiritual suffering.

I used to believe that the effort of thinking, the mystery of life, and the intellectual problems it poses were the most difficult things one had to cope with. Now I know there is nothing worse than lack of sleep.

I used to believe that the search for Truth was the most important thing in life, but now I'm sure that bread is the most urgent need of our existence.

So now you know that I had to go to the war and spend two weeks fighting in order to understand the most basic things about human nature. People who haven't fought in a war can't know the basic truths about men and life. If I survive this freezing hell, I'll never really believe anything said by anyone who hasn't been in a war—neither philosophers, writers, nor scientists.

My friend Bogdan tried to convince me that there will be no more wars when socialism is victorious throughout the world. If this happens, then people will sink into lies and fantasies. If men have no more wars to fight, then they'll only produce food and things for their houses. Great art and profound wisdom will die out. Please don't imagine that I've read this somewhere! Anyway, if I come back from the war I'll bring you my True Observations, and then you'll see what my "reading" has been!

On purpose, I did not want to begin this letter with the most important thing that has happened to me in the war. My friend Bogdan Dragović has been seriously wounded, and I don't know whether he's still alive. They say that three hundred wounded from our division were taken prisoner, and Bogdan was in that dressing station, in a village on Suvobor. That night when Bogdan was wounded, and the scene in the shepherd's hut when he was lying by the fire with our platoon commander whom one of the soldiers killed, because he wouldn't retreat until he was ordered to do so—that night crushed me completely. That night I became a scoundrel, a murderer, and a deserter!

Milena dear, you must forgive me for having been so violently opposed to your being in love with Vladimir Tadić. That was my peacetime naiveté, my lack of understanding of the basic things in human existence. If there is anything which might be considered human happiness, it must be love. We are happy to the extent that we love and are loved. So let me give you a soldier's wartime counsel: go on loving, Milena! Go on loving, and don't be afraid of what's going to happen tomorrow.

Your affectionate brother,
Ivan

Dear Dad,

I think you made a mistake in sending me to the Sorbonne, and never taking me to your village. I am troubled by my lack of sincerity toward you. There's one "truth" which I should tell you. Since I was in the eleventh grade in high school, I've been ashamed my father is in politics, because to me politics seems a baser passion than the passion for acquiring wealth, and the profession of a politician less honorable than that of a businessman. I wanted to tell you this in Kragujevac, after we had supper in that inn, when we went out into the street. But I didn't want to hurt you.

Passing through our mountain villages, where we've often had to spend the night, I've recalled the political discussions between you and your friends at our house. For all of you, politics means the liberation and unification of all the Serbs and South Slavs, and also progress, morals, and democracy. But I never once heard you mention the wretched poverty of our people. Do you know, Dad, how horribly poor our people are? One can despise these people, or else one must really fight to deliver them from this poverty. There is only one Serbian political issue, and that is poverty! The terrible poverty of our people!

We're now retreating all the time. For me, in this horrible torment—I mean the war—killing and being killed is not the worst thing. It's that people are sometimes so disgusting. Men are killed while relieving themselves, and this is considered heroic. But there are no "sides" in war, really. In war you also fight against your own people. The staffs are frightful—like every form of government on this earth, only much worse because they have greater rights of lording it over human lives. We had one marvelous commander, but he's been badly wounded. And the soldiers—these heroes from Cer and Mačkov Kamen, capable of the highest virtue and heroism—they steal whatever they can lay their hands on, they'll wreck a peasant's farm as though it belonged to the Austrians. They'll strike anyone with a rifle butt or a bayonet for a piece of bread, a flask of *rakija*, a linen sheet. This barbarism in the name of the fatherland and liberty pains and disturbs me. This abandonment of all decent instincts, this crazy selfishness, this dreadful despair bred by war! I don't know what to think, Dad. Are we really that sort of people? Or are all people like that? I'm confused by my own confusion. Where did I grow up? On what basis was I brought up to be a patriot and a decent human being?

Forgive me, Dad. In truth, I'm not now reproaching you for anything.

Good-by, Dad.
Ivan

When Tola Dačić was told that his son Miloje was alive and well at his position in the rear guard, but that he would not be able to get through to him, he took his flute out of his bag and played it to proclaim his joy. Then he set out to visit the villages in which the soldiers were resting, going from house to house, from distillery shed to cowshed, from the barn to the inn, to cheer them up and make them laugh and be merry.

"Listen, my boys, the Fritzies are at their last gasp. What's the matter with you soldiers? Why are you glowering like someone cut down your fruit trees? A man with blackness in his heart is only half a man, but the Devil and the plague will flee from a man that's merry. So strike up a song, dance, and tell some jokes—at least we Serbs have no shortage of them!"

He played his flute for them. Some of the men swore at him and pushed him away, but some joined hands and danced with gusto. They did so less from joy than sheer boredom and pigheadedness. When they got tired they shouted at him, but he just went on further, through the lanes and yards, gathering an audience:

"Now listen to what I have to say, my boys. I've got three sons in General Mišić's army, and I had one with Stepa: that was Živko, he stayed at Cer. I'm talking to you now as a father, and telling you that if any man on this earth is unlucky, it's no good his going fishing or to a wedding, let alone to war against the Austrian emperor. All people, I tell you, are either lucky or unlucky. That's how it is, nobody knows why. There's folks whose seed will sprout if they throw it on stone, whose cattle multiply, in whose houses two boys are born to every girl. The hail won't spoil their vineyards, and sickness won't set foot in their houses, though it's killing everybody in the neighborhood. If they tread on a thorn they don't get pricked; they can go through a nest of vipers and not step on a single one. Now Živojin Mišić, your commander, is such a man, a general who looks just like us peasants. Luck has transformed his life, folks. If he wasn't a lucky man, he wouldn't have risen from a peasant to a general, and he wouldn't have beaten the Turks and Bulgarians either! What's more, if he wasn't a lucky man, the King wouldn't have given him command of the First Serbian Army. You can all shit on my grave when I've gone, if you folks too aren't lucky under his command. When you get going again, you won't stop until you get to the Drina. The tide has turned, my boys, I'm sure it has."

He trudged through the lanes, chatting about the Russians and good luck, but more about good luck because that was what he believed in, and for that he didn't have to show proof. When he wasn't talking he played his flute, and he drank whenever he was offered something.

Passing a haystack, he noticed a soldier trying to rape a woman who was swearing and defending herself with a pitchfork. Tola Dačić came up to the fence, thrust his head over the stakes, and muttered:

"Don't try to stop him, my girl, I hope you're not just dreaming he's a man! Give him a little bit of what you've got, and your house will never lack anything it needs. He's a soldier, he's defending your home and children, he might be killed tomorrow on your doorstep. What have you got there anyway? It isn't a monastery that you've got there under your skirts! He's a Serb, young. Hasn't it occurred to you, if you've got any sense, that your own man is probably chasing someone else's wife around a haystack right this minute?"

The woman brandished her pitchfork and banged it on the fence; Tola just barely managed to dodge it.

"I'd like to see a Fritzie on top of you, you stinking bitch!"

A corporal came up and put his hand on Tola's shoulders: "I've orders to take you to the regimental commander."

"But why do you have to *take* me? I'll go myself! I'll be right glad to see the commander of such a furious army, and hear him talk."

The corporal took him to a fine house where, while still in the doorway, he noticed some officers sitting round a laden table; they were in a good mood.

"God bless you, gentlemen!"

Not all the officers returned his greeting. A burly officer with a large mustache, whose rank he couldn't see, rose at the head of the table.

"So you're the gaffer spreading rumors among the troops that the Russians have reached Smederevo!"

"Yes, I am. And they've got there, too! Or if not today, they'll be there tomorrow evening, that's for sure."

The officers grinned and looked hard at him.

"Do you know, gaffer, that Vojvoda Putnik has given out an order that anybody spreading false rumors and upsetting the soldiers is to be brought before a court-martial?"

"All credit to him, but he hasn't got that order right. Now's the time, sir, when the only wrong lies are those that make the Fritzies out to be better than they are, and spread news about their victories and frighten the soldiers."

"Our soldiers don't need any lies, you silly old man! We don't want to deceive ourselves."

"But we have to deceive ourselves, sir, if there's nothing else we can do."

The officers' lips twitched; this encouraged him.

"Do you know what a soldier feels like, gaffer, when he realizes he's been deceived?"

"Yes I do. Then you have to give him something to help him along. When a man's in trouble, sir, he'd rather you deceive him with some good news than leave him in misery with the truth."

The regimental commander came closer to him: "You're an incorrigible liar, gaffer! What'll we do tomorrow, if the soldiers don't believe us when we tell them the truth?"

"If the soldiers won't believe the truth, they should be beaten. You've got the power, so punish them; beat those who don't believe you. It doesn't hurt anyone for long if he's beaten on account of the truth. Then he'll believe that his seniors are right. And a man has no greater satisfaction, sir, than to take pleasure in that truth!"

"Well spoken, gaffer! You're the biggest clown I've met in the war! Take off your bag and sit down. Have a bite to eat, and wet your whistle!"

Mišić held the telephone receiver in both hands; he looked at the clock on the table and read his disposition to the divisions: ". . . I have decided that on December 3, at 3 a.m., the entire army should launch an attack on the enemy. To this end I give orders . . ."

He sat reflecting, visualizing the terrain and the positions of the whole army according to the arrangement of the divisions. The army was now rested; the men had eaten their fill and caught up on sleep, mended their shoes and socks, and got rid of some of the lice. According to the orderlies, the soldiers had already had enough of lying about and were roaming through the yards, hanging around the women. The men of the first levy were wrestling in the haylofts, while the recruits were playing games with the village boys. In their warm rooms the officers were drinking, playing cards. Meanwhile, the cannon shells were being piled up.

However, according to reports from all the divisions, the Austrians were coming down from the mountain through the woods and along the streams in long, dense columns, taking cover from the eyes and field glasses of the Serbian sentinels and rear guard, sneaking along the ditches. The columns were longest on the right wing of the army; they were preparing to strike a blow toward Milanovac. Tomorrow, obviously. They had not left any reserves on Suvobor; they were moving forward with all the men they had.

But Field Marshal Oscar Potiorek despised and underestimated him frightfully! He was convinced that he had crushed the First Serbian

Army, and now was rushing forward to claim the victory for which he had already been publicly decorated in Vienna. But he had made a whole series of mistakes and errors of judgment. Now I've got the measure of you, Oscar Potiorek! Field Marshal, you should never collect your army near an enemy whose troops are already assembled and ready to launch an attack, even if you are much stronger. You've forgotten the experience of your ancestors in 1809 and 1870. And don't you know, or have you overlooked, the lessons of Napoleon's victories over your ancestors? Tomorrow I too am launching an attack. Yes, tomorrow.

He added to his instructions the words: "Heroes, with full hope and faith in God, advance!"

The clock ticked louder and louder, echoing through the room; the minute hand raced and flew: it was now twenty past three, and already the gray light of dusk was covering the window. He would call Vojvoda Putnik at exactly half past three. Was there anything he had not foreseen?

He looked at the positions: the main blow would fall on Prostruga: this was the direction of his strategic concentration. There the issue would be decided. There he would shatter Potiorek's army, break its back on the crest of Suvobor. Then he would pursue the scattered remnants to the Kolubara, to complete annihilation. Annihilation? Dare he set himself such an aim, even for survival?

Still the minute hand raced; its clicking sound echoed through the room; twenty-eight minutes past three. He picked up the telephone receiver, and dialed firmly.

"Give me the High Command, please. Mišić speaking. I want to inform the High Command of my decision. At three o'clock tomorrow morning I am launching an attack on the enemy with the entire army."

"You're still standing by your decision to attack tomorrow, Mišić?"

"Yes, Vojvoda, definitely."

"Well done, Živojin Mišić! That's how one should act at times like this. Splendid! I'll order the other armies to attack, too. We've no other alternative. If it's not the right time now, then time has run out for Serbia! Just tell me the directions in which the divisions are going to strike. Yes, I'm listening. Very good, yes, very good. That's right. And the direction of the main thrust, Mišić? Prostruga-Lipovača. Fine. Tomorrow is going to be your day. Perhaps the kind of day when a military leader justifies every war before God and history, and merits not only the recognition of his fatherland but the forgiveness of the mothers and orphaned children of the fallen soldiers. Can you hear me, Mišić? Please give orders to the other armies to attack tomorrow at three a.m. in full strength."

"It will be done at once. You can discuss the start of the attack among yourselves by telephone. Do you know that the Austrians are making a solemn entry into Belgrade tomorrow? We abandoned Belgrade today. Well, I hope we'll spoil their parade and their festive mood! Only please don't forget to keep in touch with the other armies and act in concert with them."

Mišić put down the receiver. He could not hear the clock. With a trembling hand he added to his dispositions: "The remaining armies and parts of the Užice Brigade will attack at the same time."

Dragutin brought in some wood.

"Tell me, Dragutin, will it be too late to sow wheat in a few days?"

"Well, in bad years and by bad farmers wheat can be sown even two days before Christmas."

"Bring me some apples. And hurry!"

He could feel his voice trembling. He couldn't talk to Šturm and Stepa about the beginning of the attack in such a state. He summoned Hadjić and asked him to do the talking, then went to the window to calm himself by looking out at the hills; they were dissolving into the dusk as if arching their backs.

"The Third Army can't attack before eleven o'clock, sir."

"Nonsense! Who but an idiot would launch an attack at noon? Tell him we can't wait."

Once more he looked intensely at the hills, at the quiet and darkness spreading ominously over the surrounding space.

"The Second Army can't attack before eleven o'clock either, sir."

"Well, I'm going to start at the time I've fixed. Please tell them that."

Hadjić's shouting down the chiefs of staff of the other armies over the time disturbed him; he wanted quiet, he wanted to be able to listen to the damned passage of time that threatened to destroy his will and spoil his plans. Hadjić told him that General Šturm, the commander of the Third Army, could not attack before nine o'clock. He picked up the receiver:

"For God's sake, Šturm, what can we do if we don't start till nine? Just imagine the soldiers waiting till nine o'clock to start an attack intended to pierce the front!"

"And just you imagine, Mišič," General Šturm shouted, "the position of a commander who gives orders to his division commanders at seven in the evening that they're to start an offensive at three o'clock in the morning! I ask you, when will the regimental commanders get their orders, and how much time will they need to work out their dispositions and inform the battalion staffs?"

"And what are we going to do, Šturm, if Potiorek takes it into his head to attack my army early tomorrow morning, at six o'clock, say? And everything points to the fact that he does intend to do that. Can you hear me, Šturm? It's the one who attacks first who'll win the battle."

"I'm not going to prophesy about the outcome of tomorrow's battle, and I'm telling you plainly that I'm not going to give my troops orders that can't be carried out. The orderlies won't even be able to get to the staff headquarters by three o'clock. Can you hear me, Mišić?"

"So what's the earliest time you could get your army ready to move?"

"I could manage it by nine; that means without complete preparations, and taking considerable risks."

"That's too late, Šturm, much too late!"

"And even then I'd be acting in full awareness of having given orders whose execution I don't believe in. Can you hear me, Mišić?"

"The risk is the same for both armies. Not to attack at daybreak. If we don't attack, we won't have time to take any risks at all. Then it will be too late to do anything. This is the point I want to make to you and Stepa. Let me know what you decide to do."

Krsta Smiljanić: "My division is in no state to attack at three o'clock, sir. The ground is broken and craggy, and the troops will get lost in the dark."

Mišić: "At daybreak the Austrians will attack. Can you hear me, Krsta?"

"I must tell you most emphatically that I cannot attack before seven o'clock."

"You are to act according to my orders, Colonel."

Ljuba Milić: "I have to report that it's not possible for me to carry out your orders. In this fog I can't assemble troops for an assault until daybreak."

"At daybreak, Colonel, the Austrians will be ready to strike at us as we deserve. Please carry out my orders!"

Miloš Vasić: "May I ask you something, sir? Can you hear me? I beg you, sir, to reconsider the orders you have sent us! Tonight's action will decide the fate of Serbia. Let your orders issued this evening stay in the logbook of the staff of the First Army, as evidence of your exceptional spirit, boldness, and firmness."

Mišić: "Who do you think you're talking to now?"

"I'm doing my duty according to the dictates of my conscience. I would defend my convictions with my life."

"My instructions to you, Colonel, are to stake your life and your conscience on carrying out the orders you receive this evening."

"Please listen to what I have to say! If you insist on carrying out your disastrous decision, please answer this question: how will the artillery manage in the dark? It's pitch-black at three o'clock, and the fog will be like pea soup."

"I have taken the fog and darkness into consideration in my disastrous decision, as it is regarded by the staff. Also the rocky terrain, and the fact that the troops are scattered. Please act according to my orders, Colonel!"

"Hello! Is that the Danube Division, first levy? Mišić speaking. Can you hear me, Kajafa? Do you think three in the morning is too early to begin our attack?"

Kajafa: "I'm in favor of three o'clock in the morning, and may the sun warm the victor!"

"But it's difficult to collect the troops in the dark. And there will be fog at dawn. Fog, night, and rocky terrain. It'll make the artillery's job more difficult."

"All these unfavorable conditions will be much worse for the Austrians than for us."

"You're very confident, Kajafa. I have the impression that you haven't taken all the facts into consideration."

"Those who want to see darkness at noon must begin the day at dawn. Can you hear me, sir? We must catch them in their lair and scatter them among the streams in the darkness. All the psychological factors are on our side."

"I understand, Kajafa. Carry on. I'll call you again later."

Obviously Kajafa's desire to attack was stronger than his anxiety as to how he should prepare for the attack and carry it out. This was where the danger lay: time was outstripping him, and he was not working in harmony with it. He put some apples on the stove to roast. He sat down by the stove and stared at the flames and glowing embers. Stepa was for eleven o'clock; Šturm was for nine; three of the division commanders were for seven; Vasić was opposed to everything planned for the following day. Only he and Kajafa were for three o'clock in the morning. Himself and Kajafa. Perhaps at this very moment Oscar Potiorek was selecting his time for attack. He too would experience his fateful moment tomorrow. Surely he would count on the fact that the Serbians, being peasants, would get up early, so he must catch them unprepared, and attack them at six in the morning. Six o'clock? None of us is in favor of six o'clock. Perhaps there was just one time, one only, which would ensure survival and salvation.

He could hear the clock on the table: its ticking echoed through the room. What hour had fate ordained for him? When should he move in order to survive?

Flames were leaping, the embers burning: time was burning.

Danilo History-Book sat alone in the room at a long, empty table, struggling to finish by candlelight a letter to his grandfather which he had been writing for two days; he just couldn't finish his description of the charge in which, so far, he hadn't participated. But he had given his grandfather his solemn promise that he would write to him after every battle. In addition to demanding that he give an exhaustive description of every battle—they had both imagined battles only as charges—and relate "everything he had thought and said while the charge lasted," his grandfather had asked him to write in detail about the commanders, and most of all about the peasants.

But how could he, how dare he write home to Novi Sad, to his grandfather, about a Serbian defeat? It would cause them suffering and unhappiness. If he told them the truth about his own experiences at the front, how he had taken Hungarians prisoner while they were relieving themselves, how he had later listened to what they had to say, and what they had said to each other, this would have been quite disgusting and not in the least heroic. Or if he wrote in his letter about the first time he killed one of the enemy—an Austrian wading in a stream, imitating the sound of a ram with its flock, luring the hungry Serbian soldiers with a cowbell, then seizing them and killing them—this would not have corresponded at all to the "Serbian heroism" expected of him, Danilo Protić, a Serbian volunteer. Furthermore, he had been deeply troubled by his first experiences of the war. He could never forget that evening at dusk, with a blizzard blowing such as he had never read about in any Russian novel, when he and Paun and Zdravko had crept up behind two Austrians hidden by broad beech trees, their heads covered with a tent flap as they rattled the cowbell. Although he had given Paun and Zdravko strict orders that those "two rams" must be brought alive to the platoon—with the cowbell around the neck of one of them, for some reason—when within ten paces of them, he could not go through with it: he had fired a bullet into the back of the one who was hopping about because of the cold, then bashed him furiously with the cowbell. The wind was whistling through the bare beech trees, carrying wisps of snow—and there were the Austrians, shaking the cowbell, luring the hungry Serbians like a ram enticing sheep. It was the humiliation that decided him.

He gave a start; Bora had come into the room with Mirko, whom they called Wren. Caught in the act of lying, Danilo was confused.

"What? Are you at it, too, Danilo?" asked Wren from the door with a grin; he was a graduate of the Prague Conservatory, known in the Student Battalion as Wren because of his good looks and dandified appearance, the wren being a rare and beautiful bird.

"What do you mean, am I at it, too?"

"Are you writing a diary? In my battalion, today and yesterday all the surviving students have been rushing to write diaries, so there's no one to talk to."

"I'm not so vain. I'm writing a letter," he said crossly, folding up the unfinished letter and stuffing it into his pocket.

Wren hugged him and slapped him on the back. "You're alive, Danilo! You're still alive! Are you still angry with me because of what happened in Skoplje?"

"No. That was a long time ago."

"Please forgive me and forget about it. I'll pay for that sin with my life."

"Don't talk nonsense! We're at war, at the front," he said, extricating himself from Wren's embrace.

"We've all been very worried about you. Did you know that, Danilo?"

"Why so worried just about *me*, Wren?"

"We were afraid because you're such a crazy guy, with your ideas about heroism. People like you don't survive the first battle."

"Some survive battles, some even survive shitting on Suvobor," said Bora, laughing aloud as he sat on the couch.

"And there are those who don't wind up their watches because of some metaphysical fear," muttered Danilo, afraid that Bora might relate his version of how Danilo had captured the Hungarians.

"Why do you look so yellow, Wren? And you've lost weight. Are you ill?"

"No, I'm not. That is, I don't know. Perhaps I am ill," he muttered, embarrassed. He took off his overcoat and sat on the bench. "An awful lot of our fellows are getting killed, did you know that? Aca, Karadja, and Spira have all gone in my battalion. And Esperanto and Stamet have been wounded. Gliša Ruler is very ill with pneumonia. We're dying, boys, dying like flies."

"Is Esperanto badly wounded?" asked Danilo after a longish silence; Wren's arrival had put him in a state of depression.

"They say he was raked bad with shrapnel. And he knew more than half the Student Battalion put together!"

"What a shame! He was a brilliant guy, I'm sure," said Danilo.

"Oh, stop talking about people being brilliant. Our fatherland doesn't need eggheads. It needs heroes in war and thieves in peacetime. Wren has come here as a guest, so it's up to us to give him a good supper, Danilo. The whole army's going on the offensive tomorrow morning. Perhaps it will be our last supper."

"Who told you that?" Danilo asked with a start, staring at Bora, who was nervously drumming on the table with the fingers of both hands.

"The whole army knows. Orders have come through from division headquarters. In fact our new platoon leader told me. He's a Bosnian, a schoolteacher, and a socialist!"

"My battalion C.O. is a reserve officer," said Wren. He is like a mother to us students. But the regulars go after us like the Devil chasing gypsies."

"Come on, Danilo, get cracking with that supper. See if that thievish Corporal Paun can find some meat. Wren's brought a bottle of wine, and I've got some cheese and bacon. And after supper the three of us will have a game of cards. I haven't had a sniff of them since we left Boljkovci. I'm beginning to forget about tricks, and my fingers are atrophying from lack of use! And God knows what colors and numbers are on the Great Wheel now. The Galaxy must have come around full circle. Perhaps, my dear fellow corporals, Serbia will play her last card tomorrow."

"Why do we have to play cards tonight? I've come to talk to you. I'm feeling dreadful. In my platoon there's nothing I can talk about but bread and the Fritzies."

"All right. We'll have a good talk and say nothing about poker.

Actually, I'll bet the gods are playing poker up there in the stars. Just imagine a god losing a whole constellation in one game! The Milky Way, for example."

"Poker is the gamble of a desperate man," said Danilo sharply, angry that he hadn't finished his letter and probably wouldn't be able to tonight in time to send it off tomorrow, if the army started an offensive and didn't return to Suvobor.

Danilo set off in search of Corporal Paun, whose bag hadn't been empty even on Suvobor. In the doorway he collided with the courier from staff headquarters.

"Corporals Luković and Protić are to come with me at once to the platoon leader!"

Danilo sat down beside Bora on the blue couch next to a blue table with three patterned plates, some hot cornbread, and a small pan in which two wax candles were burning peacefully.

"Early tomorrow morning we start an offensive," said Lieutenant Jevtić, still speaking quietly and slowly and still smiling, but not just sadly. "This evening we'll get our detailed instructions from battalion headquarters. The platoon must get ready. But first we'll have supper together and then we'll talk about tomorrow."

Bora kicked Danilo and whispered: "What about Wren?" Then he continued aloud: "Thank you, sir. But a friend of ours from the Student Battalion has come to see us. We've asked him to stay to supper. It wouldn't be right to leave him."

"Then let's fetch him right away. There's enough for him, too. The more the merrier!"

Danilo thought of his unfinished letter; he didn't feel like supper, and still less like playing poker with Bora and Wren, who ever since the retreat from the mountain had complained about not having a third player. Bora again tried to get out of staying to supper, but the lieutenant insisted, and sent his orderly to bring Wren. He was in despair at the poor prospects of the game of poker.

"Are you a socialist, sir?" asked Bora, determined to attack him.

"Yes, I am. What about you?"

"No, I'm not. I could never associate myself with any kind of fanaticism, especially in politics." The lieutenant smiled at him mournfully; this infuriated Bora, who continued even more violently: "I can respect fanatics only when they're in the middle of an ocean hunting whales. Nowhere else. I consider that anything connected with any kind of strong belief represents the greatest danger for the world."

"And do you think our world is organized in such a way that people can be happy? That they can live as human beings should live?"

"I consider the organization of this world more or less disgusting," Bora answered. "And that's not because kings and emperors and statesmen have made it so. The world is disgusting for the very simple reason that the majority of people are utter fools. It's stupidity that's the source of unhappiness, nothing but stupidity!"

"What about war, Luković?"

"War most of all. You socialists say that war is the result of imperialism and capitalism. That's nonsense! War is a matter of stupidity, the most profound human stupidity of all!"

The lieutenant's face became even sadder. His schoolmasterish sadness infuriated Bora; there was something cunning about it. He wanted to jump up and hit him hard. What expression would his face have shown then? Despair or rage?

"You've opened your mouth to some purpose, Luković. Go on," said the lieutenant urgently.

Bora turned his face to the door, and with his well-known skill shot his spit right to the door. "Is it possible that a man like you, an intellectual, a brave man and a volunteer, can still take your socialist leaders seriously, the men who even today are voting against the war budget in the Serbian Assembly, and raising hell against the bourgeois government of Nikola Pašić? After all, we're not insects! Can you support politicians calling themselves idealists, who are against the Serbian army getting boots and weapons and medical supplies? You're opposing Pašić's policy for the war as though the Serbian army was trying to conquer Vienna and Budapest rather than defending Kragujevac and Belgrade! The Austrians are slaughtering and destroying half of Serbia, while you socialists defend your precious theories and shout at the top of your lungs that the war is the fault of the imperialists!"

"So it is, my dear Luković! For what other reasons have the Germans and Austrians turned eastward and attacked Russia? As far back as human memory goes, it has been a well-known fact that wars are waged for plunder and conquest. Even wars fought in the name of freedom have not brought freedom to the masses," said Jevtić, speaking quietly and deliberately, as though uttering the words hurt him.

Wren came in and greeted them; Danilo introduced him, and hoped that this pointless argument would come to an end and that Bora's wrath would subside. Until now he had never heard Bora talk seriously about politics. Could he manage to escape from the room and finish his letter before supper was brought in? He had broken off in the middle of the second charge, and would at least like to add: "I must stop writing now; we have had orders to move to our positions. Next time I'll tell you how my first battle ended." Since they were going to launch an offensive in which there were sure to be charges, it would no longer be difficult for him to describe his feelings precisely and with conviction. He got up to leave, but the mistress of the house forestalled him as she brought in supper. The lieutenant stopped him.

They began eating their supper, a thick chicken soup. All of them drank. Even Wren who, as Danilo recollected, had not even drunk anything that last night in Skoplje; he had been the only one sober in the Sloboda café, and so had taken the whore Fanika away from Danilo. Danilo hadn't thrown him into the Vardar, because he had been amazed that this "refined musician," well known throughout the Student Battalion as a faithful fiancé and sentimental lover, should have taken the cheapest prostitute in Skoplje!

Bora seized every opportunity to oppose the lieutenant, while for some reason Wren took his side; this made Bora even more impatient with Jevtić's ideas and way of thinking. He was irritated too by Wren's prattle.

"By the annexation of Bosnia and Hercegovina, of course," said Wren, speaking a bit too loudly, "Vienna—German and Catholic—revealed her firm intention of wiping out the Serbian people. She moved against Serbia full of religious and racial hatred. People ought to know that."

"That's right, my boy. That's the aim of Catholic, Hapsburg imperialism—the annihilation of the Serbs. A depressing state of affairs for the twentieth century."

"It's terribly difficult and painful to be a Serb!" exclaimed Wren, obviously excited by the *rakija*.

"It's a bit depressing to be a Serb, gentlemen!" interrupted Bora, bending over his plate of soup.

Danilo was surprised: he had never yet heard Wren, the rather taciturn "refined musician," talk like this; and he would swear that Wren had never drunk *rakija* before in his life. Now he was drinking one glass after another. Danilo felt he must listen to him.

"You haven't forgotten, have you, that neither the Emperor nor the government declared war on Serbia according to correct diplomatic practice and international law. It was Berchthold, one of the ministers, who declared war on Serbia!"

"Yes indeed!" said Jevtić. "Those Great Power bastards so despise us Serbs that they don't even consider us worthy of being told, with their dastardly hypocrisy, that we're going to be annihilated—and by a punitive expedition, at that! Punitive expeditions haven't been used in Europe since the Wars of Religion!" Unlike Wren, the lieutenant still spoke slowly and quietly, and seemed on the verge of tears.

"And did you folks know that Baron Gölz, the Austrian ambassador, didn't even listen to Pašić's reply to Berchthold's ultimatum? Did you know that?" Wren flushed with indignation.

Obviously moved, the lieutenant spoke quietly, as though to himself: "I forget all my sufferings when I think that I'm the friend of those who killed Franz Ferdinand. A future European emperor. A deer hunter, who planned to crush the Serbs, conquer the Balkan peninsula and the Dardanelles, and then turn against Russia!"

Supper ended in an atmosphere of quiet agreement. The lieutenant was dejected, as though he had just concluded a lover's monologue, and didn't attempt to detain them. He told them to get some sleep, and he would wake them when it was necessary.

Outside in the dark, Danilo announced firmly: "I'm just not in a state to play cards now."

"You really mean that, you damned spoilsport?"

"Bora, I don't want to play cards either," said Wren. "Don't push me, I'm not going to. I'm drunk—and desperate, too. I came over this evening to confess something. You're my closest friends. Tomorrow I'll be killed. I've decided that I must get killed."

"For God's sake don't talk nonsense, Wren! I can't stand drunken confessions and drunken suicides."

"Why are you so stupidly cruel, Bora? Why can't you try to understand? I'm desperately unhappy." Wren burst into tears, which touched Danilo.

"What's up?" he said putting his hand on Wren's shoulder; he wanted to see his face.

"Danilo, do you know how it all turned out—my big success with Fanika, when you were my rival? You remember how we wanted to have a fight on the bank of the Vardar because of her, when we left the Sloboda? Actually, you wanted to throw me in, because Fanika asked me to go off with her, and took me by the arm."

"Yes, you were a son of a bitch, all right! I was sitting with her the whole evening, everything was fixed up that we'd go to her house, then you, the faithful swain, sat down next to her after midnight and went for her like a young calf! At first I thought it terribly funny."

"I don't know what came over me. It was the last night in Skoplje—the next day we were leaving for the front. The whole battalion was rushing after women. I really don't know what came over me! I'm deeply in love with my fiancée; I adore her; she's a lovely girl, pure and innocent. She's my first love."

"Well, you haven't betrayed your country, you sanctimonious musician!" retorted Danilo.

"Piss on your faithfulness to your fiancée!" said Bora, seizing him by the arm. "You'll surely win at poker tonight!"

"That night Fanika gave me a massive dose of syphilis! I'm full of pus. That's why I'm determined to get killed."

"Because of syphilis? You're going to sacrifice yourself for the fatherland because of syphilis? Bravo, most noble patriot! And wouldn't it be wonderful if you also got the Karageorge Star, because of syphilis!" Bora was trying to giggle.

"Bora, I'll knock you down! I've told you a hundred times that on occasions like this I can't stand your cynicism," said Danilo, pushing him away.

"You think I can stand it myself?"

"What's this life and freedom worth to me?" stammered Wren, weeping in the darkness. "I'm going to get killed in the first charge."

From the road, a sentry called to them to halt, and asked them for the password. But none of them could remember the password for the night before the offensive.

"Adam, get up! The shells have arrived!"

It was Uroš Babović, shouting above his head. Adam uncovered his head and raised himself on his elbows, but remained lying in the manger under his blanket and the straw.

"The whole army's going to attack tomorrow! We've got orders to prepare for a three-day march."

Uroš Babović rushed outside, but Adam crawled reluctantly out of the manger and went out under the roof of the shed, and felt thoroughly dejected by his own wretched appearance. How could he go to the attack in this state, and what about his horse? In an Austrian overcoat, and on this sorry nag—not on my life, he thought. Yet the coat was new; he had taken it from a dead Austrian and put it on, together with an Austrian cap, so he could hang around behind the front line and look for Dragan. This new Austrian coat he immediately exchanged for a Serbian overcoat, burned and torn, for which he gave a sum of money as well. Then he wiped Corporal Jakov's blood off his breeches and set off for Takovo in the wake of his squadron to exchange his nag, and buy something that looked like a real horse: an animal that could carry him to Valjevo, at a gallop if need be; an animal that would be able to catch up with the division staff—which would surely be the first to flee and the last to advance—if they captured Suvobor. Suvobor would be taken, it must be—that was what everybody wanted. You could hear it and see it, suddenly the idea was in everybody's head: the most gloomy and downcast had become vociferous and noisy; the most exhausted had had their sleep; the most hungry had eaten their fill. In a barn some ten soldiers had gathered round a woman, going after her skirts like rams after a ewe. But who would have any chance today to pinch a woman's knee in competition with the sabers and epaulets of the officers? And if these women in Takovo, young and old, had a dozen legs each, they wouldn't have been enough to give one leg apiece to every soldier of the first levy.

On the main road through the village the soldiers were crowding round a supply train, shouting, threatening, hugging each other, throwing their caps in the air, kissing the oxen, peeping into the carts. Then he understood: the shells were here. He went up to see for himself; the soldiers had their arms full of shells and were kissing and caressing them as though they were young lambs or sucking pigs. He couldn't restrain himself from passing his palm over the shells, and letting his fingers linger on the light yellow rim of the finely turned cartridge cases, as though feeling their thick, metallic pulse. He carried them in his veins as he went from yard to yard, from stable to stable, looking hard at the horses; finally he selected one and offered to swap, and to pay ten dinars, too. Then he offered twenty. But the silly fool would not accept his offer. Then he offered a sergeant a ducat for a sorrel horse. At first the man didn't believe him, until he stretched out his hand with the ducat. The sergeant suddenly became serious, took the ducat, and said that first of all he wanted to see what he was getting in exchange. Adam ran off to get his nag and rode back on it. The sergeant burst out laughing:

"You're a fool, Katić! But I haven't cheated you. Just give your horse a good rubdown and clip its tail."

Adam quickly and happily rubbed down the nag he had given to the sergeant, and rode off on the sorrel horse. He realized at once it was lazy; still, it looked like a horse. He gave it some oats, and lit a cigarette while he listened to it eating. He didn't like the way it took its food: it ate voraciously, like a hired man from a mountain village. Well, perhaps it would do at least until they got to Valjevo.

Some soldiers came past, and dogs growled. Someone was playing a fiddle, which reminded him of Prerovo and its assemblies and church gatherings, and how he and Dragan had jumped over a gypsy's cart and pulled down the canvas roof. He went out of the barn and set out to walk to the village. He would have a decent supper. He went into several yards but came back out again, then finally found a clean house with a clean-looking housewife. But the house was crowded with soldiers milling around the fireplace and the women, eating, drinking, telling coarse and stupid jokes; the dogs were puzzled and didn't bark. So he went through three hamlets, but couldn't find a single house not crowded with soldiers, or a single housewife willing to prepare some roast chicken. He suddenly felt a strong desire to eat chicken livers roasted on embers. But no housewife was willing to go catch a chicken in the dark for any money. He was angry and disappointed; then in the distance he caught sight of a lamp down the slope. The squadron was due to assemble there, so it couldn't be anyone but the staff.

He hurried through the orchards and meadows; the ground was frozen, which made walking and a stealthy approach easy; the darkness suited him, too. These nights with a light frost were good for visiting timid women, kept under the watchful eyes of their in-laws; and also for visits to women who, after tying up the dogs and giving them a piece of bacon, waited, without a sound and hardly breathing, behind the sheepfolds and cowsheds, impatient to raise their skirts as soon as possible, then lower them just as fast, and steal away to the house and their bed.

When he reached the lamp, he regretted coming; judging by the buildings and the dog, it was a poverty-stricken household. But he had no alternative. He knocked on the door and called out.

An older woman opened the door; she would be sure to have pity on a soldier, and judging by her head scarf, she was neat and tidy.

"Do you accept guests, auntie?"

She looked at him sternly for a long time, from the threshold of a lighted room. Behind her back he noticed a little boy and a little girl on a bed; they sat up and looked at him.

"If I could just get warm, auntie."

"Come in, my boy," she said in a gentle, kindly voice.

"Are these your grandchildren?" he said as he entered.

"Yes, they are. Are you married?"

"No, I'm not. Where are your son and daughter-in-law?"

"My son's in Stepa's army; and my daughter-in-law, as a matter of fact, went to her father when the soldiers came down from the mountain. She's a pretty girl, she'd best look after herself."

Adam took off his overcoat, sat down beside the cooking stove, in which a fire had been lit, and looked around the room. The woman was clean; he would be able to get some cheese for supper here, even if she was unwilling to catch a chicken.

"I'm hungry, auntie. I'll pay you whatever you ask. We're going to attack Suvobor at dawn tomorrow. We won't stop till we get to the Drina."

"And what would you like for supper, my boy?"

"May I tell you what I'd really like?"

"Yes, of course."

"First of all some chicken livers, grilled while the chicken is roasting. I feel like eating them as a first course."

She smiled at him—a gentle, kindly smile.

"I'll get it all ready for you. You sit down and get warm. Here's some *rakija*," she said, handing him a cup.

He did not normally drink *rakija*, but this evening he decided he would. He found it very pleasant to be sitting by this blazing fire in a clean room. He said this to the woman when she returned with the slaughtered rooster. She gave a broad smile, and he noticed her fine teeth; her lips looked as though she had been drinking grape juice. When she was young she must have been a pearl among women! Her hands were plump but clean; real woman's hands, such as he liked. And her skirt was clean, as was everything else about her. It was a pity she wasn't a bit younger, at least a year younger. The pipers would be dancing the kolo tonight. She set the rooster to boil, and then began to ask questions, listening attentively and observing him even more attentively. Adam sipped his *rakija*, which had a very pleasant flavor, as if sweetened, and talked to her about Prerovo; as he talked he watched her, taking pleasure in the swiftness of her hands, her nimble movements, the softness of her smooth, milkwhite face. He had not seen an older woman with such a young face, such fine teeth, such curving lips. The girls marry young in the mountain villages, he thought, when she bent down to put the chicken liver on the grill. As soon as he finished one story, she asked him to tell her something else.

When he had finished the chicken liver—the tastiest he had ever eaten—he recollected that he had not breathed the scent of a woman's bosom since leaving Mačva, since he had been with the Kovač girl beside the tavern. After that there had been nothing, apart from the chase after that incomparable Kosanka outside Mionica. They had now been two days in a village without his feeling any desire.

Radinka put the rooster in the oven, sat down on a three-legged stool, poked the fire, and looked up at him with a very sweet expression; he was not drunk, and there was nothing wrong with his eyesight. He began to talk in detail about Dragan; tears welled up in his eyes. She listened carefully, looking at him more and more amiably. He remembered that Draginja, made a widow at the beginning of the war with the Turks, was no younger than this Radinka, nor were her teeth so white—like those of a young girl. He looked at the bed: when would the grandchildren get off to sleep?

She asked him whether he had a girl friend. This confused him: why should she ask him that? He could feel his cheeks burning. He told her that he didn't, which was true. He couldn't tell her now that he loved a student by the name of Natalia, but that she wouldn't look at him because he was a peasant. Radinka reproached him for not having a girl friend, and this somehow excited him. Actually he hadn't asked her where her husband was. He did so now—in a whisper, so the grandchildren couldn't hear; they were struggling not to fall asleep. She replied aloud, with a sigh, that she had been early left a widow. She placed his supper on the table, took the roasted chicken from the oven, and with her face rosy from the fire smiled at him so avidly that a piece of bread stuck in his throat. Those children couldn't be grandchildren—impossible! She lied to me, he thought, seeing I was a soldier; everybody knows what soldiers are; they would smash up kneading troughs, and certainly not overlook such a robust and nimble young woman with a full bosom and solid legs. She was a really good woman, God bless her! He could hardly eat his supper and did so slowly, no longer feeling hungry. She cut up the chicken, selected some pieces, and silently offered them to him. Only Vinka knew how to offer in this mute fashion, and to rouse him by indicating with her eyes her own desire, and how long she had been waiting.

He stopped eating and pushed away the unfinished chicken. She was silent, staring at the glowing embers in the oven; the flames gave a ruddy color to her face, making it younger. Her lips and cheeks were flushed. Her black hair gleamed above her forehead. Those must surely be her children, girls didn't marry so young in these parts. Her husband was away at war; she had lied in talking about her grandchildren and her daughter-in-law. What a blind fool I've become in this war! She's a loyal, honorable woman; how else but by lies could she protect herself from so many lustful soldiers? He looked at those two children. The little boy, her son, was still wriggling. What repulsive creatures little boys could be, they never went to sleep when they ought to, they could go on peering and squirming till daybreak, just as though their fathers had paid them to look after their mothers! He took out a packet of cigarettes, and she handed him a burning brand in the coal tongs; over the flame they looked into each other's eyes. Her hand was trembling; the cigarette fell from his lips. She dropped the firebrand and started away from his hands, stretched out toward her breasts.

"Please go away now!" she whispered.

He got up and put out the lamp, spreading darkness over the children, and the light from the stove over her. He stood motionless; the little boy was still fidgeting in the bed. He remained in a state of confusion and bewilderment, looking down at her, as he liked best to look at a woman. That was how he had looked at Vinka, dressed only in her slip while she lay on the corn in the corncrib, the last night before he left for the front.

She had wanted it that way for some reason: in the corncrib, in the corn itself, under a pile of corncobs. Then the corncrib, full of moonlight and shadow, of gleaming and darkened corncobs, was borne away beneath them toward the Morava: her bosom had the fragrant scent of dry corn, corn silk and cornstalks. He had never been aware of that before. Weeping, she had pulled him into the meadow, the summer, the corn. Until the end of the war, until the war is over! The field murmured beneath them, the moonlight blazed, the sound of dogs barking in the village died away; then they were plunged into the war: a pile of corn rushed down upon them with a roar and buried their hot, sweating bodies. "What if you don't come back?" she kept saying from the depths of her throat. It was these words of hers that frightened him, seared him, not the mobilization order. This fear, hers and his, offended and humiliated him; suddenly hatred welled up in him, and the corncobs were intolerably cold. He jumped up from her, scattering a pile of cobs and covering her exposed belly and bare buttocks. She brushed the corn from her face, only her head was visible. She wept moonlight tears and called to him again and again. He felt a strong desire to plunge her head into the corn, but curbed it. He dressed hurriedly and dashed from the crib.

He bent slowly toward Radinka and the glowing embers, trembling as he came nearer and nearer to her terrified face. She was ready to cry out at the approach of his hands, which passed over her lips with outstretched fingers; then fondled her breasts: she rolled off the stool onto the earthen floor, but he thrust his hands into her bosom and threw her into the darkness. As she sank into it, he noticed her smile, a flame in the light of the embers:

"Do you want me—do you want to make love?"

"Yes."

"Do you want me badly?"

"Very badly."

"Come with me to my room."

She extricated herself from his arms and stole away into the room, and he followed, crawling in through the slightly opened door. She spread something on the floor, shut the door to the kitchen, then crooned before him in the darkness:

"Now come to me, come to me, my soldier!"

Mišić was alone in the room, where he had almost extinguished the lamp: it gave him pleasure to look at the firelight in the stove, and to walk about the room bathed in its ruddy glow. The apples on the stove had burned while he wrangled and hesitated over the time of the attack; he could not, dared not, insist on his first decision to attack at three. Influenced by Kajafa's excessive enthusiasm to start at three, and the refusal of Šturm and Stepa to move before eleven, he had altered his decision, and agreed that the offensive should start at seven. After splitting the difference with regard to the time, he felt more relaxed; his hesitation about the timing had made it impossible for him to concentrate on other worries.

He cut through an apple with his small knife, and walked over to the window to listen to the arrival and departure of the couriers, the horses galloping along the highway, and the passage of a supply train toward the front; then he came back to the stove and stared at the flames, his mind totally absorbed in asking himself whether he had undertaken all possible measures to ensure that the will power of his opponent should be wavering before noon, confused and unsettled by nightfall, and subject to his will in two days' time. He did not hear the various section chiefs come in until they spoke; he replied to them as briefly as possible.

Just before midnight he was startled by the ringing of the telephone.

"Putnik speaking. Mišić, are you still convinced that your main operational plans really are right, and will lead to victory? And that the measures taken to carry them out are the very best ones possible?"

"Yes, I think they are; in fact, I'm sure they are."

"Have you got any strong reason to make any changes?"

"The thing that worries me most is the time when the attack should be launched."

"Yes, I'm worried about that, too."

"Seven o'clock is late, Vojvoda."

"I'm afraid that it's too early. Is it possible for the entire Serbian army to get ready to mount an offensive in a few hours, in view of the weather and terrain, and the wide area over which they have to operate?"

"We must start then. We've no alternative."

"What we *must* do should be what we *can* do."

"I'm sure that we can do all that tonight, Vojvoda."

"My feeling is that Potiorek won't move to the offensive tomorrow. The day after, perhaps. So you really needn't worry any more about what time you start the attack."

"Yes, I'm listening, Vojvoda."

"The only sensible operational plans and decisions are those which seem quite usual to the subordinate commanders, and feasible to the troops. Tomorrow's battle may be decided by a single tenacious platoon, or even a single section making a charge. There comes a time in war when a single soldier may decide the fate of an army. Can you hear me, Mišić?"

"Yes, Vojvoda, I believe that, too."

"I would have no fears for the outcome of our enterprise if every soldier knew that tomorrow he as an individual could win or lose the war for Serbia. Good night, Mišić!"

Mišić continued to hold the receiver to his ear: calling to each other in the distance, the operators sounded suffocated. In front of the staff headquarters the cobbled flags clicked under the horses' hoofs, as couriers and orderlies arrived from other headquarters and left for the positions. Was there any order he had failed to give the army? Had he said anything about sleeping? Yes, that was it, they must sleep! And from that sleep, daybreak would come for the Serbian First Army. He dialed.

"Hello, Drina Division! Mišić speaking. Have you finished all your tasks, Krsta? In ten minutes I want you all to be lying down. Tell the regimental commanders that they're to go to sleep immediately. Good night, Drina, I'll wake you up. Hello, Morava Division! Why aren't you asleep, Ljuba? One sleeps before a wedding, but it's better to pray before an important battle! Go to bed at once and rest as long as possible. Good night, Morava! Give me the Danube Division, first levy. Is your division sleeping, Kajafa? I'm very sorry I've woken you up. Yes, that's right. No, I don't believe in jobs that go on till midnight either. Actors and poets are nightbirds. Oh yes, and politicians and gamblers, too—you're right about that. But with plowmen and farmers and craftsmen and us soldiers—all people who work hard and live serious lives—it's early to bed and early to rise. Sleep well, Kajafa, you and all your division! I want the commander of the Danube Division, second levy, please. Aren't you in bed yet, Vasić?"

"I don't believe that I'll be able to sleep at all tonight, sir!"

"For God's sake, why not, Vasić? How can you dare not to go to sleep tonight?"

"I have in front of me a telegram which will reach you by the normal channels in a few minutes."

"Read it to me at once."

"I have reflected deeply on all aspects of the attack we plan to make tomorrow. I am now convinced, as I was at the discussion in the staff headquarters, that it would be best to wait for the enemy in strong positions and crush him, then move to the attack. That is the surest way to success and the salvation of Serbia."

"Go on, Vasić, I'm listening."

"I gave you all the fundamental reasons for this yesterday."

"I know those. Now tell me the reasons which don't seem so important, but which are bubbling and simmering in your head."

"I still can't convince myself, even tonight, that the greatest risk can also be the wisest course of action."

"Tell me, Vasić, what is the worst thing you think about me tonight? You're a man of honor. I'm listening."

"Yes, I'll tell you that, too, sir. Unfortunately you can't see that a man's greatness does not lie in the greatness of his mistakes. That is disastrous, for you and for us."

"Perhaps. Well, thank you, Vasić. But what can be done about it? The world has been created in such a way that the people with the greatest fallacies often have the greatest rights, too. Fortunately for the First Army and our people, my fallacies and my rights can only last a few days longer. Now please tell the regimental staff officers to go to sleep, and put out your lamp immediately and go to bed. Blink your eyes, listen a few moments, then go to sleep. Good night, Vasić!"

He put down the receiver and went out into the corridor to see whether Hadjić and the other staff officers were asleep. The sleepy sentries and orderlies stood at attention; the lamps hissed, shadows flickered on the walls. He could not tell these soldiers to go to sleep.

The world was so created that not everybody could sleep. Shuddering from cold, he returned to his room, took up his watch from the table, and put out the lamp.

Since you already know the limits of my rights, Vukašin, do you know what is waiting for me, and for me alone, if the First Army should be defeated? Disgrace; yes, eternal disgrace. That is the punishment of the commander of a defeated army. The soldiers get their portion of suffering and hardship, but they can live through it. But to live through and survive the disgrace of the commander of a defeated army is very, very difficult. Everybody remembers it. If only you knew, Vukašin Katić, how desperately afraid I am tonight! I am the biggest coward in the First Army. No one else is tormented by such fear. And not a single soldier in Potiorek's army feels the fear that I do, my friend.

Moving as quietly as possible—very slowly, so he couldn't hear his own movements—he went over to the bed; also as quietly as possible, he lay down on it fully dressed and covered himself with a blanket and his overcoat. He could not stop shivering. He clenched his watch in his hand to muffle the sound of its ticking. If only instead of his watch he had a tuft of Louisa's hair, and were listening to her breathing instead of its ticking, he would have fallen asleep immediately. But he could not sleep for his shuddering: Rudnik and Suvobor seemed to be arching upward. The slopes rose in waves, the heights plunged downward and sank; rivers and paths crisscrossed and intertwined. The land shivered: its teeth were chattering.

6

———

Aleksa Dačić, at the head of a grenade party, was dragging himself along a stream in the darkness just before dawn toward an Austrian machine-gun nest on a small hill covered with mountain pines. He was familiar with that craggy hill from the battle waged by his platoon in the rear guard of the regiment; and he was very familiar with the stream up which he was now stealthily crawling, sweating under his bag full of grenades. It was along this stream that he had fled with Ivan Katić when Katić had lost his glasses; then they had gone back to look for them, barely escaping with their lives. From that hill above them he could hear the sound of coughing. He stood still.

"Shh! We're getting near!" he whispered, restraining with his hand one of his comrades who was walking heavily and sniffing continually. "Sit down!"

He remained standing, straining his ears to catch the sound of coughing up above him in the darkness. Yes, they were awake. They'll realize we're here when we start moving over the crags, and they'll train their machine-gun fire on us. He needn't have come on this wild goose chase. No, he needn't have, but he just couldn't restrain himself when Captain Novaković, the battalion commander, had wakened the platoon, lined them up in the dark, and asked with a cigarette in his mouth:

"Is there anyone here who'd like me to decorate him today with the Obilić Gold Medal for bravery?"

He hadn't been able to see any of their eyes in the darkness.

"Do you mean to say that among fifty Serbs there's not a single hero?

So who am I going to take with me today when I break through the Austrian positions, you motherfuckers?"

That oath had roused Aleksa like a box on the ears, and he shouted: "I'm ready for anything, sir!"

"And you are the only one?" the commander had shouted.

"No, he isn't. What Aleksa can do, so can I," said Miloš Rakić, a cross-eyed soldier from Jagodina who ever since they had been on Baćinac had tried to outdo Aleksa.

"Any more volunteers? Who do you weaklings think I'm going to break through the front with today?" said the commander as he walked along the ranks, hissing at the soldiers. "Come along with me, you two."

He took them past two more platoons, shouting and threatening; a few more volunteers came forward. Then he led them to headquarters and looked at them for a long time by the light of the lamp. They stood against the wall. Finally he spoke to them calmly:

"If our regiment's going to break through the Austrian positions, we must wipe out a well entrenched machine-gun nest and hold that hill until the regiment occupies new positions. Aleksa will lead the assault squad."

Someone behind his back was quietly whistling; he had been whistling ever since they set out: the man was shaking in his shoes.

"Who's that whistling? We're not going to church!"

"It's me. Why shouldn't I whistle? By noon we'll know where we're going to spend Christmas," replied Miloš Rakić.

From the silence above them came the hoarse sound of some Austrians coughing; a frozen stream babbled alongside. They had to go forward.

"You must go like weasels, like squirrels!" whispered Aleksa, and started to move forward slowly; the stream seeped into his heart and gurgled through his veins. "When the Serbian cannon fire their first shells, throw your grenades at them," the commander had said. But what if the Austrians sensed their presence and began to shoot before the Serbian cannon opened fire? Aleksa halted, and told the others to sit down. He sat down on the snow and breathed in the dense fog. Miloš was again whistling; someone else was whispering how last night he'd "laid a real nice bit of skirt in the manger." This whispering and whistling disturbed Aleksa; he told them to be quiet. Miloš Rakić went on whistling.

"If the Austrians realize we're here, I'll throw a grenade at you, you hear?"

He did not hear Miloš Rakić's retort. He felt like a cigarette but dared not light one. So he groped for a twig in the darkness, broke it off, and began to gnaw it. He hadn't managed to tell Ivan Katić what orders he would have to carry out at daybreak; just last night they had been talking in a way he didn't usually talk to his superiors.

Miloš had stopped whistling. Two Austrians coughed above them. Underneath them in the darkness the stream gurgled noisily under the ice and seeped into his heart.

Danilo History-Book and Bora Jackpot formed their sections into a firing line in the murk and fog, and waited for the order to charge. They were lying on the frozen surface of the snow staring at a few fires burning feebly in the fog; up above them were the Austrians.

When I get to that fire on the left, I'll light a cigarette, thought Bora; then he got up and moved away to the right, toward Danilo. Two more hours to wait; it was hard just to look silently at those fires floating in the mist.

To Danilo it seemed that those fires were eyes that had watched him draw up his section and were now taking aim at him. He got up and moved to the left, toward Bora. It would be well over an hour before they would charge; he just could not wait for "that hour" without Bora, without his friend.

As they walked toward each other, they warned the soldiers not to cough, talk, or smoke. Then they met.

"I've been looking for you," whispered Bora.

"And I've been looking for you," said Danilo. He seized Bora's hand but immediately released it, frightened by this desire for contact. What the devil's the matter with me? After all, this isn't my first battle. But it would be his first charge—that charge which, in his letter to his family two days ago, he had not been able to describe with conviction and excitement.

"I wound up my watch when we set out," whispered Bora, pulling Danilo by his sleeve to make him sit down at his side.

Danilo sat down, so that their shoulders and knees were touching. Each thought: he's trembling. They pressed still more firmly against each other to calm themselves. For a long time they just gazed at the dying fires sinking, plunging, floating in the mist toward the sky.

"It's still dark. But it's not six o'clock yet. I don't hear the roosters."

"We've eaten them."

"What about the dogs?"

"The dogs fell asleep just before daybreak."

"I wonder what they're thinking around those fires?" said Bora, taking his watch out of his pocket and holding it to his ear. He didn't wish now to deprive himself of any presence, any memory, any sorrow. Let his father count aloud those seconds to the first salvos from the cannon, and the bugle summoning them to charge.

They were both thinking about their homes, warm rooms, beds. Danilo took a handful of snow and clutched it: his brothers and sisters would be asleep, as though there were no war. An innocent sleep. All the girls would be asleep in spite of the war. But perhaps his mother was up. His grandfather, too, if he was on his estate. He would begin his letter: *You were sleeping soundly while I was lying in the snow, under Suvobor.*

"What do you think was the first thing that made man measure time? What was the first reason?"

"People started to measure time for purely practical purposes. There wasn't any ulterior motive. Just a question of practical usefulness."

"I don't think so. The man who made the first clock was neither a merchant nor a craftsman nor a military leader. The first man who had a wish to measure time and listen to it passing must have been a man who had known the depths of despair, a man more despairing than the prophets of the Old Testament. A man obsessed with death."

"I don't believe that," said Danilo; he could feel Bora's hand on his knee: it was trembling. Something was going to happen to him. Even last night, when they learned about the offensive, he had begun to behave strangely. He made fun of the new commanding officer, offended Wren, and wanted to have a fight because they didn't wish to play poker.

"Nothing important or lasting began for an insignificant reason; I'm sure of that, Danilo," said Bora, leaning more firmly against his friend: Danilo was not trembling from cold. He wanted to see his face, to see his eyes. Last night he had said three times: "Something important is going to happen. Something that will go down in history—you'll see."

"Perhaps it was a man in love who invented the clock. Someone who was waiting for a woman, or going to see her. What about that, Bora?"

"I don't think so. Lovers aren't bothered about time. They think with their eyes."

They fell silent and looked at the enemy fires leaping up in the fog.

In his head Danilo composed the letter he had begun: Immediately after midnight we took up our positions and waited for daybreak, when we would charge. In the pocket of my friend who was lying beside me, his watch was ticking away . . . What was it ticking away? Time? But this was banal, not true either. A watch does not show anything. Its time is not human time. The only time that exists is *my* time. And what is my time now? While waiting for the bugle to sound the charge, I listened to his watch. Very unconvincing; they'll suspect that I'm lying. How can you listen to a watch in someone else's pocket? Only fear has ears to hear a watch like that. Instead of all this fuss about the watch, I'll write: I was waiting for the bugle to sound the charge and looking at the campfires in the enemy lines. It was like the night before the battle of Borodino. His father, who knew *War and Peace* by heart, would laugh aloud; his grandfather would start to cough at those sentences. But what he said there was true.

"Take care of yourself today, Danilo."

Danilo gave such a start that Bora's hand fell from his shoulders. "Why should I do that?"

"No special reason. Just that we must be careful today."

"But it's precisely today that I won't be careful. Today I'm going to fight to make history, I assure you."

"And what shall we do with your little wooden horse?"

"My little wooden horse?" stammered Danilo after a slight pause. "We will do what we agreed on that freezing cold night on Maljen. If I get killed, you'll go to Novi Sad and tell my family that I was killed in a charge; you must say it was in a charge. Then you'll take the little wooden horse which my grandfather gave me as a present on Saint Vitus' Day, when I finished the first grade of the primary school. And you'll keep it for your son. That all right with you, Jackpot?" He tried to sound lighthearted as he spoke the last sentence and put his hand on Bora's knee.

"Yes, that's all right with me, Danilo. Let's leave it like that for the time being. But after the war we won't say anything to anybody about your little wooden horse."

Bora brought his face nearer and looked hard at Danilo; he seemed to be smiling. Ever since they had heard about the offensive, he looked strange. And he smiled for no obvious reason, as though smiling in his sleep. How could he keep up Danilo's courage? And what could he give Danilo as a memento?

They stared at the fires in silence. The Austrians were extinguishing their fires, as if they were killing them. They heard a whistle up above in the fog. As if obeying a command, they both stood up and said:

"Take care of yourself today."

"You, too."

Crouching over, they hurried back to their places in front of their squads.

"I don't like it that our platoon is staying with the regimental reserve," said Sava Marić to Ivan Katić in a worried voice, as he handed him a shelled walnut.

"Why not?"

"Because the reserve fights both its own battle and the C.O.'s, too."

They were sitting under the roof of a shed, between vats filled with fermenting plums; around them in the limpid darkness the soldiers were wrangling as to when was the best time to cook *rakija*.

"And what is the C.O.s battle, Sava?"

"That's the most costly of all battles, sir. It's fought for the officers' promotions and medals."

Ivan Katić could not quite grasp this, but because of his own anxiety about going into battle without a spare pair of glasses, he had no wish to prolong this conversation with Sava Marić, who was unusually talkative that morning at daybreak. He had pestered Ivan with questions about what sort of people the French were, and how they were different from the Serbs. But Ivan couldn't tell him anything at all significant. Sava's curiosity simply aroused in Ivan a violent, burning sadness at the thought of Paris, that city now beyond his reach, that dream-like amalgamation of freedom and beauty, and the exciting illusion that there was nothing in this world one couldn't do. That was how it seemed to him, and how it seemed to all young men in that city. My father believed that, too, he thought. Never again would he stroll through the Latin Quarter with a book under his arm, listen to the organ in Notre Dame, walk through the Tuileries, and experience the heady sensation of seeing women's smiles, like rosy foam, on the pavements of the Boulevard Saint Michel. No, of course I don't regret coming back, he thought; I've no regrets at all—I had to come.

On the road, an infantry column was passing on its way to the lines; some officers were shouting and swearing at the soldiers because they wouldn't stand aside to let them pass with their horses. Ivan could hear blows and groans.

"Do you hear those blows, Sava?"

"Yes, I do. And the man that's doing the thrashing has the right to do it; and the man that's getting thrashed has to put up with it. He's got to learn sense, and keep out of the sight of bloodsuckers."

"Then what does freedom mean to you, Sava? What are you dying for? Perhaps the poor wretch whom that blockhead of an officer is bashing with his saber will be dead in two hours."

"Freedom?" said Sava, as he cracked a walnut. "Who can say what he means by freedom? For me it means not being afraid to love and respect, those things which in my soul I feel I must love and respect, according to the wisdom given me. And not being afraid not to love and respect what I don't want to." He handed Ivan a shelled walnut.

"And do the soldiers, I mean the peasants, feel like that about freedom?" Ivan took the walnut but didn't eat it.

"Everybody has his own kind of freedom, Mr. Katić. I know what mine is."

"Forgive me, but what is it, exactly?"

"Well, put it this way. For my own folk, I'm willing even to be a servant. But with a stranger I don't even want to be a landlord, or to lord it over him in any way. When a Serbian tax collector wants the skin off my back, when a Serbian officer beats me, then I'll curse him and do my best to deceive him. I'll keep out of their sight. For instance, when we've got a government that's no good, like we have now, if you can't change it, cheat it! But perhaps it will be changed. As you know, we've changed kings and rulers several times in less than a hundred years!"

"But what more is there to your freedom, Sava?"

"Sir, I want to sing when I feel like singing, and to cry when I feel like crying. I want to do what I feel like doing. That's what I'm fighting for."

Ivan was struck dumb. For ten years at home he had listened to his father and his friends, professors and doctors, talking about the national aims of Serbia; he had heard about the war aims of politicians, officers, journalists, radicals, and socialists, but nobody had ever said like this peasant: I'm fighting so that I can love and respect the things that I love and respect. Yes, there was some point in dying for Sava's war aim.

"Do you like the smell of fermenting plums, Mr. Katić?"

"Yes, I do. I love the smell of fruit when it's rotting and fermenting. Those smells of peasant houses, barns, distilleries," he stammered untruthfully.

Sava did not agree with the soldiers who asserted that you should not cook *rakija* before the first frost. Ivan listened to their wrangling, which was conducted in serious tones, as though they were discussing the very essence of matter. As he listened to them he breathed in the smell of fermenting plums for the first time in his life.

At dawn, as the daylight was struggling to break through the dense fog, Mišić was riding onto the slope above Milanovac, toward the positions of the Morava Division, accompanied by a few of his officers. At the top of the slope he stopped to look at the area in which his army would operate; everything was bathed in mist—no good for the cannon. It was very quiet: not a cock crowed, and no dog barked. He looked at his watch: it was six o'clock. If Field Marshal Oscar Potiorek had also decided to begin his offensive today, then he too had planned to start at seven. The two armies would collide as they advanced; and the one with the cooler commander and the bolder soldiers would win. Then Putnik's midnight warning would become a reality: the battle could be decided by a platoon, a section, or one fearless soldier.

The officers around him were silent. He wanted to ask them why. But he did not wish to begin this day, which was just dawning, with such a mistake. The frozen ground crackled beneath the horses' hoofs, echoing as far as Suvobor; they were going uphill, sinking into the fog, in which the trees were dissolving and the path had completely disappeared.

The platoons had already occupied their positions, he thought; then he saw them: the infantry, staring mutely at the fog, with their bayonets fixed; there were extra shells beside packing cases, behind the gunners who were fussing nervously with the mechanism of the sights; the battery commanders had their headphones on, and were checking their communication with the field telephones; the officers kept looking at their watches. Was there anything that he, the commander of the army, had not thought of and foreseen, any necessary measures he had not taken? He did not know. Had he any forebodings? He did not want to answer this question, not even to himself.

He had had no dreams last night, though for a moment he had managed to stop the movement of Rudnik, Rajac, and Suvobor, which had been colliding, changing places, and getting mixed up with one another all night long. They had thrown off the divisions placed on them, but he had replaced them according to his dispositions for the attack.

But he had got up on his left leg, damn it! He looked at his watch:

half past six. He must be on the ground, standing on his feet, when the cannon started firing. He pressed his horse to a gallop along the slope, into the fog. He couldn't stand the thundering noise and the dust of several horses galloping. He came to a forest and stopped his horse. He could not see the end of the forest; the oaks beside the path were tall and strong. Among them he would wait for the battle to start. He dismounted.

"Wait for me here," he said, and went into the forest. The frozen surface of the snow cracked under his footsteps, echoed through the forest as in an empty church. He walked a bit further, so that his officers could not see him, so that not a living soul could see him. He would choose a tree for this moment; he looked for a powerful oak with a clean trunk and no dead branches. He found a good one, and leaned his arm against its cold, dark brown firmness. He breathed this oak tree into his nostrils, knelt down, removed his cap, put it down on the dry turf, crossed himself, and pressed his forehead against the tree trunk:

"O God our Creator, I have done what is within my power and knowledge. I know that it is very little for our survival. Do Thou, if Thou dost exist, work the miracle."

He remained with his forehead pressed against the oak tree, listening to the beating of his heart; the forest around echoed with its pulsation.

Bora Jackpot was lying down in the snow, staring into the fog and listening to his watch: if the timepiece had not been invented, perhaps there wouldn't have been any wars. In the chronicle of evil that was recorded history, everything of any significance had its origin in the fear of time. That loathsome creature, man, had become a plunderer, a robber, a philosopher, and had introduced war on this earth, all out of his horrible fear of time. And what did this so-called Serbian offensive mean in the infinite stretch of time, in the Galaxy? We'll put bullets into some goddamn Austrians, and they'll do the same to us; we'll shout and yell, and then rot. Meanwhile the Great Wheel goes whirling around. The Galaxy has been flung into infinity. But here and now, in the very instant of the first light which is about to appear, we will simply begin shitting and slaughtering. Here am I, supposed to be a section leader. I'll be ordering these peasants to hurl themselves at the Austrians and get killed. Perhaps my father is sitting on a tiny cog of the Great Wheel, a cog much smaller than a pin, sitting there without his head, which stayed on the earth with the ax, stayed in the fatherland. He gave a shudder, and pressed his forehead against the snow. My guts will rot today. I should have left some memento for Danilo History-Book. A card, at least. The jack of hearts. Bora, you wretch, you shit.

Danilo History-Book was lying down in front of the soldiers, fighting off a sense of foreboding; he did so by concentrating on hatred of the enemy. He recollected all the reasons for this hatred, but now they didn't seem very compelling. He recalled the scorn shown to the Serbs in Vienna, about which their new commanding officer, and also Wren, had spoken the previous evening. Well, a man might fight a duel for the sake of pride and honor. But to go to war—and such a war as this? Only if one felt hope. One could have high hopes, that early December morning, of expecting a salvo from the cannon. And the bugle calling them to charge. He would begin his letter: While I was waiting for the bugle to sound the charge, I remembered my grandfather's dearest wish.

Second Lieutenant Jevtić materialized out of the fog, smiled at him, and beckoned him to come join him. Danilo jumped up, trembling—but not only from cold; he was caught again at an inopportune moment.

"Another ten minutes," said the lieutenant in a quiet voice, smoking avidly.

Danilo straightened his belt and put his bag in position. Somewhere down below, in the direction of the village, a dog began to bark in the fog: a powerful, deep-toned bark. Was it threatening someone, defending itself, or simply conveying a warning? He felt agitated as he listened to it; that dog was warning of something extremely important. The lieutenant was also listening anxiously, and the soldiers, too. Some of them took off their caps and crossed themselves. Some of them looked sternly at Danilo, as if looks could kill. If it had been dusk and not dawn, he would have crossed himself, too. The lieutenant smiled at him: he was saying something, and pointing to the sky. Danilo did not understand what he was driving at. The dog went on barking.

"It's going to be mild today. It'll be a glorious day, you'll see!" said the lieutenant, rather too loudly.

Danilo wanted to express his doubts about the glorious day, but suddenly a booming sound over his head made him sway, and he was bent double from the firing of the cannon, whose shells were exploding in the Austrian positions higher up in the fog. A wave of groans echoed through the first light of day.

"That's our cannon, boys! Go on, give them a good bashing, don't spare the shells! So there is a God, after all! All power to your elbow, gunner! We've been waiting for our Serbian cannon to blast their guts! Go on, gunner, don't spare the shells! I don't care if they double the taxes after the war—I'll pay up! I'd give half my estate for a few crates of shells!"

The soldiers shouted and threw their caps in the air.

This was it, the real thing: Serbia's hour of greatness. Those are the words I'll begin my letter with, said Danilo to himself. He quivered, tears welled up in his eyes, he felt like embracing his men.

The cannon went on firing without a pause. Second Lieutenant Jevtić said: "When you hear the bugle, rush forward as if going into a field of corn. Can you peasants hear me? Never mind if they pepper us with shells. We'll go forward as though we were going through an apple orchard when there's a wind blowing! Do you hear me, boys?"

"Yes, we hear! We'll do it!"

"Anyone that gets behind must hurry to catch up. And whoever's in front is not to wait for anyone till he gets to the top of Suvobor!"

"Why shouldn't we wait at the Drina, sir? Suvobor is too near!" interrupted Bora Jackpot, infuriated by the lieutenant's talk of "corn" and "apple orchards" and "wind"—schoolmasterish heroics and words meaningless in the face of death. They made him feel ashamed in front of the soldiers, behind whom stretcher-bearers were standing. The bugle sounded the charge. The lieutenant raised his hand and shouted:

"Charge!"

He rushed up the slope in front of his platoon, brandishing his revolver. Bora Jackpot too hurried up the bare slope, vowing not to lie down under the bullets until the lieutenant did so. Because of the shells, he couldn't hear the rifles and machine guns. Danilo had rushed out boldly in front of his section, spurring himself on and strengthening his conviction by constantly repeating: This is the real thing—the real thing at last! Bullets began to hiss around him. The lieutenant shouted:

"Charge! Hurrah!"

The bugle shrilled angrily. The soldiers yelled, "Hurrah!" Danilo shouted, too, as he ran toward the forest looming out of the fog.

"Lie down, Danilo!" said a voice in the distance.

He turned around: it was Bora who was calling to him. Danilo fell down in the snow and opened fire on the enemy trenches some hundred paces away. Shells were bursting behind the Austrian trenches. This overshooting filled him with despair. The lieutenant again gave the order to charge. Danilo got up.

"First section, forward!" Jevtić commanded. "Second section, rapid fire!"

Danilo then ran toward the smoking barrels; he would not stop till he got to the enemy trenches. From a standing position he fired at an Austrian trying to escape from the trench; he felled him. Then he aimed at a helmet behind the ridge.

Bora Jackpot stumbled over a piece of turf, fell on a rock, and groaned: had he broken his leg, or was he wounded? The soldiers caught up with him. They'll think I'm frightened, the bastards! He must get to the trenches, right up to the gun barrels; he simply must. He got up, began to run, and overtook his soldiers. A few rifles were shooting at him; he would be safe if he jumped into the trench and took away their rifles. He fell down in the snow in front of the smoking rifles trained on him, and gave a convulsive shudder; he didn't know why he was lying down—only a few more steps and he'd be there. He fired, then stopped: the sky came looming out of the fog, the forest grew right up to the sky, the bare treetops were burning the blue expanse. I'm dying, he thought. The sky burst asunder above his head, hideously blue and shining. The Austrians ran through the fog, rushing upward toward the bright, shining blue. His soldiers pursued them and jumped into the trench.

From the Austrian trench Danilo History-Book was shooting at Austrians who were trying to run away into the wood, into the fog which met them as they came down from the mountain ridge. The Serbian cannon pounded at the fog and the Austrians.

"Forward! Rapid fire! We're still after them!" shouted Jevtić.

Aleksa Dačić and his assault squad did not manage to get up to the machine-gun nest unobserved, though two of the Austrians never stopped coughing. As soon as the first Serbian shells fell on the Austrian positions, the machine gun began to chatter over the mountain pines, where Dačić and his squad were edging along "like weasels." Aleksa gave the order: "Follow me! Surround it!" In a few leaps he reached the entrenched gun, and at the same time won the bet of three packets of tobacco that he had made with Miloš Rakić: he was the first to throw a bomb behind the stone wall.

"Where are you, whistler?" he cried.

Miloš Rakić answered from his right: "I've got two here."

Two more grenades reverberated, after which the machine gun was silent.

"Mine was the first!" cried Aleksa defiantly.

Up above them, behind the stone wall, they could hear groaning.

"Give yourselves up, brothers!"

Somebody threw one more grenade. Aleksa ordered, "Form a firing line!" Then they surrounded the stone summit of the hill, shouting loudly: "Come out into the clearing!"

Instead of soldiers, the attackers could see only four clenched fists waving above the stone wall.

"Heads up! We want to see all of you! Stand up, you Austrian pisspots!"

Someone fired a bullet at one of the fists. With this shot two of the fists sank behind the stone, and one bareheaded Austrian rose up, thrusting his hands into the fog. Aleksa Dačić jumped on the machine gun.

Those whom Dačić did not mow down with the machine gun were raked with rifle volleys by his squad. Serbian firing lines came hurrying up the mountain side and surrounded the fir grove. The fog, descending from the summits of Suvobor, coagulated in the streams.

And where's that goddamn battalion commander to see what I'm doing now? said Aleksa Dačić to himself, as he opened a case full of ammunition. What price a medal for bravery, for Christ's sake! For what I've done just now I should be promoted to sergeant and get the Karageorge Star! To hell with those bastard officers—a bunch of cowards and thieves!

As though scared off by the Serbian cannon, the fog moved down from Rudnik and Suvobor and thickened into a great dense skein above the Morava, rolling along the river's meandering course. A mild, bright day rose over the earth, with the sky forming a wide, deep arc above the mountain and the great battle being fought there. An autumn day such as could not have been hoped for, ousted from its proper sequence; a day that had yielded before the sudden onslaught of a winter bursting upon the warring land ahead of time, cutting short its season, lashing it with snow and north winds; and now that day, lost in infinity, had flown down this morning over Serbia like a wild goose over a newly sown field.

General Mišić was hurrying to the headquarters in Milanovac with his staff to hear the first reports from the commanders. Behind his back the increasingly furious clangor and thunder of the battle reverberated over the mountains, while in front of him the valleys were filled with concentrated light and quiet.

It was no matter of chance, he was sure, that a day like this had greeted the start of the offensive: it was unforeseen and unexpected, as was the First Army's attack. It was a gala day like a great feast day, a moment of salvation. He saw something festive in everything that met his eye—trees, houses, the earth itself. Now he was sure of success.

He rode through Milanovac with a smile on his face; people greeted him anxiously and listened intently to the battle. Still smiling, he passed through the staff headquarters, leaving behind him a murmuring crowd of astonished officers: it was the first time they had seen him smiling. He went into his own room; Dragutin, who was staring at the stove, did not hear him.

"What a day! Have you seen it, Dragutin?" he asked, saluting him and smiling broadly. "No worry about sowing something today, is there?"

"Yes, sir, you could start sowing today—that is, if tomorrow's the same as today. For another two or three days, in fact," said Dragutin seriously, and then went out into the corridor.

"That's right. We want another two or three days like this," said Mišić as Dragutin left. Then he sat down at the table to be near the telephone. The room was full of the battle. The First Army was doing its work well; he could hear its heart beating, its fist striking.

Hadjić called out from the doorway: "An excellent start! Excellent, sir! I've got reports from all the divisions."

"How could they not make a good start on such a day!"

Hadjić read the reports from the division commanders. Mišić could visualize the First Army climbing up toward Rajac and Suvobor along the entire front—a bit slowly, but still they were climbing, leaving booty and prisoners behind. My will rules that front, he said to himself, not listening to Hadjić's exclamations of joy. Potiorek was offering resistance, and was not yet put out of his stride. We must strike at his main force, he thought, and annihilate his will.

"Just a minute, Hadjić. I want to write the orders to the divisions for tomorrow."

"Isn't it early for that, sir? It's only noon."

"No, it isn't early. This day isn't going to end for us."

"We just have to chase them off that slope, and that'll be enough for today. Those were the orders for our battalion," said Second Lieutenant Jevtić with a smile; he was talking to Danilo History-Book and Bora Jackpot while they all took cover.

"It certainly is enough, sir. We've charged six times today, and climbed six slopes," said Bora Jackpot, who was hungry, thirsty, and tired.

"It's not enough, sir! We've broken their back, and should pursue them till midnight," said Danilo. He felt neither hunger nor fatigue; when he felt thirsty, he ate some snow.

They were standing under the cover of the platoon firing line, which was replying somewhat languidly to the enemy; the fire from the Serbian cannon was now much less frequent, as though the guns were tired, or had used up their ammunition. The enemy artillery had not been active on that part of the front since noon.

"Get ready—we have to charge," said Jevtić with a quiet sigh. "Protić, take your section along the edge of the wood, get behind them, then charge them from the side. Luković, hold them under rapid fire."

Danilo was pleased with his task, excited at the prospect of attacking by the flank and taking prisoners—something in which the third platoon had been unsuccessful. Seeing Danilo's expression, Bora frowned, and lit a cigarette.

"Look after yourself!" Danilo said to him, clapping him on the shoulder as he moved toward his own section.

Bora was stung by Danilo's anxiety: was it in fact a reproach? He felt like shouting after him: Russia will conquer Austria-Hungary—you just conquer your fear, my hero!

Danilo crawled over the melting snow through heavy and accurate rifle fire from the top of the slope.

"Second section, follow me! Crawl up to the thornbushes!" he commanded in a strained voice, deafened by the sound of the firing. You don't think about anything during a charge, he concluded for the tenth time that day, regretting that he hadn't finished his letter. One's feelings were really quite ordinary, and at times even shameful and disgusting. Everything was swallowed up by fear—all the writers and poets were liars. He dragged himself over the snow on his wet knees and elbows.

A soldier behind him groaned; he turned around. It was Voja, who had dropped his rifle and was making convulsive movements in the snow. The best soldier in the section. Several times he had said humbly to Danilo: "You're like a father to us, Corporal." "But I'm five years younger than you!" "Even so, you're our senior." Danilo crawled back toward him; a bullet grazed the shin bone of his left leg. He couldn't look at it, so intent was he on reaching Voja.

"Where have you been hit?"

"In the stomach, sir. Oh, God!" He made convulsive movements in the snow, staining it red.

"Stretcher-bearers!" called Danilo. "Where are you?" No one came near because of the fierce firing. "Where's your wound, Voja?"

"In my stomach. I'm done for. I'm dying, sir. Will you write a letter to my children? Bogoljub has my address."

"Yes, I'll write to them. You will write yourself. People don't die of stomach wounds. Come here, Jovanović!" The man glowered at him as at an Austrian, and didn't budge. Bullets spattered the snow. Danilo knelt down, took hold of Voja by the legs, and began to pull him along the side of the slope to where there was some protection.

"Don't go to all this trouble, sir. Just write the letter. And forgive me if I haven't always behaved properly."

"There's nothing to forgive. You're the best soldier in the section. You'll soon be all right again and back with us," he stammered.

"Thank you, sir."

Voja's face turned pale, and his eyes blinked. Danilo hurriedly dragged his limp body over the snow. He called the stretcher-bearers, cursing them as he had never cursed anyone in his life. Voja's head was now drooping sharply, dragging behind his body as though detached from it. Danilo dropped his legs and took hold of his head. A wave of tremors passed across Voja's face. Danilo unfastened Voja's jacket and put his hand on his heart: it was still. He jerked his hand, remained in a kneeling position for a few moments, then rushed up toward his section; they were waiting for him under cover. He stood still, transfixed. Voja's death is my fault, he thought. I could have taken the section lower down, where there is cover. What was the matter with me? He trembled as he looked at all his soldiers in turn; they met his glance sternly, perhaps even with hatred.

"Are you all here?" he asked.

"One of the conscripts has been wounded. They've taken him off."

The shooting from the summit above them seemed to have died down a bit. It would soon be dark; they must hurry.

"Come on. Follow me!"

He hurried through the sparse bushes along the side of the slope; occasional bullets passed high over their heads. All Danilo could think of was those tremors passing over Voja's pallid face. Behind him he could hear spurts of rifle fire.

It was growing dark. The battle was dying down, breaking into fragments; only from the west, from the direction of Ravna Gora, could they hear the firing of one last charge.

Bora Jackpot ran down from the height above, calling to Danilo.

The platoon of Ivan Katić and Sava Marić had entered the battle at dusk the previous day; after two unsuccessful charges with some losses, they had not managed to drive the Austrians from their well fortified positions. When it grew dark they retreated, downcast; the soldiers would not accept the defeat of their last hopes.

"Where are we going to go if we fall back?" they said. "General Mišić ordered us to go forward. We'll get onto that mountain, even if we all get killed!"

"We'll attack the mountain tomorrow at daybreak," said Sava, trying to calm them down; but Ivan felt as he had after his first battle—his first defeat—on Baćinac. Those moments yesterday when the mountain had loomed up out of the fog, its white snowy surface shining in the blue sky, had been for him like a vision, or a dream from long ago. Sava had called out to him:

"Look at the sky, Corporal! There's the sun! You educated people don't believe in God, but can you tell me where a day like this came from, today of all days? We haven't seen a sign of the sun for a month!"

Ivan looked around him, fascinated: the mountains with their snowy white peaks, loomed up into the light and blueness, into eternity and peace. The war, the battle, was taking place in the fog, in the foothills, in some pit at the bottom of the earth. The bright light and the intense blue brought tears to his eyes, and he took off his glasses: yes, the war would end in the fog, in the streams. No battle could be fought under this blue sky; one could not kill people in such bright light. Light of Light. That was the third section of the dissertation he planned to write. He could also include a somewhat psychological chapter, based on his war experiences, entitled "Light and Illumination." Yes, that was what he would call it: "Light and Illumination." He wiped his eyes, looked down at the dry grass, and got caught by a thornbush. Shells roared above him as they pounded the wood. Sava Marić was murmuring something behind his back, continuing a conversation begun at dawn, on the day they came down from the mountain into a village.

"War has ruined our land. Look at our awful roads, Mr. Katić, steep uphill, and slippery downhill. And the people aren't themselves at all, what with poverty and fear. Do you know how many fine people there are in these mountains?"

Ivan did not believe him, just as he had not believed him the first time they had talked. Several carts bringing wounded men from the lines passed them on the road.

The platoon spent the night in a village cemetery; the soldiers found some straw and spread it on the gravestones and collapsed tablets. So they slept, or moved about, and thought their anxious thoughts; they placed their trust only in General Mišić. Ivan listened to them, surprised that their feelings were so commonplace, and that they had this need for faith in their commander. Nobody mentioned the fatherland, Serbia, or any war aims. They talked about the war as some great evil, from which they could be delivered by a capable commander and by their own patience and self-sacrifice.

Just as last night he had sat down on a cross torn from its place and leaned his back against a tombstone, so he sat now at dawn, his limbs numb, in a blur of fatigue, sleeplessness, and cold. He looked around, then blinked again. Once more the day would dawn foggy, but not such a dense fog as on the previous day at this time. He looked at the enclosed fields on the slope, on the other side of the stream: that was where the enemy positions were. As soon as it gets light they must capture them; they must be captured at all costs—that was the order from the regimental staff. Those positions had held up the advance of a whole division. They were waiting for their cannon. "First we'll soften them up with artillery, then go for them with our bayonets." That's what the C.O. had said last night, speaking in a lighthearted tone, with that thick-skinned lightness and indifference to sacrifices which Ivan had noticed in all commanders; only in Major Stanković had it not been apparent. And the whole night I haven't thought about Bogdan! Is that possible? All human feelings have died in me. I've forgotten about Milena, too. Incredible! If Sava Marić didn't remind me of human values, I'd either be a downright coward or as brutal as Luka Bog.

"Will we be moving soon, Corporal?" a soldier asked him, peeping from behind a tombstone.

He looked at his watch: ten to seven. "Yes, very soon."

"I wish we could start. I've had it."

"You can see I'm shivering, too."

Shells roared above their heads and fell in the enclosed fields; their booming finally died away in the streams. The soldiers hidden in the cemetery talked gaily, crossed themselves, and prayed for the gunners. The enemy answered with fire from two cannon: their shells flew over the cemetery and fell in the orchards and meadows. This cannonade will shatter the morning, Ivan thought, and stretched out on a fallen tombstone.

The platoon commander climbed onto the biggest tombstone and looked at the enclosed field through his binoculars, while his orderly braced his legs. He kept up a running commentary:

"Overshot that time, the blind idiots! Overshot again! Can't see for nuts! Ah, that was a good one! And that one. Missed that time. But they've got salt on their tails now, those Austrian bastards!"

It was growing light. The artillery duel continued. Ivan began to read the inscriptions on the tombstones:

> Here lie the weary bodies of Krsta and Mioljka
> Radenko Pljakić, a marvelous reaper
> Živodarka, with kind and tireless hands
> Milorad Belić, who had a good word for every man and beast

He stared at the clumps of dirt and thornbushes around the fallen tombstones, then sought out the eyes on the photographs. None of the people in this cemetery wore glasses; they could all see clearly whatever they looked at.

An Austrian shell boomed over quite low and exploded in the road beside the cemetery. The commanding officer jumped down from his observation post on the tombstone.

Ivan did not move: if this battle—the present offensive, the entire war—could in fact take place only here, in this village cemetery, then it would assume some higher significance. Here he would not feel that instinctual terror, he would not be afraid of losing his glasses, he could cling to the tombstones and crosses.

The cannon continued to fire, but there was no sign of life from the infantry. Sava came up to him and sat on a tombstone bearing the words: *Milan departed this life aged three years.*

"Do you know the names of the different kinds of grass you're looking at, Corporal?"

"No, Sava, I don't."

"That one near your feet is called hawkweed, and the one next to it is bluecurl. The one near the child's grave is called mothersoul. And then there's some celandine. They're grasses which have a scent."

A shell roared past and exploded in the stream.

"After the war, if we come out alive and well, God willing, you must come stay with me just before we pick the plums. Then you'll see what a beautiful land this is, Mr. Katić."

Ivan settled his glasses on his nose and looked hard at Sava. Is he trying to comfort me before I die? he wondered. He thinks I'm frightened. But what grounds has he for believing I'm a coward? Or is he trying to fight back his own fear with these stories?

"You're afraid, Sava. I noticed it even last night, and I was a bit surprised."

"Yes, Corporal, I'm afraid. I'm scared stiff," he replied without the slightest hesitation.

Ivan smiled at him with a mixture of gratitude and condescension. Both of them fell silent and looked at their soldiers. The bugler was cleaning his trumpet, "to give it a shine." One man was sitting on a grave, sewing buttons on his breeches. A few of them were feverishly arranging various odds and ends spread out on the gravestones, and putting them in their bags.

An orderly came up on horseback and stopped at the end of the cemetery; the commanding officer approached him eagerly and nodded his head. Then he called the corporals.

"Don't you think it would be a good idea, Sava, for you to tie on my glasses with a piece of string, so I can't possibly lose them?"

"Yes, we'll do that, Mr. Katić. But we don't have to do it now, not until we start moving through the scrub and the woods."

"We've got orders to move," said the commanding officer, straightening his belt. "The entire platoon is to advance at a run to that big tree. From there, Katić is to go forward against the Austrians, using grenades and bayonets, while you, Marić, are to cover their advance with gunfire. Is that clear?"

"Yes, sir," said Sava.

"Get back to your places!"

They went back. Shells were hurtling over them from both directions, and guns began to spurt from left and right. Ivan stopped:

"Tie on my glasses now, Sava, just to be on the safe side."

Sava took some string from his pocket, wound it around the frames of Ivan's glasses and then around his head, tied it, and pulled his cap over the string.

The bugler sounded charge, but softly and hesitantly.

Ivan stood at the head of his section, giving the words of command, then started to run through the meadows and stubble fields toward the big tree. The Austrians didn't fire at them. Breathing hard, they reached the underbrush and the big tree. Cannon were firing over them. The commanding officer ordered both sections to continue to advance; Ivan felt a bit easier, because Sava's section was also advancing. He heard Sava give a shout, turned around, and caught sight of him behind his own section. Sava was slapping one of the soldiers! Ivan couldn't believe his glasses; he went up and heard him swearing amid a rain of blows:

"Forward march! You're lying, you coward! Forward!"

Ivan stopped short: was Sava really striking his soldiers? And now, of all times! The Austrians opened a heavy fire; the entire platoon sprawled in the shallow snow of the clearing. The commander gave the order to charge, and the bugler sounded it on his bugle. Ivan ran forward in front of his section and rushed toward the wood, as though Sava had struck him.

Some fifty paces from their trenches, the Austrians halted them with heavy fire. Ivan turned around, looking for the soldier whom Sava had struck. If that man is killed, I'll spit at Sava in front of the whole platoon, he thought. He called the first section and began to crawl toward the wood, where shells were exploding. Deafened and half paralyzed, his senses numbed, he hurled a grenade into the Austrian trenches, then remained lying down behind a bush. The soldiers did what they had to do without words of command from him. The Austrians jumped out of their trenches and fled from the enclosed field, taking cover behind the trees; they were soon scattered by shells. Ivan went after them with his soldiers, but didn't fire at them. He could see his own dead and wounded lying on the bare slope and in the field. He felt neither pain nor anger.

Still in the same numbed state, he pursued the Austrians toward Ravna Gora; the soldiers were enraged, vociferous, and full of self-confidence: they were enjoying the advance. Ivan despised himself because he could not rejoice like these men, who had their ears boxed by everybody. He was preoccupied with his glasses; he felt that now he could no longer respect Sava; he was afraid at the thought of meeting him when they halted. Meanwhile the sky was so clear and blue that even a man's hand could sully it. The light flowed into the thunder and roaring of the battle. Even in this light the killing went on.

Adam Katić—and all the other troopers, too—found this waiting in reserve hard to take. The whole of the previous day they had been floundering behind the infantry, standing still or hopping from one foot to the other in the big field where the cavalry squadron of the Morava Division had been since noon, concealed from the Austrian artillery and waiting for the assault on Rajac. Now they were beginning to feel tired, and the joy of the previous day had evaporated—the joy which had caused them to kiss each other before the squadron left Takovo, and which had lasted right up till dusk as they had listened to the roar of battle, a roar stretching from one end of the land to the other, resounding to the farthest vault of the sky. The troopers counted aloud the shells which flew above their heads, ceaselessly shouting: "Ah, now *we've* got some! Two of ours to every one of the Fritzies'! Three of ours to every one of theirs!"

But today the infantry had been climbing slowly up Rajac—at first, to the accompaniment of heavy firing, which gradually became less frequent; then they stopped on the heights and milled around the streams for a long time, or so it seemed to the cavalrymen. Now they appeared to have come to a complete standstill, although two reserve battalions had gone to the lines in the woods through which the battle extended—a battle which seemed to be flagging, to have lost its will and become no longer dangerous. It was as though the soldiers had grown utterly weary of fighting, and could hardly wait for nightfall, to be done with their exhausting and loathsome task. That was how it struck the troopers, who were standing in front of their horses or leaning against tree trunks, anxious and downcast because of their high hopes the previous day. They strained their ears toward the west: there, on Great Suvobor, the battle had thundered upward with unabated violence, from early morning on. If they could only go on like that into the night—such was the prayer of the troopers, even those who were not religious; and they watched closely every movement of their section commanders, who were pacing up and down beside their sections, obviously cross.

"What are we waiting for, sir?" asked Adam, unable to restrain himself when Second Lieutenant Tomić reached him in the course of his pacing; he was an officer who always ate candy before a battle.

"Are you in such a hurry, Katić?" he asked, with a sarcastic smile, rolling some candy across his tongue. He did not conceal his pleasure that Adam no longer had Dragan, the best horse in the regiment: it had been intolerable to his pride as an officer that an ordinary trooper had a better horse than he had.

"Yes, I'm in a hurry, sir," said Adam provocatively.

"Are the rest of you in a hurry, too?"

"Yes, we are; we're in a great hurry, sir," some cried loudly.

The sarcastic smile disappeared from the lieutenant's face; he moved the candy to the side of his mouth. "Our squadron must break out onto Rajac before nightfall; that's all I can tell you," he said aggressively, looking at Adam. He then continued on his way, his hands behind his back.

For the hundredth time Adam vowed that when the war was over and he was a civilian again, he would twice box the ears of the candy-chewing Tomić, and send his cap flying from his head; he would do it in a public place, in front of a crowded café in Niš, where Tomić was stationed. And as soon as he had boxed his ears, he would give him ten dinars for each blow. There you are, he would say, here's some money for candy! He'll become a colonel, people will still be talking about it. He didn't care if the lawyers and judges took the skin off his back, or if those blows cost him ten thousand dinars: he was determined to get even with this second lieutenant who never stopped chewing candy, for the way he made them hang around. He continued to straighten the worn saddle and tighten the threadbare girth: Dragan's saddle had been as yellow as wax, and embroidered at the edges, and his girth had been finer than the captain's belt. Even if he found Dragan, he wouldn't find his saddle. But to hell with the saddle and the girth! If only he could catch up with Dragan before they got to Valjevo.

Some twenty paces away, a stray shell burst at the very edge of the forest; it surprised rather than frightened him. It might at least drive us away from here, he said to himself, waiting for the word of command; he had seen an orderly gallop into the field and ride up to the squadron commander. Shells were falling in the field all around him, surrounding the battalion.

"Mount!" ordered the section commanders.

Adam felt easier; he mounted quickly. The commanders ordered them to salute the squadron commander, Captain Stošović, as he rode slowly in front of the ranks, rolling drunkenly in his saddle as he always did, and speaking in a quiet, clipped voice:

"This flatfooted infantry of ours can't break through the front by themselves. The Austrians won't give up Rajac. But it will give itself up, as the saying goes. Isn't that so, men? When we leave this field, take a good look at that white patch at the top of the wood. That's the Austrian howitzer. We've got to get there while it's still daylight. Whoever captures that cannon this evening, I'll decorate him with the Karageorge Star. And another star for two Austrian prisoners. Do you hear me, Katić?"

"I'll do my best, sir."

"By heaven, you've got yourself another good horse!"

"I intend to find my own horse, sir."

Adam tried to smile at him; he didn't know whether he managed it, but he could feel grief and anger coursing through his veins.

The squadron galloped out of the field in widely extended formation. While three shells exploded around it, it drew up in a meadow near the wood in which the battle was raging. Adam realized that the battle was moving to the left of him: that was where the breakthrough would be made. Bullets whistled over his head, but he didn't feel the slightest fear. He looked at the head of the squadron—at Captain Sto-šović, slumped down and rolling drunkenly in his saddle—and expected him to fall off any minute; this absorbed his attention and amused him. He would laugh aloud when he finally fell with a thud—he really would, even if afterward he had to wash his horse's hoofs with soap for ten days. He had had this punishment once for laughing while the captain made threats to the squadron because somebody had stolen some oats. They rushed into a grove of young beech trees, and slowed from a gallop to a walk. The bullets became thicker, but still passed high above them. They came upon a number of dead men; although Adam felt repulsion at the sight of corpses, now he counted them and concluded that most of them were Austrians. Between the smooth, shining tree trunks lay abandoned, ransacked knapsacks, Austrian helmets, empty cans. There was blood on the snow, here and there a frozen pool of it; and stripped and barefoot corpses, headless or grimacing. He didn't want his horse to walk in the blood, but couldn't stop him; this disgusted him. He felt a shudder running through his body.

An Austrian salvo halted the squadron behind a shallow trench from which infantry, crouching down, were firing without haste or anger. An Austrian machine gun started to yelp. No one near him fell; Second Lieutenant Tomić galloped up beside his section and ordered them to draw their sabers, shouting:

"We must trample them! Cut them down right and left!"

The bugle sounded charge, and Serbian shells flew overhead, exploding in the Austrian positions. All the men around him crossed themselves, but he would not; not because he wasn't a believer, but because he felt ashamed to pray in front of other people. He had crossed himself only once, one night when they were surrounded; then, he had really believed that he'd be killed. He drew his saber; to try it, he cut off the top of a young beech tree. He found striking people in the neck and head with a saber exhausting; his shoulders ached and his arms grew numb from the blows. For days afterward he would recollect not only the pain in his shoulders, but the crunching of bones, the scraping sound that ran through his saber and settled in the veins of his right arm, where it remained buzzing long afterward, as though his arm were hollow. He needed several good nights' sleep before the noise of slashed and broken human bones disappeared from his arm, along with the hoarse groans, and the grinding sound which lingered behind the swish of his saber and underneath his horse.

"What are you waiting for, Katić?" cried Tomić.

He could not see that candy-eater: with drawn sabers, the squadron was charging through the wood and over the Serbian trenches. He spurred his horse and hit his cruppers with the flat of his saber, then flew into the explosion of the forest, and came out into a clearing. Some fallen horses were staggering and whinnying, but he could hear the cavalrymen's "Hurrah" and yelled with all his strength, charging with his drawn saber toward the wood from which the Austrians were firing. He rode up to the first of them, and his horse on its own pursued three others; he would strike with the flat of his saber, just to knock the man down. Some Austrians turned around suddenly, flashing their bayonets to stab his horse, but the horse jumped aside. Somehow he managed to keep in his saddle; his arm grew numb from the hoarse groaning of the Austrian. He didn't know whether he had hit that man with the flat of his saber, because the horse hadn't stopped, but had chased those three other men, fleeing without their guns like dogs. He rode past them, but didn't brandish his saber. He heard a voice shouting:

"Cut them down! Don't take them prisoner!"

The horses were pursuing the Austrians through the wood; he could hear shouts, groans, occasional shots—he didn't know from which side. His comrades called to him, but he couldn't find his voice to reply. From somewhere to his right he heard Captain Stošović shouting:

"Forward! Keep advancing!"

He moved toward him and caught up with the ranks; he was not in his own section, but didn't want to look for it now. People around him were talking jubilantly, saying that the front had been pierced and that shots could be heard on the very top of Rajac. He strained his ears: up above, on the slope that they were climbing, he heard rifle fire, machine guns, and grenades at increasing intervals. The commander ordered them to keep their distance.

At dusk they came into a thicket; he was sweating and his horse was in a lather. They swung into the last volley of the last Austrian ranks. His cap fell off. His horse reared and began to whinny as if wounded, but still didn't stop. He slashed with his saber as he charged at the

Austrians, the bushes, and the darkness. He knocked against a fallen tree trunk and fell across his horse; he felt a dull pain in his chest, and saw sparks in the darkness. He thought he heard Tomić cursing and swearing at him as he chewed his candy.

When he came to he felt cold, and his teeth were chattering. There was a sharp pain in his cheeks: with his hand he felt a cut and smeared blood on his face. Had a bayonet caught him? He could not remember when, or how. But there was a terrible pain in his chest: he must have been hit there. He was breathing in short gasps. There seemed to be pain in his ribs, too. He ran his hands over his body: his jacket was dry. He took a deep breath, as deep as he possibly could. Only his head was wounded; he was relieved. He felt the wound, but it turned out not to be a wound either! He listened: his horse was breathing deeply in the darkness behind his back. Up above he heard two or three shots, a shout, and someone singing. He got up: there was nothing wrong with him! He had fallen off his horse across that tree trunk, hit his head on it, and lost consciousness. Tomić would certainly think he'd been killed. But I'll buy him that candy, he thought, when we enter Valjevo. He went up to his horse, patted and stroked him, and ran his hands over him. "Why did you shriek like that?" he asked aloud in a joyful tone. Someone near him began to cough; there was a sound of snow rustling and creaking. He waved his hand to take his saber, but it was not in its sheath. Quickly he removed his gun from his shoulders: there were people moving among the trees.

"Who's there?" he shouted in a loud voice.

It was some men running hurriedly: perhaps some of the Serbian infantry whom they had passed during the first assault. He fired his gun high in the air, just to frighten them. The frozen surface of the snow crunched under their feet. He mounted his horse and rode after the men who were fleeing; his hands were trembling. If they had fired some shots, or at least given a shout, he would not have felt so afraid, he assured himself as he rode through the thicket, which parted in front of him as though he were driving a herd of cattle. He came out into a clearing: from the refraction of the snow, the clear sky, and the stars, he could see groups of men fleeing through the clearing. He fired at them, and spurred his horse in the direction of the silent fugitives. He caught up with them, rode beside them, then halted with his gun trained on them:

"Who are you?" he shouted.

He heard a few words of German spoken in frightened tones.

"So you're Fritzies, are you, damn you! Does anyone here speak

Serbian?" No one answered. "I'm asking you if anybody knows Serbian? I'll trample you down!" They crowded together, about twenty of them. He could not see their weapons. "Hands up!" He fired above their heads, his teeth chattering with fear at this crowd of people who didn't understand him, and whom he didn't understand. They seemed to be raising their arms. He repeated his command. They put their hands up.

What should he do now? Never had he felt such fear. Never. He wanted to tell them this, to take vengeance on them for this fear. At the top of his voice he called to his companions in his section, calling their names in turn; they were echoed back by the stream. He was also answered by a revolver shot from the wood behind the stream; while from the slope he heard a bugle sound the assembly—it was like a sound coming from the sky. Far away to the west, he could hear the rattle of machine guns. What was he to do with this crowd?

"Lie down!" he shouted, and again fired over their heads.

The Austrians crowded together, a black mass on the snow. He tried to count them. He forced his horse around the prostrate Austrians, who were beginning to cough. This coughing calmed him: they were cold down there on the snow, and had colds; they were human, after all. His fear subsided, and he cleared his throat. But he didn't stop riding around them. The silence and darkness of the wood tightened its grip on the clearing. There was no escape. He looked at the sky, as if seeking for some way out. The stars seemed very near, he could not take his eyes off them; there was something intimate about them as though they were shining from the houses of Prerovo. He stroked the horse's neck and talked to him affectionately, in a whisper, so the Austrians couldn't hear. He wanted to say something to them as they lay there, to explain why they had to lie there: they were human beings, after all; damn it, they were soldiers, too! But it was not his fault that they didn't understand Serbian, that in this world men were so stupidly made that they couldn't all explain themselves to one another in words. What could he do about that now? Was it his fault they had to lie in the snow until daybreak? And I must stay on my horse all night, going round and round, as though turning a water wheel on the Morava. It's easier for them down there in the snow, than for me spending the whole night on horseback. They must see that, if they're ordinary human beings.

"Give me the Danube Division, second levy. Mišić speaking. Good evening, Vasić. Congratulations!"

"And I must congratulate you, sir. You have proved that Clausewitz was right, that the greatest risk can be the wisest course."

"It would be nearer the truth, Vasić, to say that I haven't taken any risks with Potiorek. And there's certainly no special wisdom in having faith in the commanders and the soldiers of the First Army, as you and your division have proved. We haven't beaten the Austrians yet, but we'll surely be on the crest of Suvobor by nightfall tomorrow. Don't you think so?"

"If there are such things as miracles in human experience, there's certainly been one among the troops of my division. Those same soldiers who a few days ago were refusing to obey orders, running away, and firing at their officers, are today overflowing with enthusiasm and can't wait to rush at the enemy. A magnificent spectacle! With troops like this we can go straight to the Drina, sir."

"You're right, Vasić. But first of all, tomorrow you must take Suvobor and Mujov Grob. Do your utmost to report to me by noon."

"Hello! Danube Division, first levy. Is that you, Kajafa? Speak louder, I can't hear you. First of all, tell me what you think of the enemy this evening?"

"Yesterday they were confused, but full of impetuosity. Today they seem sluggish, somehow. They're full of despair. Prisoners are behaving like they've been saved from something."

"Have you received my orders? And what do you plan to do tomorrow?"

"My plan, sir, is to carry out your orders in the morning, and in the afternoon to work for the glory of my division."

"Well, before you're drunk with glory, hurry up toward the crest of Suvobor. Can you hear me, Kajafa?"

"Give me the commander of the Drina Division. Mišić speaking. I've been waiting to hear from you since noon, Smiljanić."

"My division hasn't moved a step forward since noon. And the left column had to withdraw to Ručić. The enemy have reorganized and are resisting firmly, sir."

"The enemy is in its death agony, and resisting with the strength of a dying man. Still, that strength is not without danger. The Drina Division is now fighting the battle of the entire First Army. Can you hear me, Smiljanić? If you win the battle for the army's main line of communication tomorrow and get right under Prostruga, the First

Army can decide the fate of the Serbian offensive. I can't hear you. Hello! I can't hear you."

He put down the receiver and quickly began to write a report to the High Command:

"Early this morning a successful start was made in a strong offensive by the entire First Army. Plenty of booty and prisoners. Fear has struck at the heart of the enemy. Penetration into the main watershed has already begun. Please give the necessary instructions to the other armies."

He paused to ponder why he had heard nothing from Vojvoda Putnik since the previous day. He's still not sure whether we'll succeed, a real Doubting Thomas. Or perhaps it's because of the feelings of earlier times that he doesn't say anything. There's no escape: our fates are always inseparable.

His adjutant, Lieutant Spasić, summoned him to supper. Even now this young man was gloomy, the only person on the staff who showed no sign of rejoicing; his mood and expression were the same as when they had withdrawn from Suvobor.

"Have you had some bad news from home, Spasić?"

"No sir. If you would permit me, sir, I should like to join the ranks."

"Right now your dissatisfaction is necessary to me on the staff!"

The previous evening Danilo History-Book had been wounded in the arm on Dubovi. It had been his fiercest battle since the offensive began; it was only in the third assault, when Bora Jackpot's section had silenced the machine gun, that they had been able to jump into the trenches and chase the survivors into the brush. These men would not surrender even when a bayonet flashed against their chests. Meanwhile, at the beginning of the last assault, Danilo had felt a burning sensation above the elbow of his left arm. Some sort of red-hot club had hit him on the arm; he staggered, blacked out for a few moments, and dropped his gun. His arm hung down, aflame with the heat of his blood. So this was it. He did not feel frightened, nor was he unhappy; perhaps he even felt rather pleased to receive such a wound. Soldiers ran past him, shouting "Hurrah!" He picked up his gun but dropped it again. He didn't wish to stop: his soldiers were already throwing grenades into the Austrian trenches. Danilo ran toward the trenches, catching up with them; he could no longer shoot, but he gave the words of command. Only when it began to grow dark, and the last gun in the platoon was silent, did he separate himself from the victorious fury of his soldiers and go off in search of Bora Jackpot.

"I've been hit, Jackpot!" he cried as he came up to him.

Bora was sitting on the edge of a trench, smoking two cigarettes at once. "So have I."

"But I really have been wounded, honestly!"

"Come sit beside me. That was an awful slaughter. I've lost four men killed and five wounded. Those Landstürmer regiments are made up of hand-picked warriors. And they smoke foul tobacco. I'm smoking two of their cigarettes because they're like one of ours."

"I've been wounded in the arm, honest I have. Look how it's bleeding!" Danilo twisted round, bent down, and stuck his limp, bleeding arm in Bora's face.

Bora felt his damp, sticky hand.

"You're a damn fool! When were you hit?" He jumped up. "Have you had your arm bandaged?"

"No, I haven't."

"You really are the biggest idiot! And you're even boasting about it! Where were you wounded? And where's that medic? Milenko, where are you? Tell Milenko to come here quick with some bandages. Do you really want to saddle me with that little wooden horse, you idiot?"

"That's enough; no need to panic. I've been wounded—so what? That's why I'm here."

"This really takes the cake. I've been right to despise heroes and seducers ever since I can remember. They're nothing but self-centered braggarts!"

Danilo fell silent, not so much because of shame provoked by Bora's words, as because of an exciting thought: it would be so much easier if in another charge he could be wounded, say, in the thigh; then he would write to his grandfather: I'm fine! No need to worry about me. I've been wounded twice, on both occasions in a charge.

Milenko, the medic, bandaged his arm; then Lieutenant Jevtić arrived, hugged him like an older brother, and whispered in his ear. For a long time the three of them sat on the edge of the trench, warming themselves beside a fire, looking at the other fires scattered over the mountain side, and taking stock of the day's progress. Finally the lieutenant and Bora wrangled a bit about England and socialism, but Danilo was silent. Pain and self-pity had now taken possession of him, and a belated feeling of fear: after all, his left armpit was not so far from his heart; his wound hurt and he was shivering. Bora wrapped him up in some tent flaps and sat beside him all night; as he kindled the fire, he said: "As soon as it's light, you're to go to the division dressing station." Danilo didn't argue with him, but had firmly resolved not to leave his section until they'd taken Suvobor. He dozed a bit, then fell into a light sleep, and a confused dream of exciting desires, imagining how he would enter Novi Sad as a liberator, the commander of a platoon, riding on a white horse to please his grandfather; he would be thin and exhausted, and have an enormous mustache. The girls would garland him with flowers, his friends would call out his name . . .

The next morning, before they set off to attack the positions taken by the enemy on the previous night, he would not go to the dressing station, although his wound hurt with a dull, strong pain. He did not hesitate for a moment, although Lieutenant Jevtić tried to persuade him to go, talking to him like a father. Bora Jackpot scolded him furiously, cursed him and insulted him, and even spat at him scornfully with his well-known, idiotic skill, as he set off to join his section; then he quickly disappeared into the wood, with his head bowed. They did not see each other after that. The platoon moved forward toward the summit of Suvobor; the battalion drew together; the regiment twisted its way through the woods, plodded through the streams, and climbed upward over the slopes and rocks, chasing the Austrians before them with gunfire and charges. Their prisoners were driven along behind them like a flock of sheep, with two soldiers to every fifty prisoners. So they continued right up till dusk, when from the summit of Great Suvobor they were greeted by a number of entrenched machine guns backed up by two batteries.

The battalion halted at the edge of a sparse beechwood, in some shallow trenches abandoned a few days before, where they found the frozen corpses of some Serbian soldiers not yet covered with drifting snow. The Austrians pounded them with gunfire, aiming at the tops of their heads, but they managed to keep out of sight.

Danilo didn't go into the trench; he couldn't lie down, and his arm hurt. He crouched beside a broad beech tree, staring at the white expanse of snow across which they must run under fire, all the way to a group of about ten old fir trees on the summit, which seemed to hang from the dark, lowering sky. The largest and finest tree was on the very top, etched against the sky like a dark, sharp-edged triangle: only its lower branches were swathed in snow. He wanted to get to that tree, to lie down beneath it and breathe in the scent of its resinous trunk. He wanted to play with the fir cones, though of course he couldn't with his left hand. He looked at his swollen fingers, now turning blue. Then he looked at the fir tree again: a lovely thing, hanging on to a cloud. Hanging on to a star, to the moon. He wanted to lie down on its fallen leaves and listen to the wind, to spend the whole night alone under the fir tree. Bora Jackpot would be cross because all night long I listened to the wind in the fir tree, to the yearning sound of its breathing in the darkness. Like that first night on Maljen with Casanova, Molecule, and Tričko—half of us already dead. And by the time we get to the Drina? Early tomorrow morning I'll write a short letter home. He looked at his soldiers: they were taking aim without haste, going about their task seriously. Nobody spoke. Shells spurted in the wood and roared through the ravines. Since noon the battle had moved quite high up, in fact it was being fought in the clouds. Once more he stared at his fir tree. There were eleven trees altogether, but not one was as tall or had such a perfect shape as his.

"Protić!" the commander shouted from behind his back, standing in the shelter of a beech tree. "The battalion is going to charge. Our platoon is making straight for the fir trees."

"Wonderful!"

"What's wonderful about it?"

"We'll get to the fir trees first!"

The officer frowned as he looked at him.

"I'm not joking. Just look at that beauty in the middle! And just think . . . Really it would be great if the war would end with an assault on those fir trees, with their capture. Forgive me, just an idea."

"Listen, Protić, you hand over your section to Corporal Paun, and stay here until we've finished the job."

"Out of the question, sir. I intend to lead my section."

Lieutenant Jevtić withdrew his face behind the beech tree. He thinks I'm irresponsible, thought Danilo. And Bora thinks I'm an egotist and a braggart. What the devil's the matter with them today? There was a strong wind blowing, whistling through the bare branches. Somewhere near him a dry branch was creaking, like that night on Maljen when he opened his heart to Bora while the snow drifted around them, and deserters called from the stream to the soldiers to run off home. It seemed to him that the fir trees on the summit were beginning to sway.

The bugle sounded the charge. The platoon commander ran out in front of the ranks, turned around, and shouted:

"Forward!"

Danilo jumped up with a yelp of pain and began to run through the wood, then down a hollow with small pine trees; bullets were whizzing past. Half unconscious from pain, and holding his gun in his left hand, he moved in ever deeper snow through a glade, then up a slope toward the fir trees on the skyline. He didn't turn around. Behind his back he heard someone shout "Hurrah!" but he couldn't shout, it would have sounded like a groan. That would make it impossible for them to keep up with him; he would get to the fir trees first. It was less than a hundred paces now. The top of his fir tree was swaying.

But why had he fallen? Had a sack fallen on top of him? It was a tree trunk right on the small of his back, across his thighs. Nothing was happening near him; the battle was far away. He tried to get up, but some enormous, burning, roaring weight rolled him into the snow. The fir tree had overturned, broken loose from the ground, and was toppling over him. Was this it? The real thing? The end? He rose up and dragged himself on his elbows toward the fir tree, which was bending down nearer and nearer to him. He must get to it. The moonlight was frozen, there was a wreath of sparks. That was them firing. But where's my gun? My God, where is it? I left it in the wood!

He thrust his head into the snow, into something red and yellow. He began to cry. Am I really crying? He looked in his pocket for his handkerchief and pulled it out, but the wind whipped it out of his hand and blew it away. The ground under him was sinking, and he with it; the snow was dissolving into darkness. As he fell, the fir tree burst into flame, into creeping plants in Kamenica, sunflowers on his grandfather's estate, dandelions. He called out to Bora Jackpot. No one heard him—there wasn't a soul in the silence. Pigeons were flying from a mulberry tree; a flock of crows was perched on another; one of them hovered on a branch right over his face, flew up into the sky, and then descended straight toward him. Behind the earth, the spark went out.

Mišić sat bent over the telephone, holding the receiver; he was putting off the moment when he would dial the High Command and speak to Vojvoda Putnik. He recalled their quarrel over the withdrawal from Suvobor; he heard every word as it was squeezed through the wire, torn up by the wind, eroded by the distance, and choked by the sound of coughing. During the past few days Putnik had been particularly troubled by asthma; his authoritativeness and superiority

—which at any sign of resistance spilled over into contempt—had been especially spiteful and malicious. He also recalled Prince Alexander's threats: those shouts demanding subordination to the Prince's will, rather than to the convictions of the High Command. In his despair he had repaid insult for insult, speaking as he had never spoken to a subordinate; using a word which could not be written in the records of the First Army, but must surely have appeared in those of the High Command. After the war the operators, when drunk, would relate this incident in confidence, and with their own embellishments.

Until this moment he had never given so much thought to that quarrel with the High Command. Could it be that this exultation was adding a little extra savor to his feelings of victory? He put down the receiver and lit a cigarette; he would call when he had smoked it. Loneliness was the fate and curse of every man who held power exceeding that of the majority of human beings. Only in front of a woman, his mother or his wife, would he have dared now to unbutton his general's jacket. He could show contempt for an opponent, for all opponents. He could exult a little in vengeance. Was there nothing else to victory but this feeling of joy? Presumably there was more to it than that. There must be. Did victory mean freedom to feel scorn and vengeance? To possess rights transcending all laws, to fulfill wishes beyond all rights and customs? Did victory mean freedom to sink to our lowest depths? Yes, it did. But he would not have it that way. At this moment he dared not give way to feelings of victory. If his mother were alive, or if Louisa were here with him, perhaps he could savor these moments by being silent while they simply looked at him. If only a woman's hand could touch him now with a little tenderness, all this uneasiness seething within him would immediately be stilled. Then he would inform Vojvoda Putnik in a calm, firm voice that the First Army had won the battle for Suvobor. He would call him when he had smoked half of his second cigarette.

However, during the three days of the offensive, no event had had the same significance as the morning of the first day, when he had hurried into Milanovac to hear the reports of the division commanders about the first phase of the battle. There was nothing to compare with that mild autumnal sunshine which had swept the fog away from the front and packed it into the basin of the Morava, thus revealing the Austrian positions to the Serbian cannon. The bare woods and empty fields had been bathed in a gala atmosphere. The road was filled to the brim with hope. How much it seemed like a great festival, or some Sunday from his youth! In the blue depths of the sky above the dark shapes of the mountains, in the infinite silence up there while the battle thundered and echoed, and his horse had suddenly stopped in front of a large elm tree just as he was entering Milanovac, he saw and felt something which completely wiped out the boundary between life and death. Just for a moment he believed in immortality.

He extinguished his half-smoked cigarette, cleared his throat, then firmly dialed the number of the High Command and asked to speak to Vojvoda Putnik:

"Mišić speaking. Hello! Mišić speaking."

"Yes, Mišić, I'm listening."

"My troops have broken through onto the mountain ridge Prostruga-Rajac-Suvobor. The battle for Suvobor has already been decided, Vojvoda. Can you hear me?"

"Yes, Mišić, I'm listening."

"The enemy's strategic dispositions have been broken up. The First Army is now established in a central position facing the wings of Potiorek's divided forces. This breakthrough must be turned into a knockout blow against the Austro-Hungarian army in Serbia. Can you hear me, Vojvoda?"

"Go on, Mišić. Tell me all you have to say."

"I am determined to pursue the enemy resolutely into the valley of the Kolubara."

"That would be very dangerous! It would mean taking a risk beyond your strength and outside your competence."

"I don't understand you, Vojvoda."

"The Užice Brigade has met with fierce resistance, and the enemy has had some success against the Third Army as well. The Second Army hasn't moved a step from its first positions."

"Then please give them orders to advance at all costs. Otherwise my breakthrough will remain in the sphere of tactical significance."

"I have already given them orders to this effect. And you must halt on the Suvobor ridge, gather up your troops, and give them a rest."

"But surely if my army penetrates deeper in the direction of the Kolubara and threatens the enemy's flanks, that would be of great assistance to the Third Army and the Užice Brigade. Potiorek would have to retreat on the entire front."

"But failure to penetrate further toward the Kolubara would imperil the victory on Suvobor. You know very well that depth of penetration need not only measure the strength of the attacker; it may be a tactical trap on the part of the defenders. Then our offensive would be a case of the wolf eating the donkey. Can you hear me, Mišić?"

"The soldiers don't want to stay on the mountain."

"Potiorek's men didn't want to stay on the mountain either, and the price they paid for coming down from Suvobor was to lose it. The rest of the price for their hastiness they will pay in the next few days—when according to my strategy all Serbian armies are in action. Do as I have told you and stay on Suvobor ridge."

Anxious and confused, Mišić put down the receiver: Vojvoda Putnik had not shown great pleasure. His subordinates found his extreme caution hard to bear; but did not everybody praise it after the event? Or was his vanity stronger than his obligation to give just recognition to others? Did he perhaps remember their quarrel over the withdrawal of the First Army from the Suvobor ridge? Whatever it was, he dared not oppose him today.

He decided to postpone lunch, and asked for some apples and lime tea. He wrote orders to the divisions for the next day in the spirit of Putnik's instructions, but hinted that the attack would soon be continued; he praised the success and mutual harmony of the commanders. While deciding what to write in the last sentence, he smoked two cigarettes; finally he wrote: "I would be glad to hear your opinion concerning the most appropriate time for moving the main force, according to the prevailing circumstances."

After lunch he was roused by a call from Kajafa: "Before receiving your order to halt I had already given my division orders to continue pursuit, to go on chasing the Austrians until their hearts give out. Can you hear me, sir?"

"Yes, I'm listening, Kajafa."

"I'm pushing forward in the direction Rajac-Dobro Polje-Cugulj, toward Baćinac."

"Why have you done this, Kajafa?"

"Because the enemy is disorganized and fleeing in confusion. The enemy is beaten, sir. I can see that quite clearly."

"But first we've got to consolidate the victory already won, secure the flanks, and wait for the other armies. We are only one part of the Serbian front."

"That's true, but it's our duty to turn this victory into a victory for the entire Serbian armed forces. And we can do that only if we extend the victory already won."

"Any imprudence or impatience now might be fatal. A man must be courageous and stand firm in defeat; but in time of success he must be wise and cunning, Kajafa."

"Forgive me for speaking beyond my competence. But I consider it out of place and dangerous to bother with wisdom in time of war. Perhaps it can come into consideration at the end of the war. But during the war, only courage will never go wrong."

"People rarely lack courage when it's a question of survival, Kajafa. Potiorek didn't lack courage in capturing the Suvobor ridge, but he did show lack of wisdom as a commander."

"He lacked many things required for victory. His army has all the qualities that lead to defeat."

Mišić removed the receiver from his ear in order not to listen to Kajafa's reasons for pushing the enemy. He was in fact opposing Kajafa with Putnik's arguments. He moved the receiver back to his ear and heard him say:

"I maintain that there is no serious reason why we shouldn't follow up our victory and push forward to Valjevo. Can you hear me, sir?"

Mišić put down the receiver again. Now Kajafa was bolder than Mišić, now he was acting according to his convictions, and opposing Mišić as Mišič himself had opposed Putnik a few days before. Mišić dared not do that today. Now Kajafa was bold enough to do what Mišić no longer dared to do, just as a few days ago Mišić had been bold enough to do what Putnik dared not do. He trembled, and his eyes filled with tears.

A bird which had flown in from Rudnik banged against the window and chirped from pain as it tumbled headlong down the wall. Mišić's trembling became like a burning fever; his forehead was bathed in sweat. He shouted into the receiver:

"Hello, Kajafa! I approve your orders! Carry on with the pursuit!"

He could hear a buzzing sound and a squeak in the distance. He put down the receiver without waiting to hear what Kajafa had to say.

Hadjić came into the room and spoke to him from the door; he was in high spirits: "We've captured six officers today, two thousand soldiers, four machine guns, three cannon, and two mountain howitzers."

"Today the First Army has finally recovered its faith in itself. It can't be beaten any more. Hadjić, please see that Professor Zarija puts it down in the army records," he said with conviction.

Until midnight he continued to wrestle with the problem: should he halt and consolidate his gains, or should he pursue Potiorek to final defeat? At midnight he wrote instructions that all divisions were to continue to pursue the enemy; then he summoned Professor Zarija to occupy his sleepless hours with his clever accounts of books that he, Mišić, had never read and would never wish to read.

After the death of Danilo History-Book, Bora Jackpot was so overcome with grief that he could barely walk; he was no longer even tormented by fear during battle. He kept silent, and avoided Second Lieutenant Jevtić; he was particularly irritated by the commander's official "socialist" grief for a "fellow man," which he expounded by stressing Danilo's virtues of courage and dignity. During the assault on Great Suvobor, that very morning, they had quarreled about where to bury Danilo; Bora wanted Danilo buried where he had died—on the very spot where he had dug his arms and head into the snow in his death agony, "like a wild beast"; but Jevtić, with his "schoolmasterish romanticism," commanded that he should be buried among the fir trees on the mountain top. Bora was so infuriated and filled with despair by the lieutenant's funeral oration, delivered over the hastily buried corpse and accompanied by a salute fired by his section, that he ran up to him, his throat constricted with pain, and hissed into Jevtić's weeping face:

"My friend Danilo wasn't a virtuous man, I assure you, sir! He was cowardly in front of the officers. And he was always spouting catchwords about national feeling. That's why we called him 'History-Book.' "

Jevtić was stunned.

"Yes, sir, that's how it was! In actual fact Danilo History-Book loved women more than he loved the fatherland. As for his heroism, it was the heroism of a fool, which he showed clearly enough by the way he died!"

He left the lieutenant dumbfounded. That day he didn't speak except to give a few orders during the fighting; he restrained himself until nightfall, then covered himself with a tent flap in an abandoned trench and wept his heart out. Until that moment he had not had the slightest idea how much he loved Danilo History-Book.

That morning the regiment was moving over Maljen; icy rain had been buffeting them since dawn, and a north wind whipped their eyes. Their wet clothing and boots froze; their breeches crackled as they walked, and the tent flaps in which they were wrapped rattled as if made of lead. Their mustaches froze, and the damp hair underneath their caps; drops of rain froze on their faces, and soldiers fell down on the frozen snow. There was less and less swearing and laughter in the column; the men felt helpless, and humiliated by their helplessness, on this black ice. They could hardly wait to catch up with the Austrians, so they could halt and dig themselves in in the frozen snow. Bora Jackpot too wanted this as he walked at the head of the column, behind the lieutenant on horseback. The lieutenant offered his horse to Bora so he could rest a bit.

"I've never mounted a horse in my life and have no intention of doing so now!" he said firmly. "In any case, I find using domestic animals for national ends—for King and country—disgusting!"

He stared at the fir trees and the clearings, trying hard to recognize them and to guess at the position of the First Battalion, to which Casanova, Molecule, and Tričko had been assigned. If only he could have found Casanova and Molecule, and covered them with a bit of earth! They had surely been stripped to the skin; they had had new clothes, good boots, and sergeants' overcoats. To lie dead and naked in the snow and rain was surely the most terrible humiliation a human being could experience in the entire Galaxy!

In front of them, behind the grove of fir trees, rifle fire spurted and a machine gun began to yelp. The platoon halted. Jevtić dismounted, then tripped and fell in the underbrush. He laughed as though he had slipped while skating. What a pitiful and comical creature man was!

"Lie down!" shouted Jevtić to his platoon, as he himself got up.

The soldiers rolled over to the edge of the wood; Bora Jackpot, already frozen, did not wish to lie in the frozen snow. He stayed where he was, caught by gunfire, and lit a cigarette. The bullets were infrequent and high above their heads. He caught sight of a big clearing behind a row of fir trees, alongside the road through the woods. Had he already seen it during the withdrawal? A battle had erupted in the woods, over toward Maljen.

An orderly from battalion headquarters brought some written orders to Lieutenant Jevtić. He read them, then reflected for a while.

Is that high and mighty army commander thinking up some plan for us to make a detour through the streams, or to roll downhill and break our necks? wondered Bora, waiting for Jevtić to speak.

"Get into battle formation. Luković, you seize the fir trees by the clearing!"

"Is that all?" said Bora caustically, and summoned his section to set out behind him.

They came upon an old shallow trench filled with snow, and snuggled down inside it; Bora could see corpses scattered over the clearing. He left the trench and walked slowly from one slain man to another.

Most of them were wearing only shirts and undershorts; only those corpses clad in ragged peasant blankets and breeches, with emptied multicolored bags, looked as they should look. There was frozen blood, and frozen mustaches moistened with blood. Shrapnel wounds frozen over. Some of the dead were already powdered with drifting snow, from which protruded their naked, livid behinds: the disgusting sign of a man's presence. There were letters scattered around, and torn photographs and bits of string, dirty rags, and empty bags thrown among the corpses. Poverty-stricken Austria, reduced to thieving! So you strip the corpses, too, turning them over for a rag, a piece of hardtack, a cigarette. This filthy Europe! So you too will dress in the stinking, bloodstained rags of dead Serbian peasants. Petty thieves! He stood in the center of the clearing and twice shot out his spit—at the whole world.

He heard his soldiers calling to him and turned around. A battle was raging among the fir trees. He could not hear what they were saying; they were waving their arms, beckoning him to run to them. He turned around to face the firing: a line of Austrians appeared from behind the fir trees, shooting at him. He threw himself down in the snow beside a burly corpse wearing only a shirt; this man's exposed chest and bloody head were his only cover. Bullets spurted furiously around him and sank in the snow, or pierced the frozen corpse. Bora tried to dig himself in, scratching at the ice and breaking it with his knees and elbows, while a hail of bullets whipped around him. To be dead: that was the end of everything. He scarcely breathed as he lay there with his face against the frozen surface of the snow, the crown of his head against the chest of the corpse. He felt as though he was a hill in a deserted plain. His section began to fire furiously. Would they be able to stop the Austrians? He would be taken prisoner; he had been ready for anything in the war except that. What if a German bent over him with a bayonet? A stupid way to end, the most stupid of all. The bullets no longer fell near his head, but hissed above him. Slowly he raised his head and peered over the corpse: the Austrians were lying down by the edge of the fir trees, shooting. Who would be the first to charge? If Danilo History-Book had been alive, he wouldn't have given it a second thought. He counted the Austrian rifles: about fifty, no machine gun. What is Jevtić waiting for? Does he know where I am? My God, death is stupid: just corpses lying side by side. I suppose they won't have time to strip me. But if the Fritzies don't do it, my own side will, the Serbs. The corpse twitched. Ah, they've noticed me, they're trying to hit me. He dug his head into the frozen snow and tried to bury himself. He hated and despised himself. Danilo had died like a fool, but "heroically"; I'll just have a hole in me like an idiot! What inane funeral oration will that schoolmaster pronounce over me, without even a corpse! He'll break into a sweat when he has to expound my virtues!

The gunfire died down and finally ceased. Once more he raised his head, heavy and repulsive, above the chest of the dead man. Before he could even catch a glimpse of the Austrians, a bullet whistled by; he hit his head vindictively on the frozen surface of the snow. A number of guns fired; his section answered with a volley. He no longer dared to raise his eyes: nothing for it but to wait for a bullet to get him as he lay there playing dead. Or should he stand up and let the bullet go through him? Which death was preferable, less idiotic? Ever since he had first learned his letters, he had detested stupidity and stupid people more than anything: he would choose the less stupid alternative. He would wait for his bullet, as though already a corpse. No heroics. He would be a sacrifice. He would think about the Galaxy, and how the Great Wheel was revolving. He could not feel it; in his fear he could not even believe in his own cosmology. A trifling, miserable invention!

Once more the firing ceased around the clearing, but spread through the woods. It was not yet noon: someone had to charge. His teeth chattered from cold. He lay down on the ice, his whole body trembling violently. The Austrians would see that he wasn't a corpse yet and they'd rake him with gunfire. He made a supreme effort to keep rigid and stop his teeth from chattering. His body grew numb; he almost lost consciousness. Since Danilo's death he had not wound up his watch; last night it had stopped. He stretched his hand toward his pocket and placed it on his watch. He dug away the snow with his fingers so he could plunge his hand in his pocket and feel for his watch. The firing started up again: he didn't hear the first bullets. Did they see me move? he thought. But he must wind up his watch and listen to it; then let them kill him—a corpse listening to his father's watch.

His section opened fire; the Austrians were now firing aimlessly. He wound up his watch and held it against his ear, close to his face; it was as though he was restoring to life the heart inside the corpse. His teeth stopped chattering. He heard the bugle sound the charge; he knew the bugler. He heard shouts of "Hurrah!" He raised his head: the Austrians were firing an answering volley, and not yet retreating. He turned toward his section: they were in full retreat, with many casualties. If my men move once more, I'll get up and run like crazy toward them. Yes, it's a stupid thing to do, but less contemptible than to breathe in the stink of a frozen corpse, and act the part of a dead man even while waiting for death. He put the watch back in his pocket. He summoned the full force of his will to do the one thing possible in this Galaxy—to commit a final act of folly: he rushed toward his section through the frozen clearing, over the bodies of the dead men.

All the division reports spoke of victory: Kajafa had taken Baćinac, and was now above Mionica, impatient and angry at being halted in his pursuit of the enemy; Vasić had captured Maljen; Smiljanić was on Milovac and pressing forward from Gukoš along the valley of the Ljig; Milić had burst out onto Mednik and Vis, and was descending to the Gukoš–Gornja Toplica highway. This meant that the First Army was now getting close to the Kolubara and Valjevo. Carried away by enthusiasm, the troops could not stop their pursuit of the disintegrating enemy. Meanwhile the High Command reported that the Užice Brigade had broken through their front and were pressing on toward Užice and Kosjerić; the Third Army was pushing the Austrians relentlessly toward the lower Ljig and the Kolubara; the Second Army had begun the battle for Konatica.

The staff headquarters was full of the noise and celebration of victory; right in front of Mišić's door, adjutants and orderlies were telling dirty jokes. Songs could be heard in the cafés and lanes of Milanovac, and ever longer columns of exhausted prisoners were passing along the highway. When he brought him tea, apples, and wood, Dragutin coughed purposefully, indicating that he had something important to say. Apart from his adjutant Spasić, always a silent shadow, only he, the commander of the army, was anxious and gloomy, and didn't even have the will to conceal it. Several times his mother had said to him: "It's hard for you, my boy. You've got the sort of nature that fears the worst. Like me. You can never really rejoice about anything. Are you afraid of something, Živojin?" Her small, wrinkled face would twitch, and tears would glisten in her close-set blue eyes. "Yes, I'm afraid," he would whisper.

True, after his arrival in Mionica and the time of testing on the Ribnica bridge, he had felt considerable anxiety—especially after the defeat on Suvobor, and that night before the attack; but never, he was sure, had he felt such a sinking feeling inside himself or such trepidation as he felt now. A kind of feverish presentiment of evil, a fear born of victory, possessed his whole being. The victory had been achieved, and was still being achieved, far more easily and quickly than he had expected in his most soaring flights of hope and self-confidence.

All human victories, he felt instinctively, carried within them—according to their size and significance, and the sacrifice and suffering invested in them—their own process of justice: vengeance on the victor. That was their price, their retribution, the price paid for the pain and suffering of the defeated, the punishment exacted from the victor for his joy in victory. What price would the First Army have to pay for so many successes in battle, regardless of the fact that the battle was being fought not for military glory, but for the survival of the Serbian people? What punishment would be meted out to him for his victory over Field Marshal Oscar Potiorek, who had already celebrated his victory in Vienna?

He sat at the table, numb and motionless, moving only to light or extinguish a cigarette, which he smoked simply by balancing it on his lower lip. His hands lay unheeded on the table as he gazed at the dark, lowering sky that pressed against the window.

While Potiorek had shown only the will to win and thought with the logic of the stronger, Mišić had been able to foresee his intentions. But now Oscar Potiorek was thinking not only like a commander on the defensive, a commander whose front had been pierced and whose army was demoralized—killing women, children, and old men as it retreated through the villages; now Oscar Potiorek was feeding his will power only on thoughts of revenge. For he was a victor whose victory had unexpectedly turned into defeat in the course of just three days— a commander who must be tormented by vanity, shame, and despair. Now it was impossible to foresee his intentions.

That morning's reports from the divisions about the statements made by prisoners were quite contradictory. A sergeant from Dalmatia affirmed that they were beaten to their knees, and in such headlong flight that it would be impossible to catch up with them this side of the Sava. But an Austrian, a captain in the regular army now commanding a battalion, reported that their failure was the result of momentary exhaustion and depletion in numbers; fresh troops and reserve forces would arrive any day, and tomorrow or the day after they would begin a counterattack. The Dalmatian's statement expressed much more affection for the Serbs and desire for their victory than evidence of an Austrian defeat; that of the Austrian showed hatred, threats, and desire for vengeance. Mišić dared not fully believe either.

What was the least risky course of action now? He had not been afraid of risk when he abandoned the crest of Suvobor and announced his decision to move to an offensive, at a time when a Serbian defeat was imminent and inevitable in the opinion of all those who judged by the visible evidence. So why was he afraid to take a risk now, when most of the facts and the general situation suggested that a Serbian victory was imminent and inevitable? But then, he had not made those decisions involving risk solely on the basis of visible facts and the general situation. In what direction should he move the army now? Should he attack, to prevent Potiorek from withdrawing to the Drina, or should he push him toward Šabac, in a northerly and northeasterly direction? If he moved down into the Kolubara valley with the entire army, might not Potiorek start a counteroffensive?

Hadjić came into the room heavy-footed, and gave a verbose account of reports from the divisions which continued to speak only of victory. He had decided to reproach him because of the optimism of the staff, but then Hadjić read out a directive from the High Command, according to which the First Army was to swing its entire front toward the west. Although this order resolved his most pressing anxiety, and would involve greater concentration of the army and a shorter front, and also the acquisition of reserves, he still felt no relief, and his feeling of uncertainty was as strong as ever. The more convincingly Hadjić interpreted this order from the High Command, the more incomprehensible it seemed to him. To be left alone again, he told Hadjić to begin at once preparations for moving the staff to Boljkovci.

After the war, all the professors would be wiser commanders and greater strategists than he was; all the cadets of the military academy would state precisely in their examinations what the commander of the First Army should have done on December 7, 1914.

He wrote the shortest orders he had yet issued to the division commanders since the beginning of the offensive, and different from all those he had written before—addressed to each commander individually. Since yesterday their telephones had ceased to ring: they had gone off over Suvobor in the wake of their divisions.

He rose from the table, his whole body stiff. Slowly and painfully he moved to the window, and looked at the mountains in the gathering darkness.

As the Morava Division approached the Kolubara, battles became increasingly short and infrequent, the columns of prisoners longer, and the booty more abundant and varied, including things unknown to the Serbian soldiers. Perhaps the only person in the cavalry squadron not in high spirits was Adam Katić, who became more and more uneasy as his hopes faded of finding some cavalry unit or division staff—the one place where Dragan was likely to be. Instead, his squadron took captive groups of mud-stained, poverty-stricken infantry, or a supply train with enormous, skinny nags which stood motionless in the ditches, or lay down in the frozen puddles, like cattle. The horses they captured were such as to arouse in him only contempt for the Austro-Hungarian Empire.

Adam Katić could not feel the slightest pride or pleasure in the fact that he was recommended for the Obilić Gold Medal and for promotion to the rank of corporal for his "unquestionable heroism" in capturing an enemy section on Rajac—which had been publicly announced by Stošović, the commanding officer, in front of the entire squadron. He did not even feel like exulting over that candy-chewing officer, Lieutenant Tomić, who had avoided him after the incident on Rajac. It was not only because of his grief over Dragan that Adam took no pleasure in his prospective medal and promotion: he did not feel he had done anything on Rajac to deserve the Obilić Gold Medal for bravery; in fact, he thought he had done more to deserve it on at least ten other occasions, when none of the officers had noticed. The only good thing about the medal was that it would shut up Aleksa Dačić a bit and stick his nose in the ground; that is, if they ever met again alive. But if Aleksa asked him why he had got the medal, he would not conceal the truth from him; he hated telling lies. He did not see why he should lie about any of his war experiences, since he had always believed, throughout his twenty-one years, that the only thing worth lying about was a woman.

Whenever possible he went up to each new column of prisoners, offered them *rakija* and tobacco, and asked:

"Have any of you fellows seen a really fine black horse anywhere between Rajac and Suvobor? A horse with white fetlocks and a big white flower on its forehead?"

The prisoners would look at one another and shake their heads, unable to understand him; a few Czechs and Croats could hardly wait to tell him all they knew. And more. When they told him stupid lies, he would spit and walk away. He was impatient to hear the command to move on toward the Kolubara and Valjevo; most of all he placed his hopes on their entry into Valjevo: there he would find division headquarters, colonels and generals, and perhaps among them Dragan.

As soon as they left Gukoš, General Mišić—together with the operational part of the army staff and a company of cavalry as escort—were overtaken by an orderly bringing telegrams from the High Command. In front of a jumble of overturned munitions carts, slain horses, and little piles of infantry ammunition scattered about in the mud, Mišić stopped to read the telegrams.

Prince Alexander, the Commander in Chief, speaking in the name of the King and praising Mišić most generously, declared him promoted to the rank of vojvoda.

A sharp, burning sensation of exhaustion, striking like a blow, prevented him from removing his eyes from the telegram. It was not joy alone that produced this feeling: there was something else, never experienced before, some vague and overwhelming sensation in his head. Are you afraid of something, Živojin? He had been hearing his mother's voice ever since they started on their way. He raised his eyes: Baćinac was moving away in the distance, sinking down into the mountains toward the Drina.

"Allow me, Vojvoda!"

Smiling and excited, the orderly handed him his vojvoda's baton; the road between the high hedges became filled with enthusiastic approval, and one of the officers began firing shots from his revolver. These shots and the rejoicing dispelled the mist in which he seemed to be enveloped, and restored his habitual sternness. He said sharply:

"Dragutin, take that and stuff it in my knapsack!" Then he turned to the officers: "It's not a good thing, gentlemen, when the High Command is in a hurry to distribute decorations!"

At a rapid pace he rode his horse down the road, which was jammed up by the Austrian defeat, its surface washed away by the rain. It was the same road along which he had traveled with such difficulty by car, traversing crowds of refugees and other evidence of the Serbian defeat, to take over the command in Mionica. Now, from the Gukoš side, he looked around.

Once more Serbia was overturned, but this time toward the north and west, leaning forward toward the Sava and the Drina, scattering the Austro-Hungarian army away from Rudnik, Suvobor, and Maljen—an army now in headlong flight from the ever fewer bullets of the First Army, fired in anger and revenge. Behind the soldiers stretched a cold, metallic silence under a dark, lowering sky, heavy with snow which hadn't quite begun to fall and bury the slaughtered men and animals, fill up the trenches and shell holes, and block the roads over which the war was moving.

He made his way more and more slowly along the road jammed with overturned cars, broken carts and fiacres, cannon, gun carriages, field kitchens, and ambulances full of abandoned wounded men, the dead, and the dying. He rode slowly, avoiding the corpses of soldiers and horses, abandoned guns, field tools, and boxes of military archives. As he looked at all this his heart was very heavy—so heavy that for the first time since he had passed along this road, he felt no desire to stop at the wild pear tree where he had taken his captain's examination, and look at Baćinac and his native village Struganik. Even the wind had not escaped the scars of battle: undergrowth and boundary hedges were as still as if turned to stone. No birds anywhere. On the earth and in the sky, he was eagerly searching for a crow.

If the snow did not fall soon, people would not dare to go along the roads; until the woods and orchards were in leaf once more, clothing Serbia with greenery, this quiet following such great destruction would frighten them, one and all, day and night.

In the village, with its broken gates and burned fences, and the doors of houses opened onto a dark, gaping void, not a single dog barked; no cattle remained to bellow, nor a solitary cock to crow in that abysmal silence through which the road meandered tortuously in the mud, choked with the disordered monstrosities of defeat. Nothing in the world has such power to create senseless disorder as an army gripped by fear and a desire for vengeance; nothing exacts such punishment from the land as soldiers in headlong flight. Apart from the silence in front of him, what else was there to his victory?

The Austrian prisoners, ragged and mud-stained, lay in the ditches or sat beside the hedges, their rifles thrown down before them on the road. As he came along with his staff they got up with bowed heads and dangling arms; the wounded merely raised their heads, then sank down into the dry sharpness of the hedge.

Behind him, on the Third Army's front, a widespread artillery battle was beginning; its thunderous rumble spattered the silence of the muted battlefield of his own army. Šturm and Stepa were lagging behind—especially Stepa—lagging dangerously, unable to move forward. But two days ago he himself had not dared to do so; he had not been bold enough to risk everything on a big victory, and had made it impossible for Kajafa to carry through his task as well.

"Vojvoda Mišić, it was in this plum orchard that you saved me from one hell of a beating," said Dragutin quietly and confidentially, bringing his horse alongside so that their legs brushed.

Mišić was silent and frowning for a long time. He felt something inside him that he did not wish to acknowledge: this was the first time someone had addressed him as vojvoda. The person who had done so was Dragutin; perhaps it was a good thing that he, rather than anyone else, had done so.

"That's right, Dragutin. You were standing against that plum tree above the shell hole when I caught sight of you from the car."

"The first church we come to, I must light a candle for that officer."

"What? That second lieutenant who was beating you with his belt in such a despicable way?"

"Yes, for him, poor man. He was killed on Rajac three days ago, so they tell me. A shell got him. Nothing left of him to bury. And he was a really handsome young man, God rest his soul."

Vojvoda Mišić was startled: perhaps he was a bit to blame for the man's death? God knows how many men's deaths I'm guilty of, he thought. I am a villain and an accomplice.

"Light a candle for him in my name, too, Dragutin," he said, deeply moved. Then he thought: how many mistaken orders have I given since I took over the First Army? And which of my orders has caused men to die needlessly?

His vision became blurred as he approached some wrecked fiacres, an overturned motor car, and three carts full of wounded Austrians, now dead. He wanted to stop there and sit down by the hedge to recollect all the battles he need not have fought.

In Mionica they stopped in front of the inn where he had taken over the First Army from General Bojović. A few elderly people came out of the inn; taking off their hats or fur caps, they shouted excitedly:

"Three cheers for the Serbian Army! Long live Živojin Mišić!"

He saluted them, remembering his tight-kneed, staggering steps from Prince Alexander's car to the threshold of the inn, then full of civilians who were grumbling at Bojović because of the retreat.

"We won't stay here now. Let's go to another inn. We'll go to the town hall," he said, and set off in the direction of the Ribnica bridge, where he had won his first battle for the army: a battle against chaos, when he had separated the fear of the refugees from the fear of the soldiers, and implanted some semblance of order amid great misfortune. He had never climbed a steeper slope than this level ground from the inn to the bridge, bearing the entire road from Rudnik to Mionica on his shoulders.

Women, children, and old men came out of the yards, calling to him and greeting him. But the sound of their voices was blotted out by the thunder of cannon from Breždja, the bleating of sheep and lowing of cattle from across the Ribnica, and the shouts and curses on the riverbank in front of the thronged bridge, just twenty-four days before. A shudder ran through his body at the recollection of how he had passed through that cleft in the close-packed crowd of soldiers and refugees—that funnel which slowly opened and widened in front of him in the dusk—allowing him, together with Spasić and Drugutin, to pass over the empty bridge above the roaring Ribnica, and to order the soldiers to line up on the bank in the muddy cabbage field, with the rain pouring down in the gathering darkness. What would happen now if Dragutin started to play his flute? The stone bridge rumbled from the pounding of horses' hoofs. Under his overcoat he was trembling violently. Would Dragutin begin to play? He looked at him: Dragutin was lost in thought, and his face was sad. Was he remembering how his playing had caused those despairing soldiers to fire at him out of the darkness?

"Dragutin, were you very frightened by those bullets fired at you in the dark, when you were playing your flute here?"

"No, sir. I didn't seem able to feel frightened. It was that kind of day, for me."

In the cabbage field on the bank of the turbid Ribnica, where he had created the orderly ranks of a battalion from a fleeing rabble and planted the seeds of order in chaos, there were about ten dead bodies scattered in the mud and cabbage leaves—peasant women, young boys, and bareheaded old men; their fur hats were caught on some willow trees. Were the murderers having fun with their victims, or did they wish to frighten passers-by? He stopped his horse; all the others did so, too.

"It's as if they had caught them stealing cabbages in Franz Josef's kitchen garden!" said one of the officers angrily.

Mišić set off again, to stop the conversation behind his back. Women in mourning, young boys, and old men ran out onto the road from nearby yards and shouted: "Long live the Serbian army! Long live our liberators!" And as soon as they recognized him: "Long live our general, Živojin Mišić!"

He wanted at least to smile at them. But black flags hung under the eaves of the houses; it seemed as if no house was without one. He saluted the people. He had been riding a long time and felt a sudden exhaustion; he could hardly stay in his saddle.

In his instructions to the army for the next day he would say: pursue them to the Drina and the Sava, without stopping. Chase them until you have no breath left in your body. Punish the Austrian punitive expedition, punish it savagely. Punish those men who came to punish us only because we were determined to survive.

The local people kept running out onto the road; the men carried flasks of *rakija*, and the women had bread, apples, and plums in their aprons. When they recognized him they cried out his name.

Yes, punish them, but justly. A victory that lacks justice is no true victory. He who feels only hatred cannot be just. But how can a man be just in these days? Is such a thing possible? How could one be just after so much death?

Mišić looked at his watch: it was three in the afternoon. He would be able to get to his home in Struganik before the light failed and see what was left there, and who from his big family was still alive. First of all he would go to his mother's grave. If she were alive, she would not rejoice at his promotion to the rank of vojvoda today, not at all. Her eyes would fill with tears, her lips would remain tense and silent. He would go straight to his mother's grave and spend a little time in silence beside her tombstone, which was narrow and bent as she herself had been in her lifetime. He would place his hands on the mound of earth, sunk in the grass, beneath which she lay.

Without his glasses, Ivan Katić stood beside Aleksa Dačić in the middle of his squad's firing line; he was in a trench alongside a field path, staring at the blurred outlines of the bare field, over which meandered a long wisp of darkness on the grim horizon of his field of vision.

"Where are they now, Aleksa?"

"About a gunshot's distance from us. Now they're passing through some undergrowth."

"And how many are there?"

"About a hundred of our boys, I'd say. I don't know how many Fritzies, damn them! About a hundred also, I suppose."

Ivan leaned against the edge of the path and strained his eyes even more, staring through the sparse undergrowth at the restless wisp of darkness which was infiltrating the grayness of the sky and pouring over the dark shapes of trees, undergrowth, and slope. It was as though he was dreaming. The fields were there, yet they weren't fields. His fear was not true fear; the pain in his forehead was not real pain. This day was not like all the days he remembered.

In fact, this day had had no daybreak; night had gone, taking the dawn and the first light with it, but leaving behind an inn full of dead Austrians and Serbs, the corpses of horses behind the inn, and slaughtered women and children in the ditches. For him the night had actually come to a violent end before he lost his glasses. It had all happened in a surprise attack on the headquarters of an Austrian alpine brigade, with their supply train and field hospital—in that terrible hand-to-hand fighting with rifle butts and bayonets in the darkness, and the mad rush after the enemy staff officers fleeing with their wounded, when one hit out in the dark at every voice and every groan. In that dark, burning tumult something had hit him on the head; there had been an explosion of breaking glass like a grenade, then everything became numb and silent. When he became aware that his face was wet and saw that the lamps were lit, he was lying in the arms of Aleksa Dačić, who was swearing at somebody as he put him down on the bench of a schoolroom desk. He noticed the blackboard, lit by a lamp, and a teacher standing beside it, wearing the uniform of an Austrian officer. Some dream! The class was making a terrible noise, like just before the holidays.

"Lift your head up so I can bandage it," said Aleksa, waking him. "There you are, Corporal. Somebody hit you with the butt of a rifle."

"But my glasses!" he had said with a groan, jumping up before he had even felt to see if they were there. "Where are my glasses?" He stood up among the desks. Aleksa, holding a lantern, gaped at him and muttered a curse. The noise in the classroom suddenly stopped. An Austrian officer wearing glasses was leaning against the blackboard. "Where are my glasses?" he asked, seizing Aleksa by the jacket. Aleksa didn't hear him, but one of the soldiers shouted:

"It's true, so help me! The corporal's lost his goddamn glasses!"

He had passed both hands over his face to see if they were there, holding them against his eyes for a long time. But somehow he couldn't cry, not when there was so much misery all around. When he removed his hands from his face, there were Austrian officers standing against the wall beside the blackboard; he couldn't see their faces clearly, but the tallest of them was wearing glasses. He stared at this lucky man. Then a soldier came up to that lucky man, and very gently—just like Ivan's mother when he was in bed, and in that dream—very gently and carefully took off the glasses and handed them to Ivan:

"See if this Fritzie's glasses are any good, Corporal."

Would he actually take a man's glasses from him?

"No, they're no good," he said, without further reflection, marveling at the Austrian officer's indifference.

He had sat down at the desk and stared at the blackboard lit by a lamp. The soldiers were whispering to one another as they kept guard over the captured officers. Aleksa sat down dejectedly in the last desk, like the biggest dunce in the class. Perhaps this was all a dream?

"I give you my word, Corporal, I'll get back your glasses if I have to go to the Drina!" said Aleksa. "I won't go back to Prerovo if I don't find them. Now wash your face—it's covered with blood. Did they whack you on your forehead with a rifle butt?"

"I've no idea." He washed his face; the bruise on his forehead hurt. Then he looked around the school playground: those heaps of darkness were dead Austrians. He heard some people making a noise and set off in that direction to look for Sava Marić. Daylight, with its many colors, was already visible. He went up to one of the ditches: they were indeed the dead bodies of women and girls; and one boy beside a gate.

"When did they do this?" he asked.

An old woman leaning against the fence answered his question: "Last night, just before you came."

"But why did they do it?"

"Might is right, my boy!"

Wanting to see the woman's face clearly, he moved toward her, but she took off quickly down the road. Then he leaned against the fence. Standing among a crowd of soldiers from both sides, Sava Marić was shouting:

"I won't allow you to take boots and overcoats from the Austrians! Only blankets and tent flaps!"

"Do we have to go barefoot to the Drina, Corporal?"

"Indeed you do. You go barefoot in your own land, and you can fight barefoot for your freedom!"

"Just look at that ditch and see what they've done to our people! And they take every goddamn thing! This is a big village and you can't find a kilogram of flour."

"Listen, Stefan. I want one of those Fritzies to feel ashamed of himself when he sees us! Let him feel ashamed because he can't respect himself, and repent his evil deeds. We're a serious people, we are!"

"We're a blind people, Sava!" cried Ivan from the ditch. Then he turned to go back to the school. He called to Aleksa Dačić.

"Will you stay beside me, Aleksa, until my father sends me another pair of glasses?"

"Of course I will, Corporal! We're both from Prerovo, aren't we? We're neighbors."

Ivan was struck speechless by these words: Austria-Hungary was vanquished, the war was over. Momentous words and fundamental conclusions about people welled up in his mind. He could have jotted them down in his notebook, but just then the commanding officer's orderly ran up and led them into a house:

"Can you see well enough to command your section, Katić?"

"Yes, I can."

"Then go with them at once to the end of the village. There's a battalion of Austrians moving against us from the next village. They want to capture the staff."

Ivan Katić stared at the shapeless heaps which were shouting, wailing, and yelling: "Vorwärts! Vorwärts!"

"What's happening now, Aleksa?"

"The kids are all excited. They want to run away. Can you hear the row they're making?"

"And how far away are they, Aleksa?"

"Not more than two hundred paces."

"No one is to shoot till I give the command!" cried Ivan. Then he asked quietly: "Is that all right, Aleksa?"

"How can we shoot our own people? You see those boys there? If it was only women and old men!"

Women were crying out and calling for help, just on the edge of his vision.

"What are those women doing, Aleksa?"

"The Austrians have got hold of them by their shoulders, and they're pushing them in front."

"Can you see the Austrians' heads? Can we aim at their heads?"

"How can you hit a man's head, damn him, when he's bending down and hiding behind a woman?"

"Are they beating the children?"

"Yes, they are. They've each grabbed one child and they're pushing him in front like a young ram. But the children have spotted us. So have the women. That's why they're making such a row."

"Why are the Austrians shooting?"

"There's two officers walking behind them, firing their revolvers. Look—the Austrians have taken the children up in their arms! My God, Katić, what's going on?"

"What are you waiting for, boys? Shoot!"

"Who's that shouting, Aleksa?"

"An old man. Poor devil! Someone's beating him with a rifle butt!"

"Shoot that Austrian! Aim your gun at him."

"How can I shoot when the bullet will get two women as well?"

"What'll we do, Corporal—clear out? How can we shoot our own people?" cried the soldiers.

The sound of wailing and shrieking, mingled with German oaths, came nearer.

"We'll wait for them here, then go for them with our bayonets!" said Ivan to the soldiers.

The field was dark with wailing, weighed down by the sky.

"What are you Serbian soldiers waiting for? Shoot them! It doesn't matter if we all go."

"Is that the same old man, Aleksa?"

"Yes, it's him. And there's a woman laughing. Probably gone crazy. The one in the middle with a white head scarf. The children are putting their hands over their eyes. And the Austrians are hiding behind them, damn their guts! Should we make a bolt for it, Ivan?"

"Shoot, boys! You're Serbs—shoot!"

"Aleksa, I'll go with the first section and take them by the flank. But don't open fire until I start shooting from behind their backs."

"It's too late, Corporal."

"No, it isn't. First section, follow me!"

"I'll go. You can't see."

"Yes I can, Aleksa. I can see."

Ivan ran along the trench by the field path, followed by a few soldiers.

Aleksa swore in despair; he didn't know what to do. He took aim at an officer who was lagging behind his own firing line and the groups of Serbs. The Serbs were suddenly silent. The two armies aimed at each other over the heads of women, children, and old men; they took aim, but didn't fire. Then Aleksa decided what to do, and shouted:

"Look here, Fritzies! Go back to where you came from! I give you my solemn word we won't shoot!"

They stopped, but said nothing. The Serbian people were silent, too, standing some fifty paces in front of the rifles of their own army.

Aleksa looked for Ivan, but couldn't see him. He stared at the women in front of him: above the heads of the women and old men moved the bayonets of the Austrians' rifles, trained on the Serbian soldiers. If they fire, he thought, then we'll have to. We'll kill our own people. Once more he shouted:

"Listen to me, Fritzies! If you won't go back where you came from, then we will! Give me your oath in the name of your Emperor that you won't shoot until we get into the village!"

The Austrians still didn't speak, nor did the Serbs. A magpie swished past them, took fright, and flew high up in the sky. Then Ivan's section rushed at the Austrians from behind, from a considerable distance. Aleksa kept his gun trained on the officer. Ivan's section shouted: "Hurrah!"

The Austrians were confused. The people began to wail, then rushed toward Aleksa's men and sprawled in the meadow. Aleksa fired at the officer; in the confusion he didn't see whether he'd hit him. He gave the command to charge. Then the charging and slaughter started in the field.

Sava Marić came up with his section; a squadron of Serbian cavalry also rushed up to pursue the Austrians over the bare field, to take prisoners and to kill. By dusk, the village of the people whom the Austrians had used as shields was liberated.

When twilight came, and quiet descended on the abandoned village and the weary soldiers, Aleksa cried out in alarm: "Where's the Corporal? Where's Ivan Katić, damn you all?" He ran from house to house, from soldier to soldier. "When did you last see him? Where was he when you saw him?"

The soldiers shrugged and said nothing; they didn't know when Ivan Katić had disappeared. No one had seen him killed. A few men asserted that they had seen him running after three Austrians into a large enclosed field. They hadn't seen him since.

Aleksa reached the field with a few soldiers. It was now dark. He called Ivan's name. Silence. The soldiers shouted:

"Ivan! Corporal!"

They joined hands and walked slowly through the field, feeling with their feet, stumbling over bushes, calling Ivan's name. They crossed the field several times in all directions. When they reached the end they stopped. There was not a sound.

Aleksa broke away from the rest of the soldiers and went slowly into the field, into the darkness and silence. He wept aloud.

Vojvoda Mišić entered Valjevo with his staff early in the morning. He rode at a rapid pace in the center of the staff column, trying not to look at the bodies of men and horses lying about on the dripping cobblestones of the street. He tried not to count the houses with black flags hanging from their eaves, smashed doors and windows, and burned and broken fences. And he made an effort not to see the wounded Austrians lying on the pavements with their heads on the doorsteps of shops and workrooms.

He was soon recognized by the local people who knew him well and wanted to greet him personally. He avoided their eyes and looked at the head of his horse, which was tossing in rhythm with its footsteps. It was in Valjevo, he recalled, that he had spent the pleasantest and most carefree years of his life, as a peacetime division commander; he had been happy with Louisa and the children, his authority had been unchallenged among the officers, and he had been widely respected by the townsfolk. When he left Valjevo, after his transfer to the General Staff as Putnik's assistant, the whole town had come to see him off. He could hear people calling his name, and shouts of "Long live Živojin Mišić!" But he just looked at his horse's head, and tried to keep his thoughts on that undeserved triumphal departure from Valjevo. How easy and delightful it was to enjoy unearned recognition!

As if to rid himself of these memories, he walked briskly into the district court where the High Command had been accommodated a month before. As he walked along the dirty corridor, he remembered that difficult and extraordinary meeting of the High Command, when Vojvoda Putnik had made his choking plea for peace; when Pašić had picked up all the tricks, like the winning partner in a game of *tablonet;* and Vukašin Katić, who had spoken with greater wisdom than anyone else, had probably put an end to his political career. He stopped at the entrance of the courtroom: some irresistible force was drawing him inside. He told his adjutant to have a room prepared for him and see that it was well heated, then went into the courtroom: the floor was covered with broken glass from the windows, torn and burned paper, along with cartridge belts and empty bottles; against the walls was some straw on which people had lain, and on the judge's podium, little heaps of human excrement. He leaned against the doorpost and thought about Field Marshal Oscar Potiorek, about Vienna, Europe, and Western culture. But he quickly left the room, feeling vaguely ashamed but proud at the same time. He gave orders that some prisoners should be brought in to clean up and scrub the courtroom, then walked up and down the corridor while he waited for his room to be prepared. He was probably capable of much wrongdoing in this life, he reflected, but he could never have served an occupying power. It would be better to be a slave.

By noon the news had spread all through Valjevo that Živojin Mišić, the commander of the First Army, had arrived; a large crowd gathered outside the staff headquarters, eager to see him, to hear his voice and greet him. People were shouting his name in the streets, cheering him as their liberator, the man who had vanquished Potiorek; but he sat crouched over the stove in his room, smoking and thinking. He never stopped smoking. Hadjić came in and told him that the assembled townspeople of Valjevo wanted him to show himself so they could greet him, but he refused: "Tell them I'm very busy."

Hadjić came in again with the same request.

"Tell them that in a few days Vojvoda Putnik will arrive in Valjevo. Then they'll be able to greet the man who most deserves their thanks," he said firmly.

Hadjić came back with a plea that he would at least come stand at the entrance to the court.

"Tell them that King Peter will come to Valjevo, and then they'll be able to greet the man to whom the glory rightly belongs," he said sharply.

Only when the rejoicing outside seemed to be turning to dissatisfaction, and his determination to stay inside had reached the point of pigheadedness, did he put on his overcoat and cap to go out. Accompanied by his adjutant and Hadjić, he stood on the stone steps, which were crowded with people rapturously shouting:

"Long live our liberator, Živojin Mišić!"

He stood at attention, his face stern, and saluted. He remained in this position for a few moments, then went back to his room to write his report to the High Command:

The enemy continues to withdraw toward the Sava and the Drina, now offering practically no resistance. All commanders report that the enemy has left in the greatest disorder. Everywhere on the roads there are large quantities of ammunition, especially artillery shells, munitions, carts, cannon, etc. Groups of enemy soldiers who at first concealed themselves in the villages are now surrendering of their own free will. Captured officers report that the enemy no longer has complete units, but only fragments of units mixed up with one another, retreating in all directions. In addition to crimes committed against a population who have done nothing to deserve them, the enemy has shown exceptional persistence in destroying our farms, violating our women, and defiling our houses and public buildings.

It was his first night in newly liberated Valjevo, but he couldn't sleep. He tried to write a letter to Louisa, but apart from the state of his health, he couldn't think of anything to say. He wrote a few indignant lines to Vukašin Katić about the inadequacy of the government, and invited him to come to Valjevo as soon as he could. Since the beginning of the offensive, he remembered, he had not asked Vasić about Ivan; he had not asked about his own sons either. Had he not in fact determined Ivan's fate by one of his directives?

The telephone was silent, which irritated him unbearably; it was some days since he had talked with the division commanders. He wanted to take the first opportunity of admitting his error to Kajafa, and settling scores with Vasić. How should he reward those who deserved recognition? Surely that was what promotion and decorations were for?

He must go into the courtroom and stay there a while, just being quiet. Dragutin told him that the prisoners had given the room a good cleaning and scrubbing, though the broken window glass had not been replaced. Dragutin opened the door for him and carried in a lamp. Mišić told him to put the lamp on the floor, then leave him alone. He shut the door and began pacing up and down the courtroom: what had he done that his grandsons would not forgive?

His footsteps reverberated through the cold, empty courtroom, the floor of which was still damp. The light from his cigarette glowed in the darkness. He continued walking up and down, until the first jackdaws began cawing on the dome of the district court and on the roof of the prison.

His adjutant Spasić and his orderly Dragutin stood leaning against the doorpost in the corridor, dozing as they listened to the vojvoda's uneven footsteps.

Adam Katić was riding alone toward Zvornik, following the river Drina; he rode under a low, glowing sun, along the edge of the snow-covered heights of Bosnia; from time to time, but not very often, he heard muted rifle fire. The road became increasingly choked with overturned munitions carts, gun carriages, and exhausted horses lying beside metal boxes or collapsing in ditches, or on the snow-flecked mud, or in freezing puddles. As soon as he saw a black horse in the ditch he slackened his pace; he did so although he didn't believe his horse could be among the slaughtered and exhausted nags marking the route by which the Austrians were now fleeing Serbia. Some people in an ambulance shouted something to him in German; the rest of the wounded were weeping. He spread his arms in a gesture of helplessness and spurred his horse forward. A group of Austrians came out onto the road in front of him from a field of unharvested corn, holding their hands above their heads. He stopped his horse and looked at them: they were unshaven, ragged, and mud-stained—a sorry sight. How could such wretches have set in motion so much evil and tyranny?

"Any of you know Serbian?" he shouted. "I won't do you any harm. You needn't be afraid. Just tell me whether you've seen a big herd of horses, five hundred of them? I'm told they passed this way this morning. Where have they gone?"

The Austrians gaped at him in silence.

"So not one of you knows Serbian, yet we've licked you!" he said, angry and despairing.

He spurred his horse and hurried on, leaving the Austrians standing in the ditch beside a pile of ammunition chests, their hands upraised.

At a large bend in the Drina he encountered a sudden volley of machine-gun fire from behind a poplar wood. He pulled up his horse against a broad elm tree beside the road, listened to the firing, and looked at the setting sun.

Those must be the last positions, he thought. How could he avoid them? And where was he to go next? It would soon be night. All his efforts, from Takovo right up to this elm tree, had been useless. The soldiers would now go home on leave over Christmas, and he would be condemned as a deserter by a court-martial.

He heard bursts of rifle and machine-gun fire, as though an attack was being repulsed; also, the whinnying of horses. Must be a cavalry charge, he thought. Since he had been in the war—and he had taken part in charges by a whole cavalry division—he had not heard such loud whinnying. Then some horses without riders ran out into the field toward him. He pressed his horse into a gallop in the direction of the poplar trees, toward the horses which were fleeing from the woods, some with saddles and some with only headstalls.

"Those are the horses!" he said aloud, and dug his spurs into his nag.

He rode into the poplar wood and rushed toward the firing, toward the ever louder and more fearful whinnying. At the end of the poplar wood his horse stopped short: on a large, bare sandbank near where the Drina had overflowed its banks, there were hundreds of horses tied together, milling about: whinnying, pulling in all directions, slipping, treading in the river, moving back in waves toward the poplars, tearing loose and trying to run away, jumping on top of each other, standing up on their hind legs, rearing toward the glowing sun and then falling down on the corpses, the dead bodies of the horses which blackened the sandbank and the shallows of the river.

Adam was momentarily blinded and deafened by the whinnying; then he heard bullets flying past his head. Not more than a hundred paces from where he was standing amid the seething mass of horses on the sandbank, Austrians were firing at him with their rifles while their machine gun mowed down the horses. He jumped from the saddle, removed his rifle from his shoulders, and hit his horse with the butt to make him gallop off into the poplars; then he took cover behind a broad tree trunk, and aimed at the murderers of those horses. Two or three soldiers returned his fire inaccurately, while the rest slaughtered the horses with their machine gun, forcing the survivors to swim down the river toward Bosnia. Those that managed to break away and gallop off into the poplar trees or the river were killed by volleys of gunfire. Adam aimed at the man firing the machine gun, but without success; he was spattered with dead bark from the trunk, splintered off by the Austrian bullets. He fired, then turned around to look at the sandbank. The black mass of horses was gradually sub-siding: only some ten of them still stood with their front legs on their dead comrades, whinnying at the river, the mountain, and the expiring sun. Adam's teeth chattered and his brain was clouded; perhaps he was dreaming. Then the last horses fell; the machine gun had slain the last of the rearing, whinnying mass. The piles of black corpses grew still. The firing stopped. Adam dropped his gun, frightened by the silence. The noise of the Drina mounted to the glowing clouds. A squad of Austrians in fighting formation ran up to a tall tree beside the river and disappeared into the darkness of the poplar wood.

Adam stood up, his knees shaking, and tried to run toward the slaughtered horses; he felt as though he was dreaming. He stood still when he came to the first corpses. He could not go over them; it must be a dream: that death rattle, those convulsively twitching hind legs, those attempts to get up, the dead falling on top of the dead. The horses lying in the shallows were biting the stones and spitting out sand and pebbles. But he was looking for Dragan: that was not a dream. Blood spurted from the wounded animals, they collapsed and died with rattling throats and wide-open, staring eyes; he was dreaming again. With his bayonet he cut loose their halters and straps, and separated the dead bodies; he tramped through pools of blood, looking for a head with a big flower between the eyes. In some of the eyes he noticed a burning fire left behind in the sky, either from the sun or the Austrians—who could tell? He shuddered at the sight of that fire in those staring eyes; perhaps he wasn't dreaming after all. His breeches were damp and his shoes squished with water or blood—he would find out which when he woke up. He looked hard at the hoofs and shins, but they were all white, or perhaps they weren't; it was just that night had fallen while he was dreaming. All the horses were black; he wasn't dreaming. He stood above a horse that was beating its head on the ground. He listened to its last death agony, its expiring sighs. He would have cried out, but he had no voice. He bent his finger to whistle, but no sound came. The corpses of black horses grew bigger and bigger: haystacks, huge piles of corpses. A whole mountain of dead black horses. The sound of the river was hushed; perhaps it had stopped flowing. The fire in the sky died out, and smoke spread out over the mountain and the river. He stood transfixed by the silence and darkness.

A flock of wild geese flapped and squawked above his head, and fell down into the shallows near the slaughtered horses. The geese honked; he was alarmed and frightened by their boldness, their strength, their life. Then another flock of wild geese cut through the silence of the sky and dropped noisily into the river, splashing their wings in the water.

When had he gone hunting wild geese on the Morava with his grandfather? Had he ever been able to shoot at those beautiful, swift-flying, all-seeing creatures with green crests on their heads?

The wild geese honked and beat their wings around the dead horses. His ear caught the sound of yet another flock squawking across the sky. He raised his gun and fired at a swift tuft of darkness above him, underneath one of the stars. That shot, perhaps the last fired by the First Army, shattered the banks of the Drina like a field cannon. A dark spot sagged, and his gun slid from his hand in fear that his shot had gone home; but the wild goose rose again in a curving upward flight, honking as it flew, and went back alone toward the east, to Serbia. He felt easier when he realized he had missed.

He slung his gun over his shoulder and set off toward the poplar wood where he had left his horse; he jumped over the slaughtered animals or walked around them. The Drina rustled behind his back; a flock of wild geese flew over his head, humming in their flight.

At eleven o'clock on December 15, Vojvoda Mišić wrote to the High Command:

"According to the latest reports from the entire area of our western front, the last broken remnants of the enemy have been driven across the Drina and the Sava, so that this area is now completely cleared. The defeated enemy is keeping watch on his frontier with small patrols of Landstürmer regiments."

He summoned the chiefs of all the army services and told them that telephone communication with the division commanders must be established within three days. He cut short their sharp assertions about the lack of material for telephones:

"Gentlemen, the First Army has ended its battle, at least for now. The time is approaching when there will be little to do, at which point a commander has the right to give even such orders as cannot be carried out!"

They left the room in silence, smiling but bewildered.

He heard a bugle from the street, something that sounded like a funeral march. For three days in succession funerals of women, and occasionally of a man, had passed along the street like a supply train. He went to the window: it was an officer's funeral.

Vojvoda Mišić stood at attention and saluted; his jaws were tightly clenched. At least this man's grave would be known, which was by no means a small thing, he said to himself. Dragutin brought in some wood and threw it in the stove; he must turn around and face him.

"Well, what have you to say to me, Dragutin? Do you want to go on leave?"

"It's not yet time for thinking about our houses and our own affairs, sir. Every since Gukoš I've been thinking: well, we've somehow managed to get rid of the Fritzies. For those who are still alive, things will be very much like before, only a bit worse. Because we've lost a great deal, we're poor as church mice now. The government will go on like it used to, making us pay taxes. The clerks have got to have their salaries and the government's got to pay them, so it won't go short. The merchants will fleece us peasants twice as much as they used to. Our officers will get promotions and medals, which is right and proper. The soldiers will get leave, for a longer or shorter time, depending on Franz Josef and Vojvoda Putnik. Anyway, they'll be able to do some plowing, to mend the fences and sheeppens, and talk with the women and old men. And spend a little time with their children. Then back to the army. But this great struggle of ours for Serbia, sir, it's the oxen that are pulling it along, I really mean that, sir. If we hadn't had oxen and cattle to drag bread and shells and ammunition and the other things you need to fight a war—to drag them through all that mud and misery and awful weather—we couldn't have done anything to the Fritzies, not a darned thing. So please, sir, if you can, when you're giving out an order praising the soldiers, just spare a word for the Serbian oxen, for the farm animals of Serbia, sir. Do it in God's name, and in the name of justice. I've seen a lot of heartless people, sir, but I never yet saw an ox that had no heart."

"You're right, Dragutin, absolutely right. Tell me, that year when you sowed the wheat two days before Christmas, what kind of a yield did you get?"

"They never remember a better harvest in Mačva than that year."

"Bring me some apples, Dragutin."

The next day, December 16, Colonel Hadjić came into his room in the evening, his face wreathed in smiles. Without preliminary greeting he cried:

"Two telegrams from the High Command! And it's hard to tell which has better news!"

"Then read them to me in the order of their official numbers," said Mišić, lighting a cigarette.

"The recapture of Belgrade," began Hadjić, declaiming rather than reading, "brings to a successful conclusion a great and at the same time glorious period in our operations against Austria-Hungary. The enemy has been crushed, scattered, defeated, and completely driven away from our territory. The troops must now have a period of rest, with better food and accommodation, and also assemble the necessary material resources and prepare for further operations. I therefore give orders—"

"And what orders does Putnik give in the second telegram?" interrupted Mišić; but the happy expression on Hadjić's face did not change. "Tell me the most important thing in the second telegram."

"You're to go at once to Belgrade, by the fastest means of transport available, to ride at the head of the army with His Majesty King Peter, and make a triumphal entry into the liberated capital as victor! The telegram is signed by the Commander in Chief, His Highness Prince Alexander."

Mišić looked down at the table, reflected for a few moments, then said firmly:

"Go ahead and carry out the instructions in the first telegram exactly as given. And reply to the second in my name as follows: 'The commander of the First Army wishes to thank the Commander in Chief for the honor and recognition conferred on him. He considers that the honor of making a triumphal entry into Belgrade with the King should go to a commander whose staff is nearer Belgrade.'" He was silent for a moment, then added: "Tell them that my health is not satisfactory either."

Hadjić looked at him in amazement: "If I may say so, sir, I would suggest—"

"You may comment only on Putnik's instructions in the first telegram."

"You have forgotten that the mayor is arranging a ceremonial banquet in your honor this evening. It's time you were setting out."

"You shall represent me at the banquet. And take with you as many staff officers as possible."

Hadjić left the room in silence.

Mišić bent over the table, glad to be alone, and immersed himself in the anxious thought that had tormented him since leaving Mionica: when a small country defeats a big one, when a weaker army crushes one more powerful than itself, can any good come of it in the future? No, it cannot. The victor will be savagely punished for transgressing the law of this world. Can Serbia have any hope of peace, after defeating the Austro-Hungarian Empire? Vengeance awaits us, inescapable vengeance.

Outside, in front of the staff headquarters, shots were being fired from guns and revolvers; officers and soldiers were celebrating the victory. He shut his eyes to keep back the tears; his whole being became paralyzed with a feeling of sadness he had never experienced before.

The sounds of shooting and rejoicing moved away from the staff headquarters and spread throughout Valjevo. Once more he felt a desire to go to his family home in Struganik, to sit beside the fireplace and poke the fire, to listen to it, to bake potatoes in the ashes and to crack walnuts. That was how he wanted to celebrate the quiet that for a short time had descended on Serbia.

There was a timid knock on the door. One of the junior officers, he thought. He would have to ask him to come in.

Professor Zarija entered. He had never seen such a stern expression on his face.

"What's happened, Professor?"

"May I have a word with you, Vojvoda, if you're not too busy?"

"Sit down, Professor. Tell me what's on your mind." He offered him a cigarette and lit it.

"We've now become a great nation. A great European nation. That's an epoch-making event, Vojvoda."

Mišić frowned as though something had scratched his face: how could anyone say such things now? But Zarija's unusual thoughtfulness restrained him from interrupting.

"After our victories over Turkey and Bulgaria, and now over Austria-Hungary, we Serbs have at last become a real nation in the historical sense of the word. We've had great defeats and great victories. We've won the right to our own dignity—and to a few misconceptions about ourselves, too! Our history, Vojvoda, has everything that you find in the history of great nations. Significant truths and closely guarded secrets. Great individuals and powerful men. We've now got the necessary conditions for great literature, art, and thought. You know, Vojvoda, if a nation doesn't produce one great book about itself, that's a sign that it has nothing worth remembering. You don't agree with me?"

"Perhaps that's how things are, looked at from your point of view. But I consider that in war it's not difficult to win a battle. Anyone who is prepared to die can defeat all his opponents. It's much more difficult to obtain peace and justice by means of war. Peace that is really peace—a tranquil peace, Professor."

"But surely the verdict of history will be that Serbia won the war, after twice beating the Austro-Hungarian army to its knees, and twice driving it back over the frontier! That will be the verdict of history.

Do you know what the most important thing is?" said Zarija, getting up and walking toward Mišić. "After these victories we'll no longer be an unhappy people, I'm deeply convinced of it. Our songs will be different. We'll have to change our manner of swearing! We'll no longer be malicious, cunning, and petty. Perhaps we'll be haughty and licentious, but after so much suffering we have the right to be haughty if we want to! A Serb will no longer feel like a man of an inferior race, a Balkan vis-à-vis the Europeans. Europe won't despise him any more."

"I don't like the frequent use of the word 'victory,' Professor, just as I can't bear the word 'catastrophe,'" said Mišić after a long pause. "Those words are associated with extreme feelings—enthusiasm or despair. And such feelings are painful and dangerous, Professor."

"Since you've allowed me to speak so freely, I must ask you this: surely you must feel like a victor tonight, Vojvoda?"

Mišić went over to the window, and stared at the dim, murky light of the street lamps in the darkness. People in the town were singing, firing guns, and making a lot of noise.

"I really don't know, Professor, who deserves the most credit for our recent victory. The dead most of all, of course." After a long pause he turned around. "And certainly my opponent, Field Marshal Oscar Potiorek, has contributed as much to the victory as I have. He must be a bitterly unhappy man tonight."

"Can you hear our suffering, afflicted people rejoicing? The people's hearts are bursting in Valjevo, Vojvoda!" said Zarija softly, almost in a whisper; his eyes were wet.

"Yes, I can hear it. And that's how it should be. They deserve to rejoice. But I don't know how to rejoice. That's how I was born."

Dragutin brought in the tea and coffee; they sat down at the table in silence. Mišić did not drink his tea; his head bowed over his cup, he continued in a quiet voice:

"I have come to believe that great military victories, and other events which history claims as victories, belong only to future generations. Only they have the right to enjoy them and make use of them. Contemporaries certainly cannot do so. That's how I see it. Only those interested in loot, power, and glory seek personal advantage in a military victory. A victory won by the people." He raised his head and looked hard at Zarija, who seemed even more worried. "But from reading our history and that of other nations, I concluded long ago that a struggle for freedom benefits only those for whom freedom isn't necessary, those who didn't even fight for it." He fell silent and drank his tea, then rose from the table. "Time we got some sleep, Professor."

Zarija saluted, wearily and reluctantly; perhaps he was disappointed.

"Listen, Professor," said Mišić, stopping him at the door. "You're a man of books, and you know a lot. My life runs in another channel, as you see; that's why I look at things differently. For some reason I've never been either happy or self-confident. But from the bottom of my heart I feel that a man has the right to rejoice, either when everybody around him can share his rejoicing, or over something entirely private. And in war, in our recent victory, neither of these alternatives is possible. Good night, Zarija."

The next morning the first person to come into his room to report was not Hadjić but the head of the medical section of the army staff.

"What is it, Doctor?" said Mišić, standing beside the stove. "Your battle isn't over. It's still raging. There's no lull. The wounds are still open. You didn't tell me anything about Milena Katić, a volunteer nurse."

"Well, I've got news of her. She's alive and well. She's working in the hospital here, sir."

"Send one of the soldiers to bring her here. Have you found room for those three thousand wounded Austrians?"

"Yes, we've done that, sir. I said yesterday that some cases of typhus had been reported. This morning I have received reports from ten places and hospitals where the First Army has been operating. Over sixty soldiers and civilians have contracted spotted typhus. In all the places where they were billeted or through which they passed, the prisoners have left lice behind them. Now they've spread all over Serbia, carrying a fatal disease, sowing the seeds of death. We're on the verge of a major epidemic, and it's spreading like a house on fire! That could be catastrophic, in our situation."

Mišić frowned and coughed, but he couldn't snap back at the doctor because of that strange, repulsive word, *catastrophe*. He walked to the window and looked at a flock of crows and jackdaws on the prison roof, the woodshed, and the outhouses. Were they spreading those lice, carrying death on their wings?

"So we've beaten the Austrians," he said quietly, not looking at Doctor Pešić. "Field Marshal Oscar Potiorek has not crushed us with his punitive expedition. We've held out against seven army corps. Man with his weapons of destruction has not bowed our heads. And now the louse has moved against Serbia. The miserable louse!" He shouted angrily, then returned to the head of the medical service. "Tell me what we are to do. My army can be ruined—what's left of it."

"All Serbia might be destroyed, sir—the entire country."

Mišić lit a cigarette at the stove; he crouched down and looked at the fire. Was the vengeance he dreaded already on its way? He stood up:

"It seems to me, Doctor, that from now on you should be the commander of the First Army, and of all the territory under its care. I will be simply your chief of staff. Please establish your dispositions for the campaign against the louse by noon!"

"What am I to fight with?" he said, hunching his shoulders and spreading out his hands.

"With whatever means we have at our disposal. I take it you don't think we should surrender to the spotted louse?"

The chief of the medical service saluted, and hurriedly left the room.

"O God, is this the beginning of vengeance for Serbia's victory? Our punishment for defeating a stronger nation, a Great Power?" he said aloud.

The crows and jackdaws cawed.

"How long must such things be?" he whispered fearfully. Then he put on his overcoat and went into the courtroom, to pace up and down, up and down.

The next evening, just before midnight, he had a pleasant surprise: the telephone rang. He picked up the receiver with a trembling hand:

"Hello! Mišić speaking. What did you say, operator? Well done! I'll recommend your entire team for promotion and medals. First of all give me the Danube Division, first levy. Hello, Kajafa! Mišić speaking. Can you hear me? Good evening, Kajafa! Have you had some rest?"

"I certainly have, General. But I can't sleep because it's so quiet; I'm already bored by it. Forgive me, you took me by surprise. Congratulations on your new rank! I'm happy to serve under you, sir. Can you hear me, Vojvoda?"

"Thank you, Kajafa. They say that in peacetime soldiers who've seen active service suffer from boredom and lumbago."

"I haven't yet got lumbago, but boredom is beginning to bother me. I'm not cut out for garrison duty or guarding the frontiers. I like to pursue and capture. In fact, that's why I put on the uniform."

"There's something I want to tell you, Kajafa. Your request to pursue the enemy on December 7 was absolutely justified. It was the right decision for a commander to make. Can you hear me, Kajafa? As a commander, I made a mistake on the seventh and eighth. I'll explain everything when we meet. Can you hear me, Kajafa? Hello? What do you mean, he doesn't answer? Why have you cut us off? All right, then give me the Danube Division, second levy. Yes, this is the army staff headquarters. Mišić speaking. Good evening, Vasić! I'm sorry I've woken you up, but the telephone is working again and I wanted to take the first opportunity to congratulate you on your exceptional performance. You'll be first on the list for decorations and promotion. Can you hear me, Vasić?"

"Magnanimity in my senior officers is very distasteful to me, Vojvoda."

"And vanity in subordinates is very distasteful to me, Colonel."

"For me, Vojvoda, my personal pride is more important than any recognition."

"But to me, Colonel, the most important thing is justice. And justice compels me to acknowledge that you are the boldest commander in the First Army."

"Forgive me, but I'm not so sure of that."

"Well, I am. You opposed both Potiorek and myself with equal persistence. I congratulate you, Miloš Vasić! Can you hear me?"

"In your last letter you asked me about a student corporal called Ivan Katić. I suppose he's the son of Vukašin Katić?"

"Yes, he is. What's happened to him?"

"He was reported missing in the last battle of the Eighth Regiment."

"What did you say? How did he come to be missing, for God's sake? Where? Was he killed or taken prisoner?"

"Just missing. His body hasn't been found, so it would be logical to assume that he's been taken prisoner. Are you listening, Vojvoda?"

Mišić put down the receiver and bowed his head.

While the shooting, killing, and pursuit of the enemy continued, Bora Jackpot pretended that his dead friend Danilo History-Book had been transferred to another regiment; while Bora was waiting to be hit himself by a bullet, a deeper sorrow for his friend could not flame up inside him. From the time Danilo died until he himself lay in that clearing, he had not wound up his father's watch; its hands stood at nine. That figure nine disturbed him even in the relative quiet before the great quiet of the present day, which stretched over the land between the Drina and the Sava; this quiet tormented him. With whom could he find release from this piercing grief? With the soldiers it was impossible; they had their own troubles, and were timidly expressing to one another their joy over the victory.

Feeling anxious and uneasy in the prevailing quiet, Bora resolved to go to the next village, where the battalion of Tričko and Wren was billeted, to find out if they were still alive, to hear their voices and burn up his grief with them. He felt ashamed at the thought that he was retreating from his sorrow in this metallic stillness which shrieked and buzzed in his ears. He took with him as an escort the least talkative soldier in his section, told him the object of his journey, and had him walk ten paces ahead to preclude conversation. Then he set out across the deserted field, walking along the bare, blackened hedges toward the village, which lay on the edge of the quiet, at the end of the world, beneath a low, gray, contracted sky. It was a good thing that everything around him, including nature, was as it should be that day. If the sky had been wide and blue, and the field green; if there had been wild flowers growing beside this muddy path; if a wind had stirred the leaves and grass, and birds had raised their voices in the hedges, then he wouldn't have been able to stand it, but would have wept aloud. He looked straight in front of him and breathed in the gray, dry silence, hearing nothing but his own footsteps. His companion, who was now fifty paces in front, stopped to wait for him; with a quick movement of his hand he waved to him to go on.

He thought that he heard someone calling to him in a hoarse voice. He halted. His father's voice had sounded just like that. He turned around and looked all over the quiet, empty field. An enormous old elm tree by the road stared at him with its trunk and bare branches. What was the elm feeling and thinking now? He wanted to touch the trunk of the tree, to rest his hands on its body. The elm might sigh or groan. It might scream at him, and lash him to fury with a blow from one of its branches. He began to run with his head lowered, bent over as if under machine-gun fire, expecting a branch of the elm to strike his head and croak some fearful reproach. He caught up with the silent soldier, so that he could hear his footsteps. The sky contracted still more and descended yet further; the field too bent in on itself, in the vise-like grip of the hedges. There, at the end of the world, was the village. Behind him, an abyss.

He went into the village: piles of gutted buildings. The silent soldier stopped and stared at the charred wreckage. A woman's voice called out somewhere. Bora again looked straight ahead. Someone tugged his arm:

"Bora!"

Tričko Macedonian ran out of a yard and hugged him, hugged him for a long time.

"I came to look for you. To see which of our bunch are still alive."

"Only Tortoise and I in my battalion, the First. Wren was wounded at Krupanj. After that we were only in one short battle."

"Is he badly wounded?"

"They say he'll live. He was a fool. He came out of cover and dashed right at a machine gun, like he was drunk. I suppose he thought the war would soon be over and he was in a hurry to get the Karageorge Star. A crazy musician!"

"He was rushing to his death, Tričko, old man. So in the First Battalion only you and Tortoise have lived to see the victory?"

"Yes, only us two."

"Is there an inn in this village?"

"Yes, but it's full of Austrian wounded. Ours, too. Come along to my place, and I'll find some *rakija*."

"I don't want to go into a peasant's house now. Let's go to the inn; at least it's something like a Serbian café. The one honorable institution of our freedom. Why are you frowning? After all, we went to a café just before we left for the front. Do you remember the Sloboda in Skoplje? And the Talpara in Kragujevac, and that supper with Vukašin Katić? Do you know anything about Ivan?"

"I haven't heard anything about Ivan. Please don't drag me to a café now."

"Come on, follow me! Or you take me there. After all, we're the victors. It's the one place worthy of us today."

"You can't go into the inn. It smells of pus and wounds."

"Who cares? We'll hold a memorial service for the sixth student platoon. Where are you off to, Tričko?

"Wait for me here!"

Tričko ran into the yard; the silent soldier leaned against the fence, staring at something. Bora Jackpot was thinking about Wren. When he moved toward that machine gun, he thought, he must have hated his fiancée, that lovely, innocent girl, his first love. Does he still hate her now? From the road, he spat hard and hit the fence.

Tričko came back with some cards. Bora Jackpot began to tremble, but not with the excitement he had felt at Boljkovci, or right up to the night when he had lost his father's watch playing poker with Dušan Casanova and Saša Molecule.

"Before he was killed, Casanova said to Molecule and me: 'Listen, men, if the Fritzies get me, I want Bora Jackpot to have this pack of cards. Swear to me that you'll carry out my wish.' And we swore that we would."

"But those are the cards his uncle gave him when they said good-by at Niš! They came from Paris. How many times in Boljkovci did I ask him if we could play with those very cards!" Bora took them, ran his fingers over them, and stroked them. "And Casanova would answer, 'I swear I won't touch them until we've won the war!'" The cards fell from his hand.

"And Casanova said to me softly so our host wouldn't hear: 'You know, men, after the war Europe will be a brothel thirteen stories high, but they'll build the casinos under the water and up in the sky.' What a crazy fellow he was!" Tričko bent down to pick up the cards.

"But you haven't given me the whole pack!"

"That's all we found. He was killed at dusk. We found him in the snow the next day, when we counterattacked. The Fritzies had emptied his bag and his pockets, and scattered the cards around his body."

"Anyway, all the jacks are here," said Bora, stuffing the cards into his overcoat pocket. "Now take me to the inn."

In the silence they walked along the road toward the center of the village; the silent soldier hurried on in front of them, as though on patrol duty. They came to a huge old inn with a porch. In front of it was a broken, overturned ambulance and some dead horses. Bora Jackpot read aloud the name of the inn.

"The Red Tavern. Why should it be called the Red Tavern?"

"I don't know."

Bora walked slowly into the inn behind Tričko, who was stepping between rows of wounded men lying on straw as though stacked in piles, and some tables pushed together in the middle of the huge room; there were wounded men on the tables, too, pressed against one another and covered with blankets. Those on the floor, he noticed, were covered with tent flaps. The smell of pus, blood, and the soldiers' filth filled his nostrils. He stopped to find out why some of the wounded were lying on the tables. A doctor, a lieutenant, was bandaging their wounds with the help of a medic. A wounded man groaned and swore in Serbian.

Tričko called to him crossly from the door leading into a dark corridor.

"Where are you taking me now? There's no place in Serbia where the living can celebrate the victory," muttered Bora as he followed Tričko into a kitchen containing a large built-in stove, a bed, and a table at which two officers were dozing; one had a bandage around his head, the other around his arm. An old woman was peeling potatoes by the stove.

"Have you corporals already forgotten the service rules?" mumbled the officer with the bandage around his head; one of his eyes was swollen.

"I don't understand you, sir," said Tričko.

"Why don't you salute? Stand at attention! You're talking to a captain of the first class, damn you! Are you a student?"

Tričko stood at attention, but Bora Jackpot would not. He stood leaning against the doorpost, ready for anything if the captain of the first class tried something.

"Are you a student too?" shouted the captain. One of his eyes was dull and bloodshot, and he could hardly squint from the other.

"I'm the son of Vojvoda Putnik!" retorted Bora, grinning.

The captain stared at him with his one eye, speechless.

"Have you got another room, auntie," asked Bora, speaking to the housewife.

"Yes, my boy, I have. Only I must clean it up a bit, and make a fire in the stove. There were some Austrian doctors there two days ago."

"Do you have any *rakija*? I'd like two liters of hot *rakija*."

"I haven't a grain of sugar, my boy."

"I've got some sugar," said Tričko. "Put the *rakija* on to heat at once." He bent down and whispered in her ear, then saluted and went out, nodding to Bora.

The captain of the first class made an effort to open his swollen and livid eye a little more. The old woman put down the pan of potatoes and went out into the corridor. Bora followed her, without saluting the captain. The woman took them into a room with an unmade bed, and two empty bottles of cognac on the window sill.

"Here you are, boys. I'll clean it up and light a fire right away."

"I'll do that," said Tričko. "Do you think you could roast us a chicken for supper? We'll pay whatever you ask."

"The problem is to catch one. The Fritzies shot at them with their rifles, and they flew off all over the place. But there are still a few around. If you've got a gun, go ahead and kill them. They're up there at the end of the orchard."

"Fine. Now put the *rakija* on to heat, and I'll make a fire in the stove."

"There isn't going to be any shooting of Serbian chickens. You hear me, Trička? I won't have it! I don't care if I die of hunger. I'm not going to fire a gun now. Don't you have anything else? Couldn't you give us some fried potatoes?"

"I'm preparing those for the officers. I could make you some polenta. And I've got a bit of cheese."

"You make us some polenta and put the *rakija* on to heat!" said Bora. He went back into the dark corridor and waited for the room to be cleaned and a fire lit in the stove. Leaning against the wall, he listened to the groaning and muttering of the wounded in German, Hungarian, Czech, and Serbian. As he listened, he thought: do those wounded men on the tables feel like victors? And how those on the floor must hate them now! But perhaps they all feel nothing but despair.

Bora entered the room, now cleaned up a little, and with a fire burning in the stove. He sat down at the table and began to drink the hot *rakija*, and talk about their comrades who had been killed. It was growing dark; Trička, still silent, lit a tallow candle. The woman brought in a dish of polenta and some cheese. They began to eat, and Bora continued to talk about their dead comrades, mentioning each in turn, in the order in which they had lined up in front of the barracks. He couldn't eat; taking the cards out of his pocket he began to count them.

"Don't count them!" said Trička, seizing his arm. "Please don't ever count them! Please, Bora!"

"Why?" asked Bora. By the light of the candle he could see tears in Trička's eyes; he put the cards down on the table.

"There are some things you just can't tell people," said Trička; then he began to weep, and extinguished the candle.

Neither of them spoke. The fire in the stove went out; everything was in darkness. A clamor in several languages resounded through the inn. There was a sudden scream, then groans, as in a charge by night.

"What the hell's the matter with them?" shouted a thick, hoarse voice from the passage.

"The wounded are hitting each other, Captain. They've put out the lamp and they're fighting."

"Stop that now, for God's sake! The battle's over."

Vojvoda Mišić reached the outskirts of Struganik as it was growing dark: that evening he didn't wish to see the village in the wake of occupation and liberation, after the passage of two hungry armies; tomorrow he would listen to the woeful tales of neighbors and relatives, look at the women swathed in black head scarves, and find out who had been killed. Tonight he would sit alone beside a fire in the old open hearth; he would arrange accommodation for Zarija, Spasić, Dragutin, and the soldiers of his staff in the house of his elder brother.

As he passed the first unlighted houses of Struganik, he was met by sounds of lamentation in the darkness. The dogs were silent: were they frightened, or had they been killed? He reached his apple orchard: had the soldiers eaten up those heaps of ungathered apples? Tomorrow he would go look at the apple orchard. The soil felt very heavy and resounded under the hoofs of his horse—that soil which he had once trodden barefoot with thorns in the soles of his feet. The path now seemed much narrower, the same path along which his mother had walked, her back bent under many kinds of burdens. Under the walnut trees at the end of the meadow, the path seemed to narrow down to nothing; that was where he had barely managed to reach his frightened mother, carrying his swathe of newly cut grass, when he was a second lieutenant. The walnut trees were silent in the darkness, as though slaughtered.

His sisters-in-law, nieces, and elder brother received him quietly, without obvious pleasure. He heard Dragutin whispering to them that the King had promoted him to the rank of vojvoda. He greeted them in front of the open door of the house, in the light of the fire from the hearth:

"Are you all alive?" he asked in a troubled voice.

"Yes, those of us who haven't gone off to the war. We haven't heard anything yet about those who went to fight."

He did not wish to prolong the conversation. He told them to help the soldiers stable their horses, and to prepare the distillery shed for them to sleep in. No need to bother about supper; they would fix something for themselves as soon as it was light. For himself he asked them to bring plenty of wood, and some potatoes for him to bake. He would have asked for a handful of walnuts, but tonight this would have seemed like presuming on his new rank.

He went into the kitchen, stood by the open hearth, and took a deep breath of the familiar smell of the old fireplace: the sharp, pungent smell of smoke, soot, and ash, in which he could distinguish the smoke of each kind of wood which had been burned there. Tonight he would have liked a fire of dried bitter-oak wood; it made a pleasant sound as it burned, it had a restless flame and smelled of lichen. But to ask for bitter-oak tonight would also seem like presuming on his rank of vojvoda. There was a pile of beech logs beside the hearth; a man could warm himself by many a worse fire.

He sat on a three-legged stool, still wearing his overcoat. Professor Zarija and Dragutin were talking in low voices with his brother. He told them that they must be tired, so they ought to turn in immediately. Tonight I want to be alone with the fire, he said to himself. They went out and he felt easier. He poked the fire, making the flames dance and leap up the chimney. Behind his back he thought he could hear his mother give a quiet sigh beside the kneading trough. What would he have said to her tonight? Certainly he would not have mentioned his promotion; he would have just talked about his children.

His sister-in-law brought him a pan of potatoes, and offered to bake him bread and bring him some cheese. "I'll have all that in the morning," he told her, and placed the potatoes in the hot, smoldering ash. His brother put down an armful of oakwood staves.

"Good God, are we burning staves?"

"Yes, we are. And building wood, and beams! We're burning all our finest building material; we're burning it for our freedom, Živojin."

"I don't like to pay such a price to celebrate our freedom."

"Well, *I* do! I hear the King has promoted you to vojvoda."

"Yes, brother, that's true."

"I'm sure you deserved it, Živojin, and that's what the people think."

"Well, if that honor had not come my way, it would not have been a miscarriage of justice. You could have brought me an armful of logs. I'd have gone out onto Baćinac tonight to collect wood, before I'd throw a stave on the fire. Just tell me where I should sleep," he continued, turning to his sister-in-law, "then you go to bed."

She told him that the guest room with two beds was empty; that was where he usually slept when he came to see them. Two Austrian officers had slept there, she added, but she had changed all the bedding two days ago.

He didn't tell her that he felt an aversion to lying on a bed in which Austrian officers had slept, and that he'd bring in two armfuls of straw from the hayloft, spread it out beside the hearth, and doze there between the first and third cockcrows. That's what his mother had sometimes done when it was her turn to do the morning chores.

He was alone. As he smoked, he poked the fire and listened to its crackling, always the same before it died away.

A whole grove of trees had been burned up on this hearth. A whole century of living. The immeasurable strength of earth, sky, and sun had been consumed there in flames. Then the ash had been thrown on the dunghill, and the wind had scattered it in all directions. But there still remained the smell of smoke and soot on the walls of the fireplace and the flues of the chimney. This was what remained from a wood larger than a village, through which mountain winds had roared and north winds had moaned, where summer storms had burst with all their fury, and impenetrable silence had descended when the snow fell. Birds and butterflies had flown about there; tortoises, snakes, and cockroaches had crept over the ground. And from all this there remained simply a sharp, pungent smell of smoke; this soot which was licked by the flames, along which the smoke passed on its upward climb before it finally disappeared above the rooftops. Was human life really more lasting than the life of a grove of trees? Was man more eternal than an oak or a beech tree? The span of human life on this earth was shorter than that of a beech tree, incomparably shorter than that of an oak. How many people could be like wood for building, could make something new or different? Then everything was reduced to ash, smoke, soot. The earth was nothing but an evil hearth, a wicked ashpit.

He stabbed through the flames with the poker and left no trace of them, then spread out the embers, extinguishing the remains of the fire. He made patterns in the ashes, which would last only until he threw some more logs on the fire, or the wind rushed over the hearth from the chimney. Victory, glory, recognition: what were all these before a hearth where a constant succession of people had made a fire and warmed themselves by it, to be consumed by fire in turn?

He went on making patterns in the ashes, then obliterated them. But his mother was there behind his back, leaning silently over the kneading trough and sighing quietly. A shudder passed through him. He waited for her to whisper: "Are you afraid of something, my boy? What will happen tomorrow, Živojin? What's going to happen tomorrow?" Smoke and ash. A sharp smell, nothing more.

Someone coughed in front of the door. His grandfather used to announce his arrival like that. It was as though his mother had gone out of the room. A horse was stamping in front of the house. He dug out the potatoes and picked them up; they were baked now, and he put them down at the edge of the hearth to cool. He shivered from the stream of cold air pouring over his back. He heard someone give a deep sigh; he started, then turned around. Vukašin Katić was standing in the open doorway, looking at him with fear and alarm.

"Vukašin!" he cried, overwhelmed by the look in his eyes and the expression on his face. He could hardly get up, and had no strength to walk toward him. One of his feet was in the ashes, and he was still holding the poker. A spasm of compassion and fear mounted to his throat.

Vukašin Katić dropped his walking stick on the floor inside the doorstep; he too was unable to advance toward Mišić, burdened as he was by a turmoil of love and a kind of sick hatred. Nor did he wish to conceal these conflicting emotions. He looked at Mišić standing there, with one foot in the ashes and holding a poker in his hand: he saw an exhausted, penitent man. Could it be that he was unhappy? The thought flashed through his mind that this man in front of him was not a victor and a vojvoda. He took a step forward and looked hard at him. Then he said:

"Good evening, Živojin!"

Mišić dropped the poker, stood at attention in the ash at the edge of the hearth, and with slow, weary movements saluted this father whose son had been reported missing in the last battle of the Eighth Regiment of the First Army. The fire burst into flame; the logs crackled; flame and smoke shot up the chimney.

Vukašin trembled at this greeting, but grasped its meaning and looked down at the hearth, at the patterns in the ashes. Mišić met his glance as he looked down, and became even more perplexed; it was as though he felt ashamed.

There's not a spark of joy in him, nothing to show he has any feeling of glory, thought Vukašin. Something akin to gratitude welled up inside him, something like respect and esteem, a feeling deeper than affection for a friend. He went up to Mišić and held out his hand. Mišić took it, and didn't want to let go.

"There are still grounds for hope," Mišić began, in a hoarse, quiet voice. "I've given orders to the regimental commander that Ivan's platoon make a thorough search of the entire area where the enemy were operating, and where the battle was fought that day. They found his knapsack with some odds and ends inside, and an exercise book. That will come to the army headquarters tomorrow or the day after. The regimental commander believes that he's been taken prisoner; I do, too."

Vukašin withdrew his fingers from Mišić's hand, shut the door, and sat down on the stool where Mišić had been sitting. Tears which he could not keep back poured over the patterns and footprints in the ashes. He covered his face.

"He has been recommended for the Miloš Obilić Gold Medal for bravery, for his heroism in the battle on Maljen on December 7," said Mišić, taking another stool and sitting down beside Vukašin.

"What about your children?" asked Vukašin in a trembling voice.

"They're alive." He handed Vukašin a cigarette, then a firebrand.

For a long time they smoked in silence. Vukašin felt a desire to rush out and start for Maljen. He wanted to look for Ivan; to tread the slopes of that mountain where his son had walked, and where he had disappeared. Had he actually disappeared forever? Ivan, my own son. Disappeared. Missing.

Mišić listened to him as he sobbed and stared at the fire with clenched lips. How could he comfort Vukašin? What word or gesture could he offer? He could bend the course of the war, he knew how to make an army win victories. But he had no power to alleviate a father's grief. None at all. He put his arm on Vukašin's shoulder; he was afraid that it would seem like a conventional gesture of sympathy.

"Živojin, I want you to believe me when I say that I wasn't against sending the students to the front because my son was in the Student Battalion," said Vukašin hoarsely. "It was because I myself was afraid that Serbia would lose both the war and the peace. That's how I felt. I want you to believe this."

"I do believe you. I believed you when you said it in the district court in Valjevo. And I wasn't the only one. But as I said that night in Valjevo, in times like these, we can't do only what is wise and sensible, but what must be done."

"Does a man without children have a fatherland? A man without children doesn't even need freedom. If you don't leave someone of your own behind you, Živojin, then death is the end of everything."

"There are a thousand reasons for living, Vukašin."

"But there is only one valid human reason for dying. I don't know what these human affairs are, or in what aim and purpose one can believe for all time. Only in one's children, one's son."

Mišić could see his shoulders shaking. His brother came in and stood by the door.

"Should we bring your visitor some supper, Živojin?"

"We've got some potatoes here. You go to bed."

He put some logs on the hearth and stirred up the fire, struggling to find the right words; he couldn't. "Have you seen Milena?" he asked.

"Yes, I saw her very briefly. I was hurrying to get to you as soon as possible."

"She's had a rough time of it, poor girl."

"She's alive."

Vukašin sighed, then suddenly got up. He couldn't look at the fire any more, or listen to his friend or talk. Missing. Disappeared. Gone forever. My boy, my Ivan.

He went into the darkness to look for him out there on Maljen. He went down the lane, tramped through the mud, his teeth were chattering. He wanted to and must tread that earth where Ivan had disappeared. He walked through the underbrush, over the fields, uphill toward Maljen. He hit his head against a tree, wiped his forehead. His hand was damp. He cried aloud:

"Father, my son's been killed! Your grandson, Ivan."

He continued tramping over the earth in the darkness, uphill all the time. To feel it more deeply and strongly he took his shoes off and went barefoot over the earth where Ivan had disappeared. He sank into some mud. If this was the earth he wanted to sink into it up to his thighs, up to his throat, to walk so that he plunged and dived through it and his lips and veins were full of it and he himself was that earth on which his son had disappeared—his Ivan.